Estelle Ryan

The

Dante Connection

The Dante Connection

A Genevieve Lenard Novel

By Estelle Ryan

First published 2013

Acknowledgements

This is almost an exact copy of the acknowledgements in my first book. I am so very honoured to be surrounded by amazing people. I'm truly standing on the shoulders of giants.

Anna J Kutor, for your unending and unconditional support, and your patience. Charlene, you know you own my heart. Linette, for being the best sister anyone can ask for. Moeks, for your faith in me. R.J. Locksley for editing. Wilhelm and Kasia, Kamila, Ania B and Piotrek, Krystina, Maggie, Julie, Jola, Alta and the B(l)ogsusters for all your interest and support. Iwo, for such amazing help with all things IT and hacking related. A special thank you to Jane for your love and support.

And then a very special thank you to those readers who have reached out and contacted me after reading *The Gauguin Connection*. Writing is an extremely isolated job. Receiving feedback from such amazing, gracious people have left me humbled and counting my blessings. A mere thank you is not enough to express my gratitude for each email and encouraging word. Keep them coming!

Dedication

To Anna.

Chapter ONE

"Genevieve, you have to help me. I killed two men."

"Francine?" I cringed at my redundant request for confirmation of identity. The sight in front of me shocked my sleepy brain into full alert. My hand tightened around the front door handle and I stared at the grievously injured woman in the hallway.

"Help me, please." Her voice was hoarse as if she had been screaming. Her left eye was swollen shut and her face freshly bruised.

I could not read her expressions. My throat tightened with that realisation. My connection to other people depended on my world-renowned ability to read nonverbal cues. But Francine's face was too damaged to allow much muscle movement. A cut on her cheek was still oozing blood, and she was bleeding from other places too. There were rust coloured splatters all over her clothes. I couldn't see if it was from her injuries. Maybe it was her victims'. A shudder rolled down my spine.

When the insistent ringing of my doorbell had woken me at two in the morning, I had not expected to find the woman who had been avoiding me for two weeks on my doorstep. The exotic beauty I knew to be a computer genius, an exceptional hacker and an enthusiastic proponent for conspiracy theories was weaving, looking ready to lose consciousness. I had only ever seen her looking like a supermodel. The hunched-over figure at my doorstep did not resemble that at all.

"Please?" Her whispered plea brought my attention to her swollen lips.

"But you killed two people." How could I let a killer into my home?

"It was in sel..." A gurgling cough punished her body and she reached out to me. Instinctively I recoiled, but she didn't notice. Her breathing was becoming laboured and it didn't take my three doctorate degrees to know that she needed medical attention.

"Oh, for goodness' sake." I stepped away from the door and opened it wider. "Come on in then."

"Colin," she wheezed as she staggered to my expensive sofas. I closed the door, made sure all five locks were secured in place and hurried over before she reached the living area. With an internal groan, I spread the beige mohair throw over the sofa and watched her lower herself in obvious agony. "Please get Colin here."

"You of all people know that I can't get a hold of him." I had met Colin and Francine five months ago when working on an art crime case. My life had been in danger while investigating the murders of art students. Francine had proven herself to be an invaluable asset when she offered her computer hacking skills. Skills she used for a few government agencies.

Colin, on the other hand, was a criminal. He was an accomplished thief, infamous, and honourable. In that trying time five months ago he had proved himself to be one of the good guys – a concept I had learned from my boss. Not only was Colin a thief, but he was a thief who worked for Interpol. At last count only five people knew of his unconventional job. His cooperation with the law was something neither him nor the powers that be in Interpol wanted to be known. After working side by side with him, I had thought he was my friend, but he had disappeared out of my life a month after the case had closed. That had been four months ago.

At first I had thought he had to be working on some assignment, but after not being able to contact him on the number he had given me, I had become concerned. Three weeks ago I had asked Francine if she could track Colin with her computer skills. We had met only once after that before she too started avoiding my calls. All this rejection did not sit well with me.

"How am I supposed to get Colin here if I can't reach him?" I asked.

"Send him a 911 text to the number you have. He'll phone you."

"How can you be so sure?"

Francine's facial muscles tried to draw together into a pleading expression. "Please, Genevieve. We need him. Just send that text."

Apart from my boss, Francine was the only one who called me Genevieve. Mostly, people called me Doctor Lenard. Three other people used different names for me, but that was in the past.

For a moment I studied her. As usual she was dressed in the best designer clothes, now torn and ruined by bloodstains. She favoured her left side and I wondered if she had been stabbed. There wasn't a large bloodstain in that area, so it was most probably broken ribs. I had a lot of questions about her presence on my sofa. Including the suspicion that her injuries had something to do with her reason for avoiding me. Now she was telling me that we needed Colin. I balked at the 'we'.

A pained groan and tears streaming from her swollen eyes drew me out of my thoughts and put me into action. I stomped to the kitchen, grabbed my smartphone off the counter and swiped the screen. Within three seconds I sent the text message and was staring at the little screen, waiting for Colin to call. My smartphone's screen lit up and a silly ringtone filled my apartment. I swiped the screen.

"Yes?"

"Jenny, what's wrong?" Worry raised Colin's voice from its usual deep rumble. Hearing his voice again for the first time in four months made me happy, sad and angry at the same time. But mostly angry.

"Francine killed two men."

"She... Wait... What?" He took a deep breath. "Is she with you?"

"Yes." The more he spoke, the angrier I was becoming. It limited my social vocabulary.

"In your apartment?"

"Yes."

"I'm on my way."

"I'll phone the police."

"No!" Again he took a breath audible enough for me to hear. "Let's first hear what happened."

"She killed two men, Colin. There is nothing more to it. She told me so herself. I should phone the police." My words were clipped.

"Wait a moment."

I heard some clicking noises and narrowed my eyes. Those noises not only came through the phone, but also from a window in the back of my apartment.

My lips tightened and I turned around. "I have a front door."

"That you always lock." Colin smiled as he walked to me in long strides. Something was not right. His usual confident walk seemed impeded in some way. Seeing him after such a long time overwhelmed me with all kinds of emotions which distracted me from my observations. "Hello, Jenny. Did you miss me?"

"You left me." My lips were tight, my brows pulled together and my voice cold. "After all that irrational talk about friendship, you disappeared without a word."

He studied me through narrowed eyes until I became uncomfortable. "I missed you too."

My discomfort made me reach for a change of topic. I turned to the living area. "Francine is over there."

Colin looked past me. The *frontalis* muscles on his forehead lifted his eyebrows and his mouth went slack. Textbook example of shock. He rushed to the sofa and fell on his knees next to Francine.

"Oh, honey, what have they done to you?" He gently lifted a stray strand of hair from her bloody face. Without looking away from her, he addressed me. "Get some clean towels, Jenny."

"All my towels are clean. Always." I groaned at the thought of my designer white towels. There was no conceivable way I would ever use them again. Not after they were stained by someone else's blood. With a sigh of resignation I got four soft, fluffy, brilliantly white hand towels.

"Who did this, Francine?" Colin asked.

"The hacker," she wheezed. Her good eye was glazed over and her speech slurred. "Or his thugs... security compa... systems... they go... all the systems."

I walked closer, feeling a distinct discomfort in my chest. It took a moment for me to realise the discomfort I was feeling was concern. I did not feel concern. Not usually. Concern was reserved for people we cared about. I had not known that I had grown to care for Francine. I handed the towels to Colin. "She doesn't look good. We have to phone an ambulance."

Francine jerked at my suggestion and Colin murmured reassurances to her. He gently dabbed at her face. "Francine, honey, I know someone at a private clinic. No one will even know you're there."

She shook her head and winced. "They'll get me there. He got into the systems. He knows."

"Why didn't you come to me?"

"Genevieve needs to know, Colin. She's everywhere on... he got the... systems."

Everything in my being stilled. "What do I need to know? Who are you talking about? What systems?"

Colin was frowning at Francine's strange statements, but didn't answer me. His attention was on her. "The person I know at the clinic will register you under any name I give him. We can even register you there as a man, but you need to get medical attention."

"I'll be fine." She had barely uttered the last word when another painful cough caused more tears to stream from her eyes. It took her a minute to catch her breath. "Okay, but I'll only go if Genevieve goes with me."

"What? No." Distress tightened my throat and raised my

voice. This was becoming too much for me. Francine appearing beaten up at my door in the dead of the night, Colin showing up three seconds after he contacted me for the first time in four months, and now Francine was insisting I accompany her to a hospital. "Why?"

"I trust you."

"But you trust Colin. You've known him for longer. He's also a criminal." The words shot uncensored out of my mouth. I was distraught by the intensity of the compulsion not to go to a hospital.

For a moment it looked as if Francine had lost consciousness, but then she opened the eye that had not completely swollen shut. "Please, Genevieve. Just don't let them take me."

"Who? Let who take you?" I turned to Colin. "Who is she talking about?"

"I don't know." He gently pressed the towel against her still-oozing wound. "Get dressed. The clinic is not too far from here."

"No. I'm not going." None of the books on friendship I had recently read said anything about being supportive to the types of people in my living area. "She killed two people. It's bad enough that I had you and Vinnie constantly in my life."

"Why, thank you, Jenny."

I didn't understand why he would thank me, so I continued, "I'm not going to become an accomplice, after the fact, in people's deaths."

"They tried to kill me," Francine said quietly. Colin and I looked at her in surprise. I had been sure she had lost consciousness.

"Who tried to kill you?"

"The hacker," she said.

Francine had never told me exactly what it was that she did. All I knew was that it involved hacking and other computer-related activities. She had claimed that she worked for the good guys, but a small micro-expression had left some doubts in my mind.

My ignorance concerning all things information technology often made me feel paralysed in her company. Those times I would concentrate on reading her nonverbal cues. Like now. I narrowed my eyes, but it didn't help me read her any better. Her face was simply too swollen for any natural muscle movements. "I don't know if you're telling me the truth."

"I am..." Another cough stopped her mid-sentence. Her ragged breathing was worrying, but it was when her body slumped into my sofa that my chest tightened again. I was worried about a killer. Very worried.

"She needs a doctor now, Colin," I said.

"We'll take my car." Colin stood up and again I noticed the difficulty in his movement. I wondered what had happened in the time he had been unreachable. He straightened, pulled out his smartphone and tapped the screen a few times before holding the device to his ear. "Francine's been attacked. We're here at Jenny's. Yes. Sure."

I watched Colin through narrowed eyes as he walked to my front door while talking to the other person. He unlocked the door and opened it. I recognised the voice before the large man dressed in fatigue pants and a black sweater stepped into my apartment. Vinnie.

I stormed to the front door, stopped in front of the two men and pointed an angry finger at them. "You left me. You both left me. Vinnie, I thought you were my friend. But you left me."

My accusations brought remorse to both men's faces. Vinnie looked in pain. He rocked on his feet as if wanting to move towards me. If I went by his behaviour before he had absconded, he wanted to pull me into one of his unsolicited hugs. I would not appreciate it. I was too angry.

He broke the silence, his gravelly voice regretful and his eyes sad. "Jen-girl, I'm so sorry. It wasn't an easy decision, but it was the best decision."

"What decision? Why did you have to make that decision?" I didn't understand what was happening and didn't like the feeling. Vinnie had entered my life at the same time as Colin and Francine. At first he had been my bodyguard, but later I had thought him a friend. He had left a month after Colin had cut off all contact. His last words to me had been reassurances that he would bring Colin back. "You told me that friends always wanted the best for each other. How was leaving me and then ignoring me for months the best for me? And who are you to make that decision?"

Vinnie flinched at my cold anger. "Jen-girl, we'll explain."

"Good idea." Francine's soft voice brought our attention back to the sofa. "Look at me. This could've been Genevieve. You should've told Genevieve."

Vinnie gasped as Francine hugged her side and groaned. He rushed to the sofa.

Colin closed the door. "I'm sorry, Jenny."

"It's not enough." I turned my back on him and walked to the sofa. "Vinnie, you need to take Francine to the hospital."

"We're taking her to the clinic," Colin said.

"Okay." Vinnie seemed to immediately know where this clinic was. He was on his haunches next to the sofa, talking quietly to Francine. He leaned over, carefully lifting Francine against his chest, and stood up in a movement so smooth that I stared at his legs. Vinnie was not only tall, but exceptionally strong. For a short while I had felt safe when he had been my bodyguard. Francine would be safe with him.

Colin followed them to the front door and addressed me over his shoulder. "Bring those towels, please."

"I'm not going." I leaned back and folded my arms over my chest.

"Jenny, it will be much easier if you help me." Colin was using his negotiation voice. It annoyed me.

"No."

"Please get dressed, bring the towels and meet us at the car." He opened the door for Vinnie. "We can argue about this while I'm driving our friend to the hospital for life-saving medical treatment."

If the situation were not so dire, I might have been more

offended at his undisguised attempt at emotional blackmail. Not that it would ever work on me, but it did make me think. In the months since we had first met, Francine had gone out of her way to be my friend. She had frequently met me at a bistro close to my office for lunch. Every time had been at her initiative, not mine.

"Genevieve, please. I need you." Francine's voice was weak, the pleading in her tone strong. Was this what friends did? Help each other despite very probable legal ramifications? The books didn't say.

With an angry grunt I walked to my bedroom to get dressed. Life had been much simpler before these people who called themselves my friends entered my life.

By the time I reached Colin's car, Vinnie had climbed into the backseat with Francine in his arms. I handed Colin the towels. He gently put one under her head and closed the door. He turned to me, sincerity in every micro-expression. "Thank you."

"Don't thank me yet. You left me. For months. Then you appear in my flat within seconds of me contacting you. Don't think I didn't notice that you must have been in the vicinity. We are going to have an argument while you're driving."

"I wouldn't have it any other way," he said and opened the passenger door for me. There was too much I wanted to say to him at that moment. Eventually I simply groaned and got into the high seat of his SUV. I took juvenile pleasure in pulling the door out of his hand and slamming it.

As soon as Colin pulled away from the curb, he pushed a few buttons on the dashboard screen. The sound of a phone ringing filled the car.

"Allô," a tinny, but distinctly male voice answered. He sounded awake.

"Paul? This is Andrew Marvell." Colin gave me a quick smile. I shook my head at his false identity. His use of the names of seventeenth-century English poets was how I had exposed him in the first place. I knew that if I checked,

Andrew Marvell would also be an English poet.

"Andrew?" The voice laughed. "It's been years. How are you?"

"Still invisible. How are you?"

"Still the best." His English was exceptional, the French accent barely audible. There was a slight pause. "It's two-forty in the morning. I take this is not a social call?"

"Unfortunately not. I have a friend with me who needs medical attention. She needs it without any paperwork."

"Done. How bad is she?"

"She's been badly beaten. Maybe some broken ribs, hopefully no internal bleeding."

"You know where to bring her. I'll be waiting for you."

"Thanks, Paul." Colin glanced at his watch. "We should be there in another five minutes."

Unsurprisingly the streets were empty. This time of the morning was too late for the night owls and too early for the early birds. About the only time that there was a lull in the constant movement of the city. Knowing that there was a killer in the backseat, I thought it was a good thing there were no witnesses.

After four months of fretting about Colin's safety, three months of Vinnie's absence and two weeks of Francine avoiding me, I now found myself cocooned in this SUV with them. Reunited. And infuriated. I had so many arguments that I didn't know where to start. "I'm not going into the hospital."

Colin smiled. "That only took thirty seconds."

"You timed me?"

"I had a bet with myself."

"That doesn't make sense. How can you bet against yourself? There will be no winner." I caught myself before I digressed further. "I'm not going into the hospital."

"So you said." He glanced at me. "Why not?"

I inhaled, but didn't get a chance to speak.

"And don't tell me it is because Francine killed two men. We still don't know the whole story and I do not believe you are so judgemental that you won't give Francine the opportunity to explain. I can also understand that you are extremely angry with me and with Vinnie, but you still wouldn't let that keep you from being there for your friend." His voice softened. "What is the real reason, Jenny?"

I might be the one with degrees in psychology and nonverbal communication, but Colin had a natural ability to see deep into people's psyches. It annoyed me that he knew me so well. Especially since he had not been in my life for the last four months to know me any better. Yet he knew when to push me for explanations and when to leave me be. I wished he would leave me be about going into the hospital.

"Ignoring me won't work," he said as he turned into a narrow street.

"I don't like hospitals," I said.

"Why not?"

"I don't want to talk about it." I turned away from him.

We entered the parking lot of an upscale medical clinic. Colin parked close to the entrance and turned to me. "I'm sorry, Jenny. The last four months have been hell. Part of that hell was the decision to exclude you from what was happening. I will explain everything to you as soon as Francine is taken care of. Until then I sincerely hope that you can see how much I regret all this time we've lost."

I studied his face in the harsh light of the clinic entrance and saw regret. I also saw stress lines that had not been there before. Equally important was what I couldn't see. There was no arrogance or smugness, not even a trace of humour. Whatever had happened had been bad. Colin was sitting quietly, allowing me to scrutinise his face. It was the combination of all these factors that eased my anger.

"I will accept your apology after a complete explanation."

"You guys... really weird." Francine's weak voice broke the moment. "Where are we?"

"At the clinic, honey." Colin got out of the car and I followed suit. He opened the backdoor and I could hear Francine's disjointed complaints about security. I didn't know if

I could take her seriously. She was always convinced that there was some or another conspiracy surrounding an event.

"Don't use my name. The hacker... my uncle. Colin, my uncle."

I frowned at the fragile quality to her voice. "What about your uncle? Is he in danger?"

"They stole his... oh—" She gasped when Vinnie moved and she slumped back against his chest.

The sliding doors to the clinic opened behind me. I turned as an overweight man came to us. He was wearing a white overcoat which led me to believe that he was a doctor. I never understood how doctors could smoke, use drugs or be overweight. He stopped next to Colin and peeked through the window into the car. "This your friend?"

"Yes," Colin said. This doctor showed not one cue of surprise or shock at the unorthodox situation. Instead he turned to Colin.

"Andrew, good to see you."

"Good to see you too." Colin shook the man's hand. "Thanks for helping me out."

"No problem." He leaned in and spoke to a groaning Francine. "Shall we get you inside and see what the damage is?"

He didn't wait for her response, but immediately stood back and waved at the door. A young man pushed a gurney through the entrance and hurried to the car. Vinnie exited the vehicle and laid Francine on the gurney with a gentleness belying his ruthless criminal appearance. She groaned only once in pain. The young man started pushing the gurney, but she gripped the sides and started shaking her head.

"No! Not without Genevieve. Where is Genevieve?" There was hysteria in her voice. I cringed and pushed myself against the car.

"Who's Genevieve?" Paul asked and then followed Colin's pointed look towards me.

"Jenny?"

"No."

"Jenny, come on. Francine needs you."

"No."

"She's your friend and right now she needs you." His voice was losing its apologetic gentleness. He was appealing to my rational side.

"I didn't ask for her friendship." My heart was hammering in my chest. I could taste the fear on my breath. The hated blackness frequently threatening to smother me moved into the periphery of my vision. I closed my eyes and envisioned a clear sheet of music paper. I drew the G-clef and started mentally writing Mozart's Symphony No. 5 in B-flat major. I didn't even hear Colin move until he was standing in front of me.

"Jenny, I'm here. Tell me when you're ready."

I wrote five bars of the first movement before I felt control come back to me. I slowly opened my eyes and looked into Colin's intense gaze.

"I've never had friends. I don't know how to be a friend. I must be abysmal at it, because you left me. All of you," I whispered. "And I haven't been in a hospital for fifteen years. I genuinely don't want to go in."

"Oh, Jenny." Remorse was all over his face and in his voice. "I'm deeply sorry for the pain I've caused. We have a lot to talk about and deal with. Do you think you could put your anger and your fear aside for Francine? At this moment her health, her life, should take precedence. Right?"

"Logically, yes." If only I could convince my psyche that this hospital was not going to leave me emotionally scarred like all those other times in a past best forgotten.

He leaned in even closer, his nose almost touching mine. "Use your logic and your Mozart thingie to help Francine. Please, Jenny. Do this for me."

I breathed deeply. Twice. "I'll do it for Francine."

His face relaxed. "Thank you."

"Can we maybe move this along?" Paul asked from the open sliding doors. Francine coughed again and even I cringed at the painful sound. I walked to the gurney and the orderly started pushing it towards the clinic. I was walking on the one side, Vinnie on the other, concern pulling at his face.

Once Francine's coughing stopped, she turned frantic eyes on me. "Please don't leave me. Not once. Please."

"I will only promise to go in with you and stay with you until you feel safe." This might result in me staying days in the hospital, but I was not going to promise anything more than this. "Okay?"

She swallowed with difficulty, nodded once and her body went completely slack. I followed the gurney through the doors and briefly had to call up Mozart. I could feel my heart beating in my suprasternal notch, that little hollow above the breastbone. As I followed the gurney down a brightly lit corridor, I wondered how it was possible that my promise had calmed Francine, but utterly terrified me.

Only Colin's footsteps directly behind me and the unfinished first movement of the symphony in my head were keeping the blackness at bay. I could only hope Colin and Vinnie would not desert me again.

Chapter TWO

"So, why are you scared of hospitals?"

I took my eyes off the silent television screen in Francine's private room and made sure Colin saw the disdain on my face. "I'm not scared. I merely experience a very strong repulsion towards such institutions."

"Jenny, you can colour it with whichever fancy words you want, it is still a phobia."

I slumped in the luxury lounge chair. "I don't want to talk about it."

"Oh, come on, I'm dying of boredom here. Francine's sleeping peacefully from all those drugs they pumped into her, you are ignoring me, undoubtedly doing something interesting in your head, and I'm left watching a muted news show."

"I was not in my head. I was also watching the show. It's much more interesting without the sound. Look at the president's bodyguard, the one to the left." I pointed to the screen. Neutrality and objectivity did not exist in the media, but this news programme came the closest in its reportage of current events and especially the political arena. "Can you see how he is shifting from one foot to the other? And there. He's just pulled his ear again."

"What does that mean?"

"He's bored."

Colin laughed, but quickly quieted after a glance at the sleeping Francine. It had taken two hours of probing and testing, but Paul and another doctor, a woman in her early fifties, had determined that nothing was broken or severely damaged. When the older doctor had whispered a question about why Francine had been used as a punching bag, Paul had cut her off with a glare. That had made me wonder how many unregistered patients he was treating in this clinic.

The hospital looked more like an upscale hotel than a medical facility. Each patient had their own private room. The examination room I had been forced to go into with Francine was nothing like the rooms I had spent days in as a child. At least here I had been able to focus on the tasteful art on the walls and the soft classical music filling the elegant rooms. It wasn't the usual clinical white walls and rooms filled with medical equipment.

An hour ago, they had pushed Francine into her room and she had fallen into an exhausted sleep. Vinnie had left about twenty minutes ago to shower and change. His clothes were stained with Francine's blood. I had been focussing on the muted television to order my thoughts before I confronted Colin. For the last few months I had thought I would never see him again. I didn't feel ready for this confrontation.

"Tell me more," Colin said, pulling me back to our inane discussion.

"The president is not comfortable with what the Minister of Education is saying."

"How do you know that?"

"He's looking askance at the Minister. We do that when we are suspicious of others or what they are saying. And the micro-expressions around his mouth confirm this."

"Well, I wouldn't believe anything that man says in any case."

"The Minister of Education?" I squinted at the screen. The running ticker tape at the bottom of the screen was saying that the Minister of Education was announcing budget cuts, but promised that it would not affect teachers' salaries.

"Yes, him. That man is a menace to society and is only in office because of his family connections."

"Nepotism is as old as time."

"I could maybe accept it if the person benefiting from his bloodline were competent. This man is not. President Godard should replace him."

I turned my attention fully on Colin. "I did not know you were interested in politics."

"I'm not really interested. It's not like I call France my home country, but the last elections were so rife with scandals that it was difficult to not become interested."

"Are you talking about the scandal surrounding the other candidate's wife?"

The corners of Colin's mouth pulled down. "A woman who leaves her children's care to nannies, boarding schools and drivers is no role model for any group of people. According to those reports she didn't see her seven-year-old daughter for an entire semester. That is unacceptable."

I blinked in surprise. "Do you expect a woman to stay at home and raise the children?"

Colin dropped his chin and looked at me from under his eyebrows. "Jenny, you know me better than that. I don't have any preconceived idea about family structure or role division within a family. I just believe that both parents should play active roles in the raising of their children. Not leave it to anonymous caregivers and teachers."

"Does that mean that you approve of the new president? Even before he was inaugurated nine months ago, both he and his wife were constantly in the news with their presence at their son's school activities."

"In that sense I approve of him."

"But not in another sense?" I asked.

"I don't agree with all of his policies. I do think though that he was the best choice out of the running candidates."

I turned my attention back to the television screen and watched President Godard walk off the podium, ignoring questions being shouted at him from persistent reporters. He reached his wife, a strikingly elegant woman in her late forties. The media loved analysing her fashion, parenting methods, and diet, but most of all held up the success she had in her medical career as a banner for female empowerment.

The president put his hand on the hollow of her back and

walked with her off the screen. That gesture was unconscious and significant. Not only did he immediately touch her the moment he was close enough, but she leaned into that touch. I had seen them on screen enough times to know that their relationship was one of mutual trust and respect.

"So why are you scared of hospitals?" Colin's quick change of topic caught me off guard and I almost answered him.

"Where have you been the last four months?" I countered. I was angry again and it was audible.

"I honestly missed you, Jenny."

I had also missed him, but didn't know why he would bring it up now. I was still waiting for an explanation, so I didn't say anything. I simply looked at him without blinking and without any expression. This made him smile. I didn't know why.

"With you everything is so black and white, so simple."

"That is not true. I'm fully aware of the many gray areas in people's lives, thinking and communication. I just choose to not communicate like that." I was an expert in nuances of nonverbal communication, not of verbal communication. Colin had made a point of omitting the use of metaphors and slang when he spoke to me. At first it had been difficult for Vinnie, whose linguistic use was exceptionally colourful. Both of them had respected my need for the literal use of language. The television completely forgotten, I narrowed my eyes at Colin and enunciated slowly, clearly, "Explain."

He shifted in his chair, uncomfortable. "I must first say a few things."

I never understood why people needed to announce their intentions like this. Since he was waiting for my permission to continue, I nodded.

"You are scary good at reading people and I know that you are reading me at this moment. That is why I need to tell you that I can't tell you everything." He held up his hands when I inhaled to object. "Just let me finish explaining first, please. I can't tell you everything for all kinds of security reasons."

"Which means that you went away on some Interpol

mission." I watched his face closely for a reaction and was not disappointed. I didn't know how long he had been living a life of secrets, but my pronouncement made him notably uncomfortable. He couldn't resist a quick glance at the closed door.

"Yes," he said quietly. "It was mandated by... them. I can't tell you where I went and what I did. If you ask me about this, I will have to lie to you, so please don't put me in that position."

There was infinitely more to his story than some mission he had been on. I could see it. I analysed his face and again he sat patiently, waiting for me to reach a conclusion. "Okay. I won't ask you about where you were or what you did. Anything else I can't ask you about?"

He closed his eyes for a moment, considering. When he looked at me there was only sincerity on his face. "No, not that I can think of. Let me tell you what I can before you start asking questions."

"Okay." I leaned back in my chair.

"I was sent on a mission four months ago. As usual these things happen so fast that there isn't much time for packing or goodbyes."

"But you phoned me to say goodbye." I remembered that conversation clearly. I had not enjoyed it. As a rule, I avoided telephonic conversations. I abhorred it. That one in particular had made me feel uncomfortable and powerless. "You also promised to phone me the next week."

Colin rubbed his hand over his face. "I know, Jenny. I made time to phone you. But things very quickly went south when I got there. I was there for only five days when I was made."

"What does that mean?"

He smiled. "It means that I went undercover and someone discovered that I wasn't who I pretended to be."

"So I made you six months ago when I discovered that you used all those false identities?"

He laughed softly, shaking his head. "Yes, you did. Only this time, the guys who made me were not as friendly as you."

"I'm not friendly."

An unfamiliar smile pulled at Colin's mouth. Lay people called it a knowing smile. What did he think he knew about me? I didn't like being the recipient of that smile, but waited for him to continue.

"When my cover was blown, I got beaten up pretty badly."

My chest tightened. "How badly?"

He crossed his arms. Classic blocking behaviour. He didn't like remembering or talking about this. "Bad enough that Vinnie had to come and get me out. I spent six weeks in hospital and the last six weeks in physiotherapy."

The tightness in my chest grew worse. That explained Vinnie's disappearance too. "What happened?"

"I'm not going to tell you what happened, Jenny. I can't. I'll tell you about my injuries though." His tone indicated that he was trying to placate me. My lips thinned, but I listened. "Altogether nine ribs were broken, I had some internal injuries, but it was not too bad. There was extensive damage to my right leg. The femur was broken in four places and there was, still is, a lot of muscle damage."

"That's why you're walking differently." My breathing was shallow. I was scared for him, for what had happened to him. "Is there permanent damage?"

"Oh, my leg will never look as pretty as before. The scars are quite big, but the physio helped a lot and my leg now only gets stiff when it's cold or when I'm sitting for too long. The doctors promised me that with exercise I should gain full mobility again. At least the damage to my hands was not that bad."

My eyes flew to his hands. His hands were in fists, tucked under his arms. On an inhale, he uncrossed his arms and uncurled his fingers for me to see.

"There are a few small scars, but I can't see anything strange." My breathing shuddered. I dreaded to ask. "What did they do?"

"They broke all my fingers." He closed his fists again when I gasped. "That was more painful than my leg."

"You were tortured," I whispered in horror.

"Yes." His lips thinned. "I didn't want these guys anywhere near you, Jenny. I needed to heal and to walk again before I could let you see me."

"Why?" A fleeting expression around his eyes and mouth clued me in. "You thought I would not be able to handle your injuries, that I would not cope. You arrogant arsehole."

"Jenny." He sounded shocked at my expletive. "I didn't want you to worry about me."

"And disappearing out of my life without a word didn't worry me?" A sneer pulled at my lips. "You need a few classes in psychology."

"God, I'm sorry. I didn't know how to handle it. I still don't know. That whole mission went belly up." He blinked twice. "The mission went bad and I didn't want any of that to touch you."

It grew quiet between us. I needed time to think about this, to analyse how I felt about it. This was a lot to assimilate. A question that had been nagging at me came to the fore.

"Where were you tonight when I phoned you?" I asked. The pull of his mouth and tension around his eyes gave me worrisome clues. I leaned forward and glared at him. "What are you ashamed of?"

"I'm not ashamed." He flinched at my pointed look. "Not really ashamed, rather worried about your reaction."

"My reaction to what?"

He straightened his shoulders and looked me in the eye. "I bought the apartment next to yours and have been living there for the last six weeks."

For a few seconds I forgot to breathe. With a stuttering gasp, I jumped out of my chair and walked away. I stopped in front of an exceptional reproduction of a Frida Kahlo self-portrait. I focussed on the two parrots sitting on her shoulders, hoping it would calm me. It didn't work, so I closed my eyes.

"Jenny?" Colin's voice reached me through a fog of Mozart's String Quartet No. 8 in F major simultaneously playing in my head while I mentally penned it down.

I opened my eyes and found myself sitting in Colin's chair. I didn't know how I had got there or how long I had been sitting there. He was kneeling on the floor in front of me, looking very concerned. "Are you with me?"

I stared at him. For a long time. Eventually he sat back on his heels and waited. I stared some more.

"All this time and you've been living right next to me?"

"Yes."

"Why?"

"Why what?"

"Why did you buy the apartment next to mine? It wasn't for sale."

"I made Monsieur Blier an offer he didn't want to refuse." He sighed. "I wanted to be close enough to keep an eye on you and make sure you were safe."

"Safe from whom? These people who had tortured you? And how did you plan to protect me if you were so badly injured?"

"Vinnie has also been living there."

I closed my eyes and wrote a few more bars of the string quartet. I was experiencing so many emotions, I didn't know which to allow dominance. I went with the safest emotion. "I am truly angry with you right now, Colin. You had no right to make these decisions on my behalf. You didn't make the right choice. You kept a lot of important information from me. I've changed my mind. I'm not ready to accept your apology."

"Jenny, don't be mad at me."

Colin's plea was interrupted by soft groans coming from Francine's bed. We jumped up and walked across the Persian rug to her side. Even though my anger was replaced by concern for Francine, I was not going to forget about this topic.

"Oh God, where am I?" Francine reached up and gingerly touched her face.

"You're in the hospital," I said.

Her good eye widened slightly. "How did I get here?"

"Don't you remember?" Colin asked and leaned towards her. Worry tightened his features.

"You're here too?" She looked surprised to see Colin standing next to me. It was difficult for me to ascertain what was going on in her head. I cursed the swelling on her face. Only one eye was open enough to see the pupil, but it was by no means enough to tell anything. It was also ghastly looking into an eye that was so bloodshot.

"Maybe we should get the doctor." Colin straightened and turned to the door.

"No." Francine's outburst stopped him. "I'm just disoriented, Colin. Give me a moment to get myself together."

Colin caught my eye, lifted his eyebrows and nodded his chin towards Francine in some nonverbal message. I had no idea what he was trying to communicate. Francine tried to push herself higher against the pillows, but fell back with a groan. "This really hurts."

"The doctor said that he could give you more painkillers if you woke up and needed it," I said, ignoring Colin's pointed looks.

"I don't want anything that will make me feel dull." Francine slowly inhaled and on the exhale pushed herself up to lean higher against the pillows. The pain must have been significant because her natural colour was replaced by a sickly gray pallor. She breathed slowly a few times with a clenched jaw. "God, this really, really hurts. What did the doctors say?"

"That you are badly beaten up and badly bruised. Nothing is broken, but they say that it will be a few days before you should get out of bed and at least a week before you'll move again with some level of comfort."

"Great," she said with forced joy. "So I can go home now?"

"You should stay here for at least another day," Colin answered.

As they started disagreeing about this, the ringing of my smartphone came from my handbag. I walked away from the growing argument and picked my bag off the floor. My phone was in its usual pocket inside the bag, ringing and vibrating. I took it out and frowned at the screen. Why did people not pay attention to what I said?

The purpose of having a smartphone was for me to use the camera and recording functions, unobtrusively stealing moments from people in cafés in order to study their body language at a later time. It was not for people to phone me. Apparently this did not matter to the people who considered themselves part of my life.

I swiped the screen to answer the call. "Wait." I placed the phone against my chest and turned to Francine's bed only to see her and Colin staring at me. "I'm going to take this call outside."

I left the room in search of a private corner. It was ten o'clock in the morning and the hospital was a hub of activity. After two minutes walking along the hall, I returned to Francine's room. She was still arguing with Colin, but stopped mid-sentence.

"There is no quiet place in this hospital," I said with disgust, my smartphone still clutched against my chest.

"Use the bathroom," Colin said.

Francine's upscale private hospital room came complete with its own, fully equipped bathroom. Only when I closed the door behind me did I wonder if I should've thanked Colin for his idea. I shrugged it off and brought the phone to my ear.

"Yes?" I spoke quietly, hoping my conversation could not be heard in the other room.

"Genevieve, you might want to be more polite when you answer your phone." Phillip Rousseau, my boss and mentor of six years, was speaking in his patient voice. Never a good sign.

"I don't like phones," I said and waited. When Phillip didn't say anything, I started thinking. He had been the first person in my life to treat me with any kind of respect. The least I could do was return that. I did, after all, hold him in very high esteem. "Good morning, Phillip. How are you today?"

"Good morning, Genevieve." There was a smile in his voice. He knew he had won this round. "I'm a little worried. Where are you?"

"I'm at a hospital."

"A what?" The smile disappeared from his tone. "Why are you at a hospital? Are you okay? What happened? You never go to hospitals."

Not only was Phillip my highly respected boss, but he had in some way taken on a paternal role in my life. He had also taken on worrying about me. Something I had difficulty growing accustomed to.

"I'm fine. It's not me. It's–" The bathroom door burst open. Colin walked towards me shaking his head. I asked him, "What now?"

"Who are you talking to, Genevieve?" Phillip asked in my ear.

"To C–"

Quicker than I could think to react, Colin snatched my smartphone out of my grip. Thief. He held the phone against his chest. "Who's this?"

"Phillip." Colin had met my boss during that first case. We had all had a common goal, so there hadn't been time for my boss, the head of an exclusive insurance company, to take exception to Colin, an art thief. I held out my hand. "Give me my phone."

"Not yet." He paused until I raised my eyes to his face. He looked worried. "Jenny, this thing with Francine is serious. Don't tell Phillip who you're with. At least not until you've heard what Francine has to say."

"I will not lie to Phillip."

"You don't have to lie," he said with a groan. "Just don't tell him the whole truth."

I considered myself to be a rational person, not driven by emotion. Not at all. But this had been a trying morning. And at the utterance of his ridiculous request, I was furious. Again. I schooled my face while considering my next step. On my nod, Colin handed me my phone.

"Sorry about that, Phillip." Something in my tone must have alerted Colin because he tilted his head to one side and looked apprehensive. "I am at a health facility with a person of dubious repute that I met a few months ago. We helped a mutual friend, a person with unparalleled technological skills and fashion sense. This person had a similar unfortunate experience as I did that same few months ago."

By the time I finished, Colin was scowling, anger pulling the corners of his mouth down.

"What?" Phillip's voice tightened with concern. "You're at the hospital with Colin and Francine was attacked? Is she okay?"

"I knew you'd get it!" I smiled triumphantly. Colin's lips compressed with annoyance and he left the bathroom. This petty action gave me unadulterated pleasure. "Francine is badly bruised, but she'll be okay. She's arguing with Colin at the moment, because she wants to go home and he insists she stays longer in the hospital."

"How did you get involved in this?"

I gave him the quick version of this morning's events. Including the part where Francine confessed to murdering two men. I did leave out the part where Colin had been tortured and spent months recuperating.

"Why have you not phoned the police?"

I knew this question would lead to other questions. Ones that I didn't want asked. Not until I had more answers from Colin and was less angry. "Why did you phone me on my phone that I never use for speaking to people?"

"I was worried. You're always in your office by eight o'clock. When you didn't come, I wanted to know why."

"Now you know."

"Will you be coming in today?"

"If it's not necessary, I won't. I would prefer to go home and rest. Unless there is something urgent for me to work on."

"There is a new case I would like for you to look at, but it can wait until tomorrow."

"What new case?" My mood lifted. I loved a new challenge. It would also take my mind off my new neighbours.

"Nothing urgent. A string of robberies over a period of time. It can wait until tomorrow. Take the rest of the day and go to the cinema, go shopping, go for a massage. Enjoy your day off."

Phillip was always trying to get me to go to recreational places other people frequented.

"You know I won't go to those places. Studies have shown the bacteria present on a cinema seat range from E.coli to faecal matter."

"Oh, for the love of God, stop." He sighed. "I don't know why I'm still trying. At least attempt to enjoy the time off."

I finished the call and went back into Francine's room. Colin was standing next to the bed, his arms folded, and his tongue appeared very briefly between his lips. He was smug. Francine looked resigned. It appeared as if the two friends had come to some compromise. They stopped their whispered conversation as soon as they noticed me.

"She's going to stay in my apartment until we can sort this out," Colin announced.

"The apartment next to mine?" My throat hurt as I pushed the words past my lips.

"Yes. It would be safer for everyone." Colin looked less smug now. Even though I saw constant flashes of remorse on his face, I couldn't stop being angry. "Vinnie will look after her."

"And you?" I asked, dreading the answer.

"Oh, I'll be staying with you, in my old room." His smile was charming. I hated it when he tried to be charming. "It will be just like old times."

"No, no, no, no, no." I didn't care that I sounded like a panicked stuck record. "There are three bedrooms in your apartment. You will stay there. I'm still angry with you. I don't want you in my apartment. And it took me four days of cleaning to have my place back to normal after the last time you stayed with me."

Colin's eyebrows lifted in surprise. "I left your place in perfect order."

"There were dust particles under your bed." I grunted and gave in to the urge to clarify. "Not your bed. The bed you had used. There was a smudge on the left-hand corner of the windowsill, bits of fluff from your clothes on the shelves in the wardrobe and a scuff mark on the floor under the desk."

Francine's laughter, causing her to groan in pain, stopped me. The list of dirt left behind by the thief was much longer and I truly wanted to recite it.

"Oh Genevieve, you're priceless," Francine said past another groan. She sobered and looked at me with an intensity that warned me something significant was about to be said. "Thank you for being here. I can remember asking you to stay, but also remember thinking you wouldn't."

Shame briefly touched my awareness. I blinked it away. "That's what friends do for each other."

Not even the swelling in her face could disguise the relaxation of her facial features and the genuine smile pulling at her swollen lips.

"You're my friend," she said as if announcing it. "I'm glad that I have you as my friend."

Surprise stole my speech. Here I had been thinking that they had all deserted me because I was socially unacceptable. Now I was faced with a declaration of this magnitude. I reached for a suitable riposte, but came up empty.

"You don't have to say anything," Francine said. Because her voice was still scratchy, I couldn't tell if it was hurt, annoyance or pain I detected in her tone. "I understand. And I trust you. Why else would I have asked for you to stay with me?"

"I don't know." I took two steps towards the door. I had thought that Francine had insisted on those lunches with me from a need to speak to someone unbiased. She had shared with me her life philosophies and loved that I never ridiculed her. When I hadn't agreed with her, I had told her so and presented my counter-arguments to her flawed reasoning, sometimes resulting in a fun intellectual debate.

Now she told me that she trusted me. What was I supposed to do with her trust? Phillip trusted me to do my job, but until six months ago I had never had anyone trust me with their emotions or personal well-being. How did normal people deal with this on a daily basis? From my raised heart rate and shaky breathing, I knew that I was challenged with more than I could handle.

I grabbed my handbag and walked to the door. "I have to go."

"Why?" Colin asked.

"Because I have to go. I can't stay here."

"But you promised that you'd stay with me," Francine said.

"I promised that I would stay until you felt safe." I took a moment to study her body language. "You're feeling safe. I'm leaving."

"You're a coward, Jenny." Colin shook his head. "One of the bravest people I know, but a total coward."

"That doesn't make sense at all. I'm leaving."

It wouldn't take much for me to agree that Colin was right. I was a coward. Admitting to it didn't make me stay in Francine's room though. In reality, it made me leave Francine's room without another word and hasten my steps out of the hospital.

I walked into a cold, sunny day to realise that I had no transport home. There was no rational reasoning that could get me to go back into the hospital asking Colin for a ride home. A shudder went through me at the thought of using a taxi. People thought taxis were cleaner than other public transport, but that was generally not true.

This once I would ignore my germ-anxiety and get into one of the taxis parked in front of the hospital. I wanted to get home. Away from reappearing thieves and friendship proclamations. This emotional overload had me desperate for something normal. It had been three days since I last scrubbed the bathrooms and it would be the perfect therapeutic action to deal with this.

As I gingerly got into a taxi I thought about the implications of Colin's return into my life. And Vinnie and Francine. What else were they bringing with them into my safe world? I wanted to not think about this. I wanted the simplicity of cleaning my apartment and the predictability of going to work tomorrow. The thought of a new case perked me up. If only for a few minutes.

Chapter THREE

"This is the new case?" I lifted one of the thick files from my desk. If it weren't so heavy and full of loose bits of paper, I would've shaken it at Phillip in annoyance. Instead I put it on top of the others and rested my hand on it. "Five files this size and you told me it could wait? Is this a cold case?"

"Good morning, Genevieve." Phillip walked into my viewing room and pulled a chair closer. "How are you this morning? I see that you've found the files."

When I had stepped into my office ten minutes ago, these files had been waiting for me on my long desk. Above the desk, my ten top-of-the-range computer monitors, arranged in a wide semi-circle, were dark. Apart from placing my coffee mug on its designated coaster and glancing at the files, there hadn't been time for much else. Phillip's presence in my viewing room indicated that he had requested to be informed as soon as I stepped into the building. He only ever did that when he was concerned about me.

I turned away from the files and watched Phillip place the chair at a comfortable distance from me. He understood and respected my need for personal space. "Were you being sarcastic?"

The *risorius* muscle pulled at the corner of his mouth. He was fighting a smile. "Yes and no. But I don't want to argue with you on this beautiful Tuesday morning. Let's talk about Francine. How is she?"

"I don't know."

"What do you mean you don't know?"

I was becoming faster in recognising the feeling of guilt. I pushed it away. Despite my cleaning frenzy yesterday, there was still chaos in my chest. I had worked so hard during my teens and twenties to never have this feeling, but these people had brought it all back into my life.

After I had cleaned the oven a second time last night, I had accepted the necessity to sit down and analyse what was behind my desire for hygiene. Behind the tightness in my chest. A cup of camomile tea later I had identified the predominant feeling as betrayal. What I didn't know was whether I wanted to address this with Vinnie, Francine and especially Colin. I was, however, determined to insist on a complete explanation from Colin. I also wanted to hear the full account of what had happened to Francine so I could make an informed judgement call.

As it was, her admission of murdering two people horrified me. I didn't know if there was anything she could say that would make me look at her favourably again. The fact that she was so deeply pleased with calling me her friend didn't help either. It only exacerbated the maelstrom of emotions.

"I mean I don't know. I left the hospital yesterday shortly after our phone conversation and have not spoken to her since. She was awake and arguing when I left."

"You didn't phone to find out about your friend?" He shook his head. "Never mind that. Where is Colin?"

"I don't know and right now I don't want to talk about it." The strain in my tone must have alerted Phillip. His eyebrows were raised and I knew he was concerned. I didn't want him to ask the question I saw on his face. "Tell me about the thefts."

Phillip narrowed his eyes at me, no doubt letting me know that he was allowing me to evade his questioning. He glanced at the files. "It's strange. In the last four weeks, five thefts occurred in very secure and, in two of the cases, very secret locations."

"So it's not a cold case. Were they insured by Rousseau & Rousseau?"

"Two of these cases, yes."

"Then why are we dealing with all five thefts?" My mind was

adding all the pieces together. I narrowed my eyes. "Are we doing this as Rousseau & Rousseau or are we doing this for someone else? Interpol?"

Instead of answering me, Phillip got out of the chair and opened the electronic doors to my soundproof viewing room. "She knows."

"I knew she wouldn't take long to put two and two together." The familiar scratchy voice with its crisp British accent identified its owner. Colonel Manfred Millard. He entered my viewing room, looking as rumpled as always. A beige raincoat was squashed under his arm, his white shirt looked like he had worn it for a week, and the fumbled Windsor knot of his outdated tie didn't make it up to the unbuttoned collar of his shirt. But there was a genuine smile lifting his unshaven cheeks and crinkling the corners of his eyes. "Hello, Doctor Face-Reader. Looking good as always. Still as annoying as always?"

"Hello, Manny. You're smiling, so you are not sarcastic and angry. Why do you think fondly of me as annoying?"

Manny laughed. "That is why, Doc. That is why."

Phillip rolled the third and only other office chair to my desk and motioned for Manny to sit. "I've just started telling her about the case."

My first contact with Manny had not been amicable at all. It had taken us a fair amount of time to reach any form of cooperation. He had reluctantly admitted respecting my expertise and I had had to concede to his superior investigative skills. At that time he had been working for the European Defence Agency. After that case he had accepted a position at Interpol. I wasn't completely sure what he was doing now. "Why is Interpol interested in this case? When did you get this case? Phillip, why did you not tell me about this yesterday? I could've made some progress by now."

"Whoa, hold your horses, Doc." Manny lifted his hands.

"What horses? I don't own any horses." I turned to Phillip. "Will you please answer my questions?"

Phillip's mouth was quivering again, fighting another smile. He won control. "Let me give you a quick run-down and then Manny can tell you their interest. The first theft took place four weeks ago in an elderly woman's home. She had quite a few valuable artefacts in her home, but most significant was what was in her safe. She had an Alberto Giacometti bronze sculpture, more valuable than all of the art in her home combined. We're talking close to one hundred million dollars. She was attacked, gagged and bound while two men raided her home. They took a few other pieces of the art, broke into her safe and took the Giacometti as well."

"Is she okay?" I asked.

"Traumatised, but fine. She's also furious. Her home and all the content is insured by us and protected by a highly reputable security company. She had a custom-made security system installed, maintained by the security company who had three guards on her property at all times."

"Is she a celebrity that she needs such security?"

"No, but she comes from old money. Lots of it. She never got married and has no children."

"How did the thieves enter her home? How did they get past the security system and the guards?"

"That is a mystery that infuriates the security company. Their exhaustive investigation into the event reached no conclusion. Their system showed no activity during that period. The guards were found not guilty of any neglect of duty. Their statements were supported by the evidence that no alarms were triggered even though the owner said that she had repeatedly pushed the panic button in numerous places around the house. This company is one of the most respected in the country, used by many high-profile individuals."

"The owner of this company is some family member to someone high up in Interpol," Manny interrupted. Clearly he couldn't wait any longer for Phillip to finish. "Because his company is completely dependent on its reputation for reliability, he took this to his relative in Interpol. The next day it was on my desk. That was two days ago. Once I looked at it, I knew exactly who would be perfect for helping me tie this thing up quickly, so I got in my car."

"You drove all the way here from Lyon?" I asked, knowing that Manny was stationed there at Interpol's headquarters.

"Yes. Coming here was recommended."

"They want you to work with us on this," Phillip said. "They know you have connections with the insurance industry."

"After the last fiasco, the whole world knows." Manny looked displeased with this.

I didn't want to waste precious cognitive function on understanding his annoyance. The case was more interesting. "What about the other thefts?"

"Similar stories. Highly protected, highly valued artefacts of all eras, genres, mediums. In only one other case were the owners attacked. The other three times the owners were not at home during the robbery."

"Are these professional thieves?" I asked this question with Colin's face in my mind. He might be working for Interpol, but he was still a thief. Would he be capable of doing something like this? At his own admission, he had been in the city for the last six weeks.

"Most definitely not," Manny said. "Professional art thieves will get in, take what they're there for and get out. You can ask your boyfriend if this is true."

"I don't have a boyfriend," I immediately answered. And then I understood his meaning. It annoyed me. "Colin is not my boyfriend."

Manny snorted his disdain. "Well, these guys were complete amateurs. They fooled around. In one house, they even stole iPads, DVDs and three tubs of ice cream."

"Was it the same group at all five robberies?" I asked.

"No. Two of these were committed the same evening, in two different countries."

"Two different countries? Where?" That eliminated Colin from my suspect list.

Manny closed his eyes for a moment. "One was here in France, in Lille, the other in Germany. The police also found footprints at the various crime scenes, none of them the same. Some crime scenes had only one set of footprints, different to the other crime scenes. Other crime scenes had two or more sets of footprints from different perpetrators. It is all in the reports there."

I looked at the files Manny pointed at. "So, what do these cases have in common? Except of course the theft of valuables?"

Manny had now completely taken over from Phillip. He counted on his fingers. "The thief or thieves knew exactly where to go. In the Lille house, the owner had a secret safe built into a secret wall. The wall was hidden behind a curtain, the safe hidden behind a panel covered by a valuable painting supposed to serve as a red herring."

I searched my mind for the meaning of that idiom and then nodded proudly for Manny to continue.

"None of the safes were broken, lock-picked or blown up. The thieves knew the combinations to get in. One safe had a fingerprint lock which the thief managed to override. All the homes were insured, but by different companies. Maybe the most significant similarity is that all of them employed security companies."

"Not all of our clients have security companies in their employ," Phillip said. "We highly recommend it to our clients, since they are all high-end with sometimes priceless valuables in their homes. Some people simply don't want that intrusion. They would rather take the risk and pay a higher premium on their insurance than give strangers access to their home. Even if those strangers are security guards. Most of them do however have alarm systems, even if it's only to scare away stray cats or the odd thief."

I thought about this. "What about surveillance cameras on those properties that were broken into?"

"They were also overridden. While these guys were cleaning out the safes, the entire security system functioned as if everything was normal," Manny said.

The door swished open and Angelique, Phillip's personal assistant, entered. As usual she looked elegantly formidable, except when she glanced at me. Then she looked terrified. She took another tentative step and addressed Phillip. "Sir, there is an urgent call for you in your office."

"Can't it wait, Angelique?" Phillip insisted on an informal, yet respectful work atmosphere. Angelique never looked comfortable being addressed by her first name. Everyone in the office called Phillip by his name. She refused.

"No, sir. It's Madame Lenoir."

"Her house was also broken into." Phillip jumped out of his chair. "Let me take care of this and I'll get right back."

"No problem. Doc and I will catch up," Manny said. Phillip followed Angelique out my viewing room and Manny turned to me. "So, Doc, how have you been?"

"Well, thank you, Manny. How have you been?" I was well practiced in insincere interest and the exchange of mundane questions and answers.

Manny laughed. "Are you only asking me to be polite?"

"Yes." I gave it some thought. "Actually, no. I haven't seen you in five months and you've been working at Interpol. I suppose that you have done quite a lot of interesting things. That does make me interested in how you have been."

"Um, thanks, Doc. I think." He leaned back in his chair. "Joining Interpol was a good move for me. We did a full investigation into Kubanov after that whole drama five months ago. Did you know we had a breakthrough in our search for evidence against that arsehole?"

"No." The Russian criminal disguised as a philanthropist's actions had steered me on a path where I had seen far too much of the dark side of human nature. He had been at the centre of the case that had brought Colin, Vinnie and Francine into my life. He was a man who needed to be incarcerated. Preferably forever. "What evidence?"

"It doesn't matter now. Nothing ever came from it." He sighed heavily. "When I agreed to join Interpol it was on the condition that I could pursue the Kubanov case."

It had taken weeks of Mozart to forget the terror I had experienced because of Kubanov. "So what happened to your investigation?"

"We got some solid leads that would've connected Kubanov to more international crimes. If we had been able to get our hands on that evidence, we would've had a good case against him." He slumped in his chair. "When I reached that point in my investigation, the top guys took an interest, grabbed all the files from me and said that they would get their own guy on it. Can you imagine that?"

"No." I only said this because Manny looked at me with expectation to share his disgust.

"Exactly! The bastards sent their guy and if scuttlebutt is to be believed–"

"What is scuttlebutt?" I asked.

"It's navy slang for rumours."

"You've never been in the navy. Why would you use that term? Why not just say rumour?"

Manny bit down hard on his jaw for a few seconds. "Yes, you are still as annoying as always. Rumour. There, I said it. Rumours were flying that the person they had sent in to gather the evidence on Kubanov had been killed. My case went cold after that. I wasn't allowed to pursue Kubanov anymore."

"Why not? I thought you were put in charge of your own specialised investigation unit. Did you get demoted?"

"I did not…" Manny took a deep breath. "Apparently something happened that is far above my specialised pay-grade. I have carte blanche on which cases I take, as long as it is related to white collar and art crimes."

"What about conflict with your co-workers? Wouldn't they be resentful of your power to take cases from them?" I had read that some of the fiercest competition came within law enforcement, especially investigative services.

"Not that I really care, but these guys are so overrun with cases that I've found them immensely grateful to hand anything over. I can have any case I want."

"Except the Kubanov investigation."

His face tightened with anger, but his response was interrupted by Phillip's return. He lifted an eyebrow at Manny's body language, looked at me, but didn't say anything. He sat down and glanced at the files on my desk. Manny and I had completely gone off topic.

"We have to solve these thefts, Genevieve. As soon as possible."

"Of course. Why do you sound more stressed now? Did something happen with your phone call?"

"Yes. Madame Lenoir is threatening to sue us. She has no leg to stand on, since we have nothing to do with her security at home, but it is a nuisance any which way. Now I'll have to get the lawyers involved and it will cost time and money that I don't want to waste on this."

Phillip was venting. Academically I understood the need people had for this. I sometimes needed to vent. But it was boring. I picked up one of the files and flipped through it while Phillip addressed Manny when he saw that he had lost my attention. I scanned the police reports and looked at the crime scene photos. Something caught my eye and I picked up another file. Five files later I was frowning.

"Why has this flower not been identified?" My questions interrupted Manny in the middle of some unimportant observation about rich people's sense of entitlement. Both men looked at me with raised eyebrows. I shook a photo at them. "The flower?"

"What flower, Genevieve?" Phillip asked.

"The flowers that were left at every scene." I pointed at a red flower on the mantelpiece. "It is out of focus and too far for me to identify what kind of flower it is, but the same red shape appears in all five crime scene photos."

"What?" Manny grabbed the photo out of my hand and studied it. "Show me the other photos."

I laid five crime scene photos next to each other. In chronological order. At each scene the flower was in close proximity to the safe that had been broken in to. In one photo the flower was on what I guessed to be an eighteenth-century cherry wood wall unit. In another, the red flower was on the desk in front of the wall where the open safe was an empty husk.

Manny and Phillip leaned in to look at the photos on my desk. They were too close to me, so I pushed my chair a bit back and waited. They were looking back and forth at the photos. The change in their breathing was audible as they noticed the flowers in each photo.

"Well, I'll be damned." Manny slumped back in his chair and looked at me with wide eyes. "Doc, you've just seen something that none of the detectives had noticed."

I sucked my lips in and bit down hard on them before I angered Manny again by remarking that he also had not noticed this. Phillip was still looking at the photos, so close now that his nose was almost touching my desk.

"This is most frustrating." Phillip sat up and nodded at the photos. "In some photos it looks like it could be a tulip, in others a Laeliocattleya."

"A whatsit?" Manny looked at Phillip as if seeing him for the first time.

"It's an orchid hybrid." As he looked at the photos, his lips pulled into a brief pout, indicating his uncertainty. "No, it can't be. Oh, I don't know. Manny, did the crime scene investigators bag the flowers?"

"I'll have to check the evidence catalogue."

"Could you do that now?" I asked.

"Um, sure. Do you think this is important?"

I glared at Manny.

"Oh, this is too easy." Manny laughed. "Doc, you make for such an easy target. I got your goat, didn't I?"

"I don't have a goat," I said in a tight voice. Manny and Phillip started laughing, so I had to wait until they settled. This was it. I was going to have to enrol in some course to enrich my knowledge of metaphors. I didn't enjoy being laughed at.

"Sorry, Genevieve," Phillip said. "This was very amusing."

"So I surmised." My voice was still tight. It sobered Phillip, but Manny continued looking full of mirth.

"Give me a moment to phone the office. They'll check the evidence and we might have an answer." He got up and walked out of my viewing room, chuckling to himself.

I wavered for a moment, but then decided I had to know. "What just happened?"

"Manny was only teasing you, Genevieve," Phillip answered gently.

"Why?"

"With your three degrees in psychology, you don't know?"

"Some people tease to establish dominance." I had written a paper on it in my first year in university in Tokyo.

"You know this is not Manny's intention."

"No, it would appear that his teasing would fall in the other category. It is done out of playful affection. I can see it in his nonverbal cues."

"But you don't look overly happy with it." Phillip ended his statement in a question form. In the six years he had been my boss, I had learned to interpret it as his request for an explanation.

"I don't understand it. Why would Manny feel affection towards me? I'm nobody to him."

Manny returned to the viewing room. He grunted something and put his phone in the breast pocket of his jacket.

"My guys will check these flowers." He fell into his chair. "What else did you see in those files, Doc?"

I was happy to return to a topic of a lesser emotional nature. "Apart from the flowers on the photos, I didn't see anything you don't already know, but I haven't studied the files thoroughly yet. For that I would need some time."

"Take all the time you need, Doc. Just make it really fast." Manny looked at one of the dark monitors on the wall. "It doesn't compute. From the crime scenes it is obvious that these guys are rank amateurs. Yet they knew where all the security features were, they disabled it and had their sights only set on stealing the most valuable pieces in each home. Some of them then continued to steal crap, but nothing else of true value. It is almost as if they were stealing on order."

"A crime syndicate?" I asked. This was a feasible theory.

"That would explain the differences and similarities." Manny sat up and looked more animated. "The main guy found a way to get into the security companies' systems, getting the security codes and specs for each of these homes. He employs small-time criminals to do his dirty work for him, giving them everything on a silver platter. All they have to do is get him something very specific from that home. If they choose to take anything else, it is their prerogative. Hence the stolen iPads and ice cream."

"And he gets them to leave a red flower," I said.

"Yes, I have not forgotten. The questions now are why were these houses specifically targeted? Why were those specific items so significant to the brains behind this ring? And why the flower?"

Manny's phone started ringing and he took it from his jacket pocket. A brief and one-sided conversation ensued. He ended the call and put the phone back in his jacket pocket. He took a deep breath before he faced me. "I have to go. Work your magic, Doc. Find out what connects the art, the flowers and the other things."

I ignored Manny's final order to phone him, and waved off Phillip reminding me to take breaks and eat something. There was something about this case that didn't sit right with me. My subconscious had already recognised it and I needed to get to work so that it could filter through to my conscious brain.

Chapter FOUR

"Jenny?"

I blinked at the monitors in front of me. I had been staring at the ten monitors for what felt like hours. It wouldn't come as a surprise to me if I had started hallucinating. I took a shaky breath and turned to my right. I wasn't hearing voices in my head. Colin was sitting next to me.

"What are you doing here?" I asked.

"Right now I'm appreciating the amazing equipment in this room. I had no idea you had such a set-up here, Jenny. This stuff is seriously high-tech." He glanced at the three antique-looking filing cabinets. "Maybe not everything, but you have a super-cool place here. Why didn't you ever tell me about this?"

"What would be the purpose of such a discussion?" I was annoyed. This reminded me of the first time I had met Colin. Then he had also avoided answering my questions by diverting my attention. I was not going to let it happen again. I lowered my chin and stared at him from beneath my brows. "What are you doing here?"

He smiled. "Office buildings are not quite my hang-out spots, but Phillip insisted."

"Phillip phoned you? Why?" That was odd. And suspicious.

"He is worried." Colin leaned back in the chair and awkwardly stretched his right leg out in front of him. "What's this all about? Are you okay?"

"I'm fine." I took a deep breath and lifted my eyebrows to remove the frown on my forehead. It wasn't that easy to not tighten my lips though. "What exactly did Phillip say?"

"He simply asked if I could come to the office. He said that you needed some help on a case and he thought I could give you some inside views."

I looked hard for any sign of deception, but couldn't find a single one.

"I'm telling you the truth, Jenny. But I don't think that Phillip was telling me the truth. I think something happened that got him worried and that is why he phoned me."

"I believe you."

Colin exhaled and his facial muscles relaxed. "Thank you. Now tell me what happened. Did you have an episode?"

"No."

"Okay. Then what happened?" Colin narrowed his eyes and I watched his mind work. It was fascinating to see his thoughts being represented in and around his eyes. His mouth remained largely passive. A slight widening of his eyes warned me. He straightened in his chair and looked at me with concerned intensity. "Jenny, speak to me."

"There is nothing to tell. Phillip gave me a case this morning and I'm working on it." I huffed. "I can't believe he called you in to help me."

"Tell me about the case."

"Give me a moment." I didn't have an office phone in my viewing room. Phillip was the only one in this company who talked to me. If ever something had to be said, he came to my viewing room. Short business communication was usually done via email. I opened my inbox. There was a two-sentence email from Phillip explaining that both he and Manny had agreed to bring Colin in on the burglary case. I read it twice. "Do you know that Manny also agreed to you being in this case?"

"Millard?" Colin lost some of the colour in his face. I had gotten to know him quite well during the Piros case and the weeks after that. Granted, four months had passed since, but it didn't explain the flash of fear, immediately followed by rage I saw written all over his face. "Is he also involved in this?"

"He's the one who brought the case from Interpol to us."

"Of course. I should've known."

The micro-expressions flitting across his face surprised me. I was not easily surprised. I pointed at his face and twirled my index finger around. "There is so much rage there. Before you left me I only ever saw contempt, annoyance and disgust when you talked about Manny. But never rage. What happened, Colin?"

"I can't talk about it."

"Can't or don't want to?"

"Both, actually." He looked at my finger until I realised I was still twirling it. I dropped my hand in my lap. He leaned forward. "Jenny, remember when I said in the hospital that there are certain things that I won't be able to tell you?"

"Because of the high level of security and your work at Interpol. Of course, I remember."

"This is one of those things I am not able to tell you."

"Why?" I stopped speaking when Colin shook his head. His lifted eyebrows and pointed look indicated that I was to stop this line of questioning. The slight annoyance I felt brought back the complete outrage I had experienced at the hospital.

"Uh-oh. Are you thinking again about yesterday?" Colin had his hands up, his expression pleading. "Just give me ten minutes to explain."

"What are you going to explain when you can't or won't tell me most of what happened in the last four months? Or what Manny has done to you? And how are you going to explain being my next-door neighbour?"

"I told you yesterday that I bought the apartment next to yours to make sure that you are safe."

"Safe from what? Or who?"

"I can't tell you."

On the inside I let out a frustrated scream. On the outside I simply stared at Colin. This was the control I had worked so hard at maintaining. It felt good to have it back. I didn't speak. I just stared.

"Oh, come on, Jenny." His brow had deep furrows from his exasperation with me. He sighed and rubbed his hand hard over his face. "Okay, I will tell you this: the guys who captured me have looked into my life. I won't be surprised if they found out that there is a connection between us. I didn't want to be the one who led these monsters to your door."

"So you planned to keep them from my door by moving in next to me?"

"It sounded like a good plan at the time." He smiled ruefully. "Vinnie warned me that you would be very angry with us for keeping this from you."

"He was right. You should've known better." Something he had said distracted me from my irritation with him. When it reached my cerebrum, the thinking part of my brain, I forgot about Colin's four-month absence and his new apartment. "This is it!"

I turned to the monitors and lost myself in the data on the screens for a few minutes. Colin's insistence that I speak to him pulled at my concentration and I absently waved my hand in his direction. It grew quiet next to me. Five minutes later I swivelled my chair to face him. "Tell me about Francine's hacker."

Colin looked up from his smartphone. "You are like quicksilver."

"We no longer say quicksilver. It is archaic. It is called mercury. Why would you compare me to mercury? People who have mercurial temperaments are emotionally unstable. I am not emotionally unstable."

"No, you are not. But you must admit that you are quick to change focus."

I thought about this. "That is true. Now tell me about Francine's hacker."

"I assume you are talking about the hacker she was ranting about yesterday while in and out of consciousness?" He waited for my nod before he continued. "After you left Francine refused to talk to me. She said that she would only talk to you."

"Why? I know she trusts you implicitly. Why wouldn't she tell you?"

"I don't know. No matter how I cajoled her, she would not

tell me about the mugging, who attacked her or what some hacker has to do with any of this."

"And you are here to convince me to speak to her."

"Can we please first clear the air between us?" He leaned towards me. "I know one can never go back to how things were before, but I would like for you to give me the benefit of the doubt. I didn't contact you for almost four months because my mission was sensitive and because I didn't want to put you in danger. I bought the apartment next to you because I really like your apartment building, the area and of course I wanted to make sure you were safe. I didn't tell you because—"

"You wanted to protect me."

He sighed. "Yes."

"I don't want to talk about this anymore." If this discussion continued, I would confess to him how I had thought it was something about me that had made him and then Vinnie avoid me. The words were pushing against my teeth, waiting to be uttered. I also didn't want to admit exactly how much I had missed him. And Vinnie.

"I need to know that we are good, Jenny."

"I'm not sure what you mean. I'm more than good. I'm an expert at what I do."

Colin laughed softly. "What I meant was that I need to know that things are okay between us. That you might trust me again."

"Trust is earned."

"Granted. And as I did in the past, I will show you that I am worthy of your trust."

"Agreed. Now can we please change the topic? Where is Francine?"

"She's in my apartment. She refused to stay longer in the hospital and we took her home this morning. Vinnie is with her." Regret flashed across his face. "I've already moved my stuff into your apartment. Before we argue about that, you know this is the best choice. I respect that you don't like change and that you might not want me in your apartment, but with recent events, I think it is wiser if Vinnie stays with Francine and I stay with you."

I closed my eyes and wrote three lines of the second movement, the Larghetto, of Mozart's Piano Concerto No. 27, one of the pieces I used when I needed calming down. There was something so restful about E-flat major. Once my cognitive, rational side was in control again, I processed my observations of Colin while he had been talking. My eyes flew open. "It's not about keeping me safe. This is about you not wanting to be close to Francine. Why not?"

"Gods, you are good. Francine is, how shall I say, not an excessively tidy person. Vinnie doesn't mind this, he likes cleaning up. I can't stand the kind of mess she creates. Once we were on a…" He stopped. I suspected he had been about to reveal some criminal activity. "We shared a hotel suite once and after a week I wanted to strangle that woman. Her underwear was everywhere, on the sofa, in the bathroom, in the kitchen, for God's sake. Why couldn't she keep it confined to her room? I nearly broke a leg stumbling over one of her boots lying in the middle of the living room. I even found potato chips in the bath tub. How did she spill potato chips in the bath tub?"

Colin, the accomplished thief who secretly worked for Interpol, looked flustered. It was amusing to observe.

"And don't get me started on the singing. You sing beautifully in the shower. Francine? She sounds like a drunken turkey on heat. It's terrifying." He leaned in. Pleading was evident in all his nonverbal cues. "Please, Jenny. Please let me stay with you."

The discomfort of Colin mentioning my shower singing and the confusion about an inebriated fowl temporarily derailed my amusement. His distress was genuine. "I don't like this, but will concede. Just promise that you won't kick your heels against the wooden floor when you are working at the desk in the guest room. That scuff mark was hard to remove."

He smiled. "I promise."

"Okay, so when can I speak to Francine?" I needed to find

out more about this hacker. My mind was trying to connect something, but there were pieces missing. I hoped that Francine could provide some pieces.

"Now."

"I can't leave the office now. It is still working hours."

Colin was about to contradict me, but was interrupted by the quiet swoosh of the viewing room door. Phillip walked in and studied us for a few moments. His eyes conveyed concern. I wondered if he was worried about me, about Colin's presence in his prestigious firm or whether he had made the right decision by calling Colin. I didn't know, but his frown disappeared and his breathing deepened. He pulled the third chair closer and sat down.

"Genevieve, I hope you don't mind that I phoned Colin."

"I do mind. I didn't, I don't need him."

"That is not why I phoned him." He paused. "Okay, it is why I phoned him, but not in the way that you assume. I thought that Colin might be helpful with this case. Manny agrees with me. Manny had to go back to his office, but he said that we should meet tomorrow morning to discuss this case."

The increased tension in Colin's body language was becoming distracting. Something in this conversation was causing him a lot of distress. I looked at him. Few people were comfortable with me studying them as openly as Colin. Even Phillip would flinch at times when I gazed unblinkingly at him. Colin never even shifted in discomfort. He just sat there allowing me to put together what I saw.

It was that trust that held my tongue. I nodded and turned back to Phillip. "What time tomorrow morning?"

"Ten o'clock. Will you give a report on what you've found on the burglaries then as well?"

"Sure, I will have a report ready then." I should be able to add a few interesting things once I had spoken to Francine.

"Good." Phillip turned to Colin. "Thank you for coming. I don't know what is going on between you and Manny, but he does seem to trust you. Genevieve trusts you and that is enough for me. But be careful. I don't ever want a repeat of what happened last time you were helping on a case."

"Neither do I," Colin said. "My main concern is Jenny's safety. Has always been. The case, any case, will always come second to that."

"That is exactly what I wanted to hear." Phillip got up and looked down at us. "I'll leave you kids to have fun. Do what you need to, go where you need to. Let's close this thing quickly and quietly. Before another rich old lady decides to sue us."

Before I could take issue to what he had said, Phillip left the room. Colin's soft laughter made me glare at him. "What?"

"You did not like being called a kid."

"Of course not. I'm thirty-four years old. Most definitely not a kid. And you are... I don't know how old you are." This realisation truly bothered me.

"I'm thirty-eight. And I would greatly appreciate it if you did not share this information with anyone."

"Why not? Surely your age isn't top secret?" I pulled away from him. "Or are you one of those people who define themselves by the relationship between their looks and their age? No, no. You aren't that vain. Then why the secret? I don't mind people knowing how old I am."

"Identity theft."

It didn't take long for me to comprehend. "Aha. The more information people have on you, the easier it would be for them to impersonate you, steal your credit details and take over your life. Oh my goodness, should I stop telling people how old I am?"

Colin laughed. He shook his head. "I've missed this."

"What?" I was still fretting about the danger I had put myself into by telling people my age.

"Laughing." His quiet admission pulled me out of my train of thought. What I saw on his face made my chest hurt. I wanted to say something. Do something. Maybe touch him like normal people did. None of this came naturally to me. It was achingly difficult for me to be a friend.

"I don't know what to say." Distress tightened my throat and my words came out strangled.

"You don't have to say anything, Jenny. Just be you. That's what I need right now." He cleared his throat, unconsciously announcing a change in the mood, in the subject. "Why don't I drive you home and you can tell me about the cases on the way?"

"I have my own car."

"And you have secure parking here. I'll drop you off tomorrow morning. Why put any more environmentally destructive gasses in the air?"

Before I knew it we were in a heated debate about global warming and the credence to the many varying theories surrounding it. I put the files in the side pocket of my computer bag. They barely fit. Colin took the heavy bag from me and carried it to his car. The argument gained momentum until we were halfway to my apartment and I realised that he had used this as a distraction to get his way.

I gave him five minutes of silent anger until I relented and told him everything that I had learned about the burglary cases. We were still discussing this when he guided me past my front door to the neighbouring door. A flash of annoyance returned, but I banked it. For now I needed some information from Francine.

Chapter FIVE

"So? What do you think?"

I ignored Colin's question and walked deeper into his apartment. The more I saw, the more confused I became. I stopped in front of one of the walls in astonishment. Footsteps sounded over the wooden floors and stopped next to me.

"Did you do all of this?" I asked, waving my hand around the flat.

"The interior decorating? Some of it, yes. The art? That's another story." He reached to the wall filled with masks and took an Inca funerary mask. "These masks I actually did pay for, just like you. Do you think that we bought our masks from the same guy in Peru?"

"I always wondered how you knew what it was when you first saw it in my flat."

"On the first day we met," he said. He had broken into my apartment and I still remember him studying my apartment as if it was an interesting piece of art. He replaced the mask that was an almost exact replica of the one hanging in my apartment. "Tell me what you think."

I turned my back on the mask-filled wall to face the rest of the open-space living area. I didn't know what to think. I most definitely didn't know what to say. Colin's apartment was similar to mine in layout. Admittedly, I had never been in this apartment, even though I had been living next door for six years.

The same as in my apartment, Colin's was divided into two sections. The first was a cavernous room that in my apartment hosted a living area and reading area opposite each other on each side of the front door. Colin had his living area on the opposite side and didn't have bookshelves lining the walls and forming a semi room-divider. There he had filled the walls with paintings, masterpieces if I were not mistaken. Whether they were authentic, legally obtained or forged I had no way of ascertaining. Colin was, after all, a master forger and art thief.

Deeper into the apartment, the kitchen and dining areas were on the same opposing sides as in my apartment. A corridor between these two areas led to the three bedrooms that both our apartments had. Every inch of wall space was covered in art. Oil paintings and watercolours, sketches, photography and even a mosaic that I shuddered to think some museum might be wanting back.

I took my time walking around and inspecting the front part of his apartment. Sculptures were tastefully placed on antique tables. Persian carpets covered parts of the wooden floors. Our apartments had a lot in common, yet Colin's was more masculine. And the art was much more expensive than the pieces I had collected. I placed my handbag and computer bag with my work computer on one of the dark blue sofas.

"Where are your books?" I asked.

"In my study. I set up a library and reading area there. Your place inspired me."

"Evidently."

Colin looked amused by my annoyance. I was appreciating a bronze sculpture that looked suspiciously like an original Picasso. He joined me. "Don't you like my interior decorating skills?"

"It looks to me like art is not the only thing that you copy, Mister Frey." I looked pointedly at the open area. "Should I be disgusted or complimented by this blatant display of mimicry?"

"Wow." Colin took a step away from me. "That cut deep, Jenny."

"Jen-girl." Vinnie's booming voice broke into our conversation. I turned in time to see him storming towards us from the bedrooms. "You are here."

"I am," I said. Watching the almost two-metre-tall giant coming towards me changed my emotional state. I went from annoyed to happy. Despite the last four months, I was genuinely happy to see Vinnie. I was less pleased when he didn't break his stride and he swept me into his arms. My feet lifted off the floor and I hung helpless in a strangle hold.

"I'm so, so, so, so, so sorry." He repeated this a few times in my hair. I felt his muscular body tremble with emotional overload. That was the only reason I didn't try to wriggle out of his arms. Vinnie was very kinaesthetic. He was a touch person. And he was a hugger. I didn't like being hugged. He knew it, yet was still hugging me. I really wanted to wriggle.

"Vin, put Jenny down. You're smothering her." There was humour in Colin's voice.

I felt myself being slowly lowered, but Vinnie didn't let go of me. At least I wasn't squashed up against his chest anymore. He did, however, hold my shoulders in his huge hands so I couldn't move away. At the hospital he had barely made eye contact and had avoided me most of the time. Not now. He looked me over as if making sure I was uninjured.

"You're even prettier than I remember."

"Vin." Colin groaned. I couldn't see him so I didn't know if he was embarrassed or annoyed.

"What? She is," Vinnie said, still looking at me. He leaned in until his nose almost touched mine. I quickly wrote two bars of Mozart's Serenade No. 11 for wind instruments in E-flat major to not give in to the claustrophobic panic his proximity induced. "Jen-girl, I'm sorry. Colin told me that you were hurt by us not contacting you. I knew that it was not the right thing to do, but we didn't know what else to do. It was never our intention to hurt you. You're one of my best friends, Jen-girl. I never want to hurt you."

I completely forgot about my dislike for being touched. The intensity of Vinnie's remorse overwhelmed me. That and yet another friendship declaration. This was becoming too much for me. I looked around him at Colin.

"Okay, Vin." Colin must have seen the desperation on my face. He stepped in and peeled Vinnie's hands off my shoulders.

"Let the pretty lady go. That's a good man."

The relief of having my body to myself again was immense. I stepped back and concentrated on my breathing until I had my equilibrium back. After four months of limited social exposure, I now faced the challenge once again to interact. If I didn't have my experience as a child pretending to socially fit in and my extensive training in psychology to fall back on, the feeling I had now would have been severe enough to trigger an episode. I reached for the right thing to say to Vinnie.

"You've picked up weight."

"Oh, Jen-girl, I missed you." Vinnie laughed and slapped his stomach. "I put on more muscle, not fat. Being stuck in this apartment with Colin was boring. I had a lot of time to work out."

"Oh." What else could I say to that?

Vinnie looked around the apartment. "What do you think? Cool, huh?"

The moment I saw Vinnie's chin raise and his chest puff out, understanding descended upon me. "You decorated this place."

"You don't have to sound so surprised."

I was still trying to find my way through all the emotions of these two men being back in my life. Stepping back into social interaction was not as easy as it had been for me as a child. As I had grown older, I had become less tolerant of inane social niceties. But there was no denying its importance in this situation. All the indications of remorse and the desire to make amends were in Vinnie's demeanour. I reached for my training and years of observing people. I didn't fake a smile, but I modulated my tone.

"Everything makes more sense now, Vinnie. You moved in here with Colin when he was still physically weak. That leads me to conclude that you had to move his furniture into this apartment." I knew I was on the right track. Their faces told me. "He was too weak to really care what went where and you thought copying the layout of my apartment would be an easy solution. Especially since you had more important things to worry about. Once the furniture was placed, Colin grew used to it. So, when he was strong enough, he didn't move anything."

"You told her, dude?" Vinnie looked at Colin with widened eyes.

"I only told her that we moved in here six weeks ago. The rest she all deduced."

"Pretty and smart, just like I remember."

We stood in silence for a few seconds. Then I realised they were still waiting for my verdict on the apartment.

"The apartment looks artfully decorated," I said quickly, more interested in the reason I was here. "Where is Francine?"

"Here I am."

We turned to the kitchen area. Francine was wearing black yoga pants and a matching body-hugging T-shirt. Her hair was washed and styled, diamond earrings dangling, gold watch on her one wrist and a diamond bracelet on the other. Her face was bare of make-up, yet multicoloured. And terribly swollen.

I took a step towards her. "Shouldn't you be in bed?"

"I probably should, but then I would feel like I was sick or dying or something. And it's not sexy." She pulled her shoulders back, winced and walked towards us with a determined limp. She carefully lowered herself on the large dark blue sofa. "Since my usual clothes and shoes are too painful to wear, I have to make up for it with the diamonds. And there is no way I'm lying in bed wearing these fabulous diamonds."

As illogical as it was, I knew that many women used make-up and accessories the same way soldiers of old used war paints. It was a form of readiness for battle, whether it was fighting to the death or dealing with traffic, children and corporate pressure. In my everyday life, accessories were only necessary if they were useful.

"Let's sit down." Colin's suggestion brought me out of my musings. I took a seat next to Francine. Colin and Vinnie settled on the two wingback chairs facing the sofa. They started talking about Francine's injuries, the men insisting she stay in bed,

Francine arguing that she was well enough to be walking around. It was irrelevant and boring.

A thought came to me. "Francine, shouldn't you let your family know that you've been injured?"

Fleeting expressions pulled at her swollen face. The one I took interest in was emotional pain. "No, it's okay. I wouldn't want to worry them. It's not that bad in any case."

"Why did you kill those two men?" The gentleness in my voice surprised me. It made Francine blink away tears.

She sat a little straighter and immediately grabbed the side of her broken ribs. "Vinnie, could you get my iPad, please?"

"Sure thing, doll." Vinnie got up and walked towards the bedrooms. I turned to look at Francine, waiting. She smiled. At least she tried. The cut and swelling on the left side of her mouth made it difficult for the muscles to function properly.

"I hacked into the security system of the pharmacy across the street. They have a camera aimed at the alley where I was attacked. I had to enhance the video since this was quite far away, but you can see everything. The two men attacking me, me defending myself until I had to take those bastards out." Her voice cracked on the last words. She tried to sound tough, but was not hugely successful. Vinnie returned and handed the tablet computer to Francine. She swiped the screen a few times and handed it to me. "Just tap on the play button and you can watch the whole thing. Unfortunately, maybe fortunately, there isn't any sound, only the visual."

"It's all I need," I said and tapped the screen. A grainy gray movie started playing. I watched Francine coming out of a door into an alley, followed by two couples who looked like they were partygoers.

"Pause it quickly." Francine waited until I tapped the screen and looked at her. "This is an invite-only club. They change their location almost weekly to some out-of-use warehouse or building. It's very elite and underground. This is where the morally and ethically corrupt rich go to close deals that would be way unacceptable anywhere else. Here you can associate with known criminals without anyone ever thinking anything strange. Or talking about it. Everyone there can be investigated for some kind of crime, no matter how petty, violent or white-collar complex. They're all bastards and arseholes."

I frowned. "Then why did you go?"

"I got the invite from someone I had worked with in the past. Needless to say, he is not as pure as the driven snow. He did help me expose a human trafficking ring, so I never gave him up to any of the government guys I work for." She lifted one shoulder. "Anyway, I've known that these kinds of clubs have recently been on the government guys' radars. A lot of designer drugs change hands and back-door deals are made there."

"And you thought gaining access to this shadow society would win you favour with some law enforcement agency."

"How did you…" She stopped and sighed. "Yes, I thought it would get me back in their good books."

"You were in their bad books?" I wasn't sure what this implied.

"Oh, I might have pissed off a few people when I hacked Interpol's ever-so-secure system."

"You did what?" Colin's voice startled me. He was sitting next to me on the arm of the sofa. I had not heard him move. He was glaring at Francine. "Why didn't you tell me?"

"Isn't it obvious that I would start there to look for you when you disappeared?"

"Can we stay on topic, please?" I didn't wait for them to respond and turned my attention back to the tablet resting on my lap. Francine's admission did not go unnoted though. I placed it in a special compartment in my mind to later analyse. I tapped the screen.

"No, wait," Francine stopped me once again. I paused the video for the second time. "I'll finish quickly. I was stupid to go. But I really wanted to give Interpol something to like me again, so I went. As soon as I got in, I had a bad feeling. It was as if the bouncer had expected me. I've learned a few things from you, Genevieve. I noticed his body language shift when he saw me. He glanced to a table at the back. I got in, had a quick look around and decided to leave. I wasn't there for more than ten minutes. I didn't even order a drink. If you rewind this video, you would see me go in."

"Later. Can I watch the video now?" When Francine nodded, I tapped the screen and watched. The two couples stumbled to the left as Francine moved to her right, towards the camera. The moment the laughing couples were out of sight, two masked men left the building from the same door and ran to Francine.

She must have heard the footsteps and started turning to the sound, but they were already on her. One man punched her hard in the face. She fell backwards into the arms of the taller man. He grabbed her around her waist and lifted her off her feet. The first man punched her again.

At first she allowed her body to go slack, giving both men the illusion of compliance. Her body language communicated female pleading and fear. The tall man loosened his hold slightly and the first man moved in. As soon as he was close enough, she used the tall man's hold on her as leverage and delivered a jarring kick to the other man's groin. He dropped to the ground in visible agony.

She didn't wait for the tall man to recover from the shock of her sudden display of violence. Francine fought like a martial arts student. My trainer would have been impressed with her. I most certainly was. The tall man was still holding her, his face an easy target when she slammed her head back into it. There was no doubt in my mind that move had broken his nose.

He reacted by holding her even tighter, but was not immune to a ten-centimetre heel jabbing into his foot. His mouth opened wide in a scream and he released her. By now the second man was slowly pushing himself up. The moment Francine's feet touched the pavement, she started running. The first man grabbed at her and managed to catch her left calf. It was enough to unbalance her. She slammed into the ground.

The tall man limped over as she kicked at the hand still holding her calf. Both men's body language conveyed severe aggression. She had provoked fury in them. The tall man reached her side and kicked her so hard in her ribs that I flinched. I was amazed that her injuries were not more serious. She had lost one shoe, her pantyhose were ripped and she was curling in on herself to protect her torso from being kicked. The tall man delivered a few more kicks until Francine's body appeared to relax in unconsciousness.

The first man crawled over. One of her frantic kicks must have connected with his head. He was bleeding from a deep cut above his right ear. He lifted his right hand and an involuntary gasp left my lips. He held a large knife in his hand and a sneer pulled his mouth into a cruel smile. He was going to kill her.

Obviously these men did not have a high intellect or they would've learned from experience. Francine used the same tactic as she had earlier. Still pretending to be unconscious, she waited for the first man to be close enough before she executed a sequence of elegant moves so fast I could only see flashes of moving limbs until she punched him hard in his throat. His head snapped back and he dropped to the pavement, clutching his throat. Her punch had been hard enough to cause possible damage to his spinal cord. It definitely caused his trachea to collapse. He was going to die from lack of oxygen.

The tall man stared at his comrade for a second. His nostrils flared, increasing his oxygen intake and so preparing him for action. Francine must have seen this. She grabbed the first man's knife from the pavement, jumped to her feet and staggered. She favoured her left side, her ribs causing her enough pain to inhibit her agility. The tall man reached behind him and pulled a revolver from the back of his dark pants. Francine didn't give him time to move it past his side.

With a speed that only a rush of adrenaline could provide, she stepped into him and drove the knife into his heart. How he did not see it coming or react to it, I didn't know. The weapon dropped from his hand onto the pavement and he looked down in surprise. His eyes locked on the knife protruding from his chest and he slowly went down on his knees. He looked up once at Francine before he fell over and stilled. The first man had stopped moving. The horror on her face was visible despite the grainy image. She bent over and heaved. I tapped the screen and looked at her.

"They tried to kill you."

"Yes." Her eyes were glued to the paused screen on the tablet computer. She looked pale under the bruises.

"Why?"

She looked at me. "Watch the next two minutes."

Usually I preferred to watch political thrillers or art films. Movies with absurd amounts of violence didn't appeal to me. Watching someone I had recently called my friend get beaten up was not pleasant. I steeled myself and tapped the screen again.

Francine was frantically wiping her hands on her dress. That explained the blood on her designer garment. Her movements were disjointed and I could see that she was in shock. Wearing only one shoe, she stumbled out of view.

"I went to my car and came straight here," she said softly. "Continue watching."

For a few seconds I only saw the two bodies lying prone on the pavement. A dark, shiny pool grew from the tall man's chest. Blood. I shuddered. The door opened and three men, also dressed in dark clothes, walked to the death scene. They didn't even take time to check the attackers' vitals. One man rolled out two sheets of what looked like hard plastic and within a minute both bodies were rolled and bound. One by one, they carried the bodies to the left of the camera, out of view. When they returned, they disappeared inside only to come out with cleaning equipment a few seconds later. They started cleaning the pavement.

"They spend about ten minutes doing that," Francine said. "I'm sure that pavement has never been that clean."

"What happens after they finish cleaning?" I asked, watching them scrub the pavement with hard-bristled brooms.

"Nothing. People come and go. I watched the video until it became light. No police. Nothing," she said again. "My guess is that they put the bodies in a car and got rid of them somewhere. God, I can't believe this happened."

I tapped the screen and looked at her. "You are an excessively paranoid person. Why would you go to a place like this? What made you think it was safe?"

"I got hacked." I couldn't clearly see the anger in her face, but her tight fists and hard breathing communicated it loudly. "The only way that could ever have happened is if someone had physical access to my computers. Every single one of my computers has been built from parts, none of which has imprinted hardware ID's. I also compiled my own operating system with FreeBSD…"

She must have noticed the confusion on Vinnie's face and lack of interest on mine. Colin was the only one nodding his head in understanding. Francine sighed heavily. "My computers were completely safe from external hacking. I would never, never, insert a CD or USB drive in my computer without knowing where it came from, who it came from and what was on it. In other words, someone had broken into my super-secret apartment and loaded their crap onto my computers."

"Do you know who?" I asked.

"I'm working on it. When I checked my connection logs, I noticed traces in the data. That is how I knew I was hacked. Now I'm working on finding the little bastard."

"But what does this have to do with you attending this party?"

"Ah, yes. Sorry. I get angry every time I think about some bastard breaking into my place, raping my computers, and forget what I was really talking about. This bastard had access to my entire database, so he knew all my communication, everything. A lot of success in hacking relies on psychology. You need to know what your intended victim will respond to.

Studying my communication must have made it clear that I would've accepted an invitation from my contact. So they made the invite to look like it was sent from him. Someone had wanted me to be there."

I allowed this new information to process for a few seconds. "How easy is it to hack someone's system?"

"Most systems are shockingly easy to get into," she said. "Banks, law enforcement agencies and a few other institutions have better security. Breaching that is a challenge, especially to get in and out unnoticed. Your company installed a professional security solution, which is pretty much an internet security package. This is then regularly audited by a computer security company. On top of that, the firewall and packet filter made getting into your computer a bit of a challenge, but not much."

"When did you hack into my computer?" I asked. This was the better question of many begging for answers. The other questions would require knowledge that I did not have. The fact that she had gotten past the security that Phillip had once boasted of was interesting. Phillip would be livid. I was curious.

"You're not angry that I hacked your computer?" Francine blinked a few times when I lifted my shoulders in a universal sign of indifference. "Okay. Well then. I got into your computer months ago. Why do you ask?"

"I think that someone hacked my computer yesterday. Things were different when I got to work today."

My calm announcement was met with an outburst. Vinnie jumped out of his seat, demanding to know who it was. Colin overrode any reply with a barrage of questions. I was almost amused by them attacking me with questions without waiting for any answers. Almost. Being boxed in by Francine on the one side, Colin on the other and Vinnie hovering over me was becoming too much.

I had expected a reaction, but not one so overwhelming. It made me take notice. I saw the worried look Francine gave Colin and the slight headshake he gave her as a warning. I also noted Vinnie's posture change from friend to bodyguard. This had to be connected to the secrecy between them that I had observed a few times. I wondered if it was related to the case and whether I needed to know why they were so concerned.

Chapter SIX

"I think we've all calmed down now," Colin said, sipping his coffee. They had realised that their method of bombarding me was not getting them anywhere, so Colin had suggested a time-out. While Colin had gone to make coffee, Vinnie had explained the expression to me. I liked it.

"Genevieve, why do you think your computer was hacked?" Francine asked.

"I always log off any program or site before I switch off my computer. When I switched it on this morning, I was already logged into my email account. And two of the icons on my desktop had been moved."

"Have you told Phillip?" Colin asked.

"No. I forgot about it when he and Manny came into my office. Then I lost myself in my work until you appeared. And I wasn't a hundred percent sure."

"From the little you've told me, it is not conclusive that your computer was hacked," Francine said. "But taken in the context of what has been happening, I'm convinced."

"What has been happening?" I thought back to our trip to the hospital. "Does this have to do with your uncle?"

"I think you should tell the whole story now, Francine," Colin said. "I, for one, would seriously like to know what's going on."

"Yes, of course. My uncle's house was broken into a couple of weeks ago," she said.

"Is he okay?" Colin asked.

"He's fine. Just supremely pissed off. Nobody wants to take responsibility for what he calls the royal fuck-up."

"How old is your uncle?" I couldn't keep the surprise out of my voice.

"Eighty-three. He's actually my great-uncle." She rolled her eyes. "He thinks he's still forty. My uncles tried for years to get him to move into a retirement village, but stopped when he threatened to disown them last year. His body might not be the strongest, but his mind is sharper than most thirty-year-olds'."

"Should I assume that your family is affluent?" I asked.

Vinnie snorted. "You could say that."

"Yes," Francine said. "My mother's family comes from old money. There are a lot of artworks that have been in the family for generations."

"Her family is the Lemartins," Vinnie said with meaning.

"I don't know what that means," I said when all three of them looked at me expectantly. Was I supposed to react in some way?

"They are one of the most influential families in France," Colin explained. "Old money, high standing and power."

I was about to comment on Francine's lack of social standing when I noticed the warning on Colin's face. I pressed my lips together. Francine saw this and laughed, but immediately grabbed her ribs and breathed through the pain.

"Don't worry, Genevieve, this is one of the reasons I started hanging out with you. You don't give a fig about social importance. It's annoying to be with people who are in awe of my bloodline. You're not. And you're most likely right in whatever it is you're thinking right now." She started ticking off on her fingers. "I'm financially independent from my family and they so don't like it. But that is not the biggest issue they have with me. My loving family doesn't want anything to do with me because I don't care about the stupid little elitist clubs they belong to. I don't brownnose, I don't care what other people think of me and I definitely don't care about their money."

She had become more emotional talking about her family, so I didn't think it prudent to ask about the many words she used that I was not familiar with. I did, however, understand the gist.

I had always been a social outcast. At least until I had learned to copy social behaviour. Personally, I had never felt the strong urge for belonging, but knew it was important to most people and they would do whatever it took to gain acceptance. Anyone not succumbing to social pressure was remarkably courageous in my opinion.

"You're brave," I said.

"Or just stupid," Francine said with a smile in her voice. "At least that's what my mother's family always told me. Except for my great-uncle. He is a bit eccentric and as he gets older, he supports me more."

Most often people said more by not saying something. Francine's omission of support from her parents was telling. I also observed her increased discomfort with this topic. She had seldom ventured into her personal history during our lunches.

"Back to the burglary," she said, her tone less emotional. "Two weeks ago, my great-uncle was in Monaco for the weekend when his house was broken into. Of course he is insured, and he also employs a security company to watch over his house. He has a top-of-the-range security system throughout the property, but none of the alarms were set off during the burglary. There was no visible point of entry, no broken windows and the security cameras did not record anything. Basically, the crime did not happen, except for the missing art."

I glanced at Colin. His left eyebrow was lifted and the corners of his mouth turned down. "Just like the others."

"What others?" Vinnie asked.

I told them about the burglaries that I was looking into. Colin had to listen to it for a second time. He shook his head when I finished.

"You haven't told them everything, Jenny."

"God, these burglaries are definitely all related," Francine said. "I want to find these bastards. What else is there about this case?"

"At some of the crime scenes the thieves left a red flower. The type of flower has not yet been confirmed and I'm not a botanist so I couldn't identify it from the photos. Because these cases took place in different places with different types of law enforcement agencies handling it, no one picked up on that similarity."

"You did," Francine said.

"I saw the flowers on the crime scene photos. Manny confirmed it."

"Millard?" The venom in Vinnie's voice surprised me. "He's involved in this?"

"He's the one who brought the case to Rousseau & Rousseau," I said. The glances between the three of them became too much for me. "What is going on here? You're having whispered conversations and I can see from your nonverbal cues that you have a secret you don't want me to know. Usually I wouldn't care about people and their secrets, but this happens whenever I talk about this case. It also happened when we were in the hospital. What is this about?"

"You have to tell her," Francine said. She had said this before.

"Tell me what?"

There was a moment of silence. Francine shifted next to me.

"Fine, I'll tell her," she said and immediately continued, not giving the men a chance to stop her. "The reason I insisted on having you in the hospital with me was to know you were safe. And also for you to find out what has been happening. I had hoped the men would tell you, but obviously they haven't. I think your life is in danger."

I laughed. "My life? Who would be interested in me? I sit in a viewing room all day. If I'm not analysing video footage of interviews, I'm looking for anomalies in data. How could this put my life in danger?"

"How many people have gone to jail because of your body language analysis? Or because you found an anomaly in some accounting somewhere that caused a forensic investigation?"

I was surprised that Francine knew so much about my job. I knew I hadn't told her about this. She must have learned this while illegally accessing my computer. "In the last six years?

Eleven people have been sentenced to time in prison and twenty have been given suspended sentences. There are even two people who were extradited."

Francine stared at me with her mouth slightly agape. "Wow. And you don't think that maybe one of these people could be pissed off enough at you to come for revenge?"

"My contract states that I will never be named in any legal proceedings."

"Nobody knows that you're the one who got them investigated?"

"No. So you can see how I strongly doubt that my life is in danger."

Francine's lips thinned as much as it could through the swelling. She grabbed her tablet computer and narrowed her eyes. "Two minutes. Time me."

I looked at my watch, even though I suspected her order to have been symbolic rather than serious. She was tapping away on her tablet computer. I looked at Colin and Vinnie. Maybe they knew what Francine was doing, but both of them just shrugged.

"Here." She pushed the tablet in my hands. "Look."

"It was one minute and," I glanced at my watch, "twenty-three seconds."

"Look," she almost shouted.

I narrowed my eyes at her tone, but looked at the screen. The *corrugator procerus* muscles pulled my brow lower and together. "This is my email account."

"Your secure work email account. I'm totally in your system now. Whatever is on your internal main server is mine. Anything that you've saved, worked on, emailed, it is all mine. Your contact lists, your data, anything private that you might have revealed in emails or saved on your system. I can send emails in your name, I can download all your data, I can open all your files. You are mine, bitch." She closed her eyes briefly. "Um, sorry. That one just slipped out."

"What is the point you're trying to make?" I asked.

"She's trying to tell you that even a weaker hacker could get in after some time and know everything about you within a few hours," Colin said. He lifted an eyebrow at Francine. "Maybe you should tell Jenny how you got into her system."

Francine sighed. "I was just trying to prove a point. Truthfully it would take me longer than this to hack into a secure system, especially from a tablet. When I first got into your mail server, it took me eighteen minutes. Now I had all your access data and that is why it only took one minute and twenty-three seconds."

"A rather dramatic way to make her point," Colin said. "But it shows that some hacker could get into your mail or computer, and they would know which cases you worked on, who you had investigated or audited. You are not as secure as you think. Or as anonymous."

"But these are white-collar criminals. Like you. They are not violent killers." My voice tapered off towards the end and I tried my best to not look at Vinnie. Nobody had ever said it out loud, but I was pretty sure he had committed many violent crimes in his past. Maybe not his recent past, but he was not a gentle sophisticated art thief. From bits and pieces that I had overheard and observed, I had drawn the conclusion that he might have been a mercenary. Although not the kind working for the government. I tried not to ponder too much on that.

"Did you see you have four new emails?" Francine asked.

I squinted at the screen. Indeed there were four new emails in my inbox. One caught my attention.

"What's wrong, Jenny?" Colin asked.

"I didn't order anything," I said and opened the perplexing email.

"What didn't you order?" Vinnie asked.

"Oh, she got an email that there is a package waiting for her in her mailbox." Francine was leaning closer to look at the table computer in my hands. "This email says that it has 'urgent' written on the packaging."

"You don't have mail delivered to your apartment?" Colin asked.

"No, I don't like strangers knowing where I live. I got a mailbox at this twenty-four hour office centre to limit accessibility to my private life."

"And now you know that someone with hacking skills can have full access without much effort." Sympathy softened Francine's tone. "If you let me, I can make sure that it will take the best of the best hackers days to get into your computer. And your smartphone."

"My smartphone?" I glanced at my handbag next to me. My smartphone was in its usual pocket inside the lining of my bag. "Of course. It is also a computer and has internet access, so it is equally hackable."

"And it can remotely be switched on and off. It can even record voice and video without your knowledge. And like any other smartphone, it can be used to trace your location with incredible accuracy."

Cold flooded my body. This was not a life I wanted. As it was, I already was bordering on obsessed about my safety. I had five locks on my front door and a reinforced door to my bedroom. And one for my bathroom. It had become part of my evening ritual to check all the locks. Sometimes I checked twice.

Sure, I was aware of the dangers of hackers. That was why I never opened unsolicited attachments and I never downloaded something that hadn't gone through two virus checks. I also had an antivirus programme and passwords on my smartphone. My proactive internet security attitude used to make me proud. Now these attempts seemed feeble. And useless against people like Francine.

"Jen-girl?" Vinnie's voice carried the tone of someone who had been calling me for some time.

"Yes?"

"Would you like me to go and get this package for you? I have to go to the shops in any case. We're going to need more supplies if I'm to cook for all of us."

"You don't have to cook for me, Vinnie," I said. "I'm going home."

"Which is next door and you don't have enough food in your fridge. You're staying for dinner." Vinnie stood up. "So, do you want me to get this urgent package for you?"

I suspected there was more to Vinnie's offer. My lips tightened on the realisation. "You don't want me to go out."

"No, that's—" He had the decency to look abashed when he saw my sceptical glare. "Okay, it's true, but I only want you to be safe. I honestly do have to go to the market to get some stuff for dinner, so it's no hassle to get your package."

I resented his logic and the convenience. With a lack of graciousness in my tone, I relented. "Fine."

Vinnie took the key to my mailbox and listened carefully to my instructions. One of the reasons I had chosen this specific company to have my mail delivered to was the anonymity. The shop front provided normal copy and print services twenty-four hours a day. The mailboxes were located in a secure room to the left. I had a key-card that gained me entrance to the mailbox room and a key for my specific mailbox. The only time I had ever had contact with someone in the shop front was the first day when I had collected my key-card and keys. Since then I only received an email whenever mail arrived. They wouldn't even notice if it were Vinnie who picked up my mail instead of me.

After some more shared looks with Colin, Vinnie left.

"What are you not telling me, Colin?" I asked.

"Oh, there are so many things that I'm not telling you," he answered with a smile. I did not appreciate his humour. He sobered when I just stared at him. "This unexpected package is suspicious, Jenny. Vinnie wants to make sure that everything is okay before you handle it."

"Isn't this an overreaction?" I asked.

"It's not a big enough reaction," Francine said. Her tone warned me that she was about to say something of utmost importance. I stilled and readied myself to listen and observe.

"As you know, I am known for my suspicions about larger entities at work."

"Francine, you're paranoid and think that everything is a conspiracy," Colin said.

"You say potato." She shrugged. "Because of my personal beliefs, I became even more suspicious about the break-in at my great-uncle's place. I didn't suspect the guards, because I had vetted them."

"By hacking into some law enforcement agency's system and running a background check on them?" Colin asked.

"Of course. They all came out clean. I worked through a list of who I thought could have had something to do with this. The whole event was simply too well organised. The thieves must have had some inside information. That led me to the security company. It took some time, but I found the traces in the data. Someone had hacked into their system and had spent an extended period in Uncle Franco's account."

"Your great-uncle's name is Franco?" I asked.

"Yes." She blinked a few times and returned to the topic. "The hacker is not all that good. I managed to locate him."

"You found him?" Colin asked. "You know where he is?"

"I know where he was." The corners of her mouth pulled down a bit through the swelling. "When I got a trace on him through his hack on the security company's system, I found his little nest. He tried to hide where he was with zombie computers and proxies, but I found him."

"Where is he? We should tell Manny." My suggestion elicited frowns from both of them.

"He's gone. When I got his IP address and I got into his computer it was easy to get his address." She gave a half shrug. "When I contacted my guy at Interpol, he was still too pissed off with me to act immediately to catch this guy. By the time they got to his apartment, he and his computers were in the wind."

"But can't you locate him again?" I asked. "You got into his computers before, you can do it again, right?"

She looked defeated. "The short answer is no. The slightly longer answer is that he has not switched on his computers again, so it's impossible to trace him that way."

"But there is another way?" I had heard it in the tone of her last sentence.

"I hope so. When I got into his system, I copied everything. It is as if I have his computer on mine. I know where he's been, the sites he visits most often and I'm keeping a watch for him to return there. The moment he logs in to one of those sites, he's mine. I will find him again."

"Didn't he find you too?" My question brought a scowl to her bruised face.

"Yes. But not by remotely hacking my system. He had to have broken into my place. I will get that son of a bitch. I would just like to know how and why he targeted me."

"Wait," I said, thinking of all she had told us. It was outrageous in its improbability and lack of facts. "Two weeks ago your great-uncle goes on holiday and his place is robbed. You suspect something, hack into the security company's computer system to find that they had already been hacked. Somehow the hacker now knows you know. He breaks into your super-secret apartment to get physical access to your computer, which he hacked. He then uses that information to lure you to a party to kill you."

"Exactly!" She sat up. "So you agree with me that there is a conspiracy."

"What conspiracy?" I squinted. "Wait, I didn't agree to anything. I'm merely considering the feasibility of this presumed sequence of events. I also wonder why you were considered enough of a threat to eliminate. I don't see a conspiracy."

"Well, I think that there is some conspiracy and I plan to find it."

"So where do I fit into all this? Why am I in danger?" I asked, thinking about her incoherent ramblings on the way to the hospital and her earlier proclamation.

She glanced at Colin. I didn't see his expression, but hers told me that I wasn't going to hear the real reason. "My gut is telling me that the hacking into my uncle's security company and the hacking of your company is connected. And before you shout at me, I know you don't believe in gut feelings, but my gut has never been wrong."

"I don't shout."

She smiled. "No, you don't. But you do get offended at anything that is not factual. I promise you that I will find that facts to prove that my gut is right. Until then you just have to be careful."

"Why did you hack into my computer initially?" I asked.

She squirmed a little and exhibited more nonverbal signs of discomfort. "Um, I, um, have to know what is happening in the lives of the people I care for. I just check every now and then to make sure that you are safe."

"Do all of you think I need protection?" I asked through clenched teeth. "I have seven years of self-defence training, I have a superior intellect. I might not function so well socially, but I am not completely useless."

"None of us think that you are, Jenny." Colin rested his elbows on his knees and looked intently at me. "When people care about someone, they will do anything and everything to protect that person."

"But I don't need protection."

"This douche just tried to kill me," Francine said. "He's been in your system, so yes. I think that you need protection."

"Jenny, look at what we have so far." Colin was using his reasonable tone. "Burglaries that show similarities, a red flower at each crime scene tying them together, a hacker who got not only into the security company's system, but also yours and Francine's. It also looks as if all the burglaries were ordered, as if someone is behind this all. Think, Jenny."

I pressed my fingers against my temples. I didn't want this to be true, but Colin was right. "Fine. I'll concede that it looks like this might be a syndicate. But there is still so much we don't know. So far there is nothing that connects the victims. I looked through all the police reports today and there is nothing similar. Except that these houses were supposed to be protected and that the most valuable artwork in the house was stolen."

We started arguing back and forth about what was known about the case. I got bored after ten minutes. After fifteen I withdrew into my head. Maybe a few pages of mentally written Mozart would make that connection that had been knocking at my consciousness since this afternoon. A breath before the connection passed into my consciousness, Vinnie's insistent calling brought me out of my head. I glared at him.

"Don't look at me like that. I cooked you dinner." He snorted, turned around and walked to the dining area. Colin and Francine were already seated at the table. I hadn't realised I had been in my head for such a long time. I joined them at the table.

"I also got your package. I left it in your apartment," Vinnie said as he started dishing up for each of us. The helping he put on my plate was three times as much as I could consume, but I refrained from commenting. Something else was much more pressing.

"How did you get into my apartment?" I asked.

"Oh. Um. Well." He winced.

"We all have keys to your apartment, Jenny," Colin said.

"How? I changed the locks after you left me." The looks on both their faces told me everything I needed to know. "Of course, you are thieves who are experts in breaking and entering. How often do you go into my apartment?"

"Almost never," Colin said. I believed him. "We only go in after some service people have been in. To make sure that there aren't any bugs in your place."

"Stop, just stop talking." I carefully put my cutlery on my plate. I had such tight control over my movements that my hands were shaking lightly. "I'm going to my apartment. I don't want to talk to you anymore."

Ignoring their protests, I grabbed my handbag and computer bag from the sofa and went to my apartment. There were too many things for me to process. Personal things which included my new neighbours, my new housemate, the access they had had to my apartment and everything else. Since I had never liked agonising over emotional situations, the bits of information and that connection wanting to break through to my consciousness were much more appealing. Maybe an hour in my bathtub would help my cognitive processes. It might also relax my tense muscles.

Chapter SEVEN

The bath had not been as relaxing as I had hoped. Usually a good book would be enough to settle me for the night. Not tonight. I forced myself to go to bed by eleven, knowing that tomorrow I had to be ready for my meeting with Manny. I also wanted to be rested so that I could figure out what the meaning was of the shared looks between Colin and Vinnie. But by three in the morning, I was remaking my bed for the fourth time. I had twisted the sheets out from under the mattress.

I looked down at my bed, contemplating whether it was worth getting back in. I decided it wasn't. There was work that could be done instead of me twisting and turning in bed all night. This break in my routine did not sit well with me and I walked into the kitchen, the corners of my mouth pulled down. First priority now was coffee. I placed my favourite mug under the coffee machine spout, flipped the switch and waited.

"Can't sleep?" Colin's voice right behind me startled me into a shriek. I swung around, glaring. He lifted both hands, palms up, and was trying his best to hide his laughter. "Sorry, Jenny. I didn't mean to frighten you."

I mentally wrote five bars of Mozart's String Quintet No. 4 in G minor while staring at Colin with narrowed eyes. He was standing two feet away from me, barefoot, dressed in sweatpants and a white undershirt. Sleepwear. When I felt calmer, I turned back to the coffee machine in time to stop it before it filled the mug too much. I took my coffee and leaned against the counter.

"When did you come in? And where?"

"About an hour after you left. Through the window. That might be why you didn't hear me."

I was not getting into another argument about him using the

front door. I walked around him to the dining room table. My computer bag was on its usual chair, the first one from the right. "I was actually hoping that you had changed your mind."

Colin followed me, pulled out a chair and sat down, his right leg stretched out in front of him. Only now did I notice the mug in his hand. Had he also been suffering from a sleepless night?

"You seriously thought I would change my mind?" he asked.

I sat down across from him, placed my mug on a coaster and started unpacking my computer bag. "No. I knew you had made your decision. I did, however, have an irrational moment of hope."

He didn't respond. I paused in my unpacking to look at him. I couldn't see any sign of offence or hurt, so I continued. I placed my work laptop in front of me, but didn't open it. I put a notepad in front of the computer and carefully aligned three pens to the right of my laptop. I rested both my hands on top of the laptop and looked at him.

"Why can't you sleep?"

He started to answer, but I stopped him by shaking my head.

"I can see that you are going to lie. Don't do that. Not if you want me to trust you again." As it was, I was far too comfortable with him in my space. Not until this moment had I paid attention to the fact that I was only wearing ankle-length pyjama pants and a snug purple t-shirt. It was not revealing in the least, but it felt normal to sit at my dining room table with Colin at three in morning, both of us dressed in our pyjamas. I didn't want him to break the trust slowly rebuilding by the lie I saw forming on his face.

He sighed. "Truth?"

"Please."

"I haven't slept much in the last four months."

"Since you were captured and tortured?"

"Yes." He swallowed and looked out of the dark window. "It's easier when I am awake."

"You have bad dreams."

He straightened and looked at me with a false smile. We had reached the end of this topic. I could respect that.

"What are you working on?" he asked.

I tapped the laptop. "I was going to go over my notes about the burglaries, but now I don't know if it is such a good idea."

"Why not?"

"Because of that hacker." My top lip lifted slightly in disgust. "If he has access to my system, then he'll know what I'm looking at."

Suspicious muscle movement on Colin's face had me narrowing my eyes.

"What did you do?" I asked.

His smile held guilt and humour. He nodded at the laptop under my hands. "I took this to Francine last night. She did all kind of magic things to make sure no one will ever hack your computer again."

"But she can get in. That is not no one."

"True." He shrugged. "I would rather have her on my side than anyone else."

I didn't know what to say without referring to Francine's conspiracy theories and her activities that were borderline and sometimes outright illegal. "Is it safe enough to look at my notes?"

"Yes. She said that not even Kevin Mitnick would get into your computer now."

"I don't know who he is."

"Only one of the most notorious hackers in the world."

"Oh." I thought about this. "Could he be a suspect?"

"Last I heard, he was running a security company and had written some books about hacking. I think our guy has a more personal investment in this case. The point Francine was making was that your computer is extremely difficult to hack now."

"Oh. Good." I opened my laptop and turned it on.

Colin left the table for a minute and returned with a book from my bookshelves. From the bookmark sticking out, it appeared that he had already read one third of it. He didn't dog-ear the book nor did he break the spine. I approved of his handling of my books. He settled across from me and started reading. I opened the files that I had saved the day before and stared at it. Nothing new came to me. The hard copy case files were still in my computer bag. I read my notes six times and still that connection didn't want to come. I leaned back in my chair and sighed.

"What?" Colin looked up from his book.

"There is a pattern here that my mind is seeing and I'm just not getting."

"You separate yourself from your mind?" He put the book on the table.

"Of course not." Yet again I had to explain myself in simple sentences. It was not easy. "My subconscious notices a pattern or an anomaly when I go through data. It takes time for my subconscious to process that data and communicate it to my conscious mind where I have the words to express what it is that I'm seeing."

"Oh," he said and looked towards the other side of the room. "Does everybody's brain work like this?"

"Everyone's neurological patterns are unique. For most people this is similar."

"Interesting." His eyes fixed on something close to the front door. "Hey, did you forget about your package?"

"What... Oh yes, the urgent package." I twisted in my chair to follow Colin's gaze. Vinnie had placed the package on one of the wingback chairs in the reading area. It was quite large and flat, wrapped in heavy-duty brown paper. I got up and walked over. On the package was a strong handwriting, the kind that would usually be done by a man. My address was written clearly in a thin black marker. A shiver ran down my spine. I didn't like surprises.

"Aren't you going to open it?" Colin was standing next to me, also staring down at the package.

"I didn't order this."

"So someone just sent this to you out of the blue? Who would have your mailing address?"

"I have bought a few things online that I had shipped to that address." I frowned at the flat, square package on the chair. "I didn't order this."

"So you keep saying. Well, Vinnie had it checked for electronic devices and some other things."

"What other things?"

Instead of answering me, Colin picked up the package. "Why don't I open this for you?"

"Okay." I watched as Colin shook the package and tilted it from side to side. "What are you doing?"

"Trying to guess what's inside." He smiled at me. "Want to go first?"

"It's a senseless exercise. Just open it."

His smile widened and he inspected the wrapping. "Got scissors? We'll have to cut through this."

"In the kitchen."

He followed me wordlessly to the kitchen. I retrieved a pair of scissors from its designated place in the second drawer from the left. He took it and carefully cut away the tape that held the paper at the back of the package. It took a full minute to remove the layers of brown paper. Except for my name and address, there was no other writing on the package. No indication where it had come from. Only layers of brown paper. I immediately put the paper in the recycle bin, out of view. We were left with a flat brown box.

Colin had to cut the flap open since it was also taped closed. By this point I had no idea what to expect, so when he pulled out a framed painting I only raised my eyebrows. I flattened the box and also put that in the recycle bin. I turned back and found Colin studying the painting.

"I did not order that," I said. I realised that repeating myself served no other purpose than revealing my confusion. Yet I had a desire to say it one more time. I didn't. "What is it? Is it an original?"

"This is the Beata Beatrix by Dante Gabriel Rossetti." He leaned in and narrowed his eyes. "No, this won't do."

He took the painting to the reading area and turned my reading lamp so that he could place the painting in the light for maximum viewing. I quietly followed him and stood there feeling redundant. I had no art expertise to draw on. In the six years that I had worked at the upscale insurance company, I had learned quite a bit about art. But my knowledge sadly only extended to the names of the most expensive artists and valued works of art. Those I would be able to recognise on sight. This applied to a limited number of works. A very limited number.

My expertise was reading and interpreting nonverbal communication cues. And psychology. For almost all human behaviour, I could give an academic explanation of its possible origin. Right now I could give an in-depth analysis of all the cues that led me to believe that Colin was fast forming a conclusion. It wasn't difficult to see the confidence he exuded in inspecting the painting. He knew what he was looking at and looking for. I didn't. I had no knowledge of authentic paintings versus forgeries. He did.

"This is a masterpiece."

"It's real?" Surprise lifted my voice.

"Nope. It's a masterful forgery." He straightened and looked at me. I knew that look. It caused a feeling of my heart dropping into my stomach. In actual fact, my heart was palpitating from a rush of adrenaline. "This makes me think of all those paintings that were done for Piros in our last case."

"But Piros is now in prison." I had followed his trial closely. He would not experience freedom until he died. He had been sentenced to seven successive life sentences. And that had been only for the civilian cases. The international cases against him as a military official were still ongoing. "It can't be him."

"I'm not saying that it's him, Jenny. All I'm saying is that it makes me think of one of the artists who forged work for him while he was running his art crime syndicate."

"Then who painted this?"

He turned back to the painting and looked at it for a few moments. He shook his head. "I have no idea."

"Why send it to me? What does this mean?" Questions were piling up in my brain. Suddenly I felt naked in my pyjamas. I wanted to wear something that I could run away in.

This irrational thought brought a stop to the chaos in my mind. I needed to look at this calmly.

"I don't know, Jenny. All I know is the inspiration of this painting. Well, not this painting, but the original painting. Dante Rossetti was not only an artist, but he was also a translator. He translated many Italian works of poetry, including Dante Alighieri's *La Vita Nuova*."

"That was written by Dante in the thirteenth century." As a teenager I had had an interest in medieval literature. It had lasted only three months, but Dante had made an impression. I did not remember any of his early work though. My fascination had been with his later pieces. "It was long before his more famous Divine Comedy, right?"

"Exactly. He wrote that combination of prose and verse as a very young man in love with her." He pointed at the painting. "Beatrice Portinari was the main focus of his poetry in that work, Dante's love interest from childhood. Rossetti completed this oil on canvas painting in 1870."

"I don't know whether to call it strange or interesting that both their names were Dante."

"The medieval poet's full name was Durante degli Alighieri, known to most as Dante. The nineteenth-century artist was named Gabriel Charles Dante Rossetti. He preferred to be called Dante in honour of the poet."

"Do you think this is significant?"

Colin shrugged. "No. Yes. Maybe. But this painting is interesting."

The young woman depicted on the canvas was sitting in front of a low wall with light streaming in from a window behind her. Her face was lifted upwards in what looked a meditative or praying pose, and her open hands rested on her lap in a seeming petition. A red dove offered her a poppy flower. In the background to the left was a shadowy figure holding what looked like a flame in her hand. To the right, deep in the shadows, was a male lion.

"Why do you say it is interesting?" I considered a red dove with a halo delivering a white poppy interesting. Colin's reference might be different.

"It is a perfect replica. One of the best I've seen. Except for the lion."

"What's wrong with the lion?" I leaned closer to look at it.

Colin didn't answer me. He walked to the table, sat down and handled my laptop as if I had given him permission. I hadn't. I took a deep breath and joined him at the table.

"Look." He turned the laptop, my laptop, for me to have a better view of the monitor. "This is the original painting by Rossetti."

"Oh my." I blinked a few times. "There is no lion."

"Yup. No lion." He slumped in the chair. "Why on earth would someone paint such an extraordinary work and get it wrong?"

"Because it is a message." I pointed at the figure to the right of the painting on the monitor. "What or who is supposed to be in place of the lion?"

"Dante."

"Hmm." My mind wasn't even giving me a glimmer of a connection. I continued to stare at the painting on the monitor. "And the person on the left?"

"That is Love. In Dante's *La Vita Nuova* he constantly refers to her. Here he is looking towards her. In the book Dante mourned the unrequited love he had for Beatrice right up until her death. Rossetti painted this after his wife, Lizzie, died from a laudanum overdose. She died in 1862. Both this painting and the translation for *La Vita Nuova* were done after Lizzie's death. He felt close kinship and understanding to Dante's painful mourning of Beatrice's death in that book."

"It was more than just their names binding them," I said absently. This was immensely fascinating, but I could not see any correlation to any of the previous two days' events.

"Does this mean anything to you?" Colin asked.

I went through the whole story that he had just told me three times in my head. "No, I can see no connection whatsoever."

"A connection to the burglaries?"

"You think there is a connection?" I asked in turn. "Please tell me if you see it, because I don't see it."

"I'm not seeing anything. But I do think this is far too coincidental to not be connected somehow." He shifted in the chair. "The painting is here in Strasbourg."

"The original painting?" My voice was a bit too loud. I cleared my throat.

"Yes. One of the more prestigious art galleries is holding a fantastic exhibition and this is their drawing card. It's on loan from the Tate Museum in London." His mouth indicated scepticism. "Someone from this gallery must know someone from the Tate. There is no other way that they would've gotten such a priceless piece of art for their exhibition."

"Which gallery is it?" I asked.

"La Fleur Galerie on Grand Rue."

My eyebrows shot up. I grabbed my computer and looked for a company email sent out earlier in the week. "La Fleur Galerie? This is becoming ridiculous with all these little connections. Aha, got it. Just like I thought. La Fleur Galerie is insured by Rousseau & Rousseau. I was asked to watch the interview footage of all the employees to check for any markers of dishonesty. La Fleur has done a lot in preparing for this exhibition and protecting all the artwork that will be on display there."

We fell silent for a few minutes. My mind was turning over every tiny bit of information. As inconsequential as it might seem, even the smallest thing could help me solve this painting mystery. If we were talking about things seeming too coincidental, then I had another question. "Could this have something to do with your disappearance?"

Colin flinched as if I had punched him. His reaction was reflective and miniscule. But I had been trained to notice micro-expressions. I had seen his limbic brain's honest response to my question. There was nothing he could say to make me believe he did not suspect some connection between the painting, the burglaries and his mission that had gone awry.

I watched him struggle with an answer. He must have known that I would call him out on a lie. He was debating what to tell me. I was hoping for the truth. The full truth.

My waiting got interrupted by a ping from my computer. My email account had at last opened and I had a new email. It was marked urgent, but that wasn't what concerned me.

"What is it?" Colin asked. I glanced up from the computer and noticed the relief on his face that we could focus on something else.

"An urgent email."

"Seems like there are lots of urgent things. Who is it from?"

It took a moment for me to answer. "Dante."

"Shit. For real?" He leaned in to look at the screen. "This is getting way too out there to be anything but connected."

I lifted a brow at his use of such informal language. He was clearly as taken aback by this as me. I opened the email and frowned.

Colin sat even closer to also read the message. He grunted. "What does this mean?"

"'The vengeance of those wronged shall visit upon the observers of the purity of new beginnings. Mayhap the mother of all might be their saviour.'" I shrugged and shook my head. "I don't know what this means."

"Who would write something like that? It doesn't make sense."

"It made sense to whoever wrote this," I said. In Oxford I had done an undergraduate year in abnormal psychology. This kind of behaviour had come up in a few discussions. The other students had called these people loonies. People who communicated through code, thinking they were of superior intellect, daring authorities to catch them and stop them. People who were dangerous.

It felt as if my heart dropped to my stomach.

Chapter EIGHT

"If you don't like it, you can leave." I was bored with this argument.

"You know I'm not going anywhere," Colin said, the *buccinator* muscles stretching the corners of his mouth into a sneer.

"Then stop complaining. I'm getting dressed. Manny said he'll be here in about fifteen minutes." I had phoned him despite all Colin's complaints. He had sounded strangely alert at this time of the morning and hadn't wasted a moment. He was on his way. And I didn't want to meet the grumpy Interpol man in my pyjamas. I closed my bedroom door a bit louder than strictly necessary. Colin had annoyed me.

The moment I had suggested we contact Manny, he had exhibited all kinds of hostile nonverbal cues. And then refused to explain why he didn't want me to phone Manny. This conflict between the men was fast becoming overbearing. It was a distraction that I didn't appreciate. I pulled a neatly ironed pair of jeans from my wardrobe and a soft long-sleeved T-shirt from the top of a perfectly aligned stack.

I didn't bother with make-up. I seldom did. At most I applied mascara and lipstick on a working day, but this was five o'clock in the morning. In my apartment. There was no need for frivolities. I did, however, spend two minutes carefully messing up my short brown hair. Everything else in my life was generally void of chaos, and my messily styled hair appealed to my rebellion against social norms.

Colin was also dressed and pacing the length of the open-plan living area when I left my room. His lips were pressed into a thin line. A sign of distress. Combined with the rest of his body language it was easy to come to a conclusion. I went to the kitchen to make more coffee. He joined me, leaning against the counter, arms folded and glaring at me. I was hard pushed to not roll my eyes.

"What would you have done? Who would you have phoned?" I asked softly. I didn't want to argue any more.

"Not Millard."

"That's not an answer, Colin." I turned to him and studied his face for a few seconds. "You know you can tell me."

"I know." He was silent for a long minute. "I can't. I'm sorry that you have been dragged into all this, Jenny."

"Into all what?"

"This." He waved his hand towards the computer. "The burglaries, Francine's attack, this mysterious package."

"You didn't do any of this. You have nothing to be sorry for." I knew this to be true. He wasn't responsible for any of the many reasons that had me making coffee and waiting for Manny at five in the morning. Then why did guilt and remorse flash across his face?

The doorbell interrupted any further analysis. Manny. He wasn't aware of Colin's association with Interpol. I shuddered at the thought of his reaction if he were ever to find out. In his opinion, Colin was a common criminal worthy of being thrown in prison. Knowing Manny as I did, he was not going to take kindly to being deceived for such a long period.

I opened the door and frowned. Manny was freshly showered and looked surprisingly awake. He had even shaved.

"Are you going to frown at me all day or let me in, Doctor Face-Reader?" He too was irked.

"Sorry. Please come in." I moved to the side to allow Manny in. "Thanks for coming."

"Yeah, sure. Where is it?"

"By the dining room table." After locking all five locks, I followed Manny to the dining area. Colin had brought an easel from his apartment and the painting was displayed on it next to the table. As we reached the table, Colin stepped from the kitchen.

"You." Manny didn't hide his displeasure. "What are you doing here?"

"I moved in with Jenny." His smile was smug. He was masking his rage towards Manny with disrespect.

Manny turned to me, his face an expression of revulsion. "You're shacking up with this delinquent?"

"I'm not sure what that means, but I think you are insulting me. Don't." I pointed my finger at Colin's chest. "And you must stop provoking Manny. He's here to help."

If these men were wolves, they would have been snarling and snapping at each other. They were human, so they stood there glaring, neither one the first to break eye contact. God, I hated working with men. With people.

"Let's focus on the painting and the email." I wanted to go back to what I was familiar with. Analysis, data, facts. Not emotions.

"Missy, is this criminal really staying here?"

"He's not a–"

"I'm staying here for a short time," Colin interrupted me. Interesting. He actually wanted Manny to think he was a criminal. "My apartment is currently being renovated."

I bit down on the insides of my lips. Lying never sat well with me and I was terrible at it. Colin was a good liar. A truly good liar. From Manny's face, I knew he was suspicious, but almost convinced. Again he dismissed Colin and turned to the painting.

"This it?"

"Yes, this is the Beata Beatrix by Dante Rossetti."

"Doesn't look like much." He leaned in to take a closer look, his hands locked behind his back. "So you say this is a forgery?"

"Yes." Impatience was audible in my voice. I didn't like repeating myself. I had told Manny everything about the painting and the email when I had phoned him.

He straightened and stared at me for a few seconds. Then he looked at Colin, grunted and sat down heavily on one of the dining room chairs. "I'll have to take this in for the forensic guys to look for prints. Do you still have the wrapping and the box?"

"It's in the recycle bin," I said. "But I don't want you to take the painting."

"Missy, I don't really care if you want me to take it or not, I'm going to."

"You won't find any prints on it," Colin said. "Well, you'll find our prints, but no one else's. The frame is clean and I will bet my bottom dollar that there are no other prints."

"Prints are not the only things that we can get from that painting, Frey."

"Of course not." Colin nodded in acknowledgement. "Trace elements can give us clues about the painter. The paint, the canvas, everything. Jenny, you'll have to let Manny take the painting."

I hesitated. "Okay, but I want photos of this painting."

"I'll even get my guys to print out a life-size photo of this one," Manny said. "Does that work for you?"

"Yes, thank you."

"Now tell me everything else." Manny lifted his eyebrows at us. It would seem that our ten o'clock meeting had been moved forward.

I sat down in my usual chair and Colin in the chair next to mine. I fixed an unfriendly look on him when he put his arm across the back of my chair. His territorial display did not please me. I continued frowning at him until he removed his arm and straightened a bit. He didn't move away though.

"We think that the burglary cases, Francine's attack, this painting and the email are all connected," I said, addressing Manny.

"Wait, hold up." Manny pointed one finger in the air. "Firstly, tell me about Francine's attack."

"Jenny–"

"Colin, no." I stopped him with an intense glare. "The last time I withheld information from Manny, you were suspected of murdering someone and I landed in jail. I'm not doing that again. He might be uncouth in many ways, but he is a good investigator. You know this."

Colin responded by folding his arms across his chest and scowling. He looked at the painting and nodded his head. As if I needed his permission to continue. I longed for Phillip's calming presence. He was the expert in handling people. Not me.

Manny inhaled to speak. Most likely about my insult and compliment in one sentence. I couldn't let him say something that would provoke me into another faux pas or Colin into verbal assault. So I jumped in with the full explanation of everything that had taken place in the last forty-eight hours. Francine's attack, her ramblings, the hacker and his possible connection to our burglary case and my computer being hacked. I didn't tell him that Colin had bought the apartment next to me or that Vinnie and Francine were there at the moment. At some point it might become relevant, but it wasn't a necessary detail now.

"And what do you think is the relationship between all that and the painting?" Manny asked, rubbing his shaved jaw.

"I can't see any relationship," I said. "Except that it is far too much of a coincidence that these cases, Francine, the hacker, the painting and the email all entered my life in the last two days."

'There's no such thing as coincidence," Manny mumbled. He briefly pressed the heels of his hands against his eyes. "Okay, so what do you think the email means?"

I had gone over this a thousand times in my head. Still there was no significant insight. That connection still hadn't clicked into place. I shrugged. "I genuinely couldn't tell you. I have no context to interpret this seemingly nonsensical sentence. I'm not good with speculation and conjecture."

"I am." Vinnie spoke from the front door. I had to change the locks. Again. Even if it was only to stop these people for a day or two from having full access to my apartment.

"I'm even better." Francine pushed past Vinnie and walked slowly towards us. Dressed in different yoga pants and this time a glittery silver top, she more resembled her usual supermodel self. The swelling in her face had gone down only a little, but it was enough for her high cheekbones to be visible again. "Some might call it conspiracy theories, I call it conclusions based on well-researched data. Hello, Manny. You're looking oh so dapper."

She sat down next to Manny and ran a manicured fingernail down the lapel of his jacket. He inspected her face for a second, not missing a single bruise. Then he leaned in until their noses almost touched. "Don't fuck with me, little girl. You'll lose."

I could count on one hand the number of times I had heard Manny use strong language. Once again he confirmed to me his uncanny, and well-hidden, ability to see through people's disguises. Most likely he also saw that Francine only responded to and respected strength. His way of conveying that point was with swearwords.

"A real charmer, isn't he?" Francine smiled beautifully and settled in her chair. Her body language communicated approval of Manny. I marvelled at the games people played.

"What's he doing here?" Vinnie was giving Manny the same look I had seen on his face months ago. That day he had crushed a mosquito feeding from his arm with a lightning-fast slap.

The loud groan of frustration I uttered surprised everyone. Even me. I waved my index finger at them. "I don't want this… this juvenile behaviour in my apartment. I don't know how to deal with it and frankly, it is boring. If you're going to be here, behave like the intelligent individuals I know you are. Whatever it is you have against each other, act on it when I am not around."

My outburst was clipped and louder than my normal tone. I wouldn't have been surprised if Colin, Vinnie and Francine walked out and never came back. Once I had taken that tone with a schoolmate. The rest of the semester no one had spoken to me. At the end of that semester my parents had started homeschooling me. A similar situation had taken place at my first university. And at another university. That was why I avoided social interaction.

I knew Manny wouldn't leave. He had a professional stake in the case, no personal interests. I raised my eyebrows at my three supposed friends. They had been the ones insisting on friendship. Not the other way around. I wasn't trying to make friends. I wanted to solve a crime and a mystery.

"I'll make breakfast." Vinnie was the first to break the awkward silence. He gave Manny another mosquito-crushing look. "For all of us."

The large man left my apartment while he muttered about my empty fridge and bringing food. I concluded that it was his way of conceding to my demands. Since no one else said anything or left, I accepted it to be their silent agreement as well.

"Where is he going?" Manny asked.

"To get ingredients for breakfast." I turned my attention to Francine. "Colin told me you secured my laptop last night. Could someone have gotten past that security?"

"No." She shook her head. "For that to happen, the hacker has to be better than me. That leaves a handful of candidates in the world. Why?"

The next five minutes were devoted to explaining the email to Francine. When Vinnie returned I had to repeat the story. It annoyed me, but gave me the opportunity to include the details about the painting. The thought of having to repeat this all again to Phillip later at work did not enthuse me. Francine grabbed my computer and tapped away on the keyboard, doing things I carried no knowledge of.

Vinnie got busy in the kitchen while Colin, Manny and myself tried to make sense of the email. We were just going around in circles, the men insisting on outrageous conjecture and Francine interrupting to add a theory that included a government conspiracy. This was exasperating.

"What do you mean?" Colin looked at me and I realised I had spoken out loud.

"This isn't getting us anywhere. When I draw conclusions it is because I have a wealth of data to work with. We have an email, loosely connected robberies, a hacker and a painting." The *levator labii superioris* muscles pulled my top lip up in disgust. "Everything you have just said is wild hypothesis."

"It's called brainstorming, missy." Manny only called me missy when I did or said something to anger him.

"It's speculation and conjecture," I said. "Our time would be better spent looking for other connections between these different elements."

The conversation was put on halt when Vinnie brought breakfast to the table. In less than twenty minutes he had prepared large quantities of toast, scrambled eggs and freshly squeezed orange juice and served it with a tray full of condiments and steaming coffee. We started eating. There was a small window of approximately four minutes when no animosity was observed around the table. It didn't last long.

"Why do you have keys to Doctor Face-Reader's apartment?" Manny carefully placed the knife and fork on his plate and stared at Vinnie. "Or did you also move in here?"

"Don't take that tone with me, old man." Vinnie waved his knife at Manny. "I need less than this to—"

"Vinnie." Francine's low warning stopped Vinnie from threatening a law enforcement official.

Mentally writing Mozart was much more productive than listening to their bickering. A connection was begging to be made. I didn't know whether it was related to the robberies, the email, the hacker, the painting or something else. All I knew was that it was close and there were too many distractions. Too many people in my apartment, their body language, the nuances of their threats and tones were disquieting. I felt the tension slowly drain from my muscles as I finished the Larghetto of Mozart's Piano Concerto No. 27.

"Jenny?"

I opened my eyes to find only Colin and Manny still in my apartment. The table was cleared and a quick glance at the kitchen confirmed that Vinnie had cleaned up.

"I need to go to work," I said and looked at my watch. I groaned. Two hours had passed since I decided to go into my head. "I'm going to be an hour late."

"I have an errand to run, then I'll come in too," Manny said. "I'll fill Phillip in on everything we have."

"Oh, thank you." I was relieved and grateful for not having to yet again go over the last two days. Manny didn't waste much more time with redundant greetings. It took him less than one minute to leave, but not before he gave Colin one last glare. I closed the door and wondered about the sense of locking the five locks. I did it anyway.

"I'll drive you to work," Colin said from the kitchen. He was placing our mugs in the dishwasher.

I was about to argue when I remembered that my car was still at the office. "Give me ten minutes."

Nine minutes later I was back at the front door with my handbag and work computer in its bag. Colin got up from the sofa and smiled at me. "All set?"

"I'm ready to leave, yes." I opened the door and waited outside until he locked the door with keys that I knew I hadn't given him. With an inner groan I decided not to argue about that.

He took my computer bag, slung it over his shoulder and walked down the corridor. I followed him to the elevator. We fell into a comfortable silence until we were in the car and Colin pulled into the street. He was fiddling with the controls on the steering wheel. "Want to listen to the news?"

"Why do you ask when you already switched on the radio?"

"Touché." His smile relaxed his face and he glanced at me. "I could switch it off if you don't want to listen to it."

"No, it's fine. I want to hear the outcome of yesterday's debate in the senate."

"Are they still going on about the immigrants?" he asked.

Some pop song was playing in the background. Another glance at my watch warned me that the news should be read any minute now.

"Yes, but this debate was about healthcare. The president's wife actually had a few valid points in an interview on the television a few nights ago."

"Isn't she a doctor?"

"A neurosurgeon. Since becoming the first lady she doesn't practice as much as she used to, but she's still active in her field. Actually, she's one of the best in her field."

"How come you know so much about her?"

"I watched a documentary," I said. Something in our conversation clicked with something in my subconscious. I was close to unveiling some mystery, yet it eluded me. It was unbelievably frustrating. "Turn off the radio."

"What?"

"Turn off the radio, please," I said. "I need to think."

"Should I turn on some Mozart?"

I was surprised. "You listen to Mozart in your car?"

"I've kinda grown fond of the guy." Colin squirmed a little in his seat. He was embarrassed. "Anything specific you want to listen to?"

"Do you have his Violin Sonata No. 21?"

With only a few glances away from the road, he found the piece and the sounds of the opening melody filled the vehicle. I took a deep breath, closed my eyes and leaned back in my seat. From many years of experience I had learned to not push my mind. I focussed on the sombre harmonic accompaniment of the piano and the plaintive sounds of the violin. Even though the second theme in this sonata was written in a major key, it still carried the heaviness of the grief in the opening theme.

The information connected and formed a picture that crashed into my mind. I gasped and pushed my palm against my chest. I had it. I had the connection.

"What? Jenny, what is it?" Colin started to slow down and turned on the indicator to pull off the street.

"No." I sat up. "Go. We need to go to La Fleur Galerie. Now."

"Why?"

"It's there. We need to go now." I pointed to the right. "Turn here. It is about five minutes away. We're close. We must get there now."

Colin turned into the street I indicated. His attention was taken up by manoeuvring his large SUV through the tight streets of downtown Strasbourg. "Jenny, what is going on?"

"It's a message."

"What message? What are you talking about?" Colin drove us as far as he could in a second narrow street and parked illegally. "We're going to have to walk the rest of the way."

"Let's go." I jumped out of the car before he finished his sentence. We needed to get into this medium-sized art gallery. It was located in the centre of the tourist district on a street that had been closed for traffic. I could see the corner of the building about eighty metres ahead of us and increased my pace.

"Jenny, talk to me." Colin was next to me, lengthening his stride to keep up with me. He sounded worried.

I took a deep breath. I needed to focus my thoughts. The excitement of the connection had me reverting back to scattered behaviour. To neurotypical people it didn't make sense and was often referred to as crazy behaviour. I needed to line up my thoughts in a logical manner.

"What was wrong with the painting?"

"Apart from it being a forgery, the lion replaced Dante in the painting. Everything else is exactly like the original." He narrowed his eyes. "What about the lion?"

"Lenard is a variant of Leonard which means 'lion strength' or 'strength of a lion'. That's the anomalous lion in the painting." I took a shaky breath. "The second sentence in his email says, 'Mayhap the mother of all might be their saviour'. The name Genevieve has Celtic roots with the meaning 'of the race of women' or 'mother of the race'. Whatever vengeance he has planned, he thinks I can stop it. Either stop it or play some other preventative or abetment role. And I'm sure the clue is in the original painting hanging in this gallery."

"Jesus." Colin stopped me a few metres from the front doors of the gallery. "Jenny, if this is a personal message, it could be a personal attack. I don't think it is a wise idea to go into the gallery alone."

"I'm not alone. I have you," I said and continued walking. "Besides, what could go wrong? It is an art gallery in the city centre surrounded by tourists, with security personnel, security cameras—"

"Which can all be hacked." He caught up with me and grabbed my elbow. "We should phone someone."

"Who? Do you want to phone Manny?" My sincere suggestion offended him greatly judging by his expression. Since he hadn't told me what his problem was with Manny, I chose to ignore the shimmer of guilt I felt. I pulled my elbow out of his grasp and knocked on the glass door. It was before opening hours, but I could see personnel moving around inside. It was my second, and louder, knock that got the attention of a skinny young man. I glanced at Colin. "Look at all these people inside. We are perfectly safe. I'll just have a quick look at the painting."

The door opened before he could reply. I took a deep breath and readied myself for my best performance at social interaction.

Five minutes later Colin was looking at me with a slack jaw, and the young man was escorting us to the painting. My name and credentials delivered in a kind but authoritative tone worked wonders. All with the help of years of studying, observing and practicing.

The young man led us through the front of the museum towards the back. We passed a few people, but apart from curious looks, they didn't pay much attention to us. We went up a set of stairs to the next floor. None of the rooms had doors, a few had a heavy rope preventing access. Colin was absorbing everything in our surroundings. A practiced thief.

We reached a large room dedicated to the most prominent works of art. The Beata Beatrix was in this room. I put my social skills to practice again. After only one minute's discussion, the young man agreed that I could lift the heavy rope to enter the room. He left us to call his supervisor.

Colin was right behind me, his body a loud expression of disagreement. I ignored him and stepped onto the carpet. Most art galleries favoured wooden or tiled floors. This carpet was a Persian that left half a metre of uncovered tiled floor space running the length of the walls, framing the beautiful handcrafted rug. All the walls in the room were filled with paintings from the eighteenth century, but it was the painting straight ahead that caught my attention. The Beata Beatrix was hanging in the most prominent place in this room.

"Jenny, wait." Colin's fingers brushed my elbow. He had tried to grab my arm again, but I was faster and I left him at the door, walking straight to the painting. He was not happy with me. "Seriously. Wait. Something doesn't feel right."

"You know I don't work with feelings," I said without looking back and took the last four steps to the painting. On the second last step, something clicked under my right foot.

"Freeze!" Colin's shout was what stopped me. It was so remarkable for him to raise his voice that I immediately knew to take it seriously.

"What's wrong?" I was standing with my right foot ahead of the left, most of my weight resting on the right. "Should I not move at all? Is speaking okay?"

"Don't turn around," he quickly said when I started to turn my neck. "Speaking is okay, but no moving. Okay, Jenny?"

"Okay." This was proof of my trust in Colin. Despite his disappearance out of my life, my anger towards him and my confusion about his issue with Manny, I trusted him. But I didn't know with what. "Tell me what is going on."

"Jenny, I want you to stay calm. Don't shift your weight at all. Can you do that?"

"I'm doing that. Now tell me what is going on." I was becoming annoyed with the concern I heard in his voice.

"When I tell you, I don't want you to react. I don't want you to go into your head either, okay?"

"Why not?"

"Because you rock yourself when you're in your head and that would not be good."

"Colin." My voice was low and I pushed the words through my teeth. "Tell me what is wrong."

"I think you've just stepped on a bomb."

Chapter **NINE**

"A bomb?" I almost laughed at the ludicrousness of the notion. "Colin, you can't expect me to believe that."

"Argue all you want, just don't move." I heard him move and found it very difficult to not look over my shoulder.

"What are you doing?" When he didn't answer me immediately, I spoke louder. "Not speaking to me is making me feel unsafe. That makes me want to go into my head and not come out again. If you tell me what is happening, I can deal with it rationally and intellectually."

"I'm coming to you, but I'm going to walk along the wall. I don't want to step on the carpet at all."

"Why?"

"Look at the painting. What do you see against the wall?"

"I assume you are not talking about all the paintings hanging on the wall." I let my eyes inspect the wall in front of me. I was about a metre and a half from the wall. I had actually planned on stepping right up to it, inspecting the original for clues in the message this person was trying to convey to me. "There's a thermometer next to the Beata Beatrix, which is odd. Why would they need to check the temperature? Surely it is controlled by the air-conditioning. It's rather the humidity that needs to be controlled in an environment like this."

"Look more carefully." Colin's voice was a bit closer.

"There is a wire running from under the carpet to the thermometer and from the thermometer to the back of the painting."

"Exactly."

"How is that a bad thing?"

"Without sounding as paranoid as Francine, I think that you were lured here with the clues. I'm sure there is a pressure plate hidden under the carpet where you are standing now. Again I'm merely guessing, but I'd rather err on the side of caution. I also think that those wires are leading from the pressure plate to a bomb behind the painting. Either that or…"

I didn't like the way he stopped himself from continuing. "Tell me, Colin."

"Or you're standing on the bomb."

He was standing to the right of me now, about a metre away. His eyes narrowed at the wiring and I could see in the economy of his movements that he was trying his best to not jolt anything. He took another careful step closer and leaned in to look at the wires leading from directly under my feet to the painting. He aligned his head to the wall, not touching it, trying to look behind the painting. It was the two quick blinks that made me want to crawl into my head and hide in Mozart's harmony forever.

Colin straightened and looked at me with great severity. "Do not move. Not a muscle, Jenny. Don't adjust your weight, don't change your breathing, don't even blink."

"That is impossible. Blinking is an involuntary–" I stopped speaking. He must have said this either to bring his point across or to distract me. The latter almost worked. I got the point.

"I heard the click when you stepped on that plate, Jenny. I have no idea what will happen if you move. Even just looking down could alter your weight distribution and it could set the bomb off." He took out his smartphone and tapped on the screen. "We're phoning for help."

"Does Vinnie know how to disable bombs?" I asked.

"I'm not phoning Vinnie." The pronounced curl of his lip gave me a hint before he confirmed, "I'm phoning Millard."

A few emotions pulled at his facial muscles before he tightened his lips and bit down on his jaw. People did this when they attempted control over wayward feelings. He lifted the phone to his ear.

Manny didn't take long to answer. Before Manny had time to be sarcastic, Colin started speaking. "Jenny stepped on a bomb. We are at La Fleur Galerie. I'm pretty sure she stepped on a pressure plate. Yes, a bomb. Would you like me to spell it for you? No, you cretin, she's not moving. Just send GIPN and their bomb disposal guys. And get someone to evacuate the building."

From where I was standing I could hear Manny shouting at Colin. The words were not clear, but the message was. The shouting stopped abruptly and Colin lowered the phone. "He hung up. But he is phoning the cavalry and he is on his way too."

I didn't ask about his incorrect use of cavalry. The GIPN weren't soldiers on horseback. They were an elite group of highly trained policemen and women. Much like the American SWAT teams and other emergency response teams. In the background a phone rang and I wondered if it was the order to evacuate. I turned my attention to Colin. "You should leave."

"Don't be stupid."

"With my IQ, that is not likely to happen."

He rolled his eyes. "You might have an incredible IQ, Jenny, but it is possible to be stupid as well."

"It's a harsh and ugly word, used far too much in modern society."

"I agree, but in this case it is accurate. You will indeed be acting far less intelligent than you are if you think that I am going to leave you here alone."

"According to you, there is a bomb under my feet or in front of my face. Of course I want you to leave."

"I'm not going anywhere, so you can stop that argument right now. Nothing you can say will change my mind." The jut of his jaw indicated his determination as well as his anger.

"Why are you angry?"

"Because you didn't listen to me when I told you to wait."

"Oh. Sorry." I thought about this some. "With your experience as a thief, your feeling that something is wrong is obviously derived from your learned observations and analysis of the environment around you. I was wrong to discount it as irrelevant and unimportant. But you really shouldn't call your subconscious observations feelings. That was what made me lose interest in what you were saying."

There was a slight narrowing of his eyes before he smiled at me. Whatever he was about to say got interrupted by the young man calling to us from the doorway. "We're leaving. Nobody knows what is going on, but we were told to leave you guys in here. Is everything okay?"

Since I couldn't turn around to speak to the young man, Colin took over. His smile was almost convincing as a relaxed, charming expression. "Everything is just fine. It's best if you get your colleagues out of here right now and take the morning off. I'm sure your boss will contact you when the gallery will be ready to open again."

"Okay, if you say so." I heard the doubt in his voice, but there was a bit of excitement too. It could be from the prospect of having a paid day off or from the potential raise in status he could receive from his friends if he had been at the scene of some interesting crime. His footsteps disappeared down the stairs.

"How's your balance?" Colin asked.

"I'm fine." Without moving my head I dropped my eyes to my extended right leg. "I don't know for how long my muscles will be able to hold this position."

Downstairs, the front door opened, allowing the chaos of sirens and running footsteps in. I hated not being able to turn around and see what was coming at me. All I had was Colin's expressions. The one he had now was of recognition and annoyance. Manny had arrived.

"What the fuck are you doing here, missy?"

I almost smiled at Manny's insensitive handling of such a delicate situation. And I was grateful. I would not have appreciated patronising concern in a carefully modulated tone.

Not from Manny. A muted argument between him and some stranger with a deep voice drew my attention to Colin's face. He looked amused. The argument gained volume until Manny proclaimed, "That is my girl in there. I know how to handle her and will not leave here. Tell them, Doc. Tell them that they don't need kid gloves."

I almost shrugged, but stopped in time. Not moving was a challenge. "I don't know what kind of gloves they're going to need to see if there is a bomb or to disable it. If they need kid gloves, you should let them use them, Manny."

There were chuckles behind me. Colin's smile erased the anger he had exhibited when Manny had spoken. I didn't understand the humour of this moment.

"How many people are there?" I quietly asked Colin.

His eyes zoomed in on the doorway and beyond. "Manny, a man dressed in a bomb suit, two men looking like they're from the emergency response unit and I see another two further away from the door."

"They all have guns, don't they?" I deeply disliked weapons.

"All except for Manny and the bomb-suit guy." Maybe Colin didn't see Manny's weapon, but I was sure there was a gun somewhere on his person.

"Ms Lenard?" the deep voice asked from the doorway. It sounded like his voice was coming through a speaker.

"It's Doctor Lenard to you," Manny said before I could answer.

"My apologies. Doctor Lenard, my name is Edward Henry. I am an EOD technician and am going to make my way to you."

"What is an EOD technician?" I asked.

There was a moment of silence. "Explosive Ordinance Disposal technician. I disarm bombs. Are you doing okay?"

"I'm fine."

"Can you hold still and not move?"

"I haven't moved since I've stepped on this thing. Colin told me not to move."

"I assume you are Colin?" There was no doubt in my mind that Edward hadn't addressed that question to me, so I didn't answer.

"Yes, I am."

"Sir, I'm going to have to ask you to carefully make your way out of the room."

"I'm not going anywhere." Colin looked at me when he said that.

"I have to insist."

The thought of Colin leaving me to face Edward and a potential bomb by myself caused me to make a strangled sound. I wanted to give in to the overwhelming desire to simply walk out of here. Or even better, go into my head and bathe in Mozart.

"Jenny?" Colin's eyes flew to me and narrowed.

"Please don't leave," I whispered. "Rationally I know you should not be here, but I really don't want you to leave."

His right hand lifted as if to touch me, but it stopped mid-air and then fell to his side. "Nothing and nobody can make me leave you."

"Sir, you have to leave now." The voice came from my left, the opposite path Colin had followed to get to me. I slowly turned my head just enough to have this man in view. He wore something I could only liken to a space suit.

It was a full-body suit made of material that looked impenetrable. I doubted he was able to get dressed without any help. The suit even covered his head and had a helmet with a visor. That explained why his voice sounded like it was filtered through a sound system. His hands were uncovered which, after a moment's thought, I realised must be to give him the freedom I could only imagine was needed to disable an explosive device.

That last thought combined with Edward's awkward movements in that blast suit brought home the severity of this situation. As quickly as I could without changing my balance, I focussed on Colin. I would much rather look at him than at the spaceman. I desperately wanted to reach for Mozart in my head.

"I'm not leaving. You'll just have to work with me here," Colin said to Edward, but didn't look away from me.

Edward stopped and looked from us to the doorway and back. "Who are you people?"

"I'm Doctor Genevieve Lenard and this is Colin–"

"That's not what he was asking, Jenny," Colin interrupted me and I knew it was to prevent me from revealing his surname to a law enforcement official. "We are citizens in need of your expert help. I will not get in your way, I will not comment on what you do. I'm here for Doctor Lenard."

It was the first time Colin had addressed me professionally and it didn't feel right. As much as I had hated him shortening my name at the beginning of our acquaintance, I now only responded to him when addressed as Jenny. The same as Manny calling me everything but my real name.

"Frey, are you sure about that?" Manny spoke from the door, giving away Colin's surname. "As much as I don't like you, SOP requires that you leave."

"Standard Operating Procedure," Colin said before I could ask about the acronym. Then he looked over my shoulder towards the door. "I'm not leaving. Just as you're obviously also not leaving."

"No way in hell I'm leaving Doctor Face-Reader with the likes of you," Manny said.

"It's all settled then." Colin looked back at me. "Don't get startled and move, Jenny. Bomb guy is almost next to you."

"His name is Edward," I said and turned my head a fraction. Indeed, the heavily suited man was about two metres away from me, walking slowly on the tiled floor. "Hello, Edward."

His head snapped up and he looked at me through the visor. After a few seconds' inspection he nodded. "Hello, Doctor Lenard."

"Please call me Genevieve," I said. Colin made a rude noise, but I didn't want to look at him. That would require a fast movement.

"Right. Genevieve." He stepped closer until he was within reach of the wires. "Do you have any idea what's going on here?"

"Colin thinks—"

"Only wild speculation," Colin said. This time I slowly moved my head to glare at Colin. I hated being in a situation where I was forced to count every word I said. I already had to focus on not moving to a safer place – my head. Colin didn't respond to my glare. He was looking at Edward. "If you feel along the carpet, it will be easy to locate the pressure plate."

"And you are sure this is a pressure plate?" Edward asked. "How would you know?"

Colin closed his eyes briefly. "When Jenny, Genevieve, stepped on it, there was an audible click. That and the wires brought me to this conclusion."

Edward slowly lowered himself to his haunches and inspected the carpet around my feet very lightly with his fingertips. "Would that be your wild speculation?"

"Please don't touch me," I said. "I don't like being touched and will probably move if you do."

Edward froze and there was a short silence. "I wasn't planning on touching you, Genevieve. I'm just feeling around your feet for this pressure plate. It would seem that you were correct. There is a plate. I don't know if it is a bomb though."

From a pocket Edward removed a device. It was in two parts, attached by a cable. The one part looked like one of those laser guns the traffic police used to catch people speeding. The other had a display screen and a few control buttons.

"What is that?" Colin asked.

"This is Fido," Edward said and aimed the laser gun part at my feet. "It is equal to using a sniffer dog or bees to locate explosive devices. It detects a wide variety of commercial, composite and pure explosives."

"What is its accuracy rate?" I asked. This was fascinating in quite a disturbing way. I might have enjoyed this marvel of scientific and technological development much more had I not been the one being sniffed by a machine.

"Less than three percent false alarms."

"But there is a possibility." My voice cracked and I focussed on my breathing for a few seconds.

Edward finished aiming the sensor at my feet and looked up at me. "I'm not going to let anything happen here, Genevieve."

His reassurance didn't help. How could I believe him? He was no doubt trained in keeping the situation under control. That would mean keeping me calm. In order to do that I was sure he would lie. And I couldn't read his body language under that big suit or his facial expressions, which meant I had nothing. I didn't know if I could believe him and that automatically made me not believe him. This circuitous thinking raised my heart rate and my breathing was becoming irregular.

"Jenny, look at me." Colin had moved another centimetre closer. "I wish I could hold your hand, but that might change your balance and we can't have that."

"My leg," I said softly.

"What's wrong with your leg?" Edward asked.

"Tell him to not speak to me, please," I said to Colin. A moment ago Edward's presence had been tolerable. Not anymore. Even though I knew his name, Edward was still a stranger to me. Him being so close to me was triggering behaviour I had worked hard to control. "My leg is beginning to cramp. My thigh muscles are quivering. I want to move."

Colin vehemently shook his head at Edward. I supposed the man was on the verge of speaking to me again. "Unless it is of utmost importance, don't say anything. I'll handle Jenny. She won't move."

"Handle me?" I narrowed my eyes.

"Don't go interpreting things I didn't say, Jenny. I just mean that I'll talk you through this."

"Then you should've said that. Why do people say one thing when they mean another?" I grunted in discomfort. My right thigh muscle was pulling into a knot. "Colin, my leg."

"Is a very sexy leg," Colin said. "Both of them actually."

My jaw went slack. His eyes dropped to my legs and slowly moved from my feet to my thighs. He leaned slightly to the side to look behind me. "Your arse is really sexy too. In these jeans especially. I like how it hugs your butt. Although I prefer you in your pyjamas. With sleepy hair. Stuff fantasies are made of."

I was frozen in a combination of horror and fascination. Colin had fantasies about me? He thought I was sexy? And he had said all this in front of Edward. I was sure that even Manny could hear it from his position by the doorway. There were sounds and movement next to me, but I was too absorbed by Colin's ghastly inappropriate behaviour to pay attention to it. What was he thinking saying these things?

"Yes," Colin continued. His eyes moved over my torso and paused on my chest. "It's a pity that your jacket is hiding your cleavage. The top you're wearing this morning? Wow. When you move, it moves just enough for me to see a bit of lace from your bra. Now that really got my attention. Sexy, sexy, sexy."

Then I saw it. The *orbicularis oculi* muscles contracted around his eyes. The corners of his mouth pulled to the side so quickly in a smile, I almost missed it. If I had not been so shocked by what he had blurted out, I might have caught on to it much sooner.

"You have truly stooped low, Colin." Disgust lifted my top lip and I dropped my voice. "Low."

"Whatever are you talking about, Jenny?" He gave me a lecherous look that was almost comical in its exaggeration.

"Did you in all honesty think I would believe you?"

"You almost did." His smile was genuine. "For a moment there I had you in the palm of my hand."

I sneered at the hand he waved at me. "You did not have me in the palm of your hand. You confounded me with your outrageous compliments."

"Secured." The voice behind me startled me and I almost moved. I blinked a few times and carefully turned my head to look at Edward. I had completely forgotten about him. "It's safe for you to step away, Genevieve."

He was standing to the left of the painting with clippers in his hand. The wire running from the carpet to the wall had been cut. The painting was slightly askew, which meant that he must have moved it. How had I missed this?

"It's safe? Are you sure?" I asked. I still didn't believe or trust him.

"Take off your helmet and tell her again," Colin said next to me.

Edward lifted the visor. "I can't remove the helmet by myself. Will this do?"

I nodded and studied his features. He had a crooked nose and his lips were almost feminine in their fullness. But his eyes were the most arresting feature in his face. I had only once before seen such a light blue that almost looked gray. They were framed with long, dark lashes.

"It is safe to move, Genevieve. Fido didn't detect any explosives here and I dealt with the wiring. You are safe." The truth was there. Even though I could not connect his facial expressions to his body language, his face told me what I needed to know.

"Okay." The first step I took was away from the wall, away from the painting. After being locked in one position for almost an hour, my legs did not agree with the movement. It felt as if my muscles had been replaced by a gelatinous substance. My knees buckled and my legs started to fold under me.

"I got you." Colin moved to my side with two fast steps and pulled me against him. I leaned heavily into his side, his firm embrace the only thing keeping me upright.

"What the hell happened here?" Manny stormed towards us, all his freshness of this morning gone. He bore the signs of prolonged frowning, creases on his brow and stress pulling the corners of his mouth down. "When in bloody hell did you think it was okay to start triggering bombs without letting me know first?"

Pins and needles announced the return of blood circulation and I shifted from one leg to the other. It caused a rocking motion that Colin wordlessly followed.

"Do you realise that you are saying we should inform you first before we set off bombs?" I asked, distracted. The pins and needles were becoming painfully pronounced.

Manny walked away, turned around and walked back to us. He took another step so that he was in my personal space and pointed a finger in my face. "You aggravate me."

The stress was now clearly visible all over Manny's body. I realised that I was the cause of it and it didn't feel good. I stopped moving and looked at Manny. "I'm sorry."

The rest of my apology and explanation got interrupted by Edward and his team insisting that we leave the room. They needed to make sure there weren't any other surprises under the carpet. Edward also reprimanded Manny for walking all over the carpet without a thought.

"Can you walk?" Colin asked. Being held by him like this, I became aware of the differences in our height. I was a centimetre or two taller than the average woman, but fitted neatly under his arm.

"I think so." I gave a tentative step away from Colin, but he followed me, still holding me tight against him. My legs felt much better, but I was sure I looked like a newborn filly.

Another man, also dressed in protective gear, but not a full-body suit like Edward, led us to the side of the wall, to the tiled floor. All the while Manny grumbled about me causing him to take early retirement.

The man who escorted us out of the room left us at the doorway. Manny got out his phone and within seconds was involved in an intense conversation, interspersed with barked orders. He nodded at us to follow him and walked to the entrance, every now and then glaring back at us.

In the larger space of the gallery, I stepped away from Colin. This time he let me go, but stayed close. I hated feeling this weak. I straightened my spine and pulled my shoulders back. Walking slowly to ensure maximum balance, I made my way to the front. The gallery was now filled with law enforcement people dressed mostly in black protective gear. I stopped.

"You okay?" Colin asked, touching my elbow lightly.

I turned to face him and pulled my elbows tight against my side. "Thank you."

"You're welcome."

"And thank you for distracting me with the inane talk. It worked." I tilted my head to the side. "Why did you say those things?"

"You mean telling you that you're sexy?" He smiled his charming smile. He was trying to provoke me. Again. I let my face convey my full displeasure and waited. He laughed softly. "Okay, okay. Just for the record, it isn't inane. It's the truth. But I did think that saying it in such an outrageous manner was going to be better at distracting you than getting you involved in an intellectual debate."

I stared at him. By the day my respect for this man grew. If only he hadn't had a long criminal history, I would have considered him a peer. No, I mentally corrected myself. I did consider him my peer. He might not have the same genius IQ I had, but he had a natural ability to see deep into people. Without wasting a moment, he had known the best way to get my mind off the bomb and my cramping leg and not allow me to disappear into Mozart.

"When you look at me like that I get worried," he said, one corner of his mouth lifting.

"You shouldn't be worried." I lifted my hand and after a moment's hesitation, placed the tip of my index finger on his sleeve. "What you did in there was incredible. I am deeply grateful."

Loud footsteps stopped next to us. Manny. "Would you please now tell me what the bleeding saints you were doing here?"

"Don't start with me, Millard." Colin moved just a fraction, but it was enough to form a barrier between me and Manny. "Remember that I was the one who phoned you."

"Which might be the only intelligent thing you did all day."

Not only did my expertise give me the skills to live more

unobtrusively among neurotypical people, it also enabled me to understand irrational behaviour. Manny had been frightened by the gravity of the situation. His aggression stemmed from relief rather than anger. Yet it grated on my nerves.

Colin and Manny were now involved in a very loud, very insulting argument. Both men letting off steam. With a sigh I looked around. Everyone in the gallery was moving with purpose, investigating. I found it mildly amusing that no one was paying particular attention to Manny and Colin. One of the many GIPN guys caught my attention. Something about him was familiar. I squinted and wondered if I had met him before.

The two men next to me were talking at the same time now. It drew my attention away from anything and anyone else. Neither Colin nor Manny was listening to the other, both speaking in raised voices.

I had had enough. No one noticed me leaving quietly. I needed to be in a safe place. I needed to be in my viewing room. And I needed Mozart.

Chapter TEN

It was only when Phillip sat down in one of my viewing room chairs that I became aware of his presence. A quick glance told me he was about to give me a long lecture. I knew Phillip's facial expressions well. When his bottom jaw moved from side to side and his nostrils started flaring, it spelled trouble for me. I closed my eyes and waited.

"Look at me, Genevieve," he said after what felt like ten minutes. Most likely it had only been fifteen seconds. I opened my eyes and blinked at him. Because I knew him so well, I saw the concern hidden behind the anger. "A bomb?"

"Manny phoned you." I turned back to my computer for a second to turn down Mozart's Symphony No. 24 in B-flat major. It became background music and I looked at Phillip.

"Yes, he did." Any other person might have missed the flash of a smile. I had seen Phillip's amusement. "You stole his car."

"Technically I suppose you could call it stealing. But he left the keys in the ignition, so is it really stealing?" I would have to check this.

"You took his car without his permission. It is stealing." Again the micro-smile. "He is extremely unhappy about it. Why did you take his car?"

"I was bored with him and Colin arguing. And I wanted to come and work. I could see that they were not going to bring me here without another argument, so I left. Manny's car was conveniently close to the building and had the keys in it. It was indeed timely, because I didn't want to get into a taxi." I shuddered at the memory of my recent experience. I could still smell the cheap lavender air-freshener trying to mask the smell of fast food and body odour. "How did Manny know I had taken his car?"

"GPS," Phillip said and I nodded.

"We live in a society where everyone can be watched and tracked." I liked this fact when it enabled me to do my job when I investigated an insurance fraudster. I didn't like this as much when it was aimed at me.

"Big Brother watches us all the time."

"Oh, I know that reference!" I sat up in my chair. "It comes from the George Orwell book *Nineteen Eighty-Four*, where–"

"Genevieve," Phillip held up his hand, "tell me about the bomb."

I slumped a bit. "Didn't Manny tell you?"

"He only said that you and Colin triggered a bomb."

"We did no such thing. I stepped on a pressure plate that could or could not have been a bomb. Edward said that there were no explosives, so maybe it wasn't a bomb."

Phillip slowly placed his hands on his knees and leaned a bit forward. "Who is Edward? No, don't tell me. It isn't important. What is important is that the bomb disposal unit confirmed that it was a bomb."

"Manny told you this?"

"Yes. He also said that you should tell me how you and Colin landed up there."

I told him about the painting, the email and how I had made the connection with my name and surname. And that I had obviously been right.

"But you do realise that you should've phoned Manny before you stormed into La Fleur Galerie."

"Not really. I wasn't sure about the connection. Like most connections, at first it is only a clue that leads one to something more concrete that one can then call irrefutable proof."

"Genevieve." Phillip's jaw was moving again. He took a deep breath and spoke clearly. "You need to slow down and think about this some more. On paper it is a completely different story if you pursue a clue or a connection until you have the evidence to solidify it. You are not trained to be out there."

I inhaled to argue my point, but stopped when Phillip lifted his hand. His raised eyebrows implored me to consider his point. I did. And then I groaned.

"Did I make a terrible mistake?"

"No, you didn't. You made an intelligent and accurate connection between some abstract and disjointed bits of information we had. Next time it might be better if you consulted with Manny first before you acted."

I thought about this. "Manny asked you to handle me, didn't he?"

Phillip chuckled. "Not in those words exactly, but yes. You scared him. You scared me too."

"I didn't mean to. I was just following—"

"A lead. I know. But promise me that you will speak to Manny first before you do something like this."

"I'll be quite happy to leave all the action to him. I didn't like being there."

"I'm sure you didn't." He leaned back in his chair and nodded at the monitors. "What are you working on?"

Thankful that this conversation was finished, I straightened in my chair. "The burglaries. There are too many coincidences between the burglary cases, Francine's attack and the email and painting I received."

"And you've found something to link it all?"

"Maybe. I'm not sure. This is one of those clues that needs to be solidified into factual evidence." I took a deep breath to prepare myself for this explanation. I wanted to make it as clear as possible. I hated repeating myself. Even more than that, I hated having to explain my explanations. "None of the victims share any similarities in clubs they frequented, social circles, travel itineraries or anything else. What they did have in common was that all of them used high-end insurance and security companies."

"Which makes the burglaries even more bizarre. With trained security personnel on the premises, these amateur thieves should never have gotten in. But we know this already. What else?"

"A conclusion I was bound to draw was that the thieves must have received information from within the circle of security. They received inside help, either from within the insurance companies or the security companies."

"But they didn't all use the same companies."

"True. But then I started looking at what these companies might have in common. The insurance companies didn't share any common factors that were of significance."

"The security companies did?" Phillip's voice raised in excitement.

"Yes. Look at this." I pointed to five of the monitors. "Each security company has the same badge at the bottom of their page."

Phillip leaned closer and squinted at the monitors. "What is that?"

"It is an internet security package, or like they call it, a professional security solution." This had been the connection I had subconsciously made and only fully realised when I had seen those badges. "I don't have experience or knowledge in this area, but I wonder if that software program was used to hack their systems. When Francine looked into the burglary at her great-uncle's, she discovered that the security company's system had been hacked."

Phillip's eyes grew wide before he became pensive. "Are you thinking what I think you are thinking?"

"I don't have the ability to know what you are thinking, Phillip." His smile told me I had erred. "Oh, it was one of those questions."

"Yes, it was. Now tell me what you are thinking."

"To ask Francine to use her skills and see if my hypothesis is correct."

Phillip smiled. "I thought that was what you were thinking."

The viewing room door whooshed open and Angelique

walked in, as cautious as always. "Sir, there are people here to see you. And Doctor Lenard."

I didn't know whether her distaste was for Phillip's guests, for me or that these people wanted to see me as well.

"Show them in, please, Angelique," Phillip said. The older woman left the viewing room and returned three seconds later with Manny and Colin. Neither looked pleased. At least they didn't have any signs of a physical altercation. It was a relief to see that they hadn't resorted to such boorish behaviour, even though it would've been befitting their earlier verbal onslaught.

"I could have you arrested, Doctor Face-Reader." Manny walked right up to my chair and stared down at me with narrowed eyes. His expression did not convey anger. "Are you okay?"

"I'm fine. You shouldn't leave the key in your car's ignition."

"And you shouldn't drive away in other people's cars." Manny stood back to look at the monitors.

Colin had quietly moved to my left side and sat down in a chair that I knew I had not placed there. He lightly touched my shoulder until I turned to him. He didn't speak, he just inspected my face in a manner I supposed I did at times as well. Something he saw must have pleased him because he visibly relaxed and nodded. "Glad you're okay."

"What am I looking at, Doc?" Manny asked. I closed my eyes for a second to get past the irritation of having to repeat myself. And then I did. Almost verbatim, I told them what I had told Phillip a few minutes before.

"Okay, so we need to get the cyber unit to check if this software was used as a Trojan horse to get into their systems." Manny was sitting next to Phillip to my right. Colin had stayed on my left. I wondered if my assumption was correct that he wanted to keep as much distance as possible between him and Manny.

"Or we could ask Francine," I said. Colin's breathing changed and I glanced at him. "What? If Francine wants to be involved in this, she's going to work with Manny as well."

"Francine is already involved in this, Jenny. But you might want to ask her first if she wants to work with him." He lifted his chin towards Manny.

"She phoned me this morning after breakfast, Frey." The *buccinator* muscles pulled one corner of his mouth into a sneer. "She is convinced that it is a huge government conspiracy. Apparently I am not part of that since Doctor Face-Reader here trusts me. Do you trust me, Doc?"

The question came to me so fast that I flinched. The intensity in Manny's stare alerted me that my answer was required, but more than that, it was important. I raised my eyes to the ceiling to consider my answer. When I came to a decision, I looked at Manny only to see his lips tighten and his colour change. "Why are you angry?"

"You have to think about your answer?"

"Of course. I had to consider all the levels of trust before I could answer you honestly."

Manny looked at Phillip and threw his hands in the air. Phillip only smiled.

"But," I continued, "I've come to the conclusion that I do trust you. You are competent in your profession and I have empirical evidence that you have high ethics and morals, and that the denouement of your, of our, actions is an important consideration in your decision-making process."

Manny pinched the bridge of his nose and it looked like he was trying not to hyperventilate. Eventually he just shook his head and looked at me. "Your head must be a scary place to be in, Doc."

"Actually…" I stopped, assessed and smiled. "You are accepting my trust as a compliment and returning it with a backward compliment. Okay. Although your compliment is not exceptionally eloquent."

"Why don't we move on," Phillip said. "Manny, don't you think Francine would be a better choice than the cyber unit? She's personally invested and could focus all her energy on this. I'm sure the unit has other cases they're working on as well."

"The problem is that she is personally invested," Manny said. "That is never advisable to have someone work on a case when there is any personal connection to the crime, the suspects or any aspect for that matter."

"That means I should also be disqualified from working on this case," I said. "The email, the painting, the lion, it all points to a connection with me."

"But you're not normal." Manny groaned and lifted both hands, palms out. "That came out wrong. What I meant was that you are not like everyone else who allows their emotional involvement to cloud their judgement."

"You are right on both accounts. I am not normal, not according to society's standards, and I also am perfectly capable of looking at a situation objectively."

"I wish more people had that ability." Manny turned back to the monitors. "Okay, so let's ask Francine if she would be able to find out if the software these security companies used has a virus or some other computer thingie that allowed the thieves to get inside information."

We all stared at the computer monitors, thinking. Then I remembered. "My computer was hacked."

"What?" Phillip's exclamation would have echoed if my viewing room had not been soundproofed. Oh dear. "When did this happen? Why didn't you tell me, Genevieve? Is our system compromised?"

"I don't know, I don't know. I just noticed that something was wrong yesterday. I always log out of everything and when I switched my computer on I was already logged into my email account. And two of my icons had been moved. Francine secured my laptop."

"But what about the company's system?" Phillip was notably concerned. He barely blinked when Manny's phone started ringing and he moved to the corner to quietly speak into it.

"We should ask Francine to secure it," I said. "She told me how easy it was to hack into my computer and into the company's network."

Red spots coloured Phillip's cheeks and I could see his heart beating faster in the carotid artery in his neck. His hands were in fists on his lap, belying his otherwise calm posture.

"Jenny, I think you should let me tell the rest of this story," Colin quietly said next to me. Maybe it was because he was growing concerned with Phillip's state of agitation.

"It's okay. Phillip knows me."

"Let me hear what Colin has to say," Phillip said. I was surprised and it must have shown. "I don't trust him more, Genevieve. He might possibly give it a different perspective."

"I think Francine would be a good choice for this," Colin said. "She only hacked into Jenny's computer to prove her point on how easy it was to access your system."

"It's that easy?" Phillip almost never raised his voice. Not like now.

"It doesn't look like you're doing a better job than me telling the story," I whispered to Colin. "You're upsetting him."

"He doesn't care about being upset with *me*," Colin whispered back. I was sure Phillip could hear us, which made our whispers redundant.

"Oh." I sat back in my chair just as Manny joined us. He was looking at something on his smartphone, flipping through images.

"When can Francine come in?" Phillip asked.

"I don't think she actually needs to be here to secure anything," Colin said.

"There was some sort of something on the back of the painting." Manny's off-topic announcement was delivered with a graveness that delivered a shot of adrenaline to my system.

"Was that what the phone call was about?" I asked. His demeanour had changed since his phone call. Something was wrong.

"Yes. They sent me photos." He tilted his smartphone towards us.

"If you give me your phone, I can upload it to my computer and we can all see it."

"What about the hacker? Is it safe?" Manny asked.

"I'll disconnect from the company's server and from the internet. That way nobody will have access to anything on my computers in here." I turned towards my computer and did exactly that. Once it was done, I held out my hand for Manny's phone which he reluctantly handed over. Fortunately I had the correct cable at hand and not even a minute later, the photos were up on the monitors.

"Go to the first one," Manny said. I clicked on the first photo. It was a close-up of some device. "That is the explosives box."

"There was an explosives box?" Saying those words felt strange in my mouth. I didn't even know if Manny was using the correct terminology.

"Missy, it was a real bomb. It had everything…" He pointed to the monitors. "Let's start with the third photo."

I clicked on the third photo and it filled the monitors. My eyebrows shot up and my jaw muscles lost some of their strength. Laid out on the carpet were many parts of what I supposed was the bomb. To me it all looked like electronic bits and pieces. Sinister bits and pieces. All of which could have meant my end.

"That is your bomb." Manny pointed at the monitor. "The pressure plate is that largest part. The wire connected it to the casing which was behind the painting."

"What about the thermometer?" Colin asked.

"They think it was placed there simply to make the wire running behind the painting look less suspicious. The thermometer was an empty box. That red box next to the thermometer was the bomb. Only it wasn't a bomb."

I squinted at the red box which looked about the size of a large smartphone, just thicker. "What do you mean it wasn't a bomb? You told me it was a bomb."

"The bomb guys say that the bomb had everything it needed except for explosives," Manny said.

"That is why Edward's machine didn't smell any explosives."

"Yes. The pressure plate would've triggered the explosion if you had stepped off the plate or even just shifted your weight. Some pressure plates trigger the bomb the moment it's stepped on. We were lucky."

"We were lucky because there weren't any explosives," Colin said. "Why would someone build a bomb, go through this elaborate effort to get Jenny there and not put any explosives in it?"

"Apparently he really didn't want any harm to come to her." Manny nodded at the monitors again. "The wires were neatly placed where it should have been, but the plugs weren't even connected to the receptacles on the pressure plate or the red box. Even if there had been explosives in there, it would never have gone off."

"Again. Why?" Colin asked.

"Sadly this is not the only mystery we have. Doc, go back to the first photo." Manny waited until the red box was on the monitor again. "Can you zoom in?"

"What am I looking at?" I asked as I zoomed in on the red box. Up close it looked like it could be from any material covered in shiny red paint. "I don't see anything but the box."

"Go to the next photo. They shone a black light on it and something interesting came up."

"You mean an ultraviolet light?" I clicked on the next image. This image was dark, only the outlines visible. But it was clear that it was the same object. This photo was taken up close and I didn't have to zoom in. What was visible on this image were rows and rows of numbers. "What is that?"

"I was hoping you could tell me, Doc. You're the genius." We were all leaning forward, frowning at the monitors. "The bomb guys think it is code."

"What code?" I knew that computer people like Francine often talked about writing code, but I had no knowledge of this. "I don't know how to program computers."

"That is not computer code," Colin said.

"And how would you know, Frey?" Manny glared past me at Colin. "Have another crime to add to your growing list?"

"Then what do you think it is?" I asked Colin, ignoring Manny. "Something that we need a cryptographer for?"

"Actually, yes. It might be a code, even if it's not computer code. I think that this sicko left another message for you." Colin looked away from the screen, worry pulling at his eyes. "He's playing games, Jenny. Like a cat plays with a mouse."

"That's enough," Phillip said. "We don't need anyone to get anymore scared. Let's be proactive. Do you know how to decipher this?"

I studied the strings of numbers. "They seem to be organised in batches. Look there. You can see groupings of three sets of numbers."

"I see that." Manny grabbed my laser pointer off my desk and aimed it at the monitor. "Those three are separated by one dash and a double dash separates the groupings. Well done, Doc. What does this mean?"

"I don't know." I knew I sounded defensive, but looking at rows of numbers did not enlighten me at all to its meaning or purpose. "If it is a cipher, it could be one of many. My knowledge of ciphers is not extensive, so I'll have to research this."

Colin cleared his throat. "I can help you with this."

Manny's lips tightened, his jaw jutted and the *orbicularis oculi* muscles contracted his eyes. But he didn't say anything.

"Colin, what do you know about this cipher?" Phillip asked.

"There are so many possibilities, but if I had to guess, I would say it was a book cipher," Colin said.

"Like the Ottendorf cipher?" Even with my limited knowledge, I had come across this. "But we need a book for this."

"What exactly are you two talking about?" Manny asked. From the corner of my eye I saw Colin's posture change and I knew he was going to react to Manny's annoyance. I sighed.

"I will explain. And I'll do it simply. The Ottendorf cipher gives you three sets of numbers that refers to the page, line and letter in a book. The first number indicates the page, the second number indicates the line on that page and the third number would be the corresponding number letter in that line. If you have the correct edition of the book, you can decrypt the cipher quite quickly."

"Do you think the book could have something to do with the painting?" Manny asked. It was times like now that he proved his astute detective skills.

"Possibly, but that would be gross conjecture."

"And you don't conjecturise." Manny grunted.

I held it in for a few moments, but then couldn't stop myself. "Conjecturise is not a word. Conjecture is the verb. Or you can use speculate, hypothesise, conclude, extrapolate or even guess. But never conjecturise."

The viewing room was silent. I didn't look at Colin, but knew from the change in his breathing that he found this amusing. Phillip's expression had also relaxed into the beginning of a smile. Manny? He looked exasperated.

"Missy, just tell me if you can decode this Ottoman code."

"Ottendorf cipher." I bit my lips together to stop another tirade about the correct usage of terms and vocabulary. Once I felt more in control of my tongue, I continued. "Unless I know which book and which edition to look at, this cipher is useless to me."

"But we can look at the different factors in the email and the painting and see if we can come up with a few books that could be the key," Colin said.

"That sounds like a good idea." Phillip nodded at Colin and turned his gaze on me. "Why would someone target you?"

"I honestly don't know. I don't socialise, not in real life nor on the internet. When I'm not here, I'm at home reading or working."

"What about your past?" Manny asked. "Have you worked other places, had contact with other people you could've pissed off?"

I thought about this. Whenever I found myself in a social

setting, I made a point of not speaking to anyone. And when I did, I endeavoured to apply my years of observation and training. Personally, I thought I had been quite successful, even if I could only manage for two hours at the most to uphold my level of sociability. I shook my head.

"What about the universities?" Phillip asked.

"What about it?" I asked. Manny scowled and I knew I was going to have to explain. "Sometimes I'm asked to guest lecture at a few of the universities in the area."

"And last year you wrote that paper that caused such a controversy."

"It didn't cause a controversy," I said.

"Tell me about the paper, Doc." Manny leaned forward in his chair.

"Every year I write a few academic papers. It is purely of my own interest and is not done to be published or to cause controversy. About eight months ago one of my articles was published. It was regarding the successful treatment of non-neurotypical patients. In it I made a negative remark about narrative therapy. As it happens, a professor had published a paper a few months prior that supported narrative therapy. It was in complete contradiction of my paper, but I never once referred to it. As a matter of fact, I haven't even read it. This man took it as a personal attack on his paper and went to the dean."

"The controversy?" Manny prompted.

"Phillip exaggerates. There wasn't a controversy. The professor was just indignant and I was called into a mediation meeting. Everything was settled." I groaned when Phillip loudly cleared his throat. "Okay, it wasn't a good meeting. I stayed quiet for a long time while this professor insulted my paper. I had heard that he had been going through a difficult time and I thought that explained his behaviour. But then he said that my grammar was flawed."

"And that set you off?" There was laughter in Manny's voice.

"Set me off? It made me furious. I am proficient in four languages and know for a fact that my French grammar is flawless." It had been such an inane argument and I still cringed to think how angry I had been. "After a few angry things were said, the dean stepped in and we made peace. See, it was nothing."

"Grammar." Manny slumped in his chair. "I can't see how that could be motive for bomb-making. What a strange life you live, Doc."

"Your strange is my normal." I shrugged. "A few other academics have been unhappy with my commentary on their papers, but I truly cannot see any of them building bombs."

"Just send me a list of those names so we can check them out and make sure, Doc."

"You'll be wasting your time." There was no way these unimaginative academics would resort to anything this violent. I had, however, learned to never say never. "Fine, I'll send it to you. But I'm not going to waste any more time on that. I would rather speak to Francine about the software link between the security companies and also look into this cipher."

Chapter ELEVEN

I sank down in my sofa and took a sip of coffee. It had been another night of restless sleep. My mind had refused to switch off. Not being able to speak to Francine last night only added to the frustration. By the time I had come home, she had settled in for the night and I couldn't get myself to insist on speaking to her. She needed to heal. I needed her well so she could help me.

"What are you doing up?" Colin looked sleepy as he walked towards me. He was favouring his right leg again. I assumed that sleeping caused the leg to stiffen up some. Surely he knew that he should do stretching exercises. I pushed aside my thoughts. Most times people didn't appreciate unsolicited advice.

He was wearing blue and white striped pyjama bottoms and a white vest and his hair was mussed. He stopped at the sofa and gave an uninhibited stretch combined with a jaw-cracking yawn. I envied his lack of decorum. I would be too aware of the people around me to act with such familiarity. He lowered his arms with a satisfied sound and looked at the time on the antique clock behind me. "It's not even five yet."

"I've been up for an hour already."

"Couldn't sleep?" He sat down on the sofa next to me and looked longingly at my coffee.

"Go make your own coffee, Colin." I pulled the mug closer to my chest. "I don't share."

"Not even a sip?" He gave me his charming smile. The one I hated. "Please, Jenny."

"No."

He smiled. A real smile. "You're too easy to rile."

"Then don't rile me." I sighed. "Why do you do it?"

"That is how people sometimes connect with each other.

Not everything has to always be serious. Not every sentence has to have great significance."

"I know that." I had the degrees in psychology to prove it. "I just never see the sense in teasing and bantering."

"The sense is that it helps people relax. It is fun and it is funny. It might be something you could consider."

"Why? I don't need to be funny."

"It's not about need, Jenny. It's about want. Sometimes we do things that are a complete waste of time, but it gives us pleasure."

"Like you and Vinnie playing games on my television? Although, studies have shown computer games boost auditory perception, improve hand-eye coordination and enhance split-second decision-making."

"And yet we do it only for fun."

"Why?"

Colin gave it some thought. "Don't you sometimes just want to escape from this reality? Even if it is only for a few moments. To go someplace where there are none of these pressures, problems and responsibilities."

"I have a place like that."

"Your head," he said. "What about a world that someone else created?"

"Hmm, no. When I read a truly good book, I still find so many inaccuracies in it that it is not relaxing. But I do remember reading an article about the need women have for romance novels. They stated some of your reasons to explain the high demand for such reading material."

"Wait. You never want to just get out of your own head?"

"No. Like I said, if I need a break from this reality, I go into my own head. It's a safe place."

"With Mozart."

"Yes." The front door opening stopped our conversation. Colin jumped off the chair and grabbed a bronze sculpture I had bought in Hungary. As the door opened wider, he lifted the sculpture and I mourned the damage to such a valuable piece. A long leg, dressed in denim and with a very unburglar-like pink knitted house boot, came into view first. Another step and Francine appeared. Colin lowered the sculpture and I relaxed.

Francine first looked at me and then frowned at Colin when she noticed the sculpture. "You were going to hit me with that? Do you not know the value of it?"

"Of course I know how valuable it is." He carefully put it back on the side table. It was a modern piece, the value not known by most people unless they had an abnormal, or illegal, interest in art. He adjusted it to be almost in the exact same place as before. "I just think that our lives are more valuable."

"Word." She closed the front door and joined us in the living area. The swelling of her eye had gone down with only a small bump still visible around the cut. Even that looked much better than before. The bruising though looked terrible. It was at its worst colouring with the haemoglobin in the blood around her eye changed, resulting in an angry dark blue-purple. She still moved carefully and would for a few weeks. Ribs took a long time to heal.

"What are you doing here, Francine?" Colin asked. He sat down next to me and Francine settled in the other sofa. Colin had easily accepted Francine's entrance and she was being nonchalant, as if she entered my flat uninvited every day. Did I have no privacy from these people?

"I saw the lights were on and thought I'd come tell Genevieve what I discovered."

"Wait," I said. "How did you see the lights were on?"

"If I'm on my room's balcony and twist just a little so, I can see these windows." She waved at the large windows in front of me. That meant that I would also be able to see Colin's apartment. I sighed.

"Could I have some coffee, please?" She looked at Colin. "Vinnie won't allow me to use the coffee machine in your place. He calls me a danger to any kitchen."

Colin got up. "It's because you are dangerous in a kitchen. I was in need of coffee too. Jenny, can I top you up?"

"Pardon?"

"Would you like more coffee?" His smile reminded me of our earlier conversation.

"Oh." I looked at the mug in my hands. It was almost empty. I held it out to Colin. "Yes, please."

Colin went to the kitchen and got busy there. I turned to Francine. A moment before I asked her about her discoveries, I considered my words. My conversation with Colin reminded me of my lack of social skills. My lack of friendship skills. What was the right thing to say? "How are you feeling?"

"How am I feeling?" Francine looked surprised. "Better, thanks. Yesterday was not a good day. I don't think I've ever been to bed before midnight, but yesterday I went to sleep at seven o'clock. I woke up around three this morning feeling reborn. That was when I got to working again. Yesterday I couldn't concentrate worth shit, which was why I just gave up and went to sleep."

"What did you discover?" It was hard to keep the impatience out of my voice. Small talk was so difficult. Francine's smile told me that she recognised my effort for what it was.

"The stupid idiot hacker went back to his usual haunts. He tried to mask his presence, but I got him."

"That's fantastic." I said and got up to fetch my phone. "We should tell Manny."

"I don't know where he is."

"But you said you got him." I sat back down. Colin joined us with three mugs on a tray. Next to the mugs was a plate with cookies. Vinnie's oat cookies. There was indeed some benefit to having them all back in my life and my apartment. I took my coffee and two cookies.

Francine closed her eyes and sighed. Admitting failure was difficult for most people. "He logged on only for a short while. It wasn't enough time to find him past the tunnelling and zombie computers he is using to hide his IP. But I'm watching him. He's the type of guy who won't be able to stay away from those sites. He's already proved it and I know he'll be back. I'll get him."

"Will he know that you're watching, waiting for him?" I asked. "The last time you hacked this guy, you got beaten up."

"He won't know a thing." She took a sip of her coffee. "This morning when I was poking around the stuff I had copied from his system and I saw few interesting things. I looked at his internet history."

"The sites he visited?" I asked.

"Yes. And your name came up a few times. This guy has been reading all about you on the internet."

"There's nothing about me on the internet."

"Au contraire, mon amie. There is a lot about you on the net. Every time you publish an article it goes online. All those articles are on numerous sites. Your lectures have also been blogged about, discussed on student forums and recorded by the universities."

How could I not know this? I considered myself internet-proficient. "Is there any personal information about me?"

"Not that I could find. The hacker definitely didn't find any personal information about you on the internet. He mostly just read your articles."

"Maybe he is a student," I said.

"That is not a bad assumption," Colin said. "We should get the lists of students who attended your lectures."

"Already done," Francine said. "The universities' sites were too easy to get into. I checked all Genevieve's guest lectures and got the lists of the students who had signed up for them."

"Those lists might not be accurate," I said. "Sometimes the students who signed up don't come, and others come from different faculties. There are always other professors who also attend my lectures. Usually there are not enough seats, so people sit on the floor or stand at the back."

"The lists might just give us a starting point," Francine said. She pressed her fist against her lips. People did this when they were trying to hold back something. She removed her hand, her forehead wrinkled in confusion. "Your lectures are really that popular?"

"Yes. I am considered the top in my field. Attending one of my lectures is quite a privilege."

"And I suppose the fact that you only give a few lectures a year makes it even more desired."

"I suppose it would," I said. "What else was he researching on the internet?"

"Well, he spent an unhealthy amount of time looking at porn."

"Definitely a student," Colin said. I decided not to contradict him with statistics.

"Definitely a man," Francine said. "He also looked at the weather a lot. Strange man. He visited a few websites about the president and his wife. I think it is mostly related to the elections and politics. Then he visited a few sites more relevant to this case. There were also sites about burglary and cat burglary. And a few museums and galleries, but he didn't spend a lot of time there. He didn't hack my great-uncle's security company's system again, but he did hack a few others."

"How many?" I asked.

"Four that I saw. The most recent one he hacked has over three hundred thousand clients in France. But he was looking at a specific client's file. He was looking at it for a long time."

"Do you think that will be the next target?"

"I'm pretty sure of it. I was watching him work his way through this client's file. I saw everything he was looking at. He was going through the list of the valuables in the client's house and where they were held. He copied all the security info onto his computer."

"What security information does he have?" I asked.

"Codes, passwords, where the keys are kept, everything."

"We should tell Manny." I sighed when I noticed the corners of Colin's mouth pulled down, his lips thinned. "I'm not going to argue about this. Manny needs to know."

"You're right," Francine said. "I think it's best if you deal with him though."

"Me?" I pointed at my chest.

"Can't you get this intel to him without involving yourself or Jenny?" Colin asked.

Francine's eyes widened and a gleeful smile pulled at her lips. "Oh yes, I can do that. I can do that and so much more."

My question about this died in my mouth when my front door opened again.

"It's me. Don't shoot." Vinnie walked into my apartment with one hand raised. His other hand was holding a paper shopping bag to his chest. "I come bearing gifts."

He closed the door and turned to us with a smile. Francine smiled back at him and Colin nodded at him in greeting. Something snapped in me. I put my coffee mug on the side table with a bit too much force. "You can't just come and go in my apartment as you please. What is the use of those locks if you people just dismiss the importance of it? I know that a lock is no challenge for any of you, but does it not symbolise my need for privacy? Have you no respect for that? No respect for me?"

"Aw, Jen-girl…" Vinnie walked closer with worry and guilt on his face, but stopped when I got up and shook my head.

"No, don't 'aw' me. I'm just beginning to accept your reappearance in my life and now you want me to accept your disrespect?" My hands started shaking from the emotional overload. "Forget it. I'm going to have a shower and get ready for the day. In the privacy of my room. I'm going to lock the doors and would like you to respect that."

As fast as I could, I walked to my bedroom. A moment before I slammed my bedroom door, Vinnie called out to me. "Breakfast will be ready in twenty minutes."

The slam of the door cut off his last word, but I had heard the apology in his tone. I locked two of the locks to my reinforced bedroom door and walked to the bathroom. There I also locked the door and sat down on the toilet lid. Upon consideration I had to admit that I was overreacting. What was causing this emotional reaction?

I analysed my emotions and my reactions with detached

professionalism and cringed at the truths I had to face. I was lashing out in fear that these people, my friends, were going to worm their way into my life again just to leave.

Refreshed after my shower and dressed for work, I walked into the wonderful smell of Vinnie's breakfast. It triggered the memories of when he had stayed with me and the emotional warmth I experienced confirmed yet again that I was glad to have him back. Back in my apartment and in my privacy. They were all seated at the table and obviously waiting for me. Vinnie and Francine seated on one side and Colin across from them in his usual seat.

"Good timing, Jen-girl. I have your toast the way you like it." He pointed at the chair that had become mine over the long-gone weeks of sharing meals with them. I sat down next to Colin and folded my hands on my lap. This was not as easy as I would've liked it to be. I pulled my shoulders back and looked at them.

"I'm sorry about my outburst earlier. I know that you respect me. You've only ever shown me kindness. I'm just not always good with knowing how to return it. I'm usually much more rational in my behaviour." I struggled to keep my head up, facing them. "At the moment I'm... just... I don't know how to deal with all these emotions I'm experiencing. I truly like it when you are here."

Colin put his hand gently on my clenched hands. I looked at him. His eyes and mouth showed all the nonverbal cues exhibited when talking to a loved one. I felt confused. Again. His hand squeezed mine. "We know, Jenny. You are an extraordinary person and we sometimes forget that."

"I don't," Vinnie said. He groaned when Colin gave him a dirty look. "Okay, sometimes I forget. I'm sorry that I walked in without knocking. I should've known you wouldn't like it."

I looked down at Colin's hand on mine. He was rubbing slow circles on the back of my left hand with his thumb. It was oddly calming. I took a deep breath before I looked up at

Vinnie. "I mind and I don't. When you stayed here six months ago, it was normal for you to come and go as if this was your home. I just got used to living alone again. And I don't know how I feel about all of you having a key to my apartment."

"That was not the right thing for us to do," Colin said. "I was the one who insisted on it when we came here. I wanted to make sure you were safe."

"I know. This is the reason you've given for all your unacceptable behaviour. Making me feel weak and unable to protect myself is not helping me accept this new situation any better." I looked around the table. "I'm talking about all of you. In your different ways you act as if I'm not able to look after myself. Yet I've been doing exactly that since I was sixteen. From the age of eighteen I was completely responsible for myself. All my studies were paid for with scholarships. I did not accept money from my parents. I earned extra money by doing research and sometimes that even earned me extra credit. I've travelled to every continent on this planet and I did that alone. I'm not helpless."

What I didn't tell them was the constant panic that had accompanied me with every single decision I had made. Sometimes I had spent weeks not sleeping, mentally writing Mozart before I travelled to a country for a measly five-day visit.

"I have always been determined to not allow being non-neurotypical to be a prison from which I could never leave. With your actions you are putting me in that prison. There. I've said everything I wanted to."

It was quiet around the table. Nobody was eating, they weren't even moving. The food and coffee was getting cold.

"I'm sorry, Jenny." Colin's hand tightened around mine. I nodded stiffly. "Tell us what we can do to make this better."

Vinnie nodded emphatically. "Yes, Jen-girl. I don't want to make you unhappy. How do we fix this?"

"I don't know." My tone was defensive. Never before was I

asked to explain to people how they should behave towards me. "Just… just don't treat me as less than I am."

"Oh, honey," Francine laughed. "That is impossible. You are far too much for any of us to comprehend. How about we treat you like one of us?"

I didn't think that was a good idea. They were often involved in criminal activities, which most definitely didn't make me like one of them. I thought about it some more. Francine might be implying that they treated me with the same familiarity they were showing each other. Familiarity they had been showing me, but I had perceived it as intrusive and disrespectful. Everyone was waiting for my response. "Maybe we should try this only on a trial basis. I don't know if I would understand you as well if you spoke to me the way you speak to each other."

"Don't you worry none about that, Jen-girl. I'll still use my boring vocab with you." Vinnie's shoulders lost their tension and he picked up his utensils to start eating. I must have said the right thing, because everyone seemed more relaxed. Colin gave my fists one last squeeze before he took his hand away. I was relieved. Physical affection was unknown territory for me. Even though his touch had been light, I had felt increasingly uncomfortable. The reason for that discomfort was not entirely clear.

For a few minutes I ate and listened to their light conversation. They were posing the most improbable theories imaginable about the hacker, his boss, government conspiracies and Francine even talked about aliens. My eyebrows shot up when I realised she wasn't talking about illegal immigrants.

"Phillip asked if you could secure the system at Rousseau & Rousseau. He's concerned about the safety of our clients." My sudden interruption to their speculation about life on other planets brought interesting expressions to Francine's face. "Why are you feeling guilty? What have you done?"

"Um, I… uh…" She threw her hands in the air. "That

happened before we had this talk, okay? I've already secured the system."

"You did that remotely?" I asked.

"Yes. I've also sent everyone requests to update their passwords and will give you the override password. Or should I give it to Phillip?"

"Phillip. But why did you do this? Did Phillip ask you?"

"No." She looked as if she was in pain and I was sure it wasn't physical. "I did this to protect you. Genevieve, I'm sorry. You're my friend and you are so... so superwoman. You always know what people are thinking and you are a very controlled and contained individual. You are everything Sister Agnes wanted me to be. I just wanted to do something for you, something that I'm really good at."

"Oh." I sat back in my chair, my mind racing. The new conclusions I came to worried me. "Does that mean that I'm being selfish by asking you to only tend to my needs by not protecting me? Is this something that you want to do? Is this what friends do?"

On my last question I turned to Colin. His genuine smile crinkled the corners of his eyes. "Yes, Jenny. Friends look out for each other."

"Oh. Okay." I thought about this some more. "I find this confusing. How do you keep a balance between being supportive of your friends and becoming an intrusive entity in their lives? Do you know how to do this?"

"We try," Colin said. "This is what life is about. We try and if we make mistakes, we apologise and try again. There is no either-or. Finding the balance you are talking about is fluid. It changes all the time and that is why we should keep an open mind and forgive our friends when they make mistakes. Most of the time the intentions are good, but the action may be not so good."

Any type of relationship was a mystery to me. It would appear that I had a lot to learn. I would have to research this and purchase more books.

I looked at Francine. "Who's Sister Agnes?"

Francine froze. She had clearly spoken without thinking. After a few moments she smiled, her attempt resulting in a textbook social smile. An insincere, non-genuine smile.

"Sister Agnes is the woman who guided me to the life I live now." With that, she stood up from the table. "If you'll excuse me, I have a hacker to track down."

Chapter TWELVE

I stared at the monitors in front of me. I had been staring at these monitors for the last thirty-four minutes. To no avail. Logically I knew that looking at all ten screens filled with information was not going to give me any additional data. I leaned back in my chair and allowed my mind to wander.

Yesterday had been just as unproductive as the two hours I had been working in my viewing room this morning. And it hadn't been only me. Francine was growing more frustrated with the hacker by the minute. Breakfast had ended abruptly after Francine's exit. Neither of the men had known anything about this Sister Agnes. I had thought it prudent to not pursue this. If Francine wanted to talk about her past, she could tell Vinnie. He was good at listening.

The door to my viewing room whooshed open. Phillip walked in, pulled a chair closer and sat down. "Good morning, Genevieve."

"Good morning, Phillip." I swivelled my chair to face him.

"How are you?"

"I'm fine, how are you?"

"Fine." He wasn't fine. There was too much tension in his voice. That same tension was visible all over his body and face.

"Why are we being so overly polite? Are you angry with me? Did I do or say something wrong again?"

"I just had a long conversation with Manny." He pinched the bridge of his nose. "Genevieve, why don't you answer your phone?"

"What phone? Oh, my smartphone. I didn't hear it ring."

"Where is it?"

"In my handbag, in its usual place." I got up to retrieve my handbag from the antique-looking filing cabinets and took my smartphone from an inside pocket. After replacing my bag and closing the drawer, I walked back to my chair and lifted the device in front of me. "See, here it is."

Phillip looked from me to the filing cabinet and back. He pinched the bridge of his nose again. "How many missed calls do you have?"

I sat down, checked and frowned. "Seventeen."

"Could you please explain to me why you don't have your phone close enough to hear it ring?"

"Why would I? You are the only person who might want to speak to me during the day and you are right here. I have no reason to have the phone next to me if I know no one is going to phone me. There is no one who wants to."

Phillip stared at me for a long time. Long enough for me to reconsider my answer. I closed my eyes for a second.

"Colin, Vinnie, Francine."

"And Manny," Phillip added. "He was furious that you were not picking up your phone. Promise me that you will keep your phone close at all times."

"That is a ludicrous request. I will not sleep with it next to me or shower with it in the bathroom." I slowed down when I saw Phillip's expression. The corners of his mouth were pulling down. I lowered my tone. "That is not what you meant."

"No, that is not what I meant. Let me be more specific. Would you please, for the love of all the saints and my sanity, keep your phone with you while you are working?"

"That is most of the day." I pushed back into my chair when Phillip stared at me. He was displeased. "Okay. I will promise to try my best to remember to have my phone nearby."

"Okay, now let's get down to business." He took out his smartphone and tapped on the screen.

"Yes?" Manny's tinny voice answered.

"I have Genevieve here with me on speakerphone."

"At bloody last. Missy, are you going to have your phone with you from now on?"

"I'll try," I said.

"Good enough," Manny said. "Now let me tell you what I happened in the last eight hours. Today has been quite a scoop for us. We caught us a thief."

"Am I to assume that this thief is connected to the other burglary cases?" I received a grunt as an affirmative reply. "How did you catch him? Is it a him?"

"Yes, it is a man. A young man. We caught him because someone gave a tip."

My mind immediately went to Francine. "Was the tipster male or female?"

"We don't know." Suspicion tightened Manny's tone. "I was thinking that it might be your little friend who emailed me from my own email address."

"If you are hinting at Francine in such an unsophisticated manner, I think you are right. She mentioned yesterday morning that she had knowledge of where the next burglary was to take place."

It was silent on the other side of the line for a few seconds. "And could you please tell me why you did not inform me about this?"

"I asked her to inform you and she agreed. She obviously informed you, so you have no reason to take that tone with me."

"Genevieve." Phillip gave me a warning look before leaning towards the phone. "Tell us about the burglar, Manny."

"I emailed you the video footage of his interrogation." He grunted. "His interview. That is what the PC people call it nowadays. Anyway, he is not a very bright young man. We had him in the interview room for less than ten minutes before he spilled all the beans."

I remembered the metaphor from primary school. It had never made any sense to me. "Did he tell you who the hacker is?"

"No, he didn't."

"Well, then he didn't spill all the beans, now did he?"

Phillip frowned at me again, but Manny's chuckle placated him.

"I'm pulling into your street now, so I'll be with you in a few minutes. Set up that video, Doc. I think you'll find a few interesting things there to see." Without another word, he disconnected the call.

Phillip placed his phone on my desk, but immediately picked it up again and put it in the inside pocket of his jacket. After six and a half years of working with me, he knew that I could not tolerate clutter on my desk. His smartphone would qualify as clutter. My smartphone was still lying on my lap and I didn't know what to do with it. If I were to have it within reach at all times, I was going to have to find a logical place for it. I exhaled in annoyance and then put it on the stand of the computer monitor in front of me.

Tuning back in to work, I turned to face the bank of monitors against the wall and opened my inbox. I had three new emails. Two were from Manny. I only opened the one with the attachments. Deduction told me that the other email with 'Answer your bloody phone' in the subject line was not going to be of any use. The files were large and were going to take a few minutes to download.

"Francine has been busy," Phillip said.

"Are you satisfied with her work?" She had spent a few hours yesterday afternoon in Rousseau & Rousseau explaining the new computer security to Phillip.

"She's a competent young woman," he answered. Despite my misgivings he had actually been relieved that Francine had taken the initiative to secure the company's entire system.

The quiet whoosh of my viewing room door drew both Phillip's and my attention. Angelique stood outside the room. "Mister Millard is here, sir."

"Show him in, Angelique."

She lifted her hand in a polite gesture to invite Manny in. I wasn't fooled by her apparent respectful behaviour. Angelique was uncomfortable around me and did not like Manny. He walked past her with his *buccinator* muscles pulling his mouth into a smirk. He also knew her opinion of him. The door closed quietly behind him.

"Doc. Phillip." Manny nodded at us as he pulled a chair closer. When I lifted an eyebrow at him, he grunted and moved the chair a bit away from me. "Is this fifty centimetres?"

"I would estimate that at about sixty centimetres." I tilted my head. "No, sixty-five. Yes, definitely sixty-five centimetres."

"Just play that bloody video, missy." He sat down heavily in the chair. "You can skip the first ten minutes. He only starts talking after that."

"But there might be much to learn from him in that first ten minutes," I said. "It would give me a baseline and a much more accurate read on him."

Phillip stopped whatever Manny was going to say with a chopping hand motion. "Let her do what she does best, Manny."

I ignored the sighs and grunts, and turned to the monitors in front of me. The videos had finished downloading. There were three videos from three cameras of the interview. This was even better than I had hoped for. With so many angles to watch nonverbal cues from, I would get a much better read.

I chose the video titled, 'suspect face'. Filling the screens was a room about half the size of my viewing room. Unlike my workspace, this room had bare walls, painted a cream colour. The floor was covered in what looked like blue industrial carpeting. A generic steel table stood in the centre of the room with two chairs on each side of the table.

A young man in his early twenties sat on the one side, two men dressed in suits on the other. It was easy to see who was the suspect and who were the law enforcement agents. The young man was hiding his hands under the table on his lap, slouching in his chair, trying to look nonchalant. The camera was behind the two men, aimed at the suspect's face. I had chosen the right video to watch first. I leaned a bit closer to observe.

"Where's the sound?" Manny's question broke into my concentration.

I waved him away. "If he's not saying anything important right now, I will do better just observing him."

The young man shifted in his chair, aiming his whole body at the door. He wanted to leave. I couldn't see his hands, which was a pity. We revealed a significant amount with our hands and feet. Body language had to be interpreted as a whole. Taken into context with the hands, arms, legs and feet, a frown could often mean something completely different than if it were read in isolation.

The suited men interrogating him were becoming increasingly aggressive. They were leaning forward, their chests puffed and their elbows away from their bodies. The thief had the opposite body language. His elbows were tucked in close to his sides, the insides of his arms visible. Submissive behaviour. His shoulders were hunched, ready to protect his vulnerable spots from attack. I paused the video.

"Is this his first offence?" I asked, turning to Manny.

"Yes. The kid is a total amateur. And a student."

I was pleased that Manny had confirmed my suspicion about the young man.

"Who are the men in suits?" Phillip asked.

"Police detectives. This is their case, their jurisdiction and their interview. We are just here as assistance."

My eyebrows lifted. "And there are no territorial arguments or ambitious egos impeding the investigation?"

"Some of us have evolved from the Ice Age, missy. These two detectives were pleased to have the strength of Interpol aiding them in their investigation."

"Oh. That's good then." I had said something to upset Manny. Again. The video was much more appealing than trying to work on my social skills, so I turned back to the monitors and clicked on the play button. This time I turned up the sound.

"... you don't tell us everything, your grandmother is going to be alone in her flat. Who is going to make sure she takes her medicine then?"

The young man's shoulders raised to his ears as if in an attempt to hide his head. A sign of weakness and insecurity. He was scared. Still he didn't speak. The two detectives looked at each other in silent communication. That was something that fascinated me. Couples, friends and work partners who had spent years together had the ability to read paragraphs of silent communication by interpreting a single facial expression. They didn't have doctorate degrees in reading body language, only an understanding of the other person. An understanding that stemmed from experience, trust and openness so complete that they were able to predict the other's words and actions.

The detective on the left leaned forward and rested his arms on the table. He appeared relaxed, but his eyes were trained on the young man. "If you tell us everything, and I mean everything, right now, we might be able to make this go away."

The young man's head lifted and his eyes widened briefly. "What do you mean?"

"I mean that if we get the right judge, he can enter a plea bargain with you that might mean no prison time. You might have to do some community service, but this way you can continue your studies and still look after your grandmother."

"Can I have that on paper before I tell you everything?" The student might have been a first-time offender, but he was not dumb. A lot of the tension in his body had left. "Signed and sealed is always better, my *grandmère* taught me. Especially since I don't know if I can trust you guys."

The other detective pointed at the three cameras. "This interview is being recorded as we told you in the beginning. Everything we say here, any promise we make here you can lay claim to."

"Unless someone steals the videos or destroys it." The young man shook his head. "No, I want it on paper. I've watched enough movies about this sort of thing."

The second detective dropped his head back in frustration, but the other one knocked with both fists lightly on the table. "Let's see what we can do for you."

There was a few seconds of quiet when the detectives left and the video was switched off. When it resumed, there were sheets of paper in the centre of the table.

"Now tell us what you know." The one detective had removed

his suit jacket and was leaning back in his chair. He had a notepad and pen ready to take notes.

The young man breathed heavily a few times, his mouth twitching nervously. His hands disappeared under the table in a movement that looked like he was wiping his hands on his thighs. Self-comforting behaviour.

"Things are not always easy, you know? My dad left when I was a baby and my mom died when I was ten. My *grandmère* took me in and never, not even once complained about having an angry kid in her house. She loved me, fed me and drew me out of my anger and into a dream to achieve something better for myself."

The detectives sat silently listening to the well-spoken young man.

"There was never much money. My *grandmère* baked *tartes aux fruits* and sold them to a few local cafés. People love her fruit tarts. When I turned fifteen, I took a job to start helping pay for things. When *grandmère* found out, she was furious. She wanted me to focus on my studies so I could get a scholarship. Her dream for me was to have a university degree and have a good profession. I stopped working and she baked more. I studied more than most of the kids in my class and got a scholarship."

He rubbed his hands over his eyes. I would watch this again and then I would determine if those were tears I had seen. "Last year *grandmère* was diagnosed with cancer. She had to go for intense treatments and couldn't bake anymore. I've taken on two jobs, but it doesn't cover our bills and her medicine."

"And someone offered you a way out," the one detective said. There was sympathy in his voice and body language.

"Yes. This guy phoned me out of the blue. An arrogant arsehole." He glanced at the detectives. "Sorry. But he was extremely arrogant. He said that he was better than any security system and that he could get me a gig that would give me enough money to pay for two years' tuition and *grandmère's* meds. I knew it was stupid. I knew it was a mistake, but I was just so desperate, you know?"

"Son, we see this every day," the nice detective said. "These guys choose their targets very carefully. They look for people who are in desperate need. I wish I didn't see this as often as I do."

The young man looked relieved. Validation, one of our strongest human needs, had given this student more courage to finish his tale. "He phoned me a week ago. I don't know how he got my number, but he phoned me and told me that he had an offer for me that would end all our problems. At first I said no. I didn't even wait for him to finish his pitch. When he phoned me the next day I had thought about this enough to be curious. He told me that it would be a victimless crime. That all I had to do was walk into a house, take some things and leave a flower."

A rush of adrenaline flooded my system. In the last two sentences this desperate young man had given information that confirmed our theories. Following up on what he was saying could lead us to the hacker.

"He said I would be paid twenty thousand euros for accepting the job. Once I got what he wanted me to get, I could take whatever else I wanted from the house. He even offered to put me in contact with people who could fence the stolen stuff." He closed his eyes and hung his head. "I agreed to do this. Twenty thousand euros upfront was going to go a long way to help *grandmère*. And the possibility of much more? I couldn't give up that chance."

"What did he want you to take?"

The young man patted his jacket pocket. "The list was in my pocket. When those police guys processed me, they took everything from my pockets."

The nice detective glanced at the other one who nodded, got up and left the room.

"He gave me the security codes to the gate, the house and the safe. I mean, this guy knew exactly where everything was.

It was like he was the owner of the house and he wanted to rob himself." He straightened in his chair. "Hey, do you think that is what happened? That this is some insurance scam?"

"We're working on a few different theories," the detective said. "Do you give us permission to trace your phone calls?"

"Of course." The young man nodded at the papers on the table. "I said I'll give my full cooperation. Anything you need to catch this guy."

We watched a few more minutes of the interview, but nothing of more interest was said. I stopped the video and turned to Manny. "What was he supposed to steal?"

"Two paintings, small and valuable, and a 1933 Gold Double Eagle coin."

"Oh my." Phillip adjusted his tie. A cue of distress. "That coin was designed by Augustus Saint-Gaudens. Almost half a million gold coins were minted with the 1933 date, but none were ever released into circulation. The depression had hit the US and the government had made it illegal to own these coins. They were melted down into bullion bars. A few coins did make it out into the world. In 2002 one of these coins were sold for just over seven and a half million dollars."

Manny whistled. "For a coin?"

"For a rare coin," Phillip corrected. "Oh my, oh my. You don't know what you have stumbled upon here, Manny. There is only one of these coins authorised by the US government for private ownership. Only one. If this house owner is not the 2002 buyer, then he is in possession of an illegal coin."

"Which I suppose makes it even more valuable on the black market."

"Most definitely. Where was the coin kept?" Phillip asked.

"It was on display in the library." Manny rolled his eyes. "This house actually has a library. There must be at least ten thousand books up and down the walls. Anyway, the coin was in a glass display box, protected by a motion and heat sensor that could only be disabled with a remote control which was locked up in a safe. The safe had a code and so did the remote control. There were all kinds of other laser beams and things to keep anyone from ever taking this coin. This young man was given all the codes to disable the security and obtain the coin."

"Francine isn't convinced that the hacker is very smart," I said. "There are discrepancies in his skill set which makes her think that he had help getting into the security companies' computers. His everyday skills are far inferior to hers."

"What are you saying, Doc?"

"Isn't it clear? The hacker is working for someone. A person with extensive knowledge of art. How else would they target the most valuable pieces in every home?"

"The security companies must have that information on file."

"Has anyone contacted the security companies yet? Had a look at their computers?" I asked.

"It's in the works at the moment, but it will take some time to get all the legalities done."

"What did you find from the telephone records?"

"Still working on it." Frustration crept into Manny's voice. "I wish things happened as fast as on telly shows, but we have a lot of legal stuff to sort out before we can dig into people's records. It all takes a lot of time."

"How long?"

Manny glanced at his watch. "They started working on this about two hours ago. Hopefully we'll have something by lunchtime."

I closed my eyes and allowed Mozart to take over for a few minutes. When I opened my eyes Manny and Phillip were discussing the coin. Manny was truly disgusted with the value of such a small round piece of gold.

"Is the hacker the bomber?" I asked. Both men turned to me. "Are the hacker and bomber two different people connected by something? What is the connection between the hacker and the bomber?" I took a deep breath. "Is there a connection between them and me?"

A series of micro-expressions flying across Manny's face warned me. "Doc, there is something I haven't told you yet."

My stomach felt hollow and I could feel my heart beat in my throat. I waited. The worry and regret on his face told me that it was not going to be glad tidings.

"The flower that was found at each crime scene was identified." He nodded at the monitors. "The young gentleman also had the flower on him when he was arrested."

"For the love of Pete, Manny, just tell us." Phillip was leaning forward in his chair, concern pulling his eyebrows together.

"It was a daffodil. At each scene. A red daffodil."

Chapter THIRTEEN

I faced my front door and stood there unmoving. I wondered if it was even worth unlocking the door. Had Vinnie, Colin and Francine locked all five locks? If I walked into my apartment now, who was going to be inside? Had my apartment become an open house to every one?

Allowing these questions to float through my mind was far easier than dealing with the news Manny had given me six hours before. It had been with immense effort that I had stayed in control and hadn't succumbed to the overwhelming need to escape into the black void that always welcomed me. Even now, the lure of Mozart pulled at me.

The door opened. Colin rested his hand on the door handle and looked at me. Concern pulled at his eyes and mouth. "You've been standing there for fifteen minutes, Jenny. It's time to come in."

I shook my head. Out here I could avoid dealing with Manny's news for a little while longer.

"I'll draw a bath for you. You can relax there for an hour or so. Then we'll have dinner, okay?"

His kindness and understanding were hammering away at the tight control I had on my emotions. My eyes started burning and I shook my head again.

"I'll turn on Mozart and you can listen to this while you're lying in the tub. I'll also pour you a glass of a fantastically good Merlot that I bought today." He took a step closer to me, watching me like I usually watched people when I was reading them. Some of the tension around his eyes left when I didn't move away from him. One more step and he was standing inside my personal space.

I didn't know if Manny or Phillip had phoned him. Somehow I doubted that. If he had known about the daffodils, he might have been more aggressive in his concern right now. He touched my shoulder so lightly that I barely felt the contact through my coat. Very gently his hand smoothed down my coat sleeve to my wrist. His hand felt warm and comforting when he closed it over my icy fingers.

"Let me take that for you." One by one, he peeled my fingers away from the computer bag I had forgotten I was clutching to my chest. He gently pried open my grip and took the bag. He slung it over his shoulder and held both my hands in his. "It's really bad, isn't it?"

I nodded.

"Okay then. Let's get you inside." He had to pull twice before my legs unlocked themselves and I was able to move. I followed him into my apartment and instantly felt some of the tightness in my muscles ease. When he locked all five locks, I relaxed even more. It annoyed me that three people had keys to my apartment, but I didn't mind these specific three people in my apartment. I didn't want other uninvited guests.

After the daffodil news, I craved the security of locked doors. Reality dictated that my apartment was far from impenetrable and the past few days had proven the same truth for access to my computer and smartphone. My muscles tensed up again as my thoughts entered this direction. I clamped down on it. Being this shaken was not a state I wanted to be in.

Colin pulled me into my bedroom. He had only been living in my apartment for two days, but even when he had stayed here before, he seldom entered my sanctuary. It felt strange to have him in a space that I felt protective of. It also made me feel safe. This realisation shocked me out of my silence.

"I'll take it from here, thank you." I took my handbag off my shoulder and stood with it in my hand. It had to be in its usual place, but I didn't feel like walking back to put it on the dining room chair.

Colin held out his hand for my bag. "I'll put it on the chair for you. And I'll set up your computer on the table."

I looked at his hand and blinked a few times before I handed my handbag to him. "I won't be long."

"Take your time, Jenny. I'll get dinner going and we can talk then. It's going to be at least an hour before everything is ready, so don't come out before then, okay?"

I lifted one eyebrow, immediately suspicious. "Why do you want me out of sight for an hour?"

He smiled. "There really is no hiding anything from you. Good lord. I just didn't want you to worry about Vinnie cooking in the kitchen."

"Why would I worry?" I took off my coat and handed it to Colin who took it without any change of expression. "I know that Vinnie will clean the kitchen when he's done."

"And it won't bother you that he is here? Francine will most likely also be here."

I thought about this for a moment. "It annoys me that my apartment no longer seems to be mine, but at this moment it makes me feel safe to have all of you here."

The relaxed smile on Colin's lips and around his eyes disappeared. In its place were all the muscle movements of worry. "Relax and come out when you're ready. We'll be here."

It did take me an hour to relax in the tub, consider my situation and make some important decisions. Life had taught me a long time ago that there was no such thing as status quo. Maintaining the same comfortable situation in one's life, whether it was emotional equilibrium or stability in one's career, relationships or something else, was indeed impossible. Life had always been a fluid river in my life, changing with every season and forcing me to move with it.

An overwhelming desire to fight anything challenging my routines was my first reaction every time. But it was a futile fight. I didn't know if it was more difficult and painful for me than for others, but every change felt like torture. Embracing it took some sting out of that torture, it helped me develop, helped me grow stronger. And that was what I was hoping to do. Accept yet another personal and career change in my life.

I stopped for a moment when I realised that I was rubbing body lotion almost aggressively into my legs. A calming breath later, I finished moisturising my skin more gently and hoped that I could convince myself that change was good.

When I opened my bedroom door, the smells and sounds greeting me settled something in my chest. Vinnie and Francine were in the kitchen arguing about spices. Colin was watching television. It was an unorthodox scene of domesticity. Something I never thought I would have in my life.

"Jen-girl." Vinnie held a spice shaker above his head. Francine was leaning against him trying to reach the shaker, but in obvious pain. "Tell this silly wench that you cannot put sweet basil in a sauce for a chicken dish. It is only used with vegetable dishes."

"Says you." Francine reached a bit higher, but collapsed against Vinnie with a groan. "My grandmother always put it with the chicken and it was delicious."

Vinnie pulled her against him in a gentle hug. Francine was as beautiful as a model and also as tall. Vinnie was still almost a head taller than her and he looked down at her. "That sacrilege will not take place in my kitchen."

"This is my kitchen," I said as I walked to the fridge and took out the blackcurrant juice. I took a spotless glass from the cupboard and poured half a glass. I leaned against the counter and watched Vinnie stir something in a pot while still holding Francine.

"You need to sit down and not wrestle with me. You're still a far way from being well enough to take me on." He gave her a quick hug and pushed her away from him. "And there will be no sweet basil in my food tonight."

"He's so easy to annoy," she whispered to me as she walked to join Colin on the sofa.

"I heard you." Vinnie turned around to glare at Francine. Then he turned to me with a sweet smile. "How're ya doin', sexy?"

His crazy change of accent caught me unawares and I laughed. "I'm hungry."

"Aw, Jen-girl. You sure know how to sweet-talk a man. Get the others and sit down at the table. The food will be there in two minutes."

Thirty minutes later I wished I had more space in my stomach to have a third helping of Vinnie's winning chicken lasagne. I leaned back in my chair with a satisfied groan and lifted the wine glass to my mouth. "This is a good Merlot."

"As if I would ever buy a bad Merlot." Colin winked at me.

I wondered if I had ever felt so at home with other people in my personal space. For a short moment I basked in the feeling. I knew I was going to destroy this easy companionship with everything I had to tell them. "Did Manny or Phillip phone you today?"

"Who? Me?" Colin pointed at his chest. "Why the hell would Millard phone me?"

"Because of what was discovered today." There was a shift around the table. Everyone's body language communicated a change in mood. It made me angry that I was the one to cause this.

"What was discovered, Jenny?"

I told them about the thief who was caught. I tried to keep it as concise as possible and could hear the emotionless tone in my voice. Lack of inflection could usually be traced to an overload of emotions in people. In my case it was the tight grip I had on my emotions. "Then Manny got a phone call from the crime scene investigators."

"Did they get any fingerprints from the painting and wrapping?" Colin asked.

"I don't know. Manny didn't say. The phone call he received was about the flower." I was speaking faster, trying to get it out as quickly as possible. "They looked at the flowers that were left at the crime scene. Only at three of the crime scenes were the flowers taken in as evidence. The one that young thief had was the same. All four flowers were red daffodils."

Noise exploded around the table. There was no need to explain to them the importance of that flower. They remembered. Vinnie and Francine were talking at the same time, asking me questions and using a lot of expletives. Colin had lost some of the colour in his face, his lips pressed together until they were bloodless. He stopped rubbing his right thigh when he caught me looking at him.

"Jen-girl, are you okay?" Vinnie leaned over the table and almost touched me. I leaned a bit back.

"Now I'm fine. I wasn't all that fine when Manny told me."

A look passed between Colin and Vinnie. "Dude?"

Colin ignored Vinnie's question and looked at me. "Do you think Kubanov is behind all of this?"

"I don't know." I lifted my shoulders and shuddered. Six months ago this wealthy Russian philanthropist had been the mastermind behind an impressively well-organised art forgery ring. The little that we had been able to learn about him was ambiguous. Publicly he was renowned as an altruistic oligarch, giving back to his community in various forms, especially in art and education. But there had been a dark side that we had uncovered. His ruthless, cruel, underhanded dealings were a public secret. A secret that people never admitted knowing and never talked about to strangers. It could get you killed if anyone knew that you had any knowledge about Kubanov's less stellar activities. He was the kind of psychopath who hid in plain sight. A psychopath who had an affinity for red daffodils. He scared me.

"I'm open to accept all kinds of coincidences," Vinnie said. "Four daffodils at crime scenes is too much to call it a coincidence."

Francine emptied her glass of wine and held it out to Colin for a refill. "Why are you so quiet?"

Colin took his time pouring wine into her glass. When he

stopped halfway, she shook the glass lightly and he filled it almost to the brim. "I'm quiet because I'm thinking."

I knew he was lying. He was most likely thinking, but he was quiet because of another reason. That reason had something to do with the last four months, his injuries and the secrecy around the table I was not privy to. I looked at him, excluding everyone else from our contact. "You're going to have to tell me. Soon."

"Maybe." He didn't pretend to not know what I was talking about. "Let's go over what we presently know about Kubanov."

He started counting on his fingers. "Firstly, he has more money than God. He is highly intelligent and from what we learned the last time, he likes playing with people. He has no problem using people to get to his end goal. He used all those students to paint forgeries that were sold at top auction houses. Then he killed them. He has extensive knowledge of art, something that we already said the person behind all of this would have. And he has a tendency to use symbolism."

"The daffodils in the Russian House," Vinnie said. The Russian House was the mansion in Strasbourg Kubanov had used as the European headquarters for his dealings. Before we had discovered his art-crime ring and a lot of arrests had been made. "The house was on Daffodil Street. It has to be Kubanov behind these burglaries."

"This would make sense as a theory," I said. "Kubanov would have no qualms using somebody to recruit needy, susceptible students to steal for him."

"But isn't he this behind-the-curtains kind of criminal? Why announce his presence with the red daffodils?" Francine asked.

I was afraid of the answer. It came too close to my home and those in it. Another question bothered me. "If he only works with the best, why is he using an amateur hacker? Why not someone like Francine?"

We all looked at Francine. She lifted both eyebrows. "What? Why are you looking at me? I would never work with someone like that."

"That is not why we are looking at you," I said. "We want to know your thoughts on the connection between Kubanov and the hacker."

"Oh well, that's good then." She took a sip of her wine. "Honestly? I don't know if Kubanov is involved, but I know there must be another hacker. Someone who is more sophisticated than doofus."

"How did you find out his name?" I asked, excited. "We should tell Manny."

Everyone laughed. The mood around the table lifted slightly.

"Doofus is slang, Jenny. It means fool or stupid person."

"Oh." I thought about this. "I like it. Doofus. I think I'm going to use it. It's not offensive, is it?"

"Well, you are calling someone a fool, so in that sense it is," Francine said. "But there are a lot of fools out there."

There were a few chuckles and we fell silent. My mind was sorting through all the data. "Colin said that Kubanov likes symbolic gestures. Is he the one behind the painting, the email and the bomb? If so, how do they connect to him? How do I connect to him? How do I connect to the hacker?"

"The hacker read all your articles," Francine said.

"But that proves nothing other that he might be a student," I said. "There must be another connection."

"Did you ever say anything controversial in your articles?" Francine asked. "I read a few of them, but there were some things I didn't understand at all. Most of it though sounded solid to me, not offensive at all."

"What about that professor?" Colin asked.

I shook my head. "No, that is too silly. Such a petty thing? No. If you read my articles, you'll find some that were much more strongly worded than that one. I looked at them yesterday and sent Manny a list of peers who might have been angry with me because of an article. It is nigh-on impossible to predict someone else's sensitivity to facts presented in my articles that might contradict their views."

"But you did it."

"Of course. Manny ran those names against some system looking for criminal activities and not one of them has had any suspicious behaviour."

"Recorded suspicious behaviour," Colin said with one lifted eyebrow. I immediately caught the hint.

"Granted. But these are academics, Colin. These people theorise and teach, they are not violent, bomb-building criminals." My hand gestures were becoming more animated as I talked.

"You never know what can push a person over the edge, Jen-girl."

"Send me that list," Francine said. "I have ways to look for criminal connections that Manny's guys don't have."

"Maybe you should share your ways with Manny's people. It will help them catch bad guys," I said. The succession of micro-expressions on her face told me that I had erred. Greatly. "You think they will use it against you and all other citizens in some great conspiracy to control us all? Really, Francine. That is too far-fetched. Even for you."

"I stick with my far-fetched theories and you can stick to yours." She lifted her nose just enough to ensure I noted her superiority. I smiled. After a second she also smiled. "Give me that list and I'll check it my way."

"I'll email to you." I tilted my head to the side. "Why don't you just hack my computer and take it?"

"Because I'm not going to invade your privacy like that. I only hack to protect, not to steal from you. Whatever you give me will be of your own free will." Her focus on me changed. I recognised that look. I had seen it a few times when we had had lunch, but always dismissed it as misplaced. Not anymore. The caring, concern and friendship displayed on her face stole my breath. "We'll find these people, these connections and Kubanov, and keep you safe, Genevieve."

Instinctively I wanted to deny needing help and being in danger. I thought about it for a split second and grew cold. I had to focus to not allow my mind to go into hiding. "This is about me, isn't it? Somehow the focus of all of this is on me. Why? What have I done?"

"If it's Kubanov, I can imagine that he's pissed off with you for fuc… screwing up his very profitable art-forgery business, Jen-girl." Vinnie straightened in his chair. He glanced at Colin and renewed determination tightened his lips. "We're going to get that bastard and make sure nothing bad happens to you."

"Assuming that he is the one behind the email, bomb and painting." I groaned. "This is all still crude speculation. Just because there were daffodils at these crime scenes does not mean that Kubanov is behind this. Sure, it implicates him, but we have no concrete evidence. There are too many disconnected pieces of information. I have to find what connects all of them to me."

"Do you have any ideas?" Colin asked.

I stared at him while thinking. With a shrug, I shook my head. "Nothing, just more speculation. The only so-called connection I have with Kubanov is the case we had last summer. From what we know, the art forgery ring was only one of many avenues he deals with. The gun connections we found then can lead us to the possibility that he also deals in arms. If we follow this trail and generalise, most likely he also deals in drugs. Who knows what else? So, why would one arm of his extensive illegal business make him angry enough to do something to me?"

It was quiet around the table. In their postures and eyes I could see they knew the answer as well as I did. "Psychopaths do not take well to losing. Losing face is a very strong trigger, it prompts them into all sorts of revengeful actions. Do you think he wants revenge?"

"We won't let him get close to you, Jenny." Colin lightly touched my hand.

I looked down and realised that I was gripping the table with both hands as if I planned to pull it closer. It took concentration to relax my hands enough to let go. I slid my hand out from under

Colin's and rested it on my lap. One by one, I relaxed my tense neck, shoulder and back muscles.

A ping from a phone brought some tension back. I frowned.

"That's your phone, Genevieve." Francine sat up in her chair, looking excited. "When I secured it, I also set up the alerts to let you know whenever you receive emails. That way you'll always be on top of things."

"Why would I always want to be on top of things? Oh, never mind that."

I reached for my handbag that Colin had hung over the back of my chair. It was not hung on the correct side of my chair and my handbag was not facing the right direction, but it was better than having my handbag in a wrong place. My smartphone was in its usual pocket, easy to reach. I tapped the screen and saw the notification icon. The technology pleased me. The accessibility into every waking moment of my life, not so much.

"I have a new email," I said and tapped on the screen to open my inbox. "Oh. Oh, no. It's another email from the postal service. There's another package in my mailbox."

Colin grabbed the phone out of my hands and looked at it as if he could see what was inside the package by merely glaring at the touchscreen. "What the fuck is he playing at?"

"I'll go get it. Jen-girl, can I have the keys again?" Vinnie got up and held his hand out to me. The scar on his face was standing out against the red anger in his face. His hand had the slightest tremor, caused by a rush of adrenaline. The flaring of his nostrils indicated faster and deeper breathing. He was preparing to take action, violent action. The intimidating large man hovering over me made me feel safe and I was glad that he was on my side.

I reached into my handbag again and took the keys from its own designated side pocket. Holding the keys just above his outstretched hand, I looked at him, hoping to convey my intense sincerity. "Be careful."

"Always, Jen-girl. Always." He closed the keys in his fist and looked at Colin. "Dude?"

I only caught the end of Colin giving Vinnie an almost imperceptible shake of his head. Again with the secrecy.

"Okey-dokey. I'll be back in a few." Vinnie didn't state whether it would be a few minutes or hours and I didn't ask. I wasn't particularly excited about receiving yet another mysterious package. He could take his time. Unless…

"What if it's a bomb?" I started getting out of my chair to stop Vinnie.

"Don't worry, Jen-girl, I'll make sure it's not." He gave me a quick smile, opened the door and left.

"Does he have one of those bomb sniffer machines?" I asked.

"Or something like that." Colin's cryptic answer told me that whatever testing device or method Vinnie used was most likely not legal. My shoulders dropped a little at yet another gray area, void of simple black and white rules.

"I'm going to check what else I can find," Francine said and got up. "I will find this doofus. Before the weekend is done, I'll have him. I swear."

"That would be a step closer to finding out what this is all about and who is involved," I said.

Francine nodded. "Let me know when Vinnie comes back. I want to see what is in that package."

I didn't. I truly did not want to see what was in that package. With an elegant wave, Francine left for the apartment next door. Colin and I sat in comfortable silence and I started assessing.

Now that this case had become personal, finding new clues held none of the usual excitement for me. What I was feeling was dread. It was an emotion I was intimately acquainted with. My whole life had been ruled by it. Dread that I had forgotten to lock all the doors, that I would have an episode, that I would have to be socially appropriate, that people would shun me. I was tired of this feeling.

Chapter FOURTEEN

"I've got it." Vinnie's voice boomed with excitement as he walked through the front door. "I think it's a book. Actually, I'm pretty sure it is."

I stood up from my crouched position in front of the dishwasher. Vinnie was halfway to the kitchen. A shudder worked its way through my body. "Stop. Go back, close and lock the door. Then you can bring that package."

Vinnie glanced at Colin lounging in the living area, then smiled at me. "Sorry, Jen-girl. I'm just excited about our next clue."

I turned on the dishwasher, folded the dishcloth carefully to align all the corners and hung it exactly in the centre of the small railing on the wall. Vinnie might be excited about the new clue, but I wasn't. I resented everyone and everything for bringing more dread in my life. That included the brown paper-wrapped package Vinnie was clutching in his hand.

"Secured?" Colin asked as he got up and followed Vinnie to the dining room table.

"Checked it nine ways to Sunday," Vinnie said as he placed the package on the table.

I didn't understand his words, but his body language told me that the package held no physical threat. For a moment I stood undecided in the kitchen. Anger at my irrational emotions propelled me to action. I grabbed a pair of latex gloves from the dispenser next to the sink and walked to the dining room table. "Why didn't you open it? Can you make positively sure it is safe without opening it?"

"I have ways." Vinnie's posture and tone told me to not inquire about his ways. "When I put it through the x-ray, I saw it was a book. Open it, so we can see what book it is."

The package looked innocent as it lay there on the table. I only looked at it, not touching it. "This is most likely the book that will be the key to the code on the bomb."

"And we won't know for sure until you open it, Jenny." Colin studied me for a few seconds. "Do you want me to open it?"

I almost begged him to. But I was stronger than this fear, stronger than this book.

I put the gloves on, reached for the book and sat down in my chair. As with the painting, the book was wrapped in layers of brown paper which I carefully took off. Maybe Manny would want to send this in to the labs for testing as well. Not that I had confidence that they were going to find any evidence.

I placed the last layer of paper on the pile in front of me and studied the book in my hands. Gold embossing on the leather cover brought home the significance of this book. I took a quick breath and looked at Colin. "It's Dante's *La Vita Nuova*."

The muscles in his face contracted to give me a glimpse of the micro-expression seen especially in victorious athletes. "I was right. Damn."

I turned it over. "It looks old."

"It looks really old." Colin sat down in the chair next to me and moved in close to look at the book. "Open it, let's see what it is."

I lifted the cover. Only because I was already prepared for something disturbing did I not gasp in horror. On the first page was a dried, pressed flower. A red daffodil.

"Do you still doubt that Kubanov is behind this?" Colin asked, ignoring Vinnie's string of inventive curse words. Vinnie sat down hard in the chair across from me and glared at the book.

I lifted the flower and carefully placed it on the table. "Unless someone else has a fixation on red daffodils, it makes for a conclusive argument that Kubanov sent me this. But why? Wait, don't answer that. It is an unproductive question."

I carefully paged through the book. At a later stage I would go through it much more studiously, but as it was, I didn't see anything else out of the ordinary. Returning to the front of the book, I scanned the first pages.

"Why this book?" Vinnie asked. I didn't answer him. I didn't know the answer.

Colin put on latex gloves and held out his hand. "Let me have a look at it."

I handed him the book and sat back.

"Seriously, dudes. Why this book?" Vinnie was becoming impatient with our lack of response.

Colin continued to flip through the book. "Well, Vin, the obvious answer would be the book's connection to the painting."

"Yeah, well. I didn't study history and literature and all that crap. Care to tell me how this all fits in?"

"All that crap, huh?" Colin looked up from the book to smile at Vinnie. "Okay, here is the super-condensed version of *La Vita Nuova*. Dante Alighieri saw this girl, Beatrice, when he was around nine years old and she was a few months younger. He fell in love with her, and until her death at the age of twenty-five had a love relationship with her that mostly existed in his head. It was this almost obsession with her that made him write this book, a combination of poetry and prose. All revolving around this girl and his unrequited love for her."

"Creepy, dude. Especially for a kid." Vinnie shuddered.

"Well, he wasn't a kid when he wrote this. He must have been in his late twenties. Much later in his life it is said that he was embarrassed about having written this. Most of this book is about his feelings every time he had laid eyes on her and his intense desire to just hear Beatrice greet him. Both of them got married to people arranged for them. She died really young, like I said. It was after her death that he wrote this book." Colin lifted the book. "It is filled with more angst and melodrama than a Brazilian soap opera. After Beatrice's death, Dante became very interested in literature, philosophy and politics. Quite an intense guy."

"It is also much later that he wrote his more famous work, The Divine Comedy," I said.

"Correct," Colin continued. "There are three parts to The Divine Comedy: *Inferno*, where he starts his journey in the underworld with another poet, *Purgatorio*, where he ascends from hell, and *Paradiso*, where Beatrice takes him through the nine celestial spheres of Heaven. In the last part he imagined that Beatrice was his guardian angel who both encouraged and reprimanded him in his search for salvation. Throughout The Divine Comedy Beatrice represents love and hope."

"Way over my head." Vinnie waved his hand over the top of his head. "So how does this connect to you, Jen-girl?"

"I have no idea. None of my personal history correlates to this story. My only connection to Kubanov is last summer's case. The only connection Francine has been able to find to the hacker was that he read my articles. I honestly don't know how all this connects." I was typing a bit too aggressively on my keyboard and pulled my hands back into fists. "For days I've been trying to figure it out, but I don't have enough data."

Colin waved the book at me. "We have one more thing."

"Let's see if this holds the key." I opened the computer file containing the sets of numbers left on the explosive device. "Vinnie, will you write this down?"

Vinnie reached for the notepad next to my computer. I snatched it back. This was my notepad. Only I wrote in it. I got up and took out a new notepad from a stack in one of the kitchen drawers. His smile was knowing and full of affection when he took the pad from me.

"Thanks, Jen-girl." He lifted an eyebrow. "May I have a pen or pencil?"

I handed him one of the three pens neatly aligned next to my laptop and ignored his broadening smile. "Ready?"

It took us half an hour to use the Ottendorf cipher. I gave Colin the numbers, he searched for the page, line and letter and Vinnie wrote it down. It was a slow process. I was sure that I could count the lines and letters faster than Colin, but surprised myself with restraint and patience.

"Tapping your foot isn't going to make this go any faster, Jenny." Colin glanced at my feet. Apparently I had not been as successful at hiding my frustration as I had thought. "T, that is the last letter. What do we have, Vin?"

Vinnie's face contorted into a look of consternation. He touched his nose and shook his head. "Ghurdoapv... oh, hell. I can't even say this crap. It's no word or words I've ever seen."

He shoved the notepad across the table. I lifted it and studied Vinnie's surprisingly neat printed letters. He was right. It didn't make sense. Colin tilted the notepad to also have a look. I let my mind search for the possibility of words within this scrambled mess, but nothing came to me.

"Put it in a search engine," Colin said.

"Brilliant idea," I said. Colin dictated and I placed all the letters in the Google search bar. I pressed enter. Almost immediately a page popped up suggesting other words, asking if that was what I had meant. Google couldn't find anything with those letters. I wasn't surprised.

"Maybe it is a code within a code." Colin was still staring at the notepad.

"Or maybe the dude used words and not letters," Vinnie said. "None of those numbers in the code is higher than eleven, which is the average number of words per line in a book like this."

Colin and I stared at Vinnie. These men had taught me so much in the time I had known them. Maybe one of the most important lessons was that looks could be immensely deceiving. Vinnie might look like a thug, but he was a perceptive, intelligent man.

"That's great, Vinnie. Let's start again." It took us another half an hour to get the specific word on the specific line on the specific page. Again it was tedious. This time I managed to not show my impatience.

"'Very'," Colin said. "The last word. Okay Vin, what do we have now?"

"Nonsense. Again." He groaned and shook the notepad. "It

doesn't make sense, but here it is. 'Day upon yours off light she he work throw in mine growth seen being cream stand hear a very'. See, total fucking nonsense."

"Let me see that." I took the notepad from Vinnie and stared at the words. This was a repetition of our previous attempt. It didn't make sense at all. Mentally I scrambled the words, but could not form any intelligent sentences with what was so neatly printed on the cream paper. "This is not the key."

"Are you very sure, Jenny?" Colin leaned in again to look at the notepad. I handed it to him. He moved back, but not much.

"The verb, noun and preposition combinations won't work in any form. I will continue to try, but I'm sure this isn't it. There is something else."

It grew quiet around the table.

"I have to phone Manny," I said. Again both men reacted to the name with the slightest tension. Weary of this behaviour, I took my phone and went to the living area. Manny answered on the second ring with a sound that might have been a grumbled greeting.

"I got another package." I sat down on the sofa.

"And you collected it without letting me know. You've opened it too, haven't you?"

"Yes, why wouldn't I?"

"Because the last package lured you to a bomb!" The last word ended on a yell. I heard him breathing deeply a few times, most likely trying to calm himself. "What was in the package?"

"A book. There was also a red daffodil in the front of the book. We used the code, but so far had no luck. It is not the letters or even words."

"Did you touch everything? Most likely. And now it will be even more difficult to get fingerprints and trace evidence."

"Manny." I spoke louder than usual to stop his tirade. "I opened the package and handled the book wearing gloves. You can have the paper, but for now we still need the book. I need to figure out this code."

Manny grumbled something that might have been rude, but I

couldn't hear clearly. "Put that paper in a new plastic bag and don't touch it again, for heaven's sake. I'll come around tomorrow mid-morning to pick it up and take it to the lab."

"I don't have a plastic bag. I recycle and o—"

"Just put the bloody papers in something clean that has not been touched or contaminated before. I'll see you in the morning." He abruptly ended the call. Sometimes I was ecstatic that Manny had entered my life. That way I knew that I was not the person least skilled in social interaction and telephone etiquette.

"I'm going, Jen-girl. If you guys need me, just holler." Vinnie gave me a sweet smile before he left and closed the front door behind him. I got up and locked it. All five locks.

Colin was still sitting at the dining room table. I walked to the kitchen. A cup of camomile tea would be good.

"Manny said he'll be here tomorrow morning to pick up the papers." I filled the kettle with filtered water and switched it on. "Maybe they can get some fingerprints or something off it."

"Did he say anything about the painting? Did they get any prints off that? Any trace evidence?"

"He didn't say and I didn't think to ask. You can ask him tomorrow morning."

Again I saw the subtle change in Colin when it came to dealing with Manny. I made two cups of tea, not even asking if Colin wanted any. I placed it on coasters on the table and went back to the kitchen. I returned with a bottle of aged whiskey and two tumbler glasses. I sat down next to him.

Colin looked at me with raised eyebrows. "What's this?"

"I know that some people need alcohol to give them courage. It's called Dutch courage. Other people need it to relax a bit before a difficult conversation. I thought you might want or need this."

"For what?" The micro-expressions flying across his face told me he knew. He was merely stalling.

"Tell me." I poured about an inch of amber liquid in a glass and placed it in front of him. On a coaster.

"Jenny," he started, but stopped. His mouth moved a lot and his breathing indicated deep distress.

"Tell me, Colin," I said again, gentler this time. His distress was now so clearly displayed across his body that I felt my chest tighten. Against my nature, my entire life experience, I reached out and put my hand on his forearm. His skin was warm under my hand, his muscles strong. With his other hand he took mine and enfolded it in both his. He held onto my hand as if it was a lifeline. My chest tightened even more.

I felt so inadequate to deal with this. All I could do was sit and wait until he was ready to talk. It took a long time, a tumbler of whiskey and a lot of deep breathing before I noticed the slight change in his posture.

"After that last case, Interpol was desperate to put an end to Kubanov." His voice was hoarse from stress, his hands holding mine tightly. "I'm a thief, Jenny. Not a spy. An artist, a forger. But they wanted a spy. Those bastards."

I realised that he wasn't aware of confessing his crimes to me. He was too caught up in whatever had taken place and its lingering effects. His eyes were locked on the bronze sculpture from Hungary on the side table in the living area. I knew he wasn't seeing it.

"Kubanov has been on many countries' watch lists for a long time," he said softly. "Apart from his less violent crimes, he is well known to be dealing in arms and drugs. But he's good. Until now he has been untouchable. Everyone knows, or they think they know, that he is bankrolling many syndicates, but there has not been one single trace of evidence to connect him to any of the crimes. The same as with our case with Piros in the summer. The connection between them was there, but we didn't have anything concrete to take to a prosecutor or judge to even arrest the arsehole for an interrogation."

Something clicked in my head. "But someone found incriminating evidence and you were the best person to retrieve it from Kubanov."

"Yup." The corners of his mouth pulled down in bitter

anger. "Interpol had received reliable intel of the location of this evidence against Kubanov. I was perfect for the job, especially with my reputation. I am after all a renowned thief and forger. Interpol has always encouraged me to maintain my reputation within the industry. That has opened many doors to the really bad guys."

"As opposed to the plain bad guys." I shook my head. "What is the distinction between a really bad guy and a plain bad guy?"

"Bad guys only sell forged art. They don't kill people, they don't hurt anyone."

"A victimless crime." I had heard that a lot. Thinking about the complicated life Colin was living made my mind cringe in reflex. The duplicity involved in maintaining his criminal reputation yet simultaneously finding ways to catch criminals would force my brain into a panicked spin. What price was he paying on a moral and emotional level?

"A victimless crime indeed. No one gets hurt, the insurance companies pay out and the forgers get to create art. But really bad guys, well, they're bloodthirsty. Selling art is only a means to an end. They often use art as currency for drugs and guns." He shuddered. "Or arms much more destructive than guns. They are ruthless criminals who do not care about art, creating or the beauty of a well-placed brushstroke. They induce violence all over the globe by supplying guns to developing countries. These are the people who put guns into the hands of child soldiers."

"And Kubanov is one of those?"

"Without a doubt. What sets him apart is that he actually does appreciate art. He has a fetish for it and that is why Interpol decided that I was the best guy for the job. This was a joint operation with a few other agencies and I was the linchpin. My reputation was supposed to get me close enough to Kubanov to find that evidence. They had no one else with the right connections or who was trustworthy enough."

I thought about what he had said. There were so many questions that it was difficult to limit it to one point only. My chest hurt when everything fell into place. "Oh Colin. That is where you were? You went to Russia and were captured and tortured by Kubanov?"

He nodded, but didn't say anything else. My mind was reeling with this revelation. I had known that Colin worked for Interpol, but never, not for one minute, suspected that he did any dangerous work. I had naively thought he solely stole back works of art that were taken during wartime.

"Who supplied the information about the evidence?" I asked. "What kind of evidence was it?"

Colin got up so fast, the chair tipped over and landed with a loud noise on the wooden floor. He walked to the window and stood with his back to me. There wasn't one relaxed muscle in his posture and his breathing was laboured. He grabbed the back of his neck with both hands and shook his head as if he was having an internal conversation. His black t-shirt stretched across his back, clearly showing the muscle definition. I saw his ribcage moving with unnatural breathing patterns. He was trying to regain control. I waited.

"Kubanov is a genius, Jenny. He fucked with us." He turned around, folded his arms and looked at me. "And he's fucking with us again."

"What are you talking about?"

Colin walked back, picked up the chair and sat down at an angle facing me. "He wanted me in Russia. He trickled out just enough information to titillate, specific info that would require an expert to come after it."

"And you were that expert. How do you know this?"

"I figured it out while Kubanov was breaking my fingers. And he told me some of it. He was very proud of himself." He shifted closer and took my hand in his again. I didn't mind. He was in so much turmoil, if offering my hand could help, I could get past my dislike for physical contact.

"Where does Manny fit into this?" I asked.

"He was the bastard who had received the tips. He doesn't know of my connection to Interpol, but he had the audacity to recommend that they recruit me for this job. He was going to blackmail me into helping him catch Kubanov."

"Manny told me that he was getting close to finding Kubanov when his superiors took the case off his hands and ordered him to stop investigating." I leaned a bit closer to Colin. "His recommendation and hypothetical blackmail are not the real reason for your rage. Why are you so angry with him?"

"He didn't check his intel, Jenny!" He turned his face away, struggling for calm. A few seconds later he looked at me again. "He is a bloody good detective. Why didn't he get suspicious when he started receiving all these great tips? Tips that fell so neatly in my specialisation, making me the perfect person for this job. He should've checked it all."

"Did he have time? The way he told the story, it sounded like your bosses grabbed the case from him before he could follow up on it."

"Whose side are you on? Manny's?"

"Hey." I put my other hand over his and waited until he was looking at me. "I'm not taking sides, Colin. I'm only asking questions."

"Questions that put you on Manny's side."

I straightened in my chair and pulled my one hand away. The other stayed. "You are being irrational and emotional. I don't take sides. I listen to the facts and subsequently decide what I believe to be the most neutral truth." My voice softened. "But if I had to choose sides, it would be yours."

Colin's eyes widened and then he closed them for a moment. When he looked at me, I identified emotions that I didn't know how to interpret. "Jenny, you… Thank you. Just, thank you."

We studied each other for a long time. He must have seen something that reassured him even more because his facial muscles relaxed. As did his grip on my hand. I hoped this indicated his willingness to listen to reason.

"As much as Manny grumbles and complains, I know that he respects you," I said softly.

Colin snorted. "How can you even think that?"

"It's not a matter of thinking. It's in his body language, something I know. I seldom trust what people say, but I believe what my eyes see. Manny likes you and he doesn't like that. He doesn't want to like someone he thinks is a one hundred percent criminal. He doesn't want to respect you, but he does. I would have to observe Manny when he is asked this question to know his true answer, but from what I know about him I can comfortably surmise that he would never have done anything to put you in danger like that."

"Still on Manny's side." His accusation didn't carry any resentment, rather a tinge of humour.

"I also think that Manny can be trusted with your secret."

"What secret? That I'm working for Interpol?" He was shaking his head emphatically. "No, Jenny. He can never know this."

"Why not? It would make him much more agreeable to work with."

"No." His lips closed in a thin line and his hands tightened around mine again. There was clearly more to Colin's work at Interpol and Manny's involvement than I knew about.

"Tell me what happened in Russia."

He blinked a few times. "I was told that an old contact had informed Interpol he knew where Kubanov kept his records. According to this informant, Kubanov had an entire level under his house, or I should rather say mansion, that was not shown on any plans. That basement level housed a safe room the size of an average Parisian apartment, a fitness centre, a swimming pool and another recreation area. It was supposed to be vast. Taking into consideration that his house on the ground level covers almost fifteen hundred square metres, it isn't difficult to imagine all of that fitting into an underground space like that.

"The plan was for me to go to Russia under one of my more infamous names and make contact with Kubanov. I was to offer him a twelve-carat pink diamond with its legit papers. He had implied interest in such a diamond."

"Did you have that diamond?"

"Of course I did. It came from a heist I pulled when I

retrieved some paintings stolen during the Second World War. I had help to make sure the diamond was clean. I knew that Kubanov would not be able to resist something so unique and legal. He could show it off in public knowing that it wasn't a blood diamond or stolen. Well, I arrived in Russia, dropped my name in a few places and waited. If all had gone to plan, I was going to insist on being invited to his home so that I could get an inside view of the place to see possible entrances to the basement level. I was also going to plant some bugs."

"Surveillance devices." I remembered from the time Colin and Vinnie had bugged my apartment that they didn't call these devices by their correct name. "But that didn't happen."

"No. I was there for two days when some guys broke into my hotel suite one night and forcefully took me to Kubanov's house. He does indeed have a basement level, but I never got to explore much. I was taken to an empty room and spent the next six days there. He would taunt me, asking how I liked his secret room with all his secret records. That is how I came to the conclusion that he had lured me there."

"Why you? Why the elaborate effort to get you there?"

"Why didn't he just take me out?" Colin gave me a humourless smile when I frowned. "Why didn't he just have me assassinated? I had a lot of time to speculate about it and I think that he wanted me to suffer."

"For what?"

"For ruining his art forgery business last summer." He sighed. "I don't know how he knew that I was involved in that case, and it has me worried."

"Do you think that he wants to take revenge on all of us who were involved?" My voice raised in pitch. "Is that why you are so convinced that Kubanov is behind the email, code and bomb? He is after me now?"

"I don't know what to think anymore, Jenny. But this is the direction that my thoughts are going in."

I saw his hesitation. "There is more. Tell me."

"Everything else is pure speculation. A hunch." His lips lifted in a half-smile. "You might not appreciate my wild theories."

"Usually no. But your previous hunch would have prevented me from stepping on a bomb if I had listened to you. So, tell me your wild theories."

"Okay. We already agreed that Kubanov never does his own dirty work. He has someone else, someone strategic, do it for him. He uses people. He plans every move very carefully like the best chess player. But I think that we triggered something in him last summer. I think that he took the loss of his forgery ring as a personal attack and wants to exact revenge on us. He will use his intermediaries to get to us, but ultimately he wants to destroy us personally."

I thought about this carefully. "Your theory is maybe a little too wild for my tastes. Are you sure it's not coloured by your suffering under his hand?"

"Of course being tortured by Kubanov influenced my theory, Jenny. That is why I think this game he is playing is so personal. He could've killed me here at home. He could've killed me when I landed in Russia. He could've had his thugs torture me. Why did he choose to do this himself?"

I swallowed away my fear. My intense anger and resentment at Colin disappearing out of my life suddenly seemed petty and juvenile. I was surprised when my vision blurred. I blinked away the tears and took a few shaky breaths. "I'm sorry this happened to you. I'm sincerely sorry."

He lifted one hand and carefully wiped a single tear from my cheek. "I'm okay now. I don't know if I would've survived another day if Vinnie hadn't come and gotten me out."

"How did he know to get you?"

"Vin and I have a system. If I don't check in with him at certain times, he knows something is wrong. If I don't check in with another method, he knows that there is a serious problem. He knew where I was going and when I didn't contact him, he came to extract me."

"How did he do that? I assume Kubanov's place to be extremely secure."

"Oh, it was. Fortunately Vinnie is as badass as he looks. He has a lot of connections that even I don't want to know about. He used those guys to create a lot of chaos in Kubanov's complex. It sounded like a war zone. There were explosions everywhere and I really thought the house was going to come down on top of me." He huffed a soft laugh. "It was like a movie. With dust falling everywhere, shooting coming from above, the door to the room I was in blasted inward and flew past me. Through that smoke and dust Vinnie came walking in as if he was coming over for tea."

"Did he say something insensitive?" I was sure he would have. That was Vinnie's way of relieving tension.

"He did. He asked me if I was going to lie around all day while he was doing all the hard work." A genuine smile removed some of the pain in his eyes. "He carried me out of there while shooting from the hip with an assault rifle. The guy is a regular Rambo. I honestly don't remember the first week after that. The rest of the last four months have been two corrective surgeries to my leg and hand, and lots of physiotherapy. Now you know it all."

The way he said it was with the kind of finality to indicate the end of this conversation. Possibly the end of any conversation regarding this topic. I respected that and therefore didn't ask him about Rambo.

"Thank you for trusting me with this." I realised the significance of him sharing this with me.

"Jenny, I trust you with my life. I didn't tell you about this before because I hoped that I was wrong. That my suspicions about Kubanov wanting revenge were wrong. I didn't want you to know a single thing about Kubanov that could put you in danger."

"Again with the over-protectiveness." I sat up straight and squeezed his hand once. "We'll get them. I will figure out the code, we will find whoever is helping Kubanov with these emails and bomb. We will stop him from hurting us."

Chapter **FIFTEEN**

I woke up clutching the remnants of a dream. My subconscious had tried to push through the connection it had made, but wakefulness obscured it yet again. I banged my head back into the pillow and sighed into my dark bedroom.

It had taken me a long time to fall asleep after Colin's big revelation. He had seemed awkward after that and soon retired to his room. Working hadn't helped me unwind and neither had a soak in the tub. My mind had been consumed with thoughts of what Colin had suffered through. I didn't know if I would have come out of it as relatively unscathed as he. Apart from the physical scars, his irrational anger with Manny and his rage towards Kubanov, he appeared to have dealt with that situation rather well. Considering.

I got out of bed wondering if my observations of Colin's mental well-being were accurate or not. Only time would tell. As it was, I had not once seen him act in any manner that would alert me to severe damage to his psyche. The only difference I had observed in him was that he came across more protective of me than before. Under the circumstances I deemed it understandable, even justified.

When it came to reading nonverbal cues, I trusted my judgement unconditionally. It was this judgement that I relied on while psychoanalysing the man sleeping in the other room in my apartment. Because of the hour and my house guest I moved quietly to the kitchen and winced when the coffee machine sounded louder than usual as it started spitting out an Indian blend coffee.

"It's half past four, Jenny. Don't you ever keep normal hours?" Colin's voice startled me out of my thoughts. I swung around and stared at him. His hair was mussed, but his eyes were alert. He walked into the kitchen wearing his usual striped pyjama bottoms and white vest. I had never gotten into the habit of wearing a bathrobe and apparently neither had he. It might be something I should consider. He stopped a few feet from me and gave me an inquiring look. "Jenny?"

"Oh. Yes." I felt colour creeping up my neck. My mind was wandering so much that I forgot to reply. "Sorry I woke you. I had a dream that gave me the clue to the code."

"Fantastic." His eyes widened and he stepped closer. "What is it? What does the code say?"

"I don't know. I forgot the dream as soon as I woke up."

He laughed softly. "I hate when that happens. So why didn't you go back to sleep?"

I stifled a yawn and took my coffee. "Can't sleep. Do you want coffee?"

"I'll make it, thanks. Are you going to work now?" He moved around me and took a mug from the cupboard. "What are you going to work on?"

"The code." I left him at the coffee machine and turned on my computer. Sitting down, I stared at the monitor as the computer booted up. My dream connection was lingering just beneath the surface of my consciousness. I knew that only the smallest trigger was needed to bring it blasting into my mind. The key was to find that trigger, so I did what usually worked. I closed my eyes and gave myself over to Mozart's Violin Concerto in B-flat major.

I opened my eyes and tried to calm my racing heart. A glance at the clock on my computer screen told me that I had been in my head for the last two hours. I realised that I was hugging myself tightly and still rocking. I dropped my arms and straightened in my chair.

"Have you got it?" Colin had moved a wingback chair from the reading area and was sitting a few feet from the dining room table, reading one of my books. I didn't know why he felt compelled to be closer to me. The chair hadn't been that far away. It should not have been moved. That thought made me drop my eyes to the wooden floor. Colin laughed and put the book upside down on his leg. "I didn't drag the chair here, Jenny. I carried it. So? Have you got the key to the code?"

"I think so. Maybe. Could be."

After getting gloves from the kitchen, I paged through the book, carefully studying each page. Only when I reached the last page did I pay attention to Colin's impatient breathing and movements.

"Please tell me what's going on in that head of yours. The suspense is killing me."

I looked at him. He was leaning forward in his chair, his elbows resting on his knees, anticipation evident on his face. I lifted the book. "In the whole book only one word is underlined. The first letter twice."

He got up and sat on the dining chair next to me. "Show me."

I turned towards him and opened the book on page seventy-five. I angled it towards him and pointed to the centre of the page. "'For'. That is the word that is lightly underlined. Look here. The 'f' is underlined twice."

"And that means?" He drew out the last word on an inquiring monotone.

"That there is a relationship between the 'f' and the code. What else was strange in this book?"

He thought about it. "The daffodil. I looked through the book while you were Mozarting and couldn't see anything else. I did notice the underlined 'for', but didn't make much of it."

"Firstly, Mozart is not a verb." I shuddered and then scowled when Colin smiled. "It's wrong, so very wrong, to use a name as a verb. You're distracting me with things like that. Since the daffodil and 'for' are the only anomalies in an otherwise flawless collector's piece, there is significance."

"What significance?"

"I have a theory, so bear with me. There is something crude

about this code. Just like Francine's hacker this is sophisticated and it is not. The sophistication comes from the code, but the crudeness from hiding it."

"You think there is a code in the code?"

"Yes, and the way it is hidden comes across as desperate and amateur." Which made it all the more frustrating that I could not break this code. It was time to simplify our attempts. "We tried the letters and words from those numbers to no avail. I'm thinking that the 'for' is the key to the code."

"I consider myself quite an intelligent person, but I can't see how 'for' could be the key."

"Not the preposition. Four as a number."

"Of course. You're a genius."

"This is true," I said and picked up my notepad. It took us an hour to work through two of my ideas. Neither resulted in anything coherent. It only led us to words that could never form meaningful sentences. This code might have been crude, but it was not very easy to decipher.

"What if we try numerology?" Colin pushed his hands through his hair. Already it had been messy from sleep. Now it was standing in all directions. It took us another hour to work through his suggestions that included calculations using the Indian and Chaldean systems. We added and subtracted. I was losing patience when Colin suggested one more alternative.

"Let's add four and subtract one."

"Why one?"

"There was one daffodil in the book." He lifted one shoulder in a half-shrug. I nodded. It was worth the try. By the third word, my eyes widened and my heart rate increased. By the time we got all twenty words, I was constantly shifting in my chair.

"So?" Colin leaned closer to look at my notepad.

"This is it. This is the sentence that was hidden by the code." I pointed at the words filling two lines on my notepad. "'This sweet child mine, told her end was nigh, should not have had to face her life in a run'."

"What does that mean?"

"It is a rhyme. A sad rhyme."

"Four lines of a notably simplistic poem. But what does it mean?" he asked again.

"If we take the words at face value, then I would dare to say that this man's child was diagnosed with something terminal when she was small. The tense makes me think that she is dead."

"Well, it certainly fit in with the sadness of Dante's book and Rossetti's painting."

I turned to Colin. "Does Kubanov have a child? Did he have a child that died from cancer or some other terminal disease?"

"Not that I know of. None of the background on him has ever revealed any children." He leaned back in his chair. "Doesn't mean that he doesn't have any though. Or had."

We fell into silence, but it didn't last for long. Distinct noises coming from my front door alerted me that someone was unlocking it. This time I didn't get annoyed when Vinnie stepped in, carrying two grocery bags. His head was down and it looked as if he was attempting stealth. It simultaneously interested and amused me to watch the large man carefully close the front door, turn around and take a few silent steps before he noticed us at the dining room table.

"Motherf... Do you guys never sleep? I thought I was going to surprise you two with breakfast in bed." The corners of his mouth were turned down and he stomped to the kitchen. "I'll never get to do something fun for you."

"Morning, Vinnie." I stood up and gave in to the need to stretch my muscles. I locked my fingers and stretched my arms above my head as high as I could. The pull in my back muscles was welcome and I rolled my head to loosen my tight neck muscles. I lowered my arms to find both men staring at me. The significance of my lack of inhibition felt like a punch to my usual shields of distrust and social distance.

"Go have a shower and put on some clothes, Jen-girl. Breakfast will be ready in twenty minutes." Vinnie pulled a pan from a drawer and put it unnecessarily hard on the stovetop.

"That sounds like a good idea. Gives me more time to think about the rhyme."

"What rhyme?" Vinnie turned to us and I left it to Colin to explain our discoveries of this morning.

I cut my usual shower time short when a realisation dawned on me. I rushed out of my bedroom twelve minutes later to find Francine in the kitchen arguing with Vinnie about adding some extra spices to the eggs. I ignored them and went straight for my computer.

"What's up, Jenny?" Colin looked up from where he was watching some weekend morning television show. The fake happiness in the presenters' voices grated on my nerves.

"Please turn that off. I have to think." Immediate silence followed my sharp request. I sat down in front of my computer and opened my email.

"Jenny, what's going on?" Colin was next to me, his voice controlled, concerned.

"So far the hacker and the bomber have been consistent in their behaviour. Working with that theory, it would follow that after another delivery there will be another bomb."

Francine and Vinnie had stopped arguing and were moving closer to the table. There wasn't a new email in my inbox. It didn't make sense.

"Why doesn't it make sense?" Colin asked. I had verbalised my thoughts.

"After the painting was delivered, I received an email that led us to the bomb in La Fleur Galerie. I haven't received anything yet. Why not?"

Everyone made sounds of frustration, but no one offered a hypothesis. Colin sat down next to me and stared at my computer screen. Vinnie turned back to the kitchen with a grumble. He returned with placemats and cutlery, gave it to Francine and nodded to the table. She started setting the table, forcing me to move my computer to the far side of the table. "Maybe he'll send the email a bit later."

I exhaled loudly through my nose and shook my head.

Something was wrong, a piece of information was missing.

As Francine set the table I realised that I had been rude. "Um, hello, Francine. How are you?"

Francine looked up from where she was putting cutlery on a napkin. Her smile was genuine. "Hello, Genevieve. I'm well, thanks. How are you?"

"Frustrated." Since Francine considered me her friend, I took the liberty to forgo expected niceties and be completely honest. "I wish I had more information, more data."

She sat down at the placing she had just set and left the rest to Vinnie. Her focus was on me. It was another thing that I liked about her. "Oh god, I know. I also wish that frigging hacker would log on to one of his websites so that I can find him. That should take us at least one step closer to finding the bomber guy sending emails and ultimately, Kubanov."

I studied her for a moment. She didn't seem to mind and quietly sat as I narrowed my eyes at her. She looked much better this morning. The swelling in her face was all but gone and she had managed to hide most of the bruises with clever make-up. The only time she looked anything but absolutely stunning was when her face had pulled in anger at not being able to locate the hacker yet. My mind processed that and other bits of information.

"How did you find Colin?" I asked. Next to me Colin's breathing changed and he leaned slightly forward.

"I looked for Vinnie. He's not as good as covering his tracks as Colin."

"Hey," Vinnie said loudly as he put the salt shaker on the table a bit more forcefully than needed. "I'm plenty good at covering my tracks."

"Maybe in the ways that you can think of." Francine winked at me. The muscle movement around her eyes and mouth warned me that she was about to say something that would irritate him. "I tracked you through the Italian Mama."

Vinnie stiffened and his nostrils flared. "The cooking blog? You tracked me through a fucking cooking blog?"

"A cooking blog that you have been visiting at least twelve times a day every day for the last eighteen months." The corners of her mouth were twitching. She was having fun. "Granted, you use proxy servers to make it look as if you logged in from all over the globe, but you always follow the same path on the blog."

Vinnie's mouth was slack. After two seconds of dismayed staring he shook his head. "Fucking unbelievable. But wait, if I used proxies, how did you figure out where I was? Where we were?"

"Oh, come on, Vin. Give a girl some credit. I'm good at this."

Vinnie walked back to the kitchen still shaking his head. "A fucking cooking blog. Shit, that really makes me look bad."

I stored this interesting and amusing bit of information about Vinnie. The realisation that I still knew so little about him, his background, his history, startled me. As a matter of fact, there was so much I didn't know about Colin either. A frown deepened on my brow. I knew even less about Francine. Oh, I knew a lot about her behaviour, her sense of humour, her psychology. We had after all shared many lunch hours together. I was a deficient friend. I was going to have to work harder at finding out more personal information about these people.

I turned my attention back to Francine. The anger and fear that had been present all over her face since the attack disappeared whenever she teased Vinnie into an argument. When she looked at me, her eyes were bright and the tight lines around her eyes were gone. "Once I knew the whereabouts of Vinnie, I must admit, I was stunned. Flabbergasted. Right next door to you. They were so pissed at me when I wouldn't stop knocking at their door. And then I was pissed, seriously pissed, when they didn't want me to tell you about... about living next to you."

"She knows," Colin said when she started stumbling over her words, scared to reveal secrets. "I told her everything last night."

"Oh, thank God." Francine threw her hands in the air and nearly knocked a plate out of Vinnie's hand. He glowered at her and walked around the table to put the plate in front of me. "I was wondering when you two idiots were going to see the light and let her in on what had happened over there. At least now she can understand the need for protection."

"Sorry I didn't tell you, Jen-girl." Vinnie gently squeezed my shoulder. I wasn't prepared for the physical affection and an involuntary shudder caused him to pull his hand back quickly. A quick flash of regret made me wince.

"Colin explained to me why he had decided not to tell me. Frankly I find many faults in his reasoning, but that is in the past." I looked at Francine. "Who's Sister Agnes?"

My quick change in topic brought shock to Francine's face. She shifted in her chair. "Only because you are who you are will I tell you this. My mother is Sister Agnes."

"Say what?" Vinnie grabbed a chair and sat down heavily. "I thought both your parents were dead."

Francine snorted. "My family would like that to be true. My parents are such a scandal to the Lemartins. Personally I think it is a cool story. I love my mom and my dad, and visit them whenever I can. Ours is really not a normal suburban family. My dad is a priest and my mom a nun in Brazil. My mom went there out of rebellion against her family as soon as she could. When the two of them were young, they did the naughty and I was the result. They obviously never got married and my mom stayed on in the monastery. As a little kid, I thought that all the nuns were my aunts. I had a wonderful childhood growing up in a simple, but extremely loving environment."

"Then how did you become a hacker?" I asked without censure.

"I was a teenager, bored in the monastery. I got onto the computers and found a wonderful world there. I taught myself to travel in this world and look into places that I wasn't supposed to look into. That was how I found out who my father was."

"How old were you?"

"Seven. No one realised until I was thirteen my studiousness was actually hacking." She laughed softly. "I tried a new code and accidentally cut the whole village off from electrical supply and also caused all modes of communication to collapse. It was a dark day."

Colin and Vinnie laughed in a manner that indicated she had said more than just the literal meaning of her words.

"Are you parents still..." Vinnie shrugged. "You know."

"Eeuw. No. Dad heads a congregation a few villages away and Mom is still with her old monastery. She loves to hear about the family here, but never wants to be part of this again. Both of them are happy with their lives."

I looked at this woman who was the epitome of elegance and exotic beauty. She exuded cultured class despite her childhood in a monastery. Or maybe because of it. What an interesting woman.

Vinnie was asking her increasingly personal questions. He seemed fascinated by her parental history. Francine tried to divert his attention by talking about online friends she made then and still had contact with.

"Do you have contacts in Kubanov's area?" I asked.

She sighed in relief and gave me a grateful look. "I know some people who know some people."

"You're lying. You have direct contact with people there." Her attempt at subtle deception amused and annoyed me. "Can you ask them to find out absolutely everything they possibly can about Kubanov?"

Vinnie stared at me in the same way as the other two. "What are you thinking, Jen-girl?"

"I don't know yet. The personal aspect to this whole thing makes me think there might be merit in looking into Kubanov's life."

"I'll give you everything I have on him," Colin said. He pushed in a bit closer to the table and lifted his knife and fork. "Most of the intel we had been able to gather on him surrounds his professional activities though."

"Above board and under the table," Vinnie added.

"But so far we have not been able to get a lot of info on his childhood, friends, family or anything personal for that matter." Colin pushed the scrambled eggs around on his plate. "It certainly felt personal to me when I was in that basement. I think you are right in delving deeper, Jenny."

Silence fell around the table as we started eating and I got lost in my thoughts about finding the hacker, bomber and Kubanov. Francine might just have more success with gathering information on Kubanov than she was having with locating the hacker.

Loud knocking on the front door pulled me out of my thoughts. Another body in my already people-polluted apartment. Vinnie moved to get up, but Francine stopped him with a hand on his shoulder.

"I'll get it."

Vinnie got up so fast, he scraped the chair on my wooden floors. I closed my eyes on a silent groan.

"Not to rain on your little feminist parade, Francine, but you are far from healthy enough to protect all of us if that is a bogey at the door." Vinnie pushed Francine gently back in her chair. "I will get it."

"It's most likely Manny," I said to Vinnie's back.

Vinnie grunted. "Like I said, bogey."

"Manny is not a bogey." I turned to Colin and lowered my voice. "What is a bogey?"

Colin had lost his relaxed body language, reminding me about his revelations last night. Being a friend, what was I to do? Was I supposed to force Colin to confront Manny about the perceived betrayal? Was I supposed to stay completely out of it? None of the friendship books I had read covered this topic. I didn't know what to do, so I studied Colin.

"Let it go, Jenny. I'm not dealing with this right now." He was becoming increasingly adept at reading me. I didn't know if I liked that.

"Okay," I said softly. I didn't want Manny to hear our

exchange, but he and Vinnie were arguing on the way to the table, so I didn't think he was paying attention. "I still want to know what a bogey is."

"It's a source of fear, danger or harassment." Manny looked pointedly at Vinnie when he spat out the last word. Then he lifted his nose, inhaled and turned to the table. "Breakfast? Is there any left?"

Vinnie made a noise that sounded very much like a growl. But he went into the kitchen to get a plate for Manny. The older man sat down in Vinnie's seat, next to Francine, and tilted his head at me.

"We checked out that list of scholarly types that you sent me. Nothing. Well, nothing worth mentioning. These people just read and teach."

"What about the security companies' computers?" I asked. "Have your people found anything?"

"Yes, it is just like you said." Manny looked towards the kitchen. He was impatient for the food. "I forgot to tell you, but there was a virus in the installation program that created a backdoor for the hacker to have full access to the system. At least this is what I remember from a very long and confusing IT explanation."

"And the forensics on the painting and the wrapping paper?" Colin asked.

"It's clean. Not a single print. The lab guys also didn't find any strange components on the painting. All a dead end. What about you, Doc? What have you got for me?"

It cost me a lot to not inquire into his motivation for provoking Vinnie by taking his chair. I managed to control myself and launched into the lengthy explanation of what Colin and I had uncovered in the early hours of the morning.

"So now we know that this emailing bomber is literate."

"More than literate," I said before Manny had a chance to say more. "His language patterns in the email and then in this code both show superior understanding of the nuances of the language. I would put his education level at higher than a simple university degree."

"Simple university degree." Manny rolled his eyes. "Some people don't think it's simple to acquire a university degree."

I waved away his comment. "Combined with the intricacies of the clues, he has a higher than average intellect, but is by no means a genius."

"That doesn't really help me, Doc. A face or name would be much better."

"You of all people should know how important profiling is while investigating a crime. It could very well be the profile that eliminates hordes of suspects and leads us to the true perpetrator."

"Is there any reason why we are not suspecting Kubanov?" Vinnie asked from the kitchen.

"We are," I said. "Personally, I don't believe he is sending these emails."

"I agree," Colin said. "This would be a direct link between him and the crime, something he doesn't do. No, he's using someone to hack computers and somebody else to build the bombs and send the emails."

"It fits that he would orchestrate such an elaborate plan," I said. "He would ensure that it is executed without a flaw, but there would be at least one, preferably two layers of people between him and the crime."

"So who the bloody hell is hacking computers? And who the bloody hell is sending emails and bombs?" Manny started counting on his fingers. "We know that the emailing bomber is educated and that he might or might not have a daughter who might or might not have some terminal disease."

"She might be dead already," I said, ignoring Manny's glare. He was angry even though we had so much more than we had had the day before. "Her death might have been the trigger that caused his mental devolvement."

"Still too many mights and might nots, Doc." A smile threatened at the corners of Manny's mouth when Vinnie threw a heaped breakfast plate down in front of Manny. "We need more than all this guesswork."

"Not guesswork, Millard." Colin spoke before I could express my utter disgust at having my careful analysis of data diminished to mere guesswork. "You know how Jenny's mind works. I would stand behind all of this as gospel."

Manny only huffed and continued eating. A few moments later he asked past a mouth full of scrambled eggs, "So what has your knickers in such a twist, Doc? What's not adding up for you?"

"There isn't another email," I said. I was too bothered by this to be worried about my apparent transparency. Or Manny's reference to my underwear. "After the last package, the painting, there was that email that took us to the bomb."

"You think there will be another bomb?" Manny quickly swallowed his food and glared at me. "Well?"

"Stands to reason, yes." I sighed. "Something's missing here."

No matter how hard I tried to figure out why there was no email and what the bomber or hacker's next step might be, I couldn't reach any other conclusion. It had to be another email.

"Jenny?" Colin's insistent call brought me back to the conversation around the table. I lifted an eyebrow at him. "Francine asked if you checked your spam."

"Of course not. Why would I do that? All those offers for penile enlargements and quick money are most aggravating."

"I changed the spam control settings for your email," Francine said. "When I was working on your computer, I strengthened the filters to send any email to the spam box if your computer didn't recognise the sender's address."

Francine was still busy explaining when I rushed to the far side of the table. I sat down in front of my computer. A few clicks later and I had my spam box open. I scanned past the Viagra and gambling offers. My breath caught when the email jumped out at me.

"It's here. I got another email. From Dante."

Chapter SIXTEEN

Everyone with the exception of Colin jumped up to stand behind me. I was hard pushed to not swat at them. At least Colin maintained his distance, even though he was leaning in to have a good view of the computer monitor. The concept of my privacy when it came to my computer and emails had long disappeared. It had only required one illegal, malicious hacker and one friend, Francine, for me to feel that computer protection and internet privacy had been a total illusion all along.

I sighed and enlarged the email for everyone behind me to read. Manny must have decided we needed to hear it out loud. "'The fulminant vengeance of the betrayed will visit upon those of false hope where the hogs, vocalist and weald abide.'"

"What the fuck does that mean?" Vinnie looked at the computer screen with total disgust. "Does this person not know how to speak normal English?"

"We have already established that he has a higher command of English than most users, Vinnie," I said. "This is just another code."

"A code with hogs, a vocalist and weald?" Vinnie snorted and moved back to his chair. "What the hell does 'weald' mean in any case?"

"A forest," I said. "It is an Old English word, related to Old Saxon."

"Okay, Doc." Manny straightened. The look he aimed at me conveyed expectation and urgency. "What do you make of all this?"

I looked back at the monitor and stared at the cryptic words while sorting through the influx of information. "Firstly, I think it is safe to say now that he is following a pattern. He sends a package which contains a clue, then he sends an email with another clue. The last clue led us to a bomb."

"Do you think it is the same here?" Manny asked.

"Yes," Colin said through clenched teeth. He was also staring at the monitor and I knew which word he was focussed on. "The bastard has set another bomb."

"How can you be so sure, Frey?"

"Fulminant," Colin said. He pushed his chair away from the table and got up. "You explain to him, Jenny. I'm making coffee."

"Fulminant means something occurs suddenly and or with great intensity. It can sometimes be used as a synonym for explosive in certain contexts."

Manny thought about this while looking at the email. I watched his thoughts pull at the *frontalis* and the *orbicularis oculi* muscles in his face. When the latter muscles narrowed his eyes and his nostrils flared, I knew he had come to a decision.

"Fuck! Fuck it all to hell!" He walked a few feet to the front door, returned, walked away again and returned again. "I have to phone GIPN again. What do I tell them, Doc? Where should we go?"

He didn't give me a chance to answer. His smartphone was already in his hand and he was tapping at the screen. He raised the phone to his ear and looked at me. "Well? Where the fuck should we go?"

"Millard!" Colin stormed from the kitchen straight for Manny. He stopped so close to the older man that their torsos were almost touching. He looked ten centimetres taller and much broader in the chest. These were physiological changes that took place when a man became the aggressor in a conflict. His voice was low and cold when he spoke. "Don't you fucking dare put Jenny in danger. You don't get to push her. You don't get to use her for your own agenda."

"Stand by," Manny said into the phone without taking his eyes off Colin. He lowered the phone and moved in so that their noses were almost touching. "Stand the fuck down, Frey."

Vinnie got out of his chair, his fists clenching and unclenching.

I wanted to groan, sigh and grunt in disgust, but mostly, I didn't want to have to deal with these people. Where was Phillip with his people skills and his calming presence? He would have known exactly how to defuse this situation.

I got up and warned Vinnie off with only lifting my hand. He didn't look happy about it, but he stopped and waited. I stood next to the two men facing off. Colin's nonverbal cues showed me he was on a hair trigger. The smallest mistake and there would be a physical altercation in my apartment.

"Colin, please let it go. Manny is just feeling the pressure of knowing that there is a bomb somewhere in the city." Nothing. No reaction from either of them. Logically I knew they had to hear me, but I had no indicators that this was true.

So I did what I almost never did. I put my hand in Colin's. "Please? Manny is not putting me in danger, Colin. He was rude, yes. But it's only because he wants to protect innocent people who might be in danger right now. If the bomber stays true to character, the bomb might be in a museum or a gallery. This is the type of place visited by a lot of people, especially families on a Saturday. We need to find out if there is a bomb and we need to find where it is."

Colin's hand tightened painfully around mine. He glanced at me and I took full advantage of it. I allowed all my emotions to express themselves on my face, knowing he would see it, understand it. "We can't spend this time fighting each other. If you want to protect me, you will help me figure out what this email means so that Manny can find the bomb. That way I won't even have to leave the apartment."

Some tension left his body. "Promise me you won't leave your apartment."

I tried to pull my hand back, but he wouldn't let go. "I'm not going to make such a broad promise. But I will promise that I will not go looking for any bombs."

He studied me for a few seconds before he turned to Manny. "Watch the way you speak to her, Millard. Be respectful."

"Are you done now with your little hissy fit? Should we hug before we continue?"

"Manny, your behaviour is provocative and unnecessary," I said and forcefully pulled my hand out of Colin's. "We are wasting time while you two are posturing."

That stopped Manny. He acknowledged this with a nod and brought the phone back to his ear. "Daniel? Yes, listen. We might have another bomb like we did on Wednesday. No, we don't know where it is yet. I was thinking that you should get your team and the bomb squad ready in case. Hm-mm. Yes. We are working on it now. As soon as we know, we'll give you the location."

He swiped at the screen and put his smartphone in his pocket. "So? How are we going to figure this out?"

I sat back down in front of my computer and stared at the words again. "He's talking about where the hogs, singer and forest abide. It must be somewhere that includes all these elements."

"A pig farm?" Francine frowned. "But that doesn't include the singer. Wait, let me go get my tablet. I can search for things much better with that."

I was glad she didn't want to use my computer. She got up with only a slight wince and walked to the front door.

"Where is she going?" Manny asked when she closed the door.

"Next door." I was surprised at the gasp coming from Vinnie. Then my shoulders sagged a little bit with the realisation. I looked at Vinnie until he started shifting from one foot to the other. "I am not lying to Manny. He will find out later in any case."

"Find what out?" Manny sat down and glowered at Vinnie as he also took a seat.

"Colin bought the flat next to mine. Francine and Vinnie are staying there at the moment."

Manny's eyes flashed in surprise. "Well, that might be a good thing. At least everyone is contained."

I was not the only one who took exception to Manny's phrasing. It would seem, however, that I was the only one who wanted to stay on topic. "Let's try to keep our focus on this email for the moment. You can argue and insult each other all you want at a later time."

"She's right," Colin said as he sat next to me. "Let's try to figure out where this bomb is."

Francine came back and joined us at the table with her tablet. She was swiping and tapping away non-stop. "I'm thinking that it might be a Communist-themed restaurant."

"How on earth did you get there?" I asked. The ideas that stemmed from her paranoia usually amused me.

"Two words, honey." She held up two fingers. "*Animal Farm.*"

A few times during our lunches, Francine had talked at length about the George Orwell book. She loved the writer. His work resonated well with all her conspiracy theories. "I can see where you would get pigs in there, but where would you get the singer and the wood?"

"Well, there are a few restaurants here in Strasbourg that have singing waiters. If the restaurant is one of those rustic ones with wooden décor, we have a match." She tapped away on her tablet, frustration evident on her face. "But I can't find anything like that here. Not a Communist-themed restaurant with singing waiters."

Manny was staring wide-eyed at Francine, his lips slightly parted in shock. Vinnie and Colin were smiling. I had grown used to Francine's outrageous theories that seldom were grounded in fact. I shrugged. "It was a theory. Let's try to look at the sentence as a whole."

"Okay," Colin said. "The bomber must feel that he is betrayed."

"Was," I said. "Looking at the code and the other email, I think something had happened some time ago that started all this. It was only something more recent that triggered him into action though."

"Maybe the person or persons who gave him false hope," Colin said.

"That would be too far a leap in logic for me. It is a feasible theory though." I tried to see beyond the words, but there was so little to work with. "Taking these large leaps is not comfortable for me, but I'm willing to try. In that way I would dare say that the bomb is his revenge on whoever he feels betrayed him. Where could hogs, a vocalist and weald be found together?"

"Surely it won't be somewhere in the forest. This guy wants visibility." Manny rubbed the back of his neck.

I closed my eyes, calling up the Andantino of Mozart's Piano Concerto No. 14. Maybe that would bring some clarity to my thoughts. I was only eight measures into the Concerto when I opened my eyes. Colin was moving around restlessly. It was distracting.

"What?" I asked when he sat down hard in the chair next to me.

"Could it be a painting?" He shifted closer and reached for my laptop. "May I?"

"Move it? Touch it? Work on it?" I threw my hands in the air. "Sure. Why not?"

He pulled my computer and I bit hard on my teeth at the sound of the rubber feet under the laptop dragging across the polished wood of my table. The laptop was now between the two of us, his arm in my personal space while he entered some words into a search engine.

"Look at this painting. It is a painting by John Singer Sargent, painted in 1908. It is titled Ilex Wood at Majorca with Blue Pigs. Here we have the hogs, the vocalist and the weald, but in different words. Pigs, Singer and Wood. Could this be it?"

I stared at the painting on the computer monitor. It was in definite impressionist style, a landscape with two girls in the foreground. Along the sides leading to the back were trees and the girls were surrounded by pigs one could argue were dark gray, gray or blue. It was, for the lack of a better word, pretty. Not something I wanted to hang in my apartment.

"Where is this painting?"

"It is usually in the US. At the moment it is on loan to the Museum of Modern Art here in Strasbourg." Colin sat up and started talking faster. "It is for the American-French Impressionist exhibition. The grand opening of the exhibition is tonight."

"Bloody hell." Manny was already tapping on his smartphone. "Daniel, we've got it. It's the Museum of Modern Art. Fifteen minutes? I can be there in five. Fine, fine. I'll meet you there."

It felt like there was a large piece of dry bread stuck in my throat. I didn't understand why I felt so strongly opposed to Manny going to the potential site of a bomb. Logic dictated that it was part of his job. "Do you have to go?"

"Of bloody course I'm going." He started for the door. Francine was out of her chair and in front of him before he had taken five steps.

"One minute. Just wait one minute." She pushed with the palm of her hand against Manny's chest for a second. Then she ran out of my apartment. It was not an elegant run, she was still favouring her side.

Manny turned to look at me. "Now what?"

I lifted both shoulders. "I have no idea. It seems important."

"Well, I can't stand around here all day. I have to get to the scene." He started walking to the door, straight into Francine. I got up and walked to them.

"Here we are. Let me put this on for you." Francine held out something that looked small and plastic. It was a clip-on camera. She took a step closer and before Manny could complain, clipped the camera on his jacket. "You won't even know it's there."

"You are not recording this." Manny lifted his hand to remove it and gave Francine a very angry look when she slapped his hand away.

"It is a brilliant idea. That way we don't have to worry about you, because we know exactly what is happening. We could also be of assistance if there are some other clues or maybe a trap in the museum."

Even I was impressed with Francine's reasoning. "She's right, Manny. It is a good idea. You can use your smartphone's headset to keep in contact with us. Your hands will be free."

"And you will be in my head. I don't think it's a good idea." He shook his head. "Not a good idea at all."

"It will make Genevieve feel much safer," Francine said. Her attempt at manipulation shocked me. What shocked me even more was that Manny lowered his hand and looked at me.

"Okay, Doc. I'll keep it on for you."

"Oh. Okay. Thanks." Before I could give in to the strong urge to reveal Francine's manipulations, Manny left.

"Come on, let's get connected." Francine reached out to me, but let her hand drop immediately. Instead she motioned with her head that I was to follow her to the dining room table. "I have that camera connected to my tablet, but we'll set it up on your computer. The screen is bigger and it will be easier for everyone to see."

"It would actually be much better in my viewing room," I said as I stopped at the table. Francine had taken my seat and was tapping away on the laptop's keyboard. I stood behind her, wondering why I was not more upset that she had so unceremoniously taken possession of my computer. I had always been obsessive about giving anyone access to my home, my computer, my viewing room, my life. This, which I had thought was ingrained and nigh-on impossible to change, had indeed morphed from compulsive distrust to something I had still to name.

"There." Francine leaned back in the chair and presented the monitor to us with two open palms. "He can't hear us yet, but we have visual and audio."

On the monitor was the view of Manny's hand on a steering wheel. Beyond that were the windscreen and a street flying past. Manny was driving extremely fast. It had at most been four minutes since he had left my apartment, but he was already turning into the museum's street. Again I felt discomfort in my chest and tightness in my throat.

"I sincerely hope he doesn't enter without waiting for the bomb squad."

Colin turned his chair to look up at me. "He's an arsehole, but he's smart, Jenny. He'll be fine."

I tried to smile, but my lips wouldn't cooperate. I merely nodded and looked at the monitor again. The view shook as Manny got out his car. "Oh, for the love of Pete, what are all these people doing here?"

"Who's he talking to?" I asked.

"Himself, most likely." Francine sat up and looked around the table. "Genevieve, where is your smartphone?"

"Why?"

"If we phone Manny we can put him on speakerphone like you said."

"Oh yes, of course." I retrieved my smartphone from my handbag and handed it to Francine. She stood up and handled my phone as if it were hers. I sat down next to Colin and gave in to the need to move the laptop so it was equally spaced between the two chairs. On the monitor Manny's hand obscured the view for a second and then he pulled out his smartphone.

"What now, Doc?"

"It's Francine. We have the camera going and you're on speakerphone. If you get your earpiece in, we're all set."

"Oh, bloody hell." He sighed loudly and opened the car door. It took him a moment to find the Bluetooth headset amongst a shocking number of documents on the passenger seat. Seconds later we were looking at the museum again. "Okay, you are now in my head. Happy, Doc?"

"I assume you are referring to my satisfaction with our connection and not my general state of being." I leaned towards my smartphone that Francine had placed on the table in front of us. "Then yes, I'm happy."

The camera shook with vertical forward movement. "Manny, where are you going?"

"To evacuate the building, missy. Now get out of my head until I need you or I'm disconnecting." He opened the door and the next four minutes were a flurry of activity. The security guard at the door had to locate the curator who had to be convinced of Manny's credentials. I was impressed with Manny's professional, controlled and calm handling of the situation. It was a side of him that I had not personally experienced.

People started exiting through the doors at the same time as the sound of sirens came closer. I was riveted to the monitor and only peripherally noticed that Vinnie and Francine were standing behind us. Manny was now speaking to the head of security and the curator. It would appear that there had been around forty people in the building preparing for the evening's grand opening. I hadn't been counting the people leaving the building, but an estimate had me sure only a handful could still be in the building.

The camera swung to the front doors. I recognised the two GIPN team members from the gallery. Quick introductions were made. Through the doors came a few more officers, one of whom looked familiar in a jarring way. My mind was flung back to the gallery when I had also noticed a man in a uniform who brought the same alarming recognition. If only I could place his features. If only I could put a name and date to the man who now moved off the screen.

"Doc, are you listening?" Manny's question halted my memory recall process. I had felt the name and date entering my conscious mind, but it was lost again. I must have taken too long to answer. "Bloody hell. Doc?"

"I'm here. I'm listening, Manny."

"What is the name of that painting again?"

"Ilex Wood at Majorca with Blue Pigs by John Singer Sargent." Colin answered before I could. Manny didn't acknowledge him. He relayed the answer to the GIPN leader and curator, and then the camera was moving again. Thankfully Manny was listening to the GIPN leader and staying behind the men dressed in appropriate gear.

They stopped at the entrance to a large room. The floor looked like polished cement, the walls painted a light plain colour. Lighting, cleverly worked into the ceiling fittings, lit the room. The walls were covered with paintings.

"There, that's the one." Colin pointed at a painting on the screen.

"It's on the wall to the left, Manny," I said towards the smartphone.

"We see it," Manny said. "Only speak to me now if you have something really important to say."

I didn't consider my affirmative answer to be really important, so I didn't answer. I continued watching. Manny turned around and I saw a young man wearing a blast-resistant suit. He wasn't wearing the helmet. I was about to ask where Edward was when a robot entered the room. I had once seen a similar robot on a news report about a bomb blast in the United States. I knew bomb squads often used these robots to enter buildings or rooms first.

It was a slow process and I was intrigued by the procedure that was carried out almost to a checklist precision. I relaxed a little, knowing that Manny would be safe with people who seemed to be competent in their job. After what felt like hours, but was only ten minutes, the robot had detected traces of explosives and the EOD technician was moving in. He was wearing his helmet. They had not been successful at getting the robot to handle the painting.

Manny had moved in behind one of the appropriately dressed policeman. On the monitor all we could see now was the back of his black protective uniform. Even the voices were difficult to discern. The seriousness of the situation had changed the verbal exchanges to only what was deemed necessary. Voices were clipped and often not loud enough to make out clearly what was being said.

"Doc, you there?" Manny moved from behind the policeman. "They're calling for my assist."

"I'm here, Manny. Are you sure it is safe to be there?"

"Must be if they're calling me." Manny walked past another bomb squad member and we could see where he was heading.

The EOD technician had taken the painting down from the wall and placed flat on the floor. The back was facing up and there was a device attached to it. In my ignorant, unprofessional opinion, it looked too flat to be a bomb. From what I could tell it was about the size of Francine's tablet.

"It's addressed to Doctor Lenard." The EOD technician pointed to a post-it note attached to the dark plastic box. It was larger than the normal-sized post-it notes and bright pink. On it was some writing, but Manny was too far away to have a clear view. He must have gone down on his haunches, because the painting was suddenly much closer. Unfortunately Manny was moving too much for the camera to focus so I could read what was on the note.

"What does it say?" I asked. On the monitor Manny reached for the note and paused. He was wearing his thin, black driving gloves and I wondered if it was cold inside the building.

"Is it safe to remove?" He must have asked the EOD technician because I was unqualified to answer that question.

"Sure."

The moment Manny's gloved hand touched the bright pink piece of paper the monitor lit up. It was as if someone had shone a spotlight directly into the camera. A heinous, loud hissing sound was followed by a moment of silence and then lots of shouting. The white on the screen faded to reveal the ceiling of the room. Had the camera fallen off or was Manny lying on his back on the floor? I was frozen in my chair. I could barely breathe not knowing what I was looking at, what had happened.

"Millard, what's going on?" Colin leaned towards the computer and smartphone. "Millard!"

The view on the monitor shook a little and Manny's hands came into view. As he turned them slowly from one side to the other as if in disbelief, they began shaking uncontrollably. His gloves were shredded, his hands red and bloody.

Blackness rushed at me faster than I had ever experienced it. One moment I was looking at Manny's shaking, damaged hands. The next moment there was only safe, warm blackness.

Chapter SEVENTEEN

I knew this time it had been bad. Worse than in a very, very long time. When the blackness receded and my mind returned to the reality in my apartment, it was dark outside. I was on the sofa, hugging my knees, keening softly and still rocking. It took almost a minute and a lot of rationalisation for me to stop rocking and let go of my knees.

"You're back," Colin said next to me. Close, but not touching. He had been reading, but the book now laid forgotten on his lap. His nonverbal cues told me he was worried. Extremely worried. "Are you okay now, Jenny?"

"How's Manny? Is he… is he…" I couldn't finish the question.

"The bastard is fine. He's in hospital now, his hands are pretty badly burned, but the doctors say he'll be okay."

"His hands will be okay?"

"His hands will be fine. The damage was mostly to the skin, no nerve or deep tissue damage. His gloves took most of the damage. A good thing he wasn't wearing latex gloves to handle the evidence. Those leather driving gloves saved his hands. As it is, the doctors don't think skin grafts will be needed."

"I want to see him." I stood up, but after numerous hours of sitting in one place, my body protested. Colin jumped up and caught me by my elbows just as my legs folded under me.

"Hey, slow down a bit." He gently pushed me back on the sofa. "You've been out of it for a while. Catch your breath first."

"How long was I like this?"

"Eight hours."

"How did I get here?" I looked at the sofa.

"You were rocking pretty strongly and I was scared you were going to fall off the dining room chair, so I carried you here."

He smiled at my dismayed expression. "You didn't particularly enjoy being touched. It was quite a fight to get you here."

"I'm sorry." I didn't know why I was apologising for something that was not in my control. I had worked hard to limit my exposure to things that could trigger such episodes. Watching Manny getting blown up by a bomb which had been addressed to me definitely qualified as a trigger. A trigger that I had not been prepared for.

Colin sat down next to me and took my hands in his. "Jenny, I didn't know what to do to help you. Francine researched this online and found that the best thing was just to leave you, but stay close enough so that you knew you weren't alone. Is there something I could've done differently?"

I mentally pushed away my embarrassment. "No. Oh God, this shouldn't happen anymore. I thought I had it under better control."

"So why was it so strong then?"

I considered my answer with great care. Admitting this was not easy. "It was the shock of seeing something violent happen to someone I care about that triggered my episode."

"You care about Millard?" Colin closed his eyes briefly and sighed. "Of course you care about Millard."

"I'm not being disloyal to you because I care about Manny. I know how you feel about him."

Colin stopped me by shaking his head. "I can't begin to tell you how much I don't want to talk about this, so I'm going to say this fast and hopefully never again. My anger towards Millard is not personal and it is. I believe that he should've been more suspicious about the intel that he was being fed. He should've double-checked it, he should've questioned it. But I also understand that once the big guns took over, he didn't have a say. He doesn't even know if anything came from that intel."

"He's just an easy target for your anger," I concluded.

Colin's lips tightened. "He makes it easy. But he is one of the few law enforcement types that I respect. He has integrity and a strong code he lives by and he's good at his job."

"I want to see him."

"Are you sure? He is in hospital."

"Why do you say it with such meaning? I thought you said he is okay."

"Oh, I just thought that you might want to wait until he is released because you don't like going to hospitals."

There was truth in what Colin said. I abhorred hospitals, but fleeting micro-expressions hinted at something more to his words. I gaped at him. "You are using my fears as a shield to hide behind. You are the one who doesn't want to visit Manny. Why not?"

My words caused Colin such discomfort that for a moment I thought he was going to leave. Eventually he groaned long and loud. "God, I really admire and sometimes even envy your skills. But it sucks being at the receiving end of it. Oh, never mind. Come on, I'll take you to the hospital."

He got up and held out his hand to me. His face told me he was closed to any further personal discussion. Just coming out of an episode, I didn't mind all that much putting that discussion off for later. Manny and Colin's relationship fascinated me and I intended to get back to this.

I surprised myself by putting my hand in his and allowing him to pull me up.

"Okay?" Colin asked, looking intently at me.

"I'm fine. I just got up too fast before. Can we go now?" I wanted to see Manny, to make sure for myself that he was okay. I wanted to hear him argue with me, be sarcastic and antagonise Colin.

"Sure, let's go."

The drive to the hospital was quiet. I didn't feel like talking. Colin was driving, his movements not as smooth as usual. The more we drove, the tenser his body became. I didn't have to study him to see this. It was clear even from the corner of my eye. He genuinely didn't want to go to the hospital. Or he truly didn't want to see Manny. I wasn't clear which.

We stopped in a tree-lined street fifteen minutes later. At

the entrance of the hospital I stopped. Colin held the door open for me, a puzzled look drawing his brows together. "Second thoughts?"

"Not at all." I cleared my throat. "I, um, just want to thank you."

"For?"

"Sitting with me for eight hours. For bringing me here."

Some of the tension left his body and he gave me a small smile. A genuine smile. "For you? Anything, anytime, Jenny."

"My parents used to force me to go to hospitals for tests. Every month there would be more tests to see if they could fix me." I smiled without humour. "As if I was broken. They wanted to fix me."

"And that is why you hate hospitals?"

I nodded.

"I, for one, am glad that they never managed to fix you." Colin waited until I looked at him to see his smile before he spoke again. "I like you just the way you are. Now move your butt. Let's go see how the arsehole is doing."

I almost sighed at his pugnacious behaviour when it came to Manny, but my mind was caught on his response to thanking him. I entered the warm interior of the hospital and shuddered at the unique smells that were definitive of each such institution. Colin's light touch to my elbow barely registered through my winter coat. I didn't mind the contact and allowed him to lead me. Apparently he knew where to find Manny.

We stopped at an open door to a private room. Immediately my mood lifted when I heard Manny arguing with someone about being released. I stepped into the room, forgetting about Colin. The room was surprisingly spacious, but not as nice as the room Francine had been in. This was much more clinical and reminiscent of the hospitals I had been to as a child. A cheap-looking reproduction of a Monet hung on one wall. There were two plastic chairs for visitors and a television high against the wall. A news programme was on, the sound turned down very low.

Next to the bed was a woman in a white coat trying to take Manny's blood pressure. She was short, stout and had a fierce expression on her face that I suspected was a permanent feature. Manny had a healthy colour in his face, despite the numerous little cuts and a burn on his left cheek. His left eyebrow was slightly singed and pulled into a severe scowl. He didn't notice me entering, his face turned away from the door, focussed on the nurse or doctor.

"It's just a little burn. I'll be fine at home, Doctor. I don't need to be here."

"Mister Millard, it would be much better if you were to stay the night. I strongly recommend that you don't stay alone tonight. Someone needs to observe you. You did suffer a strong blow to your head."

"Someone hit you on your head?" I asked, appalled. The doctor and Manny looked at me in surprise.

"Doc, tell the doctor here that I don't need to be in hospital." Manny tried to sit up, but the doctor pushed against his shoulder to keep him down. He scowled at her. I wondered at his lack of surprise at seeing me. He didn't even greet me. I wanted to smile.

"Are you a medical doctor?" The doctor let go of Manny's shoulder and held out her right hand. "I'm Doctor Marcell."

I looked at the doctor's hand and thought of all the sick people in the hospital, all the bacteria and viruses that she had been exposed to. I couldn't. I just couldn't.

"She's Doctor Genevieve Lenard and she doesn't shake hands," Manny said, sounding proud.

"I'm not a medical doctor," I said as I tucked my hands under my arms. "Did someone hit him on his head?"

"No." Doctor Marcell picked up the sphygmomanometer. "When he fell, he hit his head hard on the floor."

"I'm fine. I want to leave." Manny lifted his hands to emphasise his point. Both were encased in white bandages. The doctor caught one arm and fitted the inflatable cuff of the blood pressure machine on his arm.

I stepped closer to the bed, my eyes locked on the white wrappings. "What about your hands? Will they be okay?"

"As long as he follows the medical advice, takes his meds and doesn't use his hands for the next week, he'll be fine." She stood still for a moment, looking at the readings on the machine. "Your blood pressure is a bit high, but I think it might be because of your argumentative mood."

Colin snorted behind me and caught Manny's attention. "What are you doing here, Frey?"

"Looking after Jenny."

Something in his voice gave Manny pause. He looked at me and scowled.

"What's wrong with you? Have you done something that's going to piss me off, missy?"

His gruffness, rudeness and general lack of sensitivity caused an interesting reaction in me. My eyes filled with tears and an immense feeling of tenderness overwhelmed me. I blinked and swallowed.

"Oh, bloody hell, Doc. Are you crying?" Manny looked accusingly at Colin. "What's wrong with her?"

Colin stepped closer, looked at me and surprised everyone except the doctor by putting his arm around my shoulders and pulling me under his arm. "You are such an arsehole, Millard. Look at what you've done now. Only you could make Jenny cry."

For a moment I stood stiffly under Colin's arm. His hand softly rubbed my shoulder and I relaxed slightly against him. The high comfort I drew from this closeness perplexed me. Neither of my relationships with these two men fitted with any previously observed behaviours. Actually, I had to include Francine and Vinnie as well. My relationship with Phillip had always been professional and on a level that I could analyse and understand. With these four people far too many emotions were involved.

"I didn't make her cry. Did I, missy?"

"Of course you did." As Colin leaned aggressively towards Manny, he turned me away, placing himself between us. "She hates hospitals, never goes into a hospital, but she rushed here as soon as she could. And this is the way you treat her?"

"Why couldn't you come earlier?" Manny asked around Colin. "What happened?"

Colin's whole body stiffened next to me. He must have realised that he had revealed something personal that I might not have wanted Manny to know. He squeezed my shoulder. "Nothing happened. She's here now and you're making her cry. Be nice to her."

"I'm not crying," I said and wiped angrily at the one tear that made it down my cheek. "I wanted to, but I'm not. I don't understand that. Why would I want to cry when I'm happy that you are okay and rude to me?"

The doctor uttered a strangled sound and we all looked at her. "Oh, sorry. I think I will leave now."

"Make sure you get my paperwork sorted so I can leave the death trap." Using his elbows, Manny pushed himself a bit higher on the pillows. "I'm not spending the night here."

"Will you take care of him?" The doctor looked at me. I moved in closer under Colin's arm.

"Oh, we'll take care of him." The complete lack of tonal inflection made me turn my head to study Colin. He was planning something that I was sure Manny would find most unpleasant. He smiled down at me. "Don't worry, Jenny. He's not staying with us."

"I'll give you instructions on how to keep an eye on him during the night." Doctor Marcell was by the door before any of us could say another word. "I'll get the paperwork done."

"Colin?"

Manny spoke before I could ask Colin to explain himself. "I'm not staying in the same apartment as you, Frey. Doc here I can handle, but I'm not looking into your ugly mug first thing in the morning. Just take me to my hotel."

"No." There was strength in my voice. "Either you stay in hospital or you're coming with us."

"And where exactly does your boyfriend plan to put me?"

"He's not my boyfriend." I pulled myself away from Colin's comforting warmth and looked up at him. "Where do you plan to put him?"

A malicious smile pulled at the corners of Colin's mouth. "He can stay next door. There is a beautiful extra room."

As expected Manny's face turned red and for the next ten minutes the two men argued viciously. Personally I didn't care where Manny stayed. As long as he was safe and someone was looking after him. Despite Vinnie's antagonism towards Manny, he would enjoy taking care of and irritating Manny. Francine would enjoy the task even more.

The arguing in the hospital room grew tedious. I walked away from the bed and stared at the television. The new president was addressing journalists at a news conference. Staff and bodyguards were squeezed in next to him on stage. It was a triumphant day for him. He had managed to get a new bill passed, something that would bring change to the country's economic situation. Needless to say some journalists were aggressive in their attempts to solicit answers from the head of the nation.

My mind wandered away from the controversial politics on television. For the first time since I had witnessed the explosion of the bomb, I let my thoughts roam. The more I thought about it, the more questions came to mind. Questions much more important than the argument still going on behind me.

"Have you heard anything more about the bomb?" I asked as I turned around. Colin and Manny ceased their verbal assault on each other and looked at me.

"I spoke to Edward earlier. He came by. Why?"

"What did he say about the bomb?" I frowned. "Where was Edward? Why wasn't he there? And what about the young man next to you when the bomb exploded? Is he okay?"

"Slow down with the questions, Doc. Edward and his team were on a different assignment. This young chap was supposed to be almost as good as Edward."

"He screwed up?" Colin asked.

'They don't know yet what went wrong. Edward hinted at not following SOP. There will be a full investigation and the young guy has been suspended. And to answer your question, Doc, he's okay. He wore a bleeding blast suit, didn't he?"

"How was it detonated?" Colin asked.

"Remotely. They've determined that the range could not have been farther than twenty-five metres."

"That's inside the museum," I said. "Didn't the police evacuate everyone?"

"They did," Manny said. "Only members of the bomb squad and the police were in the building at the time of the explosion."

"The bomber is a policeman." I shook my head. "No, it doesn't make sense. Maybe he only wore the uniform to gain access, but none of the clues we have right now indicate that he has any connection to law enforcement."

"Generally policemen are not as poetic as this guy," Colin said.

Manny shrugged. "I agree with you on this one, Frey. There are always exceptions though."

"Have they looked at the security videos?" I asked. "Have they determined who was out of place there?"

"I didn't ask. As soon as I get out of this hell hole, I'll find out." He looked at his hands and sighed. "I might need some help making phone calls."

"I'm sure Francine will get you set up with all kinds of hands-free gadgets," Colin said. The more I thought about it, the more his suggestion for Manny to stay next door carried merit. I decided not to say it and risk another ten-minute argument.

"What about that post-it note? I can't imagine it survived the explosion."

"It didn't," Manny said. "Can you remember what was written on it?"

"You weren't close enough for me to get a good look. I never saw it. Do you remember anything?"

"It looked like a bunch of Roman numerals to me. For the life of me, I can't remember what they were."

"Hold on," Colin said and took out his smartphone. Within seconds, he spoke into it. "Hey, honey. Quick question. Did you by any chance record the whole thing this morning? Hm-mm. Great. Thanks. Yeah, see you guys later."

He tapped the screen and looked at us. "Francine recorded everything that we had seen this morning. She is busy working on the visuals to get clearer images, especially the post-it note."

"That is fantastic," I said. "I was worried that we had lost that clue."

"There was another clue for you, Doc." Manny pushed himself up again using his elbows. His hand must have touched something, because he winced with a shudder. "Bloody hell, it hurts."

'Then stop moving, idiot." Despite Colin's harsh tone and words, I witnessed concern softening his eyes.

"Tell me about the other clue." If I got them to focus on the case, they might not argue again.

"Edward said that there was a little blast-proof box attached inside the casing behind the painting. Inside the box was a sheet of paper with rows of numbers like on the other bomb."

"Can I get a copy of that?"

"I'll get the bomb guys to email it to you. They're pretty worried about these bombs in the city. There are all kinds of talks about terrorists and extremists. We won't have any problem getting the police's cooperation. Everyone just wants this to stop."

The expression on Manny's face caused adrenaline to make my stomach feel as if it suddenly hollowed out. I felt the need to hold on to something to keep myself anchored. I walked closer to the bed and put my hand on the covers.

"What is wrong, Manny? What are you not telling me?"

I didn't think his pained expression and closed eyes were connected to physical pain. It had to be bad and I braced myself for whatever he would say.

"The casing was clever. It was made so that it looked

different when it was x-rayed. It was something with lead and something else too. Edward explained it with lots of fancy-shmancy words. But the important part is that inside the casing was a delivery device that has these guys' panties in a twist."

"English, please. What delivery device?"

"It was empty, thank God, but the delivery device is perfect for a biological."

"Are you saying that it could have been a biological weapon released into the air?" Colin asked, his voice tight.

"That is the gist of it, yes." Manny closed his eyes again. He might pretend that he was okay, but there were enough indications to let me know he was suffering physically. He opened his eyes and looked at me. "Doc, we have to stop this. It's getting bigger and worse as time goes on."

"I know, Manny. As soon as I get home and have access to the videos and the notes, I'll work at figuring this out." I refused to allow my mind freedom to think about the possible consequences of a biological bomb. I had no doubt that thinking about that would debilitate me to the point of intellectual paralysis. I needed to be useful. I needed to solve this mystery.

"If there is anyone who can do it, it is you. Anything you need, Doc. We have to stop this."

"We have to figure out who is involved in this and what their motivations are," I said. "Why I am being targeted and by whom. Then we'll be able to stop them."

There was so much to think about. A burning desire to be in front of my computer pushed at me. Already a few connections were hovering around my conscious mind. But first I had to follow an idea that made me eminently proud of myself. Even Phillip would be impressed.

"Did you say I can have anything I need?" I asked.

"Anything, Doc."

"I need you to stay next door, be safe, allow us to help you and not instigate violent verbal disagreements with Vinnie and Colin." I moved a bit closer to the head of the bed, ignoring

Manny's disapproving expression. "When the time comes, I will ask you to listen and you must."

Suspicion replaced the disapproval. "Listen to what?"

"Whatever I ask you to."

He was quiet for a few seconds. "Don't I always listen to you?"

"No. You often jump to conclusions and judgements. Strong arguments are often needed to get your attention. This time I would want you to listen first."

"I can do that." He frowned at me. "Why do you think listening would be more difficult for me than staying with a gang of criminals?"

"I'm not going to argue with you. I'm going home now to figure out how we can stop this."

I didn't wait for either man to respond. The reason I had come to the hospital was to see with my own eyes that Manny was okay. He was. Not even verbal sparring with him could keep my attention away from the white walls, the smells and sounds of the hospital. Pressure in my chest gave me plenty of warning and I wasn't planning on having any more episodes today. Hopefully not in the foreseeable future.

Colin fell into step next to me only a few metres from Manny's room. "I told him his transport will be here soon. He's not happy, but he'll stay next door."

I waited until we were outside in the crisp winter air before I turned to Colin. "You are being cruel to him."

"Harmless cruelty, Jenny. Harmless." He smiled and I realised how seldom I had seen genuine smiles from him. Only for a moment did I feel guilty that I was glad that teasing Manny could take away the pain that I saw in Colin's eyes. After this case, I would speak to Phillip. He might know what I could do to make Colin smile more. Maybe he could recommend some books that I could read.

Chapter **EIGHTEEN**

"Those are the last numbers," I said. I had been in front of my computer from the moment we had arrived back at my apartment. It had taken a frustrating and exasperating two hours before the bomb squad had emailed me a scanned copy of the code left in the blast-proof box. Colin had stormed in from his bedroom when I called him rather frantically to help me with the code. "Does it make sense? What does it say?"

"Again just a jumble of words, Jenny." Colin threw the notepad on the table. "We need to take a break. It's past eleven already."

"You take a break. I need to find the key to this code." We had already tried four different ways of decoding the numbers. All failed attempts. Emotional exhaustion weighed heavily on me, but I did not want to give up in favour of sleep. "I will try another way."

"This book might not hold the key this time. Check your email again."

I opened my inbox and also checked the spam box. "Nothing. There isn't another package. It must be this book."

Colin stood up. "I'm going to take a quick shower. When I get back, you are going to bed. We can get back to this tomorrow morning after a night's rest."

I ignored him, leaned back in my chair and closed my eyes. If he wanted to give up, he was welcome to. I was determined to not allow my fatigue to halt any progress in preventing a potential disaster. Mozart filled my mind and I surrendered to its soothing sounds. I could only hope this tried and tested method would bring clarity to my problem-solving mind.

"Up we go." Colin's voice was gentle and close to my ear. I opened my eyes the moment he slid his hands under my knees and my upper back, and lifted me effortlessly against his chest. Every muscle in my body stiffened.

"What are you doing?" My voice was hoarse and it felt like I had just come out of a deep sleep, not a Mozart mind-moment.

"Taking you to bed." He started walking to my bedroom.

"Put me down. I can walk there." I didn't struggle in his hold, too scared that I might hurt his leg or that he would drop me. And my body felt lame with exhaustion.

"Oh, hush. We're almost there." He walked straight to my bed and gently lowered me until I felt the soft bedding under me. I couldn't recall ever being on my bed fully dressed. He sat down next to me and leaned a bit closer. "You are going to take off your clothes, get under the covers and sleep. No arguing."

"You didn't have to carry me. You could've just woken me up." I tried to sit up, but his warning look stopped me.

"You were tired enough to sleep upright in your chair, Jenny. I was hoping to not wake you up at all."

"How did you know I was sleeping?" He had never before thought I was sleeping when I was in my head, working out some complex issue.

He smiled. "Your head was tilted to the side and your mouth was a bit open. I think I even heard a snore or two. Now stop arguing with me and promise me that you'll go to sleep."

I closed my eyes and resisted a groan. I was wavering between annoyance and embarrassment that Colin had caught me sleeping in a chair. With my mouth open no less. "Okay, fine, I'll go to sleep."

He touched my hand and I opened my eyes. He was still smiling. "Sweet dreams, Jenny."

"You too." I knew this had been the right response when his smile deepened. He blinked once slowly and left my room. Only when my bedroom door clicked closed behind him did all my muscles relax into my bed. I didn't stay there for too long. I knew that it would take less than a minute for me to fall asleep and I needed to go through my nightly ritual to ensure a restful night.

When I woke up to the faint smell of coffee, I felt refreshed and grateful to Colin for insisting that I took a break. A quick glance at the clock on my bedside table told me that it was half past six. I had slept almost seven hours. A very good night indeed. The knowledge that I might have a good path to the clue rushed me through the shower and into the kitchen.

Colin was watching television and drinking coffee. He too looked rested when he smiled at me. "You look much better. You slept well?"

"I did, thanks." I watched the coffee machine sputter coffee into my mug. "I think I know how to decode the numbers."

"See," he said as he stood up and walked into the kitchen. "I knew you needed a good night's rest. You should always listen to me. I'm always right."

"Unfortunately I can't agree with you. I could always listen to you, but you aren't always right. I'm smarter than you and I'm not even always right."

Colin struggled to swallow his coffee before laughing. He nodded while still chuckling. "Of course you would take that seriously. I was just teasing, Jenny. I know I'm not always right."

I wondered how much of my surprise at the lightness in his tone and eyes showed on my face. It wasn't only surprise that I experienced though. Relief also made me feel lighter. It had been less than a week since Colin came back into my life. In that week I had observed the anguish in his eyes diminish a little bit every day. This morning he almost seemed like the old Colin who had first broken into my apartment.

"Teasing." I had been too distracted by the pleasant change in his mood to have noticed the nonverbal cues.

"Yes, teasing." He nodded towards the dining room table. "So, what have you got for us?"

I turned off the coffee machine, took my mug and walked to the table. "I have no rational reason to be so convinced of this, but I strongly believe that this book is the key to the second code. We just need to find how to fit it in there. So far we tried the original Ottendorf cipher with the letters, we tried the words, and we tried the words like in the first clue. What we haven't tried is working the numbers backwards."

Colin sat down next to me, pulled the notepad closer and shrugged. "Why the hell not? Let's take it from the bottom to the top."

We spent an unproductive two hours trying every which way to decipher this code. It felt like an exact repeat of the previous time. I pressed my fingers hard against my temples. "I'm missing something."

Our second attempt to break the code had given us a string of letters. Out of sheer desperation I turned to my laptop and entered them in the URL bar.

"What are you doing?" Colin asked.

"Taking a chance—"

"Oh my God, Jenny." His voice lifted in excitement as he moved closer. A webpage had opened. It was a simple black background with gold lettering in an antique font taking up most of the page. We stared at it.

"This sentence must make sense to them," I said, still staring. "Thus it should make sense to us once we find the context."

"What context can be found in this? 'The world will know that wronged men stood against a tyrant, that the righteous stood against the protected arrogant, and before this battle was over, even a god-king and his queen can bleed.'"

Familiar scratching sounds at my front door drew my attention as the door opened. Vinnie stepped through the door with an unfamiliar expression on his face. He appeared taller than usual, the smile around his mouth and eyes making the long scar on his face stand out even more. Following closely behind him was a clearly irritated Manny.

Vinnie was wearing his usual outfit of combat pants, this time dark brown. His long-sleeved black T-shirt stretched tight over his muscular torso. If I had not known his kind heart, I would have been intimidated by the strength and danger he exuded. Next to him Manny looked like a homeless man. Clean, but definitely homeless. Usually the rumpled look only extended to his undone top button, off-centre tie and wrinkled coat. This morning even his pants were wrinkled. Dark rings under his eyes added to the numerous little cuts and the burn on his cheek to make him look worse for wear.

"Good morning, sunshines." Vinnie was in a good mood. Studying the two men, I surmised that the lift in his tone came from having Manny in his territory. Most likely taking great pleasure in challenging Manny's patience. Even now I was surprised that Manny had agreed to moving in next door. I knew he would never go anywhere he didn't want to. That led me to the question of his motivation for staying with two people he considered criminals, one of whom he highly disliked.

"Morning, Vinnie. Manny, did you sleep well?" I asked, proud of my social skills.

Manny walked straight to the table and fell into a chair. "The arsehole kept waking me up, so no. I did not sleep well. I'm tired."

"And cranky," Vinnie said from the kitchen. He was taking ingredients from the fridge, no doubt to start making breakfast. "Gramps here has no appreciation for the tender care I have been giving him. He cussed at me and called me all kinds of names every time I woke his sorry arse up to make sure he doesn't go into a coma. Ungrateful old man."

Colin made no effort to cover his smile which made Manny scowl even more. I dropped my head forward with a sigh. "Please don't irritate each other. I don't know how to handle a situation like this and we have much more important things to focus on. We need to find the context of this cryptic sentence."

Manny sat up. "What cryptic sentence? Did you decode those numbers?"

"Jenny figured it out," Colin said, his smile and lightness gone. He looked at the laptop monitor and cleared his throat. "'The world will know that wronged men stood against a tyrant, that the righteous stood against the protected arrogant, and before this battle was over, even a god-king and his queen can bleed.'"

"What the bloody hell does that mean?" Manny lifted his bandaged hands in a questioning gesture. Seeing his hands made me realise how unsuited I was in caring for people. So much for being proud of my social skills.

"Um, how are you feeling, Manny?" Instead of concerned, my voice sounded businesslike. I softened my tone. "How are your hands?"

"Fine." Manny frowned at me and waved one of his bandaged hands at me. "Tell me more about this sentence. What have you figured out so far?"

"Not much," I said. "All I can think of is that this sounds very much like an act of revenge."

"It is from *300*." Vinnie walked closer, holding a mixing bowl against his chest and whisking the contents with fast expertise. "King Leonidas said this to Xerxes."

"Are you talking about King Leonidas who led a small army of about three hundred men to confront King Xerxes' army at Thermopylae?" I asked.

"Wow." Vinnie's eyes widened. "I never would've figured you to be the kind of gal to watch those movies."

"What movies?" I asked. "I'm talking about fifth-century history. What are you talking about?"

"Only the coolest movie ever, Jen-girl." Vinnie briefly stopped whisking to glance at the front door as Francine entered. "Ah, you're here. Tell them how cool Gerald Butler is in *300*, Francine."

"That hottie?" Her posture changed from her usual model poise to a sensual stroll as she walked to the table. "Ooh, in that movie he was the sexiest thing on screen for almost three years. That body."

"Enough!" Manny's hands hovered above the table. It looked like he wanted to slam them on the table, but that would have caused considerable agony. "I don't care about the actors. Tell us about this king."

"Xerxes is the bad guy in this movie," Vinnie said. "Well, I suppose in real life too since the movie was based on history.

Anyway, he had an argument with Leonidas who said to him that…"

Vinnie looked at Francine and both of them spoke at the same time. "'The world will know that free men stood against a tyrant, that few stood against many, and before this battle was over, even a god-king can bleed.'"

They ended their quotation in loud, dramatic voices. Vinnie had taken the whisk out of the bowl and held it up in the air like a sceptre. I flinched when batter dripped from it onto my pristine floors. Colin chuckled and Manny looked disgusted.

"Are those the exact words from the movie?" I asked, glaring at the two round drops on the floor. "You're going to have to clean that, Vinnie."

"No probs, Jen-girl." Vinnie lowered his hand and started whisking again. "Of course those are the exact words. A true *300* fan would never misquote King Leonidas."

"There are significant differences between that quote and this sentence," I said and took the notepad from Colin. "He used 'wronged men' instead of 'free men', the 'righteous' instead of 'few', 'protected arrogant' instead of 'tyrant' and he added 'his queen' to the promise that they can bleed. This must have meaning to the bomber."

"What meaning?" Francine asked as she sat down next to Manny.

"That's the million-dollar question," Colin said. On his request Francine repeated the movie quotation and he wrote it down on the notepad. "Okay, so I would guess that he felt that he was wronged and that he's righteous. Also that this tyrannical god-king is arrogant, protected and has a wife. Does that make sense to anyone?"

"I agree with your assumption," I said. "I'm pretty sure that the king and his queen are symbolic rather than real. It must represent someone in power, someone powerful enough to have some form of immunity against prosecution for committing some wrongdoing."

"Bloody bleeding hell." Manny slumped back in the chair.

"That is almost every single politician and rich man on this planet. And a large number of criminals."

"No, it is not," I said. "It is someone who is connected to the bomber, the hacker or me in some obscure way. I'm still of a mind that the bomber and the hacker are also emotionally connected in some way."

"And the hacker has an accomplice who is much more skilled than him. An expert," Francine added.

"That leaves us with a lot of players in this game," Manny said. "Kubanov, the hacker, his expert help and the bomber. Are we leaving someone out?"

"The guy emailing and sending packages," Vinnie said from the kitchen. Appetizing smells were coming from the kitchen and I realised how hungry I was.

"Are these all separate people?" Colin asked.

"An astute question," I said. "It is almost impossible to determine. But if we can find a connection between these people, we can find out if they are one or four people. And who they are targeting."

"I thought they were targeting you," Francine said, looking at me.

I willed away the panic threatening to steal my attention. "No, this revenge is not against me."

"How can you know this, Doc?"

"None of the Bible verses apply to me," I said absently. My mind was trying its best to connect all the bits of information I had received, but to no avail.

"What Bible verses, Jenny?" Colin asked. There was complete silence in my apartment, everyone watching me.

"Oh, the post-it note," I said. "Francine emailed me a screenshot of the post-it note that was on the bomb."

"I was able to zoom in and depixelate the image enough to have a clear image," she said.

"And you didn't tell me, missy?" Manny's voice boomed through the apartment. Colin tensed next to me and Vinnie turned away from the stovetop to glare at Manny.

"I was going to. We haven't had time to get there yet."

"When did you figure this out?"

"Francine emailed it last night. It didn't take long to decode."

"So what was it?" Manny leaned forward. I had been so focussed on the cipher that I had forgotten to even tell Colin about the post-it note.

"Two Bible verses."

Both Colin and Vinnie groaned.

"Why is it that these guys always find a way to bring the Bible into their sick fantasies?" Vinnie asked. "I bet it is some Old Testament verse with loads of blood and guts. Or maybe from Revelations about the end of the days. Everything is always so much worse with all those thou's and thy's."

"Actually you were right with your first guess. The Roman numerals pointed to two verses, both from Exodus. The first came from Exodus 20 verse 5." I opened a file on my computer. "This is the verse where God says that He is a jealous God and, I'm quoting now, 'visiting the iniquity of the fathers upon the children unto the third and fourth generation of them that hate me'."

"Even without the thou's and thy's it sounds terrible," Vinnie said. "Freaking psychos."

"The second verse?" Colin asked quietly next to me.

"From Exodus 21 verses 24 and 25." Again I read the verse from the computer screen. "Eye for eye, tooth for tooth, hand for hand, foot for foot, burn for burn, wound for wound, stripe for stripe."

"Oh, that is so definitely revenge." Francine hugged herself. "This is not good."

"Okay Doc, now tell me how you know this is not aimed at you."

"I don't have children." The blank looks I received upon my factual announcement made me groan. I was going to have to explain. "This person or persons wants their revenge to be taken out on the child or children of whoever has done them wrong."

"The god-king," Colin said. "Can't it be that you are the child unto the third and fourth generation? That you are the one who has to suffer for something your parents or grandparents have done?"

"I thought about that and no, I don't believe so."

"Sorry, Doc, just your say-so does not convince me. Tell me about your family history."

"No." I slowly looked at the four people in my apartment. "Why would I need to? I'm sure that all of you already investigated my background. I don't think there is anything I could tell you that you don't already know."

The flashes of guilt on their faces were all the confirmation I needed. Rationally I understood why they had done this. It still irked me. I grunted in disgust.

"Doc, I had to make sure you were up for the job. I will not apologise for that." The contrite look on his face belied his words. "Please tell us about your family. There might be something I missed that could be a clue."

"There is nothing," I said, louder than necessary. I breathed deeply, studying Manny's face. This time he didn't get annoyed, flinch or say something scathing. He allowed me to see his determination. "Okay, fine. But I'm not happy to do this."

"Noted."

There was an expectant silence in the apartment. Vinnie was the only one making a light noise bringing plates of food to the table. One more plate and everyone started eating. Manny was awkwardly clutching a fork in his bandaged fist. He growled when the scrambled eggs fell off the fork before reaching his mouth. When Francine offered to feed him, he gave her a vicious look and continued struggling. It failed to amuse me. I had lost my appetite and pushed the scrambled eggs around my plate.

"My maternal grandparents were farmers who had a small farm in North Carolina in the US. They were part of a farming community, never did anything extraordinary with their lives. My paternal grandparents were both British. They moved to

France shortly after the Second World War, teaching English at a primary school in a small village in the south. Also never did anything worth mentioning.

"My parents met at university in New York. Both studied law. By the time they had me they were both in the diplomatic service. Their whole lives had been very carefully constructed to never offend anyone and to impress everyone." I stopped to take a few calming breaths. I didn't want to be overwhelmed by the memories of my parents' willingness to sacrifice anything and everything to keep up appearances. It was a long time ago and I had dealt with it. I had accepted that I had never fitted into their picture perfect lives. I had been the one flaw that they had to contend with. The one imperfection in their otherwise perfect lives. They had been more than happy to get rid of that blot on their combined successes when I had decided to leave.

"Jenny?" Colin moved a bit closer, his posture protective. "Are you sure your parents never, ever made any enemies? Maybe something they did or said to someone that you don't know about? They did live international lives. They could have made enemies."

"Everyone loves them." I shook my head. I could only manage a whisper. "They are highly respected everywhere they go. I was their only enemy."

"Oh, honey." Francine put her knife and fork down and looked at me with tears in her eyes. "Some people never know when they have the biggest gift right in front of them. I'm not one of those people. None of us are."

"Right on, Francine." Vinnie's fierce look blasted right past the shields I had constructed to keep people out of my emotions, to protect myself. He leaned forward. "You're our girl. My Jen-girl."

Colin took my hand and pressed it against his chest. "They didn't deserve you, Jenny. I don't even think we deserve you."

"For once I agree with these criminals, Doc." Manny's voice was gruff. Unfamiliar tears blurred my vision. When did this quest to find a bomber become about my personal history and my relationships with the people I was sharing a meal with? I felt overwhelmed by the kindness shown to me. Panic started creeping up on me.

"Okay, let's assume that the revenge is not aimed at Jenny," Colin said. The businesslike tone in his voice removed the emotional atmosphere around the table. It became easier for me to breathe again. "So now we have to find that connection that binds all of these—"

A loud beep came from the tablet lying next to Francine's plate. She jumped in her chair and stared wide-eyed at the device for a second before she grabbed it and started tapping and swiping the screen. "Oh my God, oh my God, oh my God. I think… no, no, no… not think. He logged on. I have found the hacker! We have that fucking bastard."

Chapter **NINETEEN**

"You're just going to have to suck it up, Doc. They're only going to interview him tomorrow." Manny sat down heavily on the sofa, carefully resting his hands on his thighs. "I can't help that he's still in surgery."

This was most annoying. We needed all the information we could get from the hacker. The moment Francine had given Manny the hacker's IP address and even GPS coordinates, everything had happened so fast, my mind was still reeling. Within an hour a response team had captured the hacker. He had tried to escape and got injured in the process.

"They're still putting pins in his arm and he'll be out for the rest of the night." Manny shook his head. "Idiot. Why do they always think they can outrun the cops?"

I didn't miss the shared look of impertinent humour between Colin and Vinnie. How many times had they run away from the police and gotten away? When I had met Colin, he told me that the thrill of the crime was outwitting the system. Was outwitting and outrunning the police just as thrilling? I didn't think it prudent to ask that question. Not when the three men had reached a highly fragile truce due to this new development.

"It's a miracle he's alive after falling out of that window," Francine said, swiping and tapping on her tablet. She was sitting next to Manny on the sofa. Colin and I occupied the other sofa and Vinnie had moved a wingback chair closer to join us. Francine turned the tablet to show us the photo of an overweight young man. His hair was long and looked greasy, his T-shirt dull and wrinkled. "He's not the most athletic of young students."

"Have you been able to get more information on him?" I asked. Earlier, while Manny had been pacing up and down my apartment, speaking into the headset, Francine had been working her way into the university's database and a few other places to find out more about the hacker.

"You know the little twerp's name is Luc Alain, he's twenty-four years old and a full-time student." Francine turned her attention back to her tablet, swiping and tapping. "I found out that his major is in electronic engineering and his grades are very mediocre. I was surprised that he's not living in his parents' basement. He seems that kind of guy. His flat is registered in his name, but the records show that it was bought a few weeks before his eighteenth birthday by his father."

"Rich kid's equivalent of daddy's basement," Vinnie said.

"Word." Francine's body language and her tone told me her incorrect use of that word was an expression of agreement. It was not the first time she had used it. She smiled at me. "Now that I have his name, I will have everything on him. Like the fact that he attended a few of your classes."

"He did?" The few times I was a guest lecturer at universities, the venues were always packed. There was no conceivable way that I could've noticed him.

"Yup. He registered for two of your lectures."

"But I never had any contact with him. I would've remembered that. So why is he targeting me? What have I done to him?"

"Don't know that yet." Francine looked at her tablet again. "I've got a program running trying to find any and all connections or even possible connections between you and this little–"

"Dickwad," Vinnie finished her sentence. He looked defensive when all eyes turned to him. "What? He's that and much more. I have a few more very descriptive phrases, but out of respect for the ladies here will hold back."

"Thanks, Vin," Francine said. "So this… dickwad has a car far too expensive for a student. He has a few parking fines. All the fines were issued on the same street. Looks like he never drives his expensive car. Twerp."

"Typical geek," Vinnie said. "He most likely only drives cars on computer games, and lives an extraordinarily exciting online life. Put those guys in real life and most of them can't cope."

"I'm coping just fine, thank you very much." Francine pointed at herself. "Not all geeks are fashionless losers living off their parents."

"Sorry, darlin'." Vinnie shook his head. "You're one in a million. All the other geeks are spineless losers."

I had to agree with him. Francine was nothing like the computer specialists I had previously had the displeasure of meeting. This morning Francine was back to her old wardrobe. She was wearing jeans that I knew had a price tag that could feed a family of four for a week. At one of our lunches she had explained to me at length the better fit and value of said jeans. I still thought that my retail jeans fitted me well.

Francine's outfit was completed with a simple long-sleeved black T-shirt, a light brown thermal winter vest, a designer scarf and antique jewellery. Her brown, knee-high boots added a few centimetres to her height.

She looked like she had stepped off a fashion advertisement billboard. Her exotic looks no longer required such careful make-up as earlier this week. There was no more swelling or dark bruises. To my untrained eye in such matters, she was strikingly beautiful. And smiling sweetly at Vinnie.

"Thanks, Vin. You're not too shabby yourself." She looked down at her tablet. "Okay, back to Luc, our little twerp-hacker. He's been at university now for six years and still hasn't graduated. He changed courses twice and... oh, lookie here. He even studied literature for a semester."

I shifted in my seat, resisting the urge to tap my foot or sigh repeatedly. Interesting as Francine's discoveries might be, they were not helpful. Not without context. "We need to speak to him. To find out what he knows."

"And who helped him with his hacking," Francine said. "The dude is really not all that hot. I would like to know who helped him."

It had been an excessively frustrating morning, and the afternoon did not have a much better prognosis. I had a strong compulsion to do something, but what? My limited computer skills could not reveal a tenth of what Francine was finding with her tapping and swiping. We had gathered a legion of unconnected bits of information, none of it helpful. Not until I could find the link or links that would slide them all into place to form a holistic overview.

In the deep recesses of my mind I knew all the pieces fitted to create one picture. More often than not, my brain worked at its own pace, sifting through data. There was not much sense in forcing my brain to reach conclusions. The more I relaxed, the quicker the hidden clues would filter through to my cerebrum.

Under the present circumstances, relaxation was not easily attained. Not when this Luc Alain could bring us closer to connecting these people and events. I thought some more about the young hacker.

"Are we working on the assumption that he is the person who had contacted all the would-be thieves?" I asked.

"Oh, that," Manny said. "Yes, that young thief we caught did say that he was contacted by someone local. Francine, can you find any connection between Luc and that young thief?"

"So far nothing." Francine was the only one who treated Manny with a semblance of respect. I would even go as far as saying that she was friendly with Manny. It was evident in her nonverbal cues when she looked at him. "I've got my other computers searching and I'm looking through his history to see if by chance there are anything that might be of use."

"Exactly how many computers do you have?" I asked, distracted.

"Many," she said. "I only managed to bring four computers next door. Three are connected to form a stronger system which can search better and faster. The other one is for other work, for example where I cleaned up the image from the post-it note. My tablet is connected to the stronger system."

Something pinged in my mind. "Can I see the footage? Yesterday's footage from the camera that Manny had?"

"Sure." She got up with a wince and pressed her palm against her ribs. "It will be easier for me to bring my laptop. The screen is much larger and we can watch it here. Hang tight."

"What are you thinking, Doc?" Manny grunted at my expression. "You're going to tell me something about not wanting to speculate, aren't you? Well, don't. Please speculate. Please."

Despite the circumstances I couldn't help smiling. And giving in. "There was someone I think I recognised."

"Where? At the Modern Art Museum?"

"And at the gallery," I said. "I already looked at that footage, but couldn't see his face. I only had glimpses, but something registered in my memory. I'm sure I know that man from somewhere. Yesterday I also thought I saw him, but he looked different."

Francine's return interrupted me. Only when we were all settled at the dining room table with her laptop placed so everyone had a clear view of the screen did I continue. "There was something about his posture that looked familiar. Only in the sense that I had seen this person before, maybe met him. It's not someone I know well."

I was pleased to see that Francine had software that I was acquainted with. She pushed the computer at me after opening the video. It was her way of giving me permission to work on her computer. I recognised it for what it was. Trust. I smiled at her and aligned the computer to be exactly parallel to the edge of the table. Within a few seconds I lost myself in the program, looking for the moment when I had seen that figure. It didn't take long to find it and I let the video play.

Most of the people had already evacuated the museum and Manny was talking to the GIPN leader, another policeman and the curator. Through the glass doors three more officers entered, one of them the person I was looking for. I paused the video, rewound it a bit until I was satisfied with the screenshot.

"That's the man." I picked up a pen and pointed at the average looking policeman. He was wearing the full GIPN uniform, including the protective gear. It was the perfect disguise. Not only did he blend in with all the other policemen swarming the museum, the outfit also covered any unique features there could have been to his physique. Like a few other officers he was wearing a baseball cap, the cap pulled low over his eyes. His head was lowered so that only his bottom lip was visible.

Manny and Colin were leaning closer to the computer, squinting at the monitor. I took the video back to the moment he entered the building and played that section again. Then I rewound again and paused it.

"He's too controlled," I said. "When people are trying to become invisible they control the movements of their arms, head, their whole bodies much more than those who move about normally. If you want to catch a shoplifter, look for the person who has the least arm and head movements. Like this man. His movements are far too limited. Compare him to the officers."

I played the video and pointed out a different policeman as I spoke. "Look at this one. His movements are much more controlled than the average man you would observe in a shopping mall. But it is awareness controlling his body. He's alert, ready to act at any moment. His head is raised, his eyes constantly moving, taking note of everything and everyone. His body is loose like a boxer ready for a fight. Even though all his muscles are ready to move, it is not prompted by fear, but by training."

I pointed at the stranger, the man I couldn't place but was convinced I had met before. "Now look at him. His head is down, his arms tight against his body and his movements not as smooth as any of the police officers. He walks with confidence, but not the same trained alertness as the policemen. This man is most likely a manager or a powerful businessman. His type of posture can be seen in corporate buildings all the time. There is a level of violence or aggression in the way he carries himself, but he doesn't exhibit the same physical traits as is the norm with policemen."

"Bloody hell, Doc." Manny shifted in his chair. "Who is this guy?"

I didn't answer him. Instead I pulled my laptop closer, aligned it to Francine's and accessed the security footage from La Fleur Galerie that had been sent to me. It didn't take me long to find what I was looking for. First, I played the few seconds' worth of footage for myself to analyse. I rewound and paused it so that the man was in forward motion, but slightly turned towards the camera.

"I'm convinced this is the same man," I said. "At the gallery he wore the exact same outfit and the baseball cap again covered his face. It is obvious that he knew where all the cameras were."

"Why did you not say anything about this?" Manny sounded annoyed, but not as angry as I had expected.

"I believed, naively believed, that the police had full control of the building. That they would never allow anyone in there who was not vetted or part of the team. I am sure to not make that mistake again."

Colin was looking from one computer monitor to the other. "Are you sure this is the same man, Jenny?"

"Convinced. In the first video he slumps much more." I pointed to the impostor's hunched shoulders. "But his legs, height if he were to stand up straight, the length of his arms are the same. The little that I can see of his face on both videos tells me that it is the same jaw and the same bottom lip. His one ear looks the same, but I can't commit to that. I'm confident though that if it were analysed, the ear on this man in the gallery would be the same as the one on the man here at the museum."

"Who is this motherfucker?" Vinnie asked. He was standing behind Colin's chair. No, not standing. He was looming, glaring at the computers.

"I wish I knew," I said. "I have an exceptional memory, but in this instance I can't place him. There has to be a reason why my mind doesn't want to recall his name or the place where I saw or met him."

"Do you think it will come back to you?" Manny asked.

"Maybe if you do one of those weird in-your-head things where you rock and moan?"

"I moan?"

"What Manny is asking with such a horrid lack of finesse is if you could possibly get that memory back." Colin glared at Manny.

As a matter of fact, the only person not glaring at Manny was Francine. She was looking at me, waiting for my answer.

"I don't know," I said. "Maybe. I don't want to lose time on it though. There are more than enough other loose ends I want to look into. I would rather try to figure out what these guys' next step will be."

"But you will try to remember." It could have been a request, but Manny made it sound like an order.

I did not appreciate his tone and ignored him. "Francine, how much have you managed to find out about Kubanov?"

Manny turned his irritation on Francine. "You're investigating Kubanov? Why? How?"

"I asked her to find out whatever she could about Kubanov," I said. "Yesterday before you came here we were talking about Kubanov's role in this. Since there is indication that this is revenge for something that happened to someone's child, I thought it might be a good idea to find out if Kubanov has any children."

Manny made a disapproving noise and looked at Francine, his top lip curled. "So? Did you find anything with your law-breaking ways?"

"Oh, I found out a lot of things." The searing tone in Francine's voice warned me. Manny must have also realised something was amiss. He leaned a fraction away from her as she continued. "I found out that you divorced your third wife seven years ago. She's now happily married to a man you worked with for fifteen years. That one must have really stung."

Manny was red in his face, his lips tight, his nostrils flared.

"Wait, wait." Francine rested a manicured fingernail on Manny's collar. "Before you huff and puff and blow my little house down, let me finish. I also know every bank account you have, how much money is in each, that you have a Malaga gelato fetish and that you ordered a new Fossil watch on Amazon a week ago. The doorman of your apartment building signed for it, by the way. It will be waiting for you when you get home."

Her expression changed to sensual, but I saw the anger hidden behind it. She played with his collar, her voice sing-song. "The coup of all coups was to know how old you are. Forty-eight to be exact. Really, Manny. A man in the prime of his life should take better care of himself. You're still young and possibly virile."

It was quiet in my apartment. At first Manny had bristled with instant anger, but quickly suppressed it. He was paying close attention to Francine in a way I would if I believed someone was about to unknowingly reveal something of utmost importance.

"Little girl, you don't want to enter a pissing contest with me," he said in a quiet voice. His smile was lazy, but his eyes revealed the depth of his anger. "You might be able to freeze my bank accounts, but I can easily have you up for treason. You do good work, but a few of the governments you charm into believing they have your exclusive loyalty won't appreciate knowing that they've been sharing you."

Francine lost some of her colour.

"Yes." Manny nodded at her as if she had asked a question. "I know about you, more than you would like me to. And no, I have not told anyone."

"How do you know this?" Francine looked worried and interested.

A series of micro-expressions on Manny's face had me sitting up. Manny was even more astute than I had credited him. "He didn't know. He's been watching you and must have come to some conclusion. That last statement was a test and you confirmed his suspicions."

Francine blinked at me before leaning closer to Manny. Her tone was still hot, her eyes cold. "People so easily underestimate me. Underestimate the power I have the moment I sit behind a computer. Don't ever speak to me as if I am lower than you, Manfred Christopher Millard. I can handle, and I actually enjoy, your sarcasm and sharp tones. But treating all of us as if you are on much higher moral ground than us? I will no longer stand for that. Despite your attempts at running background checks on all of us, there is much you don't know."

I marvelled at the nonverbal communication happening around the table. None of them had any understanding of exactly how much information they were giving each other with their micro-expressions and their postures.

From where I was sitting, the nonverbal communication was unmistakable. Francine had made it clear that Manny had overstepped a line. He, on the other hand, was giving that warning and the other veiled threats from Francine serious consideration.

He nodded his head slowly as if he had come to some realisation. "I apologise."

"Now those are magical words to a girl." This time Francine's smile was wide and genuine. "I can spill all kinds of secrets when a man as old-school and macho as you utter those two words."

"How about telling him only about Kubanov?" Colin's tone carried a subtle warning.

"Ah, of course." She sat back in her chair, relaxed. "I know some people who know some people. None of them and none of my other sources could dig up any kids that Kubanov might have had. Not one child was ever registered with him as the father and there were never any rumours about a love child somewhere either. There is always a margin of error, but I'm convinced that he doesn't have any children.

"His mother on the other hand had a few kids. Kubanov is the oldest of five. Three sisters and one brother. Between him and the second child is a nine-year age difference. Quite significant if you take into account that he comes from a poor family in a small village in rural Russia. Kids were often born one right after the other."

"None of our investigation ever found out who his biological father is," Manny said. "Do you know?"

"Only rumours," Francine answered. "Apparently one of the top officials in that area used sex as payment to speed up connecting electricity to a house or heating or water. Basic amenities. Fifty years ago corruption in Russia was even worse than it is today. One man, Roman Lebedev, was one of the worst corrupt officials. He extracted payment from Kubanov's mother for giving written permission to have electricity connected to her family home. The payment resulted in the birth of Kubanov.

"His mother was staying with her parents and two sisters. They were shamed by her pregnancy and child and tried to marry her off. Unfortunately for them it took seven years to find a volunteer. She married a much older farmer who needed a housekeeper and extra hands on the farm. Life was hard for them and the first two girls died before either of them reached their first birthday. The third daughter survived, but died ten years ago in a bus accident. The youngest was another boy."

"Kubanov has a younger brother? We never found out about this." Manny sat up. "Who is he? Where is he?"

"I'm working on that at the moment. While the mother was pregnant with the youngest, the farmer died a violent death. He was attacked and brutally murdered. There were rumours that Kubanov had killed his stepfather for all the abuse, but it was never investigated or verified. Shortly after the farmer's death, Kubanov joined the military and started his illustrious career. There is a nineteen-year age difference between him and the youngest brother."

"How do you know this?" Manny asked. His tone held no censure this time, only curiosity.

"People who know people. These are people I've met online in all sorts of situations. And no, not all of them are criminals. A lot of them are gamers, some of them IT specialists and of course some of them hackers. There are also networks of people all over the internet that you can ask all sorts of questions. If you're in the right network, you can get good answers."

"Ask your questions so that we can find out about this brother," Manny said. "After the Piros forgery case, I investigated Kubanov and found out a lot about Kubanov, but never this."

"Maybe because his mother never registered the brother as her child. This just shows how one can game a system." Francine rolled her eyes. "Most likely through bribery or more sex, the mother managed to register Kubanov's brother as the son of her five-year-old daughter."

"What? How the hell is that even possible?" Vinnie asked.

"Corruption. I don't know the reasoning behind this, but Kubanov's younger brother is legally registered as his sister's son, his nephew."

"Twisted," Colin said. "On all kinds of levels."

"Is his mother still alive?" I asked.

"Nope. She died fifteen years ago. Suicide."

Silence settled around the table. I thought of the man who had started as the unwanted product of a bribe. The man who now was one of the most influential people in Russia. He was widely respected for his philanthropic works. He was also widely suspected of many criminal activities, none of which had ever been proven. Was it his origins that had shaped his life into the ruthlessness it was now? Like people with similar backgrounds, it was most likely a combination of his impoverished, abusive childhood, his fight to survive through that and his military training that had formed his psyche.

We could never discount the addictive nature of power. People like Kubanov who had been victimised often turned into bullies whenever they had their first taste of power. I would dare to posit that his first taste came in the military, maybe when he received his first rank. That was when the hunger for more power, even absolute power, would have driven him to reach the upper echelons as soon as possible. At any cost.

And with power, all kinds of complications usually followed. That he had become a brutal criminal mastermind did not surprise me at all. That he now focussed his unhealthy mind on me most definitely did come as a surprise. Finding anomalies in data, analysing potential fraudsters' body language had never seemed life-threatening to me. I had been naive.

The distant jingling of my smartphone's ringtone pulled me out of my thoughts. I gave an irritated sigh and pulled my phone out of my handbag hanging on the back of my chair. The number registered on the screen was unfamiliar. I swiped to answer. "Hello?"

"Good evening, Doctor Lenard." It was a man's voice. Deep, cultured with a hint of an Eastern European accent. I had only ever heard that voice in person once. Six months ago. Bits of disjointed information rushed to connect. I knew who the impostor was. My free hand gripped the table as adrenaline pumped through my system. He sounded so close. "Tomasz Kubanov here. How are you on this fine afternoon?"

Chapter **TWENTY**

Cold darkness threatened to take over my consciousness. The very man we had been talking about, the man I strongly suspected was a psychopath was on the other side of this phone call. I looked desperately at Colin, for what I didn't know. He responded immediately by uncurling my fingers from the table and holding my hand between both of his.

"Genevieve, are you there?" Kubanov pronounced my name in the way I hated. The French pronunciation of my name usually sounded wrong and annoyed me. Coming from this man, it sounded sick, perverted. It nauseated me.

"What do you want?" My voice was much stronger and more stable than my current emotional state. Colin tightened his hands around mine. I looked at him and mouthed 'Kubanov', in answer to the question written all over his face. His eyes flashed open in shock. He turned to Francine and started whispering to her. I didn't pay attention to them. Kubanov had started speaking again and I needed to pay attention. I closed my eyes and isolated my concentration to mentally record every word and nuance.

"Have you missed me, Genevieve? I can't say that I've missed you. It's not possible to miss you when you've been with me every single day since last summer. I even dream about you."

"Why this obsession with me? Why target me?"

"Oh Genevieve, how could you not know?" His voice was playful. "A girl as bright as you must surely have some theories."

He had just confirmed our speculation that he was behind this. I didn't want to converse with him. I pulled the phone away from my ear to disconnect, but Colin stopped me. When I frowned at his frantic hand signals, he pulled my note pad closer and started writing. If it weren't for the disconcerting phone call I was trying to deal with, I would have been incensed with the defacing of my note pad. I gave Colin a quick disapproving look, and read his slanted handwriting asking me to keep Kubanov on the line so that Francine could trace him.

I wriggled in my chair, closed my eyes again and put the phone back against my ear. "Is this your unsubtle way of asking my hypotheses on why you are targeting me?"

He laughed. "Yes, please."

Just because I was not ready for this conversation did not mean that I lacked the theoretical know-how on handling such situations. It didn't come naturally to me like it did to Phillip, but years of training and observation served to empower me. I loosened my shoulders and relaxed against the back of the chair. Against my nature, I was about to start a game.

"There are numerous reasons, most of which I have discounted," I said.

"Oh, please tell me those reasons. It would be fun to hear them." If I had been watching him on my monitors I was sure he would have been rubbing his hands together.

"I'm definitely not a random target. This is also not borne of passion, it is too well planned."

"Thank you." He sounded sincere. "I'm glad you can appreciate the genius behind it all."

I physically bit down on my tongue to not refute his definition of genius. Instead I concentrated on the reasons why criminals resorted to violence. "You are not doing this for gain, out of jealousy or out of some ideological conviction. I have nothing you want, you don't feel a sense of ownership nor do you have any ideological convictions that I might have offended."

"Brilliant! Although I have to disagree with you on one point. You do have something I want. Your expertise."

"Which you will never have access to. You know this, covet it, but accepted the perceived loss."

"You delight me, Genevieve." His approval made my stomach

turn. I did, however, know that I was on the right path with this conversation. I had his attention and if I could draw him into a conversation, he might reveal some essential information.

"I'm also not your competition, so you don't need to eliminate me. That leaves us with only a few other options."

"What are those?" He was genuinely curious.

"I will tell you if you will tell me how you got this number. There are only a handful of people I have ever given this number to. Only someone exceptionally good could've found my number."

When the line continued to stay silent for five long seconds, I thought that I might have miscalculated my move. "You are indeed a difficult person to access. In today's online world, your presence is so minimal that I had to call in help. Only your little Brazilian-mix friend is better than my guy. Or not. But that's besides the point. He was able to track your number down. As I'm sitting here, I'm looking at a little blip on my computer. You are in your flat at the moment."

Colin's hand tightened over mine when I stiffened. I breathed deeply and forced myself to relax. "You are right. I'm sitting at my dining room table."

"Is your whole little band of misfits with you? Those puppies that follow you everywhere?" He chuckled. "Give Mister Millard my regards. He was most entertaining a few months ago with his little investigation into my life."

"Why don't you tell him yourself?"

"You are much more interesting to talk to, Genevieve. Those puppies are far beneath the likes of us. They're boring." He swallowed the last words as if he regretted saying what he had. "Finish telling me about your hypotheses."

"There is another possible reason for what you are doing. The lust of killing, of watching others suffer. I think that applies to you."

"Did little Colin tell on me? Bad, bad boy."

I tried to ignore my fear. There was one more reason that motivated people like Kubanov, but I didn't want to reveal too much to him. I was playing a game and I had a strategy. "I think that you are like a big cat, enjoying the hunt, enjoying playing with your prey. For some obscure reason you have set your sights on me. You are enjoying playing games with me. It might even serve as an aphrodisiac for you. You are having fun. I think you are bored with your everyday life and decided to play a real-life type of chess."

In his laughter I heard not only amusement, but also triumph. I almost raised both my fists in victory. A rare moment indeed for me to have convinced a man such as Kubanov that I knew less than I truly did.

"Ah, Genevieve, you are a worthy opponent. Worthy. You are like cream to my already superior cup of coffee. I hope you enjoy my gift."

"Your gift?" No sooner had I asked the question than my doorbell rang. I heard chairs scrape on the floor and fast footsteps, mostly likely Manny and Vinnie rushing to the front door. I didn't open my eyes to look. "I am sure I will appreciate the symbolism in your gift."

"It was a pleasure speaking to you, my lovely." And without another word, he disconnected the call.

The loud voices from the front door couldn't even get me to open my eyes. I needed a moment to process what had just happened, a moment for my mind to analyse.

"Jenny?" Colin squeezed my hand lightly.

I opened my eyes and was pleased that I had not gotten lost in my head. Manny and Vinnie were still at the front door, their bodies blocking me from seeing who they were arguing with.

"Are you okay?" Francine asked. She was sitting across from us, her hands frozen above the laptop's keyboard.

"I'm fine. You look pale. What is wrong?"

"I traced his call. He is here in Strasbourg."

"He knew I was in my apartment."

"Your GPS is either on, or they activated it."

"Did you do that with his phone? Do you know where he is?"

"He must have been using a supremely old mobile phone.

One without GPS. I could only locate the nearest tower his phone connected to. I couldn't get his coordinates."

"Where is that bastard?" Manny stormed towards us, looking at Francine. "Do you have his address? The response team is here, ready to go get him."

"Sorry, Manny. I don't have his coordinates." Francine did not look well. I wondered if it was some residual pain from her attack.

The realisation dawned on me with a great force. "You know the hacker who helped Kubanov."

"What?" Manny's voice was too loud. He looked down at his shoes and breathed a few times loudly through flared nostrils. We were quiet. He looked up, zoomed in on Francine and lifted a bandaged hand. "Let me speak to the response team. I'll be back in three minutes, then you can tell me all about this hacker. Bloody hell."

We watched him walk to the door, passing Vinnie on the way.

"Those guys have far too much ammo on them." He sat down next to Francine. "Manny told them that there is no danger here, but they still came storming in with their guns, extra ammo stuffed in pockets all over their uniforms. I like these guys. Why are y'all so quiet? Francine, why are you so pale? Are you okay, honey?"

Vinnie's voice softened from the excited tone as he looked at Francine. The hushed conversation had ended at my front door and Manny closed it. He saw me frowning and turned back to lock the five locks. He joined us at the table, sitting down on the other side of Francine.

"Okay, now tell me what the fuck that was all about."

"Manny, you have to be more specific with your question," I said. "Are you asking me? Are you asking Francine? What do–"

"Why don't you start, missy? Tell me why Tomasz fucking Kubanov phoned you."

"To gloat," I said. "He is playing a game and he thinks that he has out-planned, out-manoeuvred us. He wants me to know that he is responsible for what has been happening. And he wants to know for himself what I know and don't know."

"Why the hell does he have such a hard-on for you?"

I flinched. "I am convinced that his motives are not sexual in nature at all."

"Millard is obviously not thinking of his language, Jenny. What he means is why is Kubanov focussing on you."

Only when Colin spoke did I realise that my hand was still in his. I pulled it back and rested both hands on my lap. "You heard what I told him. I believe that this game he is playing is very stimulating for him."

"Eeuw." A shudder went through Francine's body. "That is sick."

"Kubanov is a highly sophisticated criminal. His kind of intelligence is often found with psychopaths. His behaviour does bear resemblance of that too. On top of that, he sees himself as vastly superior to everyone else." I smiled, proud of my deception skills. "He didn't expect me to turn the game on him."

There was silence around the table. Manny dropped his chin and stared wide-eyed at me.

Colin's eyes relaxed with a smile. "Did you lie to him, Jenny?"

"No," I said. "I just didn't tell him the whole truth."

"A lie by omission is still a lie, Doc." Manny straightened. There was respect in his eyes. "Good on you, Doc. Good on you. Now tell us how you gamed him."

"Firstly, I didn't tell him that I knew he was at both bomb scenes."

"He was?" Manny was raising his voice again.

"Yes, he was the man in both videos that I thought I had recognised. I'm just angry with myself for not putting it all together earlier."

Colin waved my anger away. "At least we know that he is here and that he is playing an active role in this whole game. Is there a secondly?"

I nodded. "I told him all the reasons I thought he might be

pursuing me. He thinks that I think it is because he enjoys playing games. That he wants to win and that I am the perfect competitor. A worthy opponent, he had said. I believe that is true. But that is only a bonus for him. I didn't tell him the true reason I believe he is doing this."

"So why is he doing this?" Vinnie asked.

"I believe that it is what we had talked about earlier. Revenge. People want to exact revenge mostly for three reasons. The last reason is betrayal. I'm mentioning this first, because I don't believe it to be relevant here. The second reason is identity. If someone's identity is threatened or harmed, they want to get back at the person who presented that threat or caused that harm."

"And you harmed Kubanov's identity, his reputation, of being an invisible, invincible crime lord. You brought his illegal activities out in the open last summer." Colin's voice was tight. He was remembering.

The cognitive dissonance I experienced was very uncomfortable. I was pleased that I had exposed Kubanov's murderous art forgery syndicate. But I hated that my actions might have played a role in the trauma Colin had suffered at Kubanov's hands.

"You made him look bad and now he wants revenge for that," Colin continued. "What is the first reason for revenge?"

"Equity," I said. "This is where those Bible verses are appropriate. An eye for an eye. I had taken away from Kubanov's reputation, he wants to take away from mine. I had taken away from his business, he wants to take away from mine."

"How would he do that?" Vinnie asked.

"A man like him would have studied me, knowing that I don't care about my reputation or material things." Fear constricted my throat muscles, turning my voice softer and much more tense. "He knows about the people in my life. He mentioned Francine, Manny and Colin. I'm sure he knows that Vinnie is also here. That would be his way of getting to me. That and attempting to reach his end goal before I can figure it out. That would make me look foolish and would give him immense pleasure.

"I don't think that he only studied me. I believe that he found that you are all connected to me somehow and went out of his way to find out as much as possible about you." As I believed he had done with Colin. My lips tightened and I shook my head. "You are in danger because of your association with me."

"Bullshit!" Vinnie jumped up and glared at me. "My life was dangerous a long time before I met you, Jen-girl. You are not responsible for this asshole's behaviour."

"Thank you, Vinnie. I know this. My statement is not out of some irrational false responsibility. I was merely stating that you are targeted by Kubanov because you are connected to me."

People like Kubanov enjoyed the complexity of these games to an obsessive degree. Despite all the clues pointing to him taking revenge on me for whatever wrong he perceived I had done, I was convinced there was more. He had alluded to me being the cream in his coffee. If that were true, who or what was the coffee?

"Unfortunately I agree with Genevieve," Francine said. "I've been wracking my brain trying to figure out how somebody could have discovered where I live and then broken in. If Kubanov studied you, followed you, he would've seen us meeting for lunch at some point."

The heavy weight of reality settled on me. "It wouldn't have been him. He would've have had someone else do it, but yes, your theory is feasible. He would have wanted to know as much as possible about the people in my life. God, I'm sorry."

"It's not your fault." Colin enunciated each word emphatically.

"Let's find him before he can hurt anyone else," Francine said softly. "I think I might know a way."

As one we turned to her.

"Does this have to do with your state of shock?" I asked.

"Yes, it does." She gave a self-deprecating laugh. "I feel incredibly stupid at this moment, because I really should've seen this earlier. Oh well, this is definitely a lesson in humility. The last person I ever would've expected to be connected to Kubanov's ilk has just handed my pride to me on a platter."

"You know who's been helping the hacker?"

"Yes. Everything makes much more sense now. Twelve years ago I was, um, functioning on the fringes." She saw my one lifted eyebrow, glanced at Manny and gave me a resigned smile. "I was not always working for the good guys, Genevieve. One day a twelve-year-old boy managed to hack me. He was good, but a bit heavy-handed and I traced him. Long story short, I took him under my wing, taught him how to hide his presence, be stealthier, basically to become an exceptional hacker."

"And this is the guy helping Kubanov and Luc Alain?"

She nodded. "I was trying to trace the call from Kubanov while you were talking to him. I heard everything. The moment he called me a Brazilian-mix, I knew. When Jonas found out that I have a Brazilian-Chinese father and a French mother, he decided that my Brazilian genes were the strongest. He always called me a Brazilian-mix."

"That's his name? Jonas?" Manny had his smartphone in his hand. "What is his surname?"

"DuPont." She sounded sad. "Jonas DuPont. He is brilliant. I have not crossed paths with him in years. I haven't seen his recent work. He's made a point of being invisible."

"Like you," I said. Francine had hinted a few times at the lengths she had gone to remain unknown.

She nodded. "Yes, I suppose."

"Why did you lose touch with him?" Colin asked.

"I started playing with the angels and he was increasingly dabbling in evil. We didn't part ways as the best of friends. I don't want to hang around black hat hackers."

"Are those the bad guys?" I asked. When Francine nodded, an immediate association came. "That must make you a white hat hacker."

"I would like to think so," she said.

"Do you know where he is?" Manny asked .

"Behind his computers," Francine answered. "As I know

him, he's already disconnected the computer he used for Kubanov's hacking and is stripping it for parts. He would be using different hardware and operating systems to start his next evil invasion."

"Send me everything you have on him," Manny fumbled with something in his jacket pocket. His lips thinned in frustrated anger and he breathed deeply. "Could you please get my phone out of this bloody pocket and phone Daniel?"

Francine smiled sensually at Manny's brisk tone and leaned closer. She looked at him with a challenge as she put one palm against his chest and took her time searching for his phone with the other. By the time she had dialled Daniel, Manny was grinding his teeth. He grabbed the phone from her and pushed it against his ear.

I wasn't interested in listening to a one-sided conversation. I turned to Vinnie. "What did Kubanov send?"

"The motherfucker sent you flowers, Jen-girl." The corners of his mouth pulled down. "Fifteen red daffodils. Millard and the police dude thought it was better for them to take it and get it analysed in case there was more to the gift than just the pretty flowers."

"Fifteen?" The number resonated with some of the many bits of information floating around my brain. Was it connected to something I had already looked at in this case or was it completely disconnected? I was relieved that the curiosity of the flowers overpowered the depraved symbolism of the gift. I didn't want to lose time going into my head to regain my calm and equilibrium.

"Yup," Vinnie said. "There was no note. Just the flowers. The kid who delivered it is with the police now. He didn't know anything. The florist is his mother and she receives a lot of online orders. Since there was no handwritten note, he thought that these flowers were maybe ordered online. When they left here, they were going to his mother's shop to find out about the order."

Manny had finished his phone call and put his phone on the

table. He looked at Francine's laptop. "Did you record Doc's conversation with Kubanov?"

"Most of it." She started tapping away on the keyboard. "I didn't catch the very beginning. It took me a few seconds to set up the recording and tracing programs when Colin told me to do it."

"Can we listen to it again?"

"Sure. Let me just… Okay, here we go."

There was a lot of tense body language around the table while we were listening to the conversation. Hearing it all again only served to confirm my previous observations. It also surprised me immensely to hear the steady, almost bored, tone of my voice. I didn't think I was capable of repeating that calm conversation if asked to. It was amazing what a person could do under pressure. It might not be second nature to me, but to successfully deceive was something that I could do. And do well enough to mislead someone like Kubanov.

My pondering pulled my attention away from the table. I didn't notice the onset of it, only the full-blown anger in Manny's body when he leaned over the table towards Colin.

"What the fuck did he mean, Frey?"

Colin moved to stand up, but I swung my arm out and stopped him with my forearm across his chest. I knew what this was about. I knew the time had come. And I was not looking forward to the next few minutes.

"Manny." When he didn't look at me, I raised my voice. "Manny! Sit down. Thank you."

He glared at me only for a second before turning furious eyes on Colin.

"Wait, don't say anything yet." Hundreds of thoughts were rushing through my mind. The ones surprising me most was my concern with everyone's emotions. I turned to Colin. "Do you want Francine and Vinnie to be here for this?"

"I'm not doing it, Jenny." Colin pushed against my arm to stand up, but I wouldn't let him.

"I'm not fucking going anywhere." Vinnie folded his arms across his chest.

"Fine." I was done being considerate. I looked at Manny until his eyes turned on me. "Remember when you promised me that you would listen when I asked?"

Manny did not like where my request was going. "Now? You want me to sit back and listen now?"

"Yes, please. Don't talk until you've heard everything." To my surprise Manny nodded. He pressed his lips tightly together and sat back in his chair. He might have complied, but it had not made him any less combative.

"I'm not talking, Jenny." Colin's body was tense against my arm. I pulled my arm back awkwardly and put my palms on my thighs.

"Do you trust me?" I asked as he moved to stand.

Colin's eyes flashed in surprise and he sat back down. He lowered his head and looked straight in my eyes. "Implicitly."

"Do you trust my assessment of people?"

He sighed. He must have anticipated my next question. "Millard doesn't have clearance for this, Jenny."

"But I do?" I lifted one eyebrow. He sighed again. I didn't give him the opportunity to answer. "I have been the recipient of Manny's harsh words more times that I can count. He's not a polite, diplomatic person. But I trust him, Colin. With my life. And I know that you know he can be trusted. You were the one who convinced me of this six months ago. This disrespect between the two of you is unproductive and completely misplaced. It constantly interferes with this investigation and frankly I am tired of wishing that Phillip was here to mediate. Tell Manny or I will."

I waited out the silence, hoping that I was handling this correctly. Indeed I did wish that Phillip had been here. I did not have the calm presence he had. What I did apparently have was the ability to gain the cooperation of four strong-minded people. Vinnie was watching Colin, undoubtedly ready to act on whatever decision Colin would make. His loyalty unwavering. Francine, on the other hand, was watching this with the same look of gleeful entertainment I had seen on the men's faces when they were watching a wrestling match on television.

Colin shifted next to me. He had made up his mind. His bottom jaw was ever so slightly pushed forward, his chest pushed out. He looked at Manny. "You tell anyone and you're dead."

Thoughts expressed themselves on Manny's face. I was impressed and extremely grateful when he didn't verbalise most of the micro-expressions I observed. "I'm listening."

"You remember when you arrested me thirteen years ago? And then after only a few hours in your custody I was taken away? Well, that arrest managed to raise flags at Interpol, and the Secretary-General at that time got involved. He and two other high-ranking officials decided that I was exactly what the organisation needed. They offered me a deal and I've been working for Interpol since. Apart from the Secretary-General and a few other people, no one at Interpol knows that I even exist."

"Tell him what you do," I said when Colin stopped.

"I reappropriate art." Colin briefly closed his eyes and shook his head. I could see this was not easy for him. "Sometimes I reappropriate other things that Interpol requires. Obviously these things are often of sensitive nature. Art stolen during wars, sensitive information lost or stolen. A lot of this can have large international repercussions. These thefts are never reported since the items were not supposed to be in those people's possession in the first place. There are only seven people who know what I do." He looked at me. "Are you happy now?"

"Thank you." I looked at Manny. "We are all on the same side. If I have learned anything from working with all of you, it is that there is no black and white in doing good. I don't always understand it, but at least I don't treat anyone as if they are beneath me."

Manny was quiet for a long time, his eyes narrowed and focused on the wall behind me. His mind was putting the pieces together. It didn't take long before he came to some conclusion. More sober than I had ever seen him, he looked at Colin. "Did they send you after Kubanov?"

"Yes."

"I never had time to verify any of the intel that I had received. Was any of it correct?" Manny startled when Vinnie slammed his hands on the table and got up.

"I have to cook. Y'all stay for dinner." He stormed to the kitchen, his movements not as fluid as usual.

"What happened, Frey? What was Kubanov talking about?" Manny nodded at Francine's computer where the recording was stored.

Colin's *buccinator* muscles pulled his mouth into a sneer. "It was a set-up. I agree with Jenny that this is about revenge. I think that after the last case, Kubanov was so pissed that he wanted to lash out. My theory is that he knew you were on that case and somehow he also knew that I had been involved. He fed you some intel, just enough to gain interest. I don't think he knows that I work for Interpol, so it was possibly only his good fortune that I was sent to his place in Russia. He took great pleasure in telling me how he had planned it."

The more Colin told him about the captivity, the mansion and the rescue, the more Manny's pallor turned gray. Colin's voice was tight with remembered distress. "When that plan didn't work, I think he sat back and started planning something much more elaborate, something that in his mind would destroy Jenny."

"But why you? Why did he want you in his territory?" Manny asked.

Colin looked at me with regret. "He wanted information on Jenny. He couldn't find anything to hurt her with and thought that I could, or would, give him a way in."

"You were tortured because of me." My voice sounded distant to my own ears. "Oh Colin. I'm so sorry."

"Me too, Frey. As much as I think you're a thieving conman, I would never have sent you out on unverified intel." His brow pulled together. "Why did they do it? Send you without making sure what I had was for real?"

Stress lines along Colin's face told me that he was in the middle of a great internal struggle. It was always difficult to hold onto one's anger when the perceived perpetrator had no knowledge of the wrong done. In Manny's case, regret for the events that had taken place was in his verbal and nonverbal communication.

"When I refused to go at first, they told me the real reasons. And I was sworn to secrecy. It's all kinds of top-secret information. Not even Jenny's trust could make me tell you."

"Oh, this is delicious." Francine bounced in her chair. "A conspiracy."

"Settle down, little girl." Manny frowned at Colin. "There has always been information that some people were not privy to. I can deal with this. I don't know if I can deal with you working for Interpol though."

Vinnie's snort drew our attention. He was chopping onions with an oversized knife that I knew I had never bought. The speed and accuracy of his knife-handling was disconcerting. Especially when he continued the controlled cutting without taking his eyes off Manny. I feared for his fingers.

"Who do you work for, arsehole?" Manny asked Vinnie.

"Manny, don't antagonise." I was growing weary of being a referee. It was beyond my understanding how Phillip could enjoy this.

"I work for myself, old man." Vinnie buried the knife's point in the wooden cutting board with such force that I thought it might have gone straight through and nicked my marble countertop. "I'm loyal to no institution, only to those I choose."

Manny's attention turned to Francine. She jumped up from her chair and grabbed her laptop. "No, no, no. You and your governments with all their conspiracies will never own me. Nobody owns me. I'm leaving. I might still have a trick or five up my sleeve to find Jonas."

She left in a hurry, clutching her laptop to her chest and promising Vinnie that she'd be back for dinner. I was left with

Colin and Manny at the table. The silence turned awkward. I considered my role finished. Manny started asking Colin questions about his level of security clearance, his jobs and many other things Colin couldn't answer. Couldn't or didn't want to.

I was content that their body language and tone of voice did not warn of impending violence, so I pulled my notepad closer and started going over everything that we had discovered. All the clues had to be reconsidered in light of the new information. The emails, the packages, the bombs, the codes, the people involved. We needed to find out the next step Kubanov was planning. And what roles all these people had in his end goal, especially the hacker.

Chapter TWENTY-ONE

"I knew it!" Francine's proud voice got absorbed by the soundproofing of my viewing room. My sacred space felt crowded. Colin and Francine were sitting on either side of me and Vinnie was lurking behind us. Soon I was going to have to ask him to take a seat. His hulking size and the pacing behind me were hugely distracting. Francine wriggled in her chair. "This twerp is confirming everything I dug up."

I didn't have the energy to correct her. Even though Luc Alain had confirmed that he had recruited vulnerable, poor students to commit the robberies, it wasn't Francine alone who had discovered this. Unused to teamwork, I had to admit that working with these people had been very efficient. Together we gathered information and connected it much faster than if I had been alone.

We were watching the hacker being interviewed in his hospital room. It had taken a few tense minutes to get the detectives to aim the cameras correctly for optimum viewing. They had blamed their lack of coffee early on a Monday morning for not being good with the cameras. I had been able to refrain from asking the relevance of the day and coffee.

I needed to see as much as possible of the young hacker's body, especially his face. Eventually they had set up one camera for a close-up on his face. That shot was on the monitor right next to a wider shot from the second camera. Not only did I have a clear view of the hacker's prone body on the hospital bed, but I could also observe the detectives asking the questions. That helped in giving me context, which in turn aided me in more accurate analysis.

Manny was standing out of camera view, sometimes moving

just enough to reveal his shoes or a glimpse of his rumpled coat. He had been uncommonly accommodating when I asked him to ensure that the interview was recorded. The confrontation between Manny and Colin had changed the dynamics in our small group. Manny's easy acquiescence to my request for him to wear an earpiece so that I could ask questions and direct the interview had also been unexpected.

Since the interview had started fifteen minutes ago, I had observed the young hacker being defiant, scared, arrogant, terrified, followed by co-operative. The detectives were the same two men who had interviewed the young thief three days ago. I liked them. They were now asking the hacker for the names of all the students he had recruited. I wasn't interested in that information, so I studied everyone's body language.

"And you did this all by yourself?" one detective asked after recording a lot of names, mostly male. Again he was dressed in a suit, his short hair neat and his manner authoritative, but relaxed.

"Of course. I'm one of the best." His arrogant expression turned calculating. "Hey, maybe you could cut me a deal, you know. Like in the movies? I could start working for you guys and won't have to go to prison."

Francine pulled on my sleeve. "Tell Manny to ask him if there is any difference between MOVD and MOVQ instructions in ASM."

Without asking for an explanation, I relayed the question to Manny. He stepped into view. "If you are as good as you say, tell me if there is any difference between MOVD and MOVQ instructions in ASM."

The detectives glanced at Manny, but there was no resentment visible. They didn't mind his interference. All three men focussed on the hacker, waiting for his answer. His *corrugator procerus* muscles pulled his brow into a worried frown, his *orbicularis oculi* muscles increasing his blinking rate. He was losing confidence. Fast.

"There isn't a difference." He smirked. "It's the same command, just in different compilers."

I looked at Francine and she shook her head, a disgusted smile pulled at her full lips. I spoke into the microphone connected to Manny's earpiece. "He's wrong."

Manny stepped forward, folded his arms across his chest and leaned back. The other two detectives had been able to get the hacker chatting, to get him relaxed. Manny was quite effective at being severely intimidating. "Young man, we both know you don't know your arse from your elbow when it comes to MOVD and MOVQ instructions. Stop lying to us and start talking about the hacker who helped you. We know that you could not have done this alone."

Luc looked helplessly at the two detectives and visibly relaxed when Manny moved back into his corner.

"Okay, fine. I will tell you. Just to let you know, in some circles I am considered to be a good hacker. It was P–" He hesitated and blinked furiously for a few seconds. I made a note of this. He was hiding something. "Um, I was recommended for this job. Most things were already arranged before the Mafia dude phoned me."

'What Mafia dude?" the other detective asked. His head was shaved, a shadow of hair forming a thin line around the lower circumference of his scull. I wondered if he shaved his hair because of convenience or to hide his baldness. People's vanity fascinated me.

"The dude with the Mafia voice." Luc's answer pulled my attention away from the detective's head. "He has this deep voice and the accent makes him sound sick."

"Like he has the flu?" the bold detective asked.

"No, man, sick as in really cool. Like he was this bad-ass." He rolled his eyes. "Old people. He also sounded old. He used very correct French when he spoke to me."

"How many times did you speak?"

"Only the once. He wanted to make sure that I was on board with this thing." The corner of his mouth pulled into a sneer. "He didn't believe the word of people who trusted me. But after we spoke he was cool. He promised me that I'd get whatever help I needed to do this job. I mean, this dude was really something, you know? All powerful and shit. But since he was the guy organising everything and the guy with the money, I wasn't going to complain. That night he paid me in cash. In advance. How sick is that?"

Both detectives closed their eyes for a moment. I supposed it was in exasperation with the young man's inept use of language. I was interested in this lexicon. But the implication that Kubanov had been in direct contact with this young man was even more interesting. Was it him or one of his associates?

It was out of character for Kubanov to get involved in the execution of his plan. Even as a businessman, he would delegate the menial tasks. Or would he? Was this so important to him that he needed to personally oversee someone even as disposable as Luc?

"What kind of help did you get?" the first detective asked.

"Oh, you know. Some hacking help." With his thumb and forefinger he rubbed down from the corners of his mouth to his chin. Blocking behaviour that indicated deception. The change in the two detectives' postures told me they doubted his truthfulness.

"Some help or someone helping you to do it right?"

"Okay, fine, be like that. Yes, it was someone to help me with some stuff. I'm not that good. Not yet. But he taught me a lot of cool things. His sick skills helped me get into the security companies' systems so that I could get all the specs I needed to organise the jobs."

"Who is this guy? What is his name?" the bold detective asked.

"I only know him as DeathRabbit867. The whole hacker world knows him. He's famous. Now, this dude is really sick. He has mad skills. There are only two hackers better than him. Rumour is that one is a chick. How sick is that?"

Francine's gasp drew my attention away from the incorrect use of the word 'sick'. I turned to her. "What is it?"

"DeathRabbit867 is Jonas." She shook her head. "I knew

this, but still can't believe it. Even when I hear it from this twerp. How could Jonas stoop this low?"

On screen the detectives were insisting on a name, the handle being useless to them. I told Manny what Francine had said. "She's already working on tracking him, so it's not an efficient use of time to question him about that. Question him about the person who recommended him to Kubanov."

'The who?" Manny whispered through his teeth.

"Twice now his nonverbal cues showed that he was hiding something when he talked about being recommended to Kubanov. Either the person is in his circle of friends and is close to him or he respects this person highly. Ask him about it." I was getting agitated wasting time explaining myself to Manny. "I don't think he'll answer you, but that's okay. Ask him yes or no questions then."

Manny stepped into view and glowered at the camera for a moment. I smiled. An annoyed Manny was familiar. The complying Manny was something I would have to get used to. He took another step to the bed. Luc pushed himself deeper into the pillows.

"Who recommended you to... the Mafia dude?" The last words came out with great distaste.

"Um, some friends?"

"You're not sure? Earlier you sounded completely sure of who recommended you. You even sounded pissed off that your Mafia dude would not believe this person. Who is it?"

The young hacker's chin pushed out. "I don't know."

It was the constant touching of his ear and mouth and the sudden stillness of his hands that gave his defiance away as a lie.

"Is it one of your university buddies?" Manny asked. I almost sighed with relief that he had taken my advice.

"No," he snorted. "I don't have university buddies. They're all a bunch of losers anyway."

"Is it one of your loser buddies?"

"My buddies are not losers."

"A family member?"

"What is this? *Twenty Questions?* I told you, I don't know who gave that dude my name."

Manny glanced at the camera. I picked up the microphone. "He knows who recommended him. But you haven't asked the right questions. Not yet. Continue."

Manny glared into the camera again before turning his annoyance to Luc. "Is it one of your hacker buddies?"

Luc didn't respond, his lips tight and his hands in fists on the covers.

"Is it someone at the university?"

I jumped in my chair and pointed at the monitor. "There. Look." I grabbed the microphone. "It is someone at the university. Ask him which one."

Just as Manny leaned closer, two medical personnel stepped into the room. "Sirs, we have to ask you to leave now. The patient is still recovering from major surgery and the stress is not helping him."

The one doctor walked to the equipment attached to Luc, frowning at the display screens. "Oh, yes. You definitely have to leave. You've been here for more than an hour already. You can come back late this afternoon or tomorrow. Right now Monsieur Alain needs to take his medicine and rest."

A few more minutes of arguing could not dissuade the doctors. They were adamant. Manny shrugged at the camera. "Guess this will have to do, Doc. Hope it is enough."

"It will do." I was deeply disappointed that Manny hadn't been able to ask any more questions.

Within a minute the monitors were dark. I turned to Francine. "We have to find out who this person at the university is."

"I'll check his old laptop for that."

"What old laptop?" Colin asked.

"Oh yes, I didn't tell you. When the police were going through Luc's flat, they found a very old laptop in a hidey-hole. They brought it to our flat late last night. Manny had insisted that I immediately look at it even though it was almost two o'clock. I had a peek at it and it looks like he had been using it only at places with Wi-Fi, like cafés and restaurants." She rolled her eyes. "Just shows you what an amateur he is. A pro would have used a strong antenna to connect to other people's Wi-Fi networks. I'm sure there will be some interesting internet history on this old laptop. It might even give me some leads to find Kubanov and Jonas."

"And the person at the university," I said. "Kubanov is planning something big. In order to get ahead of his planning, we need to understand all the players involved."

"Sounds like chess," Vinnie said.

I turned around in my chair and smiled. "An apt comparison. He has a strategy, each move planned in detail. Without knowing who else is involved, we might miss essential players and the roles they are supposed to fulfil. Everyone we've found so far has been used by Kubanov towards an end goal. They all had their individual purposes and were chosen with care. Why them? Who else is there? If we put everyone together, what holistic view will we have?"

"Those are big questions, Jen-girl."

"Questions we're not going to get answers to sitting here," Francine said.

We talked for a few more minutes and agreed that Francine and Vinnie would go home. I stayed behind with Colin and for the next few hours I watched the footage again and again, making sure I hadn't missed anything. Not a verbal or nonverbal clue. I needed more information, more data to tie everything together.

Five minutes after my asking him, Colin was driving us home. Fifteen minutes later we were in his apartment. Not mine. I wanted to be in my apartment, but Francine and all her computers were in his.

We walked into her spacious bedroom and I gasped. Loudly. Colin cleared his throat behind me in what sounded like an attempt to hide laughter.

Francine looked up from where she was sitting on her bed.

She had changed her outfit. Now she was wearing a deep blue turtleneck sweater, jeans and those silly pink house-boots. She still managed to look like she was posing for a fashion magazine, her long black hair glossy and her make-up subtle, but perfect.

"Oh, hey there. Come in, come in." She got up with only a slight wince and stepped over a silver designer sandal, two different-coloured boots and too many cables to count. How was it possible that a woman as beautiful and always well-dressed as Francine could live in a room that was giving me heart palpitations? The wardrobe doors were open, clothes falling off hangers and pulled halfway out of shelves.

"I can't." I turned around to face Colin. "I can't be here. Find out what she knows and come tell me. I'll be home."

To get to the front door I had to walk past the kitchen and the living areas. I was so focussed on getting into the neatly organised safety of my apartment that I didn't see Vinnie in the kitchen until he spoke.

"Didn't think you would last long in that pigsty." He was gently stirring a pot on the stove. As soon as I noticed it, I also noticed the mouth-watering aroma. "I'm making a nice thick stew for dinner. It's been cooking for hours, but just needed to be moved around a bit."

He placed the wooden spoon on a holder and placed the lid on the pot. This kitchen was as clean as he always kept mine when he was cooking there. All the countertops were clear of clutter and without a spot. To the left of the stove was a tablet computer streaming a news programme. The tablet was angled for easy watching while Vinnie was cooking.

The sound was turned down low, but was audible enough for me to hear the interview with the president and his wife. She was laughing at an answer the president gave. He smiled warmly at her and continued talking. Vinnie wiped the already spotless stovetop. The stew bubbled gently on one plate. It didn't make sense.

"How can you live with…" I pointed in the direction of Francine's bedroom. "… that?"

Vinnie laughed. "I've known Francine for a long time. As long as she has her own space to mess up, she'll keep everything else neat. We had a nice long discussion when she first moved in here. I don't care about her room. As long as nothing breeds in there, I'm okay with it."

"Oh God." I put my hand over my mouth and spoke through my fingers. "How can you even think such a thing, let alone say it?"

"Aw, Jen-girl, you really are cute when you get all disgusted like that." He hung the dishcloth on the oven handle and stepped closer. "Did you make any more progress today?"

"No." I lowered my hand. "Do you know if Francine has found any useful information on Kubanov, the hacker and the university person?"

He looked at the clock on the microwave oven. "I checked with her twenty minutes ago and she was still working on something. She rudely chased me away."

"Then I'm going home." I had been hoping for more data, but at present Mozart might prove to be more helpful. With a small wave, I left Vinnie in the kitchen and walked to my apartment. I stepped in and felt the relief of being in my haven wash over me. My muscles lost some of its tension as I locked the five locks and went to the kitchen to make some camomile tea.

The normality of my routine settled me. By the time I sat down on the sofa facing the balcony doors, my breathing was deeper. I paged through the article I had printed out earlier, scanning the text. Mozart's Violin Sonata No. 21 in E minor was filling my apartment, loud enough for me to focus on each note. I took a sip of my tea, put the mug on the coffee table and closed my eyes. In my mind's eye I pulled up a sheet of music paper. As each note played on my sound system, it appeared on the staves, neatly written. I loved the concrete structures of Mozart's music. The stability in it made me feel safe and corresponded with my neuro-patterns.

"Jenny?"

As a child, I had never responded well to anyone attempting

to bring me out of my mind. If they had dared touch me, it usually ended up with many bruises to everyone involved and me being grounded for weeks. Therefore it was of analytical significance that I felt comfort and security rather than intrusion when I opened my eyes to Colin's voice and saw his hand covering mine.

Was I unique in having found a person whom, for some reason, I allowed to touch me and in a sense manage me? Studies would show that this was by no means an anomaly. For me it was. My behaviour had always been predictable. And as an adult, controllable. It had been the last six months, since Colin and the others entered my life, that my status quo had changed. Nothing was the same any more. Not even my intense fear and hatred for change was the same. It had softened marginally.

"Hey, Jenny." He rubbed my hands. "When you stare at me like that, I kinda feel naked."

I stiffened. "I'm not thinking sexual thoughts."

Vinnie's laughter drew my attention to the reading area. He had settled in one of the wingback chairs, reading a book. Strange.

Colin was smiling. "I didn't mean it like that. It just feels like you strip me psychologically and emotionally of everything and can see my soul."

"Oh. Sorry."

"You don't have to apologise. You just don't often study me so deeply. Usually I can see that you only analyse my expressions. This is different."

"Oh," I said again. How else was I supposed to respond to that?

"Vinnie's made some stew that we can heat up for you."

"No, no." I stopped him, emphatically shaking my head. "I need to speak to Francine."

"I'm here," she said from the dining room table. "And boy, do I have things to show you."

I jumped up from the sofa and rushed to the table. A quick glance at my watch and I was pleased that I had only been in my head for three hours. It was seventeen minutes to nine. The night was still young. And my mind was racing with the connections the last three hours had brought to me. Francine's new information might very well help to solidify the theories I had. Theories I was sure of.

"What have you got?" I asked.

"Um, do you think we could maybe turn the music down a bit?" Francine had once confessed that she had a time limit for enjoying classical music. I remembered being a bit disappointed in her then.

"Sure." I turned to Colin who had followed me to the table. "Do you mind changing the music and turning it down?"

"I'll do it." Vinnie jumped up from the chair. Recently he had been favouring my world music selection, especially Lourdes Perez. I was not surprised when the rich sounds of her voice filled my apartment. Vinnie quickly turned the sound down until it was in the background.

My eyes were drawn to the book he had left on the chair. "Are you reading Dante?"

Vinnie's back muscles tensed. He turned around slowly and I was amazed to see embarrassment colouring his cheeks. "You don't have to sound so shocked, Jen-girl. I was just curious what this fuss was all about. That's all. The book is actually not all that bad."

"Vin is a poet at heart," Colin said with a smile.

Vinnie lifted his middle finger at Colin and grumbled as he settled back in the chair with the book.

I smiled and sat down next to Francine. She had a laptop set up on the table and her tablet was at a viewing angle next to it, a wireless keyboard in front of the tablet. Her fingers were flying over the laptop's keyboard, the windows changing too fast for me to get a good look at what was on it.

"Okay." She pointed at the monitor. I was looking at something that looked like a professional presentation. "I put things together like this to make it easier to explain. So here on the first page you will see the information that I was able to get from Luc's computers. It was all the hacking history, hacking into a few institutions, the security companies, things that didn't give any new and helpful information. Most of this I already had access to when I hacked his system.

"On the next few pages you can see everything that I was able to dig up on his background." She moved from page to page as she explained. "I'm not going to repeat the things we already know about him, even though it's also here. But this is new. A list of his known associates. I got these names from his social media pages, his email contacts, his phone contacts and a few other places. So far none of those names triggered any red flags.

"His phone records also didn't show anything criminal. I reckon that he had another phone, maybe given by Kubanov. But I'm guessing and I know you don't like it." She smiled at me. "What I don't have to guess about is his financials. Definitely daddy's poor little rich boy. Every month he received an unhealthy sum from his father. And every month he spent it all by the second week. Computers, games and hacking are very expensive hobbies and that was what most of his credit card expenses were for.

"About nine months ago, I think that was around the time that he dropped out of university, he started gambling online. He was not good at that. Not at all. He drained his accounts even faster than usual. I think that might be why Kubanov recruited him. He was behind in most of his bills and from the emails between him and his daddy's accountant it looked like he was about to be cut off as well. Boring stuff."

She clicked to the next page and straightened with excitement. "But this? This is pay dirt. This is what I found on his hidey-hole laptop. So, I told you yesterday that this was the computer he used to contact Jonas. This is also where he received all his instructions, all the information and source codes that Jonas sent him and where he had a few more secrets.

I've been going through this and it just proves how amateurish Luc really is. Even at a cursory glance I saw that Jonas had given him more than just basic help. Jonas must have been in the security companies' computers and those specific files long before he sent Luc there."

Something was causing her distress. Her breathing had changed.

"What else, Francine?" I asked.

"Jonas sent Luc an email with instructions to organise a break-in at my place. They were to only insert a flash drive into my computer. Nothing else. Jonas must have really enjoyed putting one over me. Luc was to get the best thief he could, so there would be no evidence of a break-in." She shuddered. "I never suspected anything."

"But you now have proof that your previous theory was correct," I said.

"Yeah, well, it's cold comfort. I don't particularly enjoy being outwitted by Jonas. Or robbed by a dumbass. Jonas instructed him in one of the first emails to delete every email after reading it and to clean out the trash box. Fortunately for us he didn't listen to the very good advice. I don't know if it was Jonas or Kubanov who manipulated Luc into thinking that he was the one doing all this super-hacking. They totally fed his ego with some of those emails."

"Why would they do that?" Vinnie asked from the kitchen. "Why would they feed his ego?"

"No," Vinnie said. "Why would they do all the work and then send Luc in to do it again."

"If ever there were to be an investigation, that would be what would be visible. Not Jonas' initial and very covert snooping."

"A patsy," Vinnie said, nodding his head in understanding. "A real Kubanov trick."

I knew there was more. "What else?"

"Digging through all his surprisingly well-encrypted files, I found that he had another email address." Francine smiled widely. "He had a separate address to be in contact with only one person."

"Who?" Vinnie asked from behind me. I hadn't heard him move from the kitchen.

"I don't know yet. I'm working on that. As email addresses go, this is one of the oddest I have seen. I'm also trying to decode the emails."

"It's written in a cipher?" I asked.

"Yes, but it is not cryptography used for emails. It's more like your book cipher."

"What the fuck is it with these people and their ciphers?" Vinnie stomped back to the kitchen. "It's like it is 1950 in the US and thirteen-year-old boys form a little secret society in someone's tree-house with code-words to enter and ciphers to communicate. Idiots!"

I smiled. "People who enjoy playing games are often emotionally immature. They think they're superior to everyone else when in reality they're not. Being part of something seemingly exclusive plays into their illusion." I turned back to Francine. "Send me the emails and I'll see if I can decipher it."

"To be honest, I haven't tried very hard to decipher it. I only got into that email account about two hours ago."

"No problem. Just send it to me and I'll look at it." Something she had said was bothering me. "What was the strange email address?"

She looked at her computer. "alighieri@tormail.tor."

All the connections came together so hard and fast that I physically felt it. I gave in to my need to hug myself and rock gently. "It's him. It is really him. It's him. It's him."

Chapter TWENTY-TWO

It took me an unfortunate fifteen minutes to calm down. In that time Vinnie had called Manny who was now also sitting at the table. Everyone was giving me time, but the glances I managed to grab of them showed their impatience and the tension in their bodies. It was only by a microscopic margin that I held onto my consciousness and stayed in the present. How could I have been so wrong?

Vinnie placed a cup of coffee on a coaster in front of me and sat down. Francine had moved her laptop and tablet to the other side of the table. She was flanked by Manny and Vinnie. Colin was sitting next to me, eating one of Vinnie's oatmeal cookies. I rolled my head on my shoulders a few times. A few deep breaths readied me further to explain.

"It is Professor Claude Tremont. He is the owner of that email address. He is also Luc's connection at the university." My mouth was dry, the words coming out with difficulty.

"And you know this how, Doc?" Manny sat up from his slouched position and leaned towards me.

"He's the one who got all uptight about an article I wrote." I shook my head. "I just never thought that he had taken such offence at what I had written."

"Okay, wait." Manny held up one bandaged hand. "First tell me how you know that it is this professor."

"A lot of clues. The last clue was the email address that Francine got off Luc's computer. Tremont is a professor here in Strasbourg in the comparative literature faculty, his speciality is medieval and early modern literature up until the 1800s."

"That explains the book," Colin said.

"Doc, are you sure it's this professor?" Manny asked.

"It is definitely him," Francine said. The whole time we had been talking she had been busy on her computers. "I've been trying to trace the origin of the Alighieri emails, but have not gotten far. They are all over the place and I haven't had enough time to find more detailed parameters. As soon as I had the professor's name, I linked this email address to the university, his home, cafés in a five-mile radius of all his known locations. It's him. Most of his emails were sent from the university campus or his home. A few were sent from cafés in his area. It is him."

"Let's get that bastard." Manny got up from the table and fumbled in his pockets with his bandaged fingers. "Oh, for Pete's sakes. Francine, get yourself over here and help me."

Her mouth quivered as she moved gracefully to Manny. He had already awkwardly placed the earpiece in his ear and told her to dial Daniel. I smiled at his irritation about asking for help. Francine also found this highly amusing and laughed softly when she returned to the table.

"We should call him Grumpy."

"Why?" I asked and immediately waved the silliness away. "Oh, never mind. Can you get more personal information on the professor?"

"Already on it." She moved between her laptop and tablet for a minute before picking up the tablet. "Wow, this guy is educated. He even has a degree in philosophy. Okay, do you want to hear his whole background?"

"No." I was more interested in his connection to Dante. There had to be something in his life that reflected Dante or his works. "Tell me about his family history. His wife and children, not his parents."

"Okay." She drew out the two syllables while she swiped and tapped. "He got married real young to his childhood sweetheart. Oh my God, it is just like in Dante's book! They met when they were in primary school and got married while they were still students."

"Which is different from Dante and Beatrice's history. They never got married."

"But he loved her so passionately," Francine said. "I'm looking at an interview here that Professor Tremont gave to a literary magazine. He says that he felt the same love for her that he read in Dante's work. Okay, reading on. Aha, here he says that they both graduated and he continued his studies while his wife, Sophie, worked. When he started teaching at the university, Sophie fell pregnant and gave birth to a little girl."

Manny joined us again and put his phone on the table. "How long ago was this?"

"Um, they got married twenty-five years ago, had the baby when they were married for nine years, so that would be sixteen years ago." She read for a few seconds in silence. "Oh shit. Their daughter was nine years old when she was diagnosed with some rare neurological disorder."

I grabbed my computer. "This is the code that was on the gallery bomb. Here it is. 'This sweet child mine, told her end is nigh, should not have had to face, her life in a run.'"

"Bloody hell." Manny was not the only one taken aback by this. Everyone around the table had varying degrees of shock written all over them.

"What happened to his daughter?" I asked. This must have been the difficult time Tremont had gone through and people were still whispering about.

"Um." Francine scanned more of the article. "Oh God, she died. She had undergone treatment, but nothing worked. Then Professor Tremont insisted on a procedure. It was not a very common procedure, but doctors had had success with it. The surgery was successful, but... she died a week later. Oh, wow. Against medical advice, he took her home only five days after the surgery. The moment she was off the machines, he and his wife signed her out. He blamed the hospital and the doctors who operated on his daughter for the death. Um, wait. Yeah, the magazine asked the hospital to comment and they referred to a press release after the girl's death. The press release stated that they had numerous times warned the professor and his wife of the risks of taking her home, but he believed that they had made the right choice. They hadn't."

"That's so sad," Vinnie said softly. "I don't care what kind of bastard this professor is. No little girl should suffer."

"Where is his wife now?" I asked.

Francine took a moment to answer. "It's not in this article, so I'm checking the… Shit, this guy really had a rough time of it. His wife died eight months ago."

I winced. "That was around the same time my article was published. Together with his wife's death, this must have been the catalyst for all of this."

"Tell us about your article, Jenny," Colin said.

Manny groaned.

"It was well-written and made for compelling reading, I'll have you know." I knew I sounded defensive, but Manny's resistance to any and all of my explanations grated. "My article was regarding the inclusion of verbal communication and the understanding of nonverbal cues in the effective systemic treatment of non-neurotypical patients."

"Huh?" Vinnie said as Manny groaned again.

I took a moment to simplify my thoughts. "People like me are called non-neurotypical. Our brains don't work like most people's. In order for us to receive effective psychological treatment, a few elements are needed. Firstly and most importantly is the inclusion of the family. This is where I mentioned narrative therapy. It is a type of therapy that heavily relies on storytelling, which in itself I have no problem with. The issues I pointed out were that in therapy such as this, family members are not included and often do not know if any progress is being made.

"The next mention I made of narrative therapy was when I talked about the role of society as a whole in the treatment of non-neurotypicals. I said that narrative therapy holds a social constructionist belief that there are no absolute truths. I pointed out the positive and negative points in this, but ultimately criticised current society for marginalising non-neurotypicals and so excluding them in the construction of any social reality."

"Huh?" Vinnie said again and chuckled. "No, I actually understood that. It sounded very clever, Jen-girl. So why is the prof so pissed off at you?"

"He had a paper published a few months prior that fully supported narrative therapy in its entirety." I glanced at the sofa and saw the article on the coffee table next to my mug. "I read the article earlier for the first time. Now I understand his fury a bit better. In it he explained how even in Medieval times, people used storytelling to deal with their problems, understand life and communicate ideologies. He even used Dante Alighieri's *La Vita Nuova* as an example. He lambasted critics of narrative therapy." I winced. "I mentioned in my article that highly educated professionals should not write articles and declare irrefutable statements in a field they are not well-versed in. I wasn't referring to him, nor to his article, since I didn't even know he had written it, but there were enough details for him to perceive that those two sentences were aimed at him."

"Let me get this straight," Manny said, putting his bandaged hands on his hips. "In one article you lightly criticised a therapeutic method and in two sentences appeared to criticise Tremont."

"That's what I just said." I was looking at Manny's body language. He was not being territorial, so he was showing confidence and authority. For what reason?

He folded his arms across his chest and gave a strong nod. "That's it. We're throwing his crazy arse in jail and losing the key."

"You're being prejudiced and irrational."

"Actually, Jen-girl, for once I agree with the old man."

"It is obvious that he has some problems. Granted, his problems are bad enough that he's building bombs and sending me coded messages." I felt like we were missing something. "There is always so much more underneath the surface of any action."

"No, Doc. Sometimes an atrocity is just an atrocity and a nut just a nut."

I ignored that statement. I was not going to enter an argument when I knew that there was another piece of information, essential information that I needed to connect to this development. My elbows on the table, I rested my head in my hands, framing my face with my thumbs and forefingers. It wasn't difficult to tune out the conversation around the table.

The music had changed and the voice of Cesária Évora pulled me into the easy Cape Verdean sounds. It wasn't as effective as Mozart, but there was something calming about the melodies and rhythm. After the fifth song, I had it. It was a possible connection that was there to grab and unravel. I lifted my head and waited for Francine to finish telling Manny about Professor Tremont's financials. He had been living quite a modest life, it sounded.

"Who was the doctor?" I asked when she took a breath between two sentences.

"Which doctor?" She picked up her tablet and looked at me.

"The one who operated on Professor Tremont's daughter."

She swiped the tablet's screen a few times. "This article doesn't say. Give me a minute and I'll find out."

"Why do you want to know?" Manny asked.

"It's a theory. I'd prefer to not say yet."

"You and your bloody resistance to speculation."

"It was a woman." Francine tilted her head. "A Doctor Lescot."

"Her first name?"

"Um, let me check. Lili. Lili Lescot. Why does her name sound so familiar?"

My eyes narrowed as I thought about this. I needed confirmation of my suspicion. "She operated on Professor Tremont's daughter almost nine years ago, right?"

"Right."

"Was she married then?"

"I will need a minute for this." She turned to her laptop and for a few minutes the only sounds in my apartment were

Cesária Évora and Francine's typing. "Oh. Of course! Oh. Oh."

Manny sat up. "Stop saying 'oh' like that. Speak."

Francine looked up from her computer with eyes wider than I had ever seen them. "She's the president's wife."

I dropped my head back and looked at the ceiling while the men responded with colourful expletives. Watching news programmes and documentaries was often pure escapism for me. I seldom attached any value to what I was watching. Not any more. If it weren't for the documentary on the president's wife I had watched three weeks ago, I would never have made this connection. My suspicion had been confirmed.

"She only took the president's surname eight years ago when he became serious about politics. Since then she has been practicing as Doctor Godard. Also, we know her as Madame Isabelle Godard. She stopped using the shortened form of her name when her husband entered national politics." I was becoming worried about Manny's pallor. I leaned towards him. "Are you okay? You're not looking so good."

For nineteen seconds Manny swore. Strong words. Worse than Vinnie used when he burned something in the kitchen. "We need to be fucking sure about this, Doc. Already I have all kinds of arseholes pushing me to end this bombing madness. If I now add the president and his wife to the mix? It will be total bedlam."

"Manny, look at the evidence." I pointed at Francine's computer. "Doctor Godard is even mentioned in Professor Tremont's second code. He called her 'those of false hope'. He called himself 'the betrayed' and that vengeance will visit upon Doctor Godard."

"But that was for the bomb in the Modern Art Museum" Colin said. "And it exploded, but wasn't big enough to even hurt Millard too badly. How would that be taking revenge on the president's wife?"

"I don't know. There must be an explanation though." This sudden rush of connections offered even more questions. "How does Kubanov fit into all of this?"

"That motherf…" Manny shook his head once. "He must wait for now. First I need to do something about the president's wife."

"Aren't you going to phone your police buddies?" Vinnie smirked. "Or has this just gone far above your head, old man?"

"Vinnie." My tone was strong and reproving. He had the good grace to lower his head. But he also winked at me and smiled.

Manny glared at Francine. She smiled sweetly, clearly understanding his nonverbal communication, and picked up his phone. "Same number?"

His grunt was enough answer for her. For the next four minutes we listened to a one-sided conversation. I surmised that the initial disbelief was followed by very brief panic. Soon the conversation ended.

"Okay, he's going to check with GSPR where the first lady is and if all of them are safe. He'll get back to me."

"What is GSPR?" Francine asked.

"It's the presidential security detail," Manny said.

"Who were you talking to?" I asked. I was curious.

"The GIPN team leader here in Strasbourg, Daniel."

"This is worse than the friggin' US of A," Vinnie said. "FBI, CIA, NSA, GSPR, GIPN. All these stupid alphabets."

"Acronyms," I said. "When we use the… oh, you were being sarcastic. Sorry. I'm not used to you being sarcastic."

"No sweat, Jen-girl." Vinnie grunted. "No problem. I don't care what you guys do, but I'm not calling everyone G-something. It will be the president's security detail and one G for GIPN. Else it will be too many G's for my little brain."

I wanted to correct him about his high intellect when I realised he was also referring to my name. I smiled.

It became quiet in my apartment, everyone lost in thought. I was trying to make sense of this game of chess Kubanov was playing. Despite Professor Tremont's many degrees, he was simply not capable of this type of strategic planning. That was Kubanov's trait. As I had seen before and again heard during that horrid telephone conversation, he loved playing games.

"Jenny, tell us what you're thinking." Colin was smiling at me. "You're mumbling and you're blinking furiously. Maybe if you tell us, we could play devil's advocate."

My face pulled into a frown. "It's mostly hypotheses that I'm running through my mind to see which ones fit with the concrete evidence and facts that we have already accumulated."

"Yeah, yeah, Doc. We know that you don't like guessing. Just tell us so that we can spitball your ideas." Manny gave me an uncommon smile. "It means to throw ideas around for discussion. No real spit involved."

A few chuckles eased some of the tension. Even I smiled. "Apart from Kubanov exacting revenge for the perceived humiliation suffered under my hand, there has to be more. For his personality, his reasoning, this doesn't fit. Looking at the previous case, that art forgery scam had so many elements, fitting so neatly together. On the surface it seemed like a bunch of students expertly forging masterpieces, but after a lot of layers we discovered that it led to leadership in Eurocorps and the EDA being part of this."

"Being part of this conspiracy," Francine said pointedly, but quickly leaned back in her chair when we looked at her with expressions of shock and disgust. "What? It was a conspiracy."

"Granted," I said. "One that had Kubanov right at the top, orchestrating it. He was using his philanthropic reputation to hide his illegal activities. There has never been any evidence of him being involved in any crime. He has always used others to do the practical work–"

"–so that if they get caught, he is never implicated," Colin finished.

"Yes," I said. "So why is he actively involved this time? What makes it different? Personally, I think that there is more at stake for him here than just getting back at me. I'm too insignificant. I think I'm merely a bonus to something bigger."

"Any ideas?" Colin asked.

"Not yet." I rubbed my temples. "Francine, what do you

have on the president's wife? Background, work history, family history?"

"A lot." She grabbed her tablet with a smile. "No politician escapes my scrutiny. I have dirt on all of them. I must admit that I paid more attention to her husband than to her. Maybe that is why I didn't catch on to her name at first. The husband was much more important to dig into."

Manny cleared his throat, looking at Francine from under eyebrows pulled down low.

Her smile widened. "Don't worry, handsome. No one will ever know that I checked them out. And no one will ever know what I know. I just need to be prepared."

"Prepared for what?" I asked. This woman fascinated me. Her preparedness might be conspiracy paranoia, or it might have a valid premise. With her I never knew which direction she would go.

"For the Illuminati to come out of hiding after almost two hundred years of obscurity."

Vinnie rolled his eyes, Manny he shook his head, Colin laughed softly and I knew which direction she had gone this time. I found her entertaining.

"Okay, here it is," she said. "Isabella Sophia Lescot was born–"

"Maybe you should only give us more recent details," I said. "Tell us about her student years."

Francine grunted. "Okay, if you say so. She studied medicine and that is where she met her husband, Raymond. She graduated in neurology and he as a lawyer. She was quite the feminist trailblazer at university. People were surprised when she actually got married. Like you said, she didn't use his surname until about eight years ago.

"At first they both concentrated on their careers. She was hot stuff in her field and quickly became nationally and internationally known as one of the best neurosurgeons. She took a break in her career to have their only child. He is now eleven years old. She cut back on her hours, for two years working only five-eighths of the hours she used to."

She did a quick crosscheck on her laptop. "Yup, that was around the time that Professor Tremont's daughter needed surgery. That was nine years ago. Shortly after that surgery, she left that hospital and started working at another hospital. Hmm, I wonder why. Maybe the hospital accepted a bribe, or donation as they call it, from the professor and forced her to perform the surgery."

"Francine, that is outrageous speculation," I said. "You tend to go overboard with you speculation. Not everything is a conspiracy."

"But could be true." She pulled her shoulders back. "I'm not always wrong, you know."

"I know. And that is rather worrying. And paradoxical."

"Cool." That seemed to please her. "What else do you want to know? The president hasn't always been in public service. After he graduated, he worked for a private firm as a criminal defence attorney. One of his cases ended quite badly. An immigrant, who was a juvenile and a violent criminal, could've gotten off on a technicality, but Godard slipped up. This kid was sent to jail where he was killed two weeks later. Quite a scandal. Godard left that firm and started working for the prosecutor's office six months later."

"I didn't know that." Manny scowled.

"You're a Brit," Colin said with disdain. "Do you have any interest in our politics?"

"Frey, it is not like you are a French national either. You have no grounds to look down on your nose at anyone either."

I tilted my head. None of us were pure French citizens. I held two passports, one American and one French. Manny was British. The others I was convinced had more passports and more identities than I could imagine. Vinnie I knew had been born in the US and Francine in Brazil. Colin? I did not know. It bothered me.

I was annoyed that my mind had digressed so. I cleared my throat. "The documentaries I saw about the president and his wife never mentioned much of his early years or that case. If I think about it, the only information about his background started only fifteen years ago, when he was already working at the prosecutor's office. That scandal must have been uncommonly bad. I can't remember it being on any of the news programmes I watched."

"Of course you watched news programmes when you were a student." Vinnie looked disgusted. I didn't understand why.

"I did and I cannot recall anything about that."

"A cover-up," Francine said with such authority that I almost believed her. In the context of who she was, I lifted one eyebrow and waited. "Obviously this was some government conspiracy against this poor immigrant kid, and they didn't want the public to know anything, so they had a media blackout. That was still possible in the pre-social media years. I would like to see them try that today. I'm sure that the president's PR team has also advised him to never, ever mention that scandal. Ooh, now I have to find out what happened. Give me a few hours and I'll tell you everything."

Her enthusiasm about this made me smile. She genuinely amused me with her preposterous theories in direct contrast to her highly intelligent fact-finding skills and reasoning.

The jingle of Manny's smartphone brought tension back to the table in an instant. He answered it and we all leaned forward.

"Daniel, have you got him? You're fucking kidding me. Yes? Uh-huh. Yes. Okay, let me check." He placed his hand over the earpiece on the side of his head. I didn't know if that was an effective method to prevent Daniel from hearing the conversation, but didn't say anything when Manny looked at me. "They took Professor Tremont into custody fifteen minutes ago. He's en route to the police station now. They would like for you to be there for the interview."

"Me? No." The last time I was in a police station, they had locked me in a room for more than six hours. "We can stream the interview."

"Why do you look so worried? You'll be perfectly fine in the police... aah." The *risorius* muscles contracted his lips in an attempt to hide his smile. I still saw it. "Doc, no one will arrest you or leave you in a room for the night. I'll make sure of it. You'll be in the observation room while we conduct the interview. It will be much easier with you there."

"I'll go with," Colin said, surprising everyone. He rolled his eyes at the expressions around the table. "In disguise. I'll go with in disguise."

Manny mumbled something about criminals and con artists. I didn't catch everything. I was too busy weighing up my options. Logic ruled out my resistance. "Okay, I'll go if Colin goes."

Manny lifted the phone to his ear, glaring at Colin. "We'll be there in twenty minutes."

Chapter TWENTY-THREE

I didn't want to be in this observation room. My increased heart rate and shallow breathing was evidence that my entire system rebelled against being in this building. The last time I had been in this police station, Manny had insisted it had been for my own safety, yet I still considered it as being locked up for the night. I had spent six hours in an interrogation room, just like the one on the monitors in front of me.

Then it had been Mozart keeping me calm. Now it was nonverbal analysis and Colin's calming presence next to me. I glanced at the cheap clock against the beige wall. It was a few minutes before midnight. Seven minutes to be exact. On the three large monitors, I had a complete view of the room where Professor Tremont had spent the last ninety minutes not responding to any of the detective's questions.

The police station had surprised me with its up-to-date technology. The three cameras in the interrogation room were of the highest quality, providing great visuals. There were two microphones, both fully functional and giving crisp clear sounds. The software being used by the quiet policewoman sitting behind the computers was on par with what I used.

Manny stepped into the observation room and stopped a few feet away. I had been overwhelmed with relief when I had walked into this room to find it spacious. "What can you tell me, Doc?"

"The same as I told you ten minutes after you started the interview. His rage overwhelms all his responses. I honestly don't think you're going to get him to tell you anything."

Another man stepped into the room, making it much smaller. He was not as large as Vinnie, but a tall and well-built man. I recognised him from the footage of the two bombs.

"Doctor Lenard, I'm Daniel Cassel." His English was accented, but he seemed comfortable with the second language. He stuck out his hand. "Please to meet you."

Manny placed his hand on Daniel's forearm. "She doesn't shake hands."

Daniel withdrew his hand. "No problem. It's a pleasure to meet you."

"Pleased to meet you too."

He looked at Colin. "And you are?"

"Sydney Goddphin." Colin got up from the chair next to me and shook Daniel's hand. His British accent was stronger than Manny's and incredibly authentic. "I'm an associate of Doctor Lenard's. It's a pleasure to meet you."

The assessing look Daniel gave Colin indicated that Manny had not told him who Colin really was. Colin didn't even glance at Manny who was looking at me with a frown. I lifted my shoulders and refused to say anything. Colin stepped back and sat down next to me again.

When Colin had come out of his room unrecognisable in his hipster apparel, I had told him that I was not going to lie for him. He had told me it wouldn't be necessary. When I commented on his clothes, he had been surprised that I knew about hipsters. Subcultures interested me. I had to admit being surprised that he had skinny jeans, multi-coloured boat shoes and a stretched out hoodie in his usually elegant wardrobe. Even indoors he was still wearing tinted glasses and a gray knit ski hat.

"Doctor Lenard, we would like to try something different with Professor Tremont," Daniel said.

"I didn't see you in the interrogation room," I said. "Have you also been watching this interview?"

"Yes. This has become an inter-agency, inter-departmental case. It's of national security importance that we get Tremont talking."

His mention of national security triggered a question. "Is Doctor Godard okay? Safe?"

"She's at home with her family. We've alerted the presidential security detail that something might be up, so they've got extra guys at their home and will have extra security on them until this thing is sorted out. They are sceptical though. Even though President Godard is popular and his wife the nation's sweetheart at the moment, they still receive a fair number of threats." He smiled at me. "But they know their job, so you don't have to worry about her tonight."

After the last case and the involvement of the GIPN, I had read up on them. A lot of the French version of a SWAT team's training was psychology. This man must have done extremely well in that course. He knew all the right things to say and which tone to say it in. His body language was authoritative, but respectful, open and friendly. He was successful at putting me at ease. Not an easy feat.

"What would you like to try with Professor Tremont?" I asked.

"We would like for you to interview him."

"Me?" My eyebrows shot up and I put my hand on my sternum. "Oh, I think that it would be a grave error in judgement to send me. My expertise is in watching interviews and interpreting nonverbal communication. I'm not trained in asking questions to a suspect."

"Take a breath, Doc," Manny said. "Just hear Daniel out."

Daniel's eyes widened ever so slightly when Colin put his hand over my fist in my lap. He hid his reaction quickly. "Manny has briefed me on your history with Professor Tremont. We think that he would be agitated enough with your presence there that he might start speaking. In my experience, once you get a suspect to speak, it is like a dam that bursts. Everything just comes tumbling out."

"You don't have to do this, Jenny." Colin's words were soft, excluding the two men standing in front of us. His accent slipped a bit.

I took a deep breath. I looked at Colin, then Daniel and Manny. "I can't guarantee anything. I'll try to get him to talk, but I've never done anything like this before."

"She's not going in there alone." Colin's hand tightened over mine. "Who's going in with her?"

Manny gave a half shrug and his top lip curled up. He was disgusted and not committed to what he was about to say. Interesting. "We think you should go in with her."

Colin laughed. "Who are 'we', Millard? I'm sure it wasn't your idea."

"Don't push me, *Goddphin*." Manny emphasised the surname with warning. "It was Daniel's idea and unfortunately I agree with him. Tremont has seen all of us at some point during this evening. We don't want to involve anyone else at this point in the investigation and you already know the entire background."

"And?" Colin had seen the same hesitation I had observed. There was more to Manny's reasoning.

"And Doc trusts you," Manny said reluctantly. "I know that you'll look out for her."

"Aw, Millard, that's sweet."

"Don't taunt." I pulled my hands from under Colin's. "Is there anything specific you want me to ask him?"

Daniel walked to the policewoman and got something from her desk. "You can use this earpie–"

"No, no, no." The amount of bacteria on that little device had me shivering. "I'm not touching that thing. Give it to Colin."

"Who's Colin?" Daniel asked.

Manny laughed. A belly laugh. "It's her pet name for her boyfriend here. Must be some private joke or something."

I was surprised that Manny would lie to protect Colin's identity. And I was highly annoyed that the thought of an already used earpiece had me so distracted that I couldn't even attempt to lie. I might not have been successful, but I might have tried.

"I'll take it," Colin said. He glared at Manny and then turned to Daniel with his hand extended. "I'll either relay it to Doctor Lenard or ask it myself."

"Oh, that's a brilliant idea." I sat up in my chair. "Co... um... Sydney can ask all the questions."

"Doc, you and I both know that Tremont most likely won't respond to that. I think it is you who will push him into talking."

I exhaled loudly. "Fine."

I glanced at the monitors. Professor Tremont was sitting at the table, slumped. Two burly GIPN team members were watching him from their positions next to the door. Like Daniel they were wearing their full uniform. Claude Tremont looked like a sick, weak man next to these specimens of health and strength. His hair was mussed, his face drawn. As always he was dressed in brown corduroy trousers, a crisp cream dress shirt and a sports jacket.

"Time to get this show on the road, Doc."

Even though I didn't appreciate or often understand metaphors, I agreed with Manny that this was going to be a show. I felt utterly ill-prepared for this. Colin stood up and held out his hand. I looked at it. Taking his hand represented too many significant choices. Including an admission of weakness.

I got up without touching Colin's hand and stood in front of him. "No offence intended."

"Oh Jenny, none taken." He lowered his head to look me straight in the eye. "And I mean no offence. I know that you are more than strong enough to do this alone. You are brave, strong, intelligent and so far above all these yahoos."

When I nodded and gave Colin a small smile that I knew didn't convince, he gave me a genuine smile and walked to the door. I followed him. Ahead of us, Manny and Daniel talked in low voices. They stopped in front of a door on the left and waited for us to join them. It was two doors down from the observation room.

"Doc, I'll be in the observation room. Daniel and his two guys will be right outside this door." Manny paused like people did before they said something of great importance.

"If anything looks iffy, you shout and Daniel will be in there before you can say 'help'."

"That is physically impossible." My voice tapered at the end. I grunted. "It's also a saying, isn't it?"

They smiled. Daniel gestured to the door. "My guys will leave as soon as you are in there. Sydney here has the earpiece and you only have to shout and we'll be in there. Ready?"

"No. But I'll do this." I walked past the men and opened the door. It gave me a sweeping view of the room. I took one step in and stopped next to the door. This interrogation room was exactly like the one the two detectives had interviewed the young thief in. Professor Tremont was sitting with his back towards the door on a heavy duty plastic chair. His head hanging forward and his hands on his lap.

One of the burly men was next to the door to my right. He nodded to his partner who walked to the door and pushed past me. I sucked in my breath as they touched me inadvertently. I had to hold it together if I was going to succeed in my first interrogation. I felt a hand on my lower back and swivelled around to glare at Colin. He lifted both hands and smiled apologetically. I straightened my shoulders and walked to the other side of the room to take the chair across from Professor Tremont.

He didn't lift his head as I sat down or even when Colin scraped his chair on the floor. I sat for a few seconds contemplating my next move. How I approached the initial contact would set the tone for the rest of the interview. Just as I reached a decision, Professor Tremont lifted his head. First his eyes widened in recognition, immediately followed by his pupils constricting and him squinting at me. Nonverbal behaviour observed when the subject did not like what he saw or he felt threatened.

"You! You vicious bitch! What are you doing here?" Spittle flew from his mouth and landed in little sparkling drops on the table between us. "Why the fuck would they send someone like you in here to talk to me? Do they not know who you are? What you do to people?"

I was not prepared for this reaction to my presence. It was fascinating. So much rage for whatever he had perceived I had done to wrong him. I lifted my hand from my lap in a slight movement to stop Colin from interfering. His body was tense, ready for action despite his apparent relaxed pose. Professor Tremont hadn't even noticed his presence or simply didn't care.

"Do they know how you go out of your way to destroy a man, a respected man's career? Why did you do it? Huh? Why?" He didn't give me time to answer. "Do you know how hard I had to work to have the reputation I did? You ruined it all. You and your vicious paper."

"What else did I ruin, Claude?" It was evident that he had long since passed the line of rationality. I presented a convenient scapegoat for all his problems. Using his first name would infuriate him even more. I was stripping him of his profession, his achievements. These were not the kind of questions I had expected to be asking.

"You made me look weak." He changed his voice into a sing-song bully's voice. He sounded as deranged as the wild look in his eyes implied. "Oh, look at poor Professor Tremont. He had to go for therapy and he was so proud that it worked. Look at clever, genius Doctor Lenard. She wrote an article calling that therapy hogwash. He was duped. His therapy didn't help him. He is such a loser."

He slammed both hands on the table. Colin stiffened, but didn't do anything. I was glad that this interview was being recorded. Professor Tremont's behaviour was that of a psychotic break. I would like to watch it again.

"What? Huh? You got nothing to say for yourself? I thought so. You think you are above us all. You and your high IQ. You know what the people around the university call you? Huh? Sharon Stone. They call you Sharon fucking Stone."

"Why?" For once I actually knew who this person was. On the news channel I usually watched, some documentary had been advertised that was narrated by this actress. I had been bored and had researched her on the internet.

"Because she's so sexy and has a genius IQ." His smile held no humour, only rancour. "I find that so funny. Her IQ was never proved. And she admitted that she was never a member of Mensa. So there! You don't even qualify to be compared to her."

"Who do I compare to then?"

"Evil. Pure evil." Spittle was gathering in the corners of his mouth, running down one side. "Why are only women so possessed with evil? They take away everything that is important to us. You think I'm crazy, but I'm not. I know why I am here. All those big policemen are looking for Tomasz. I know he does bad things, but at least he is an honourable man. He has standards and will not allow anyone to betray him."

I felt the need to use one of Vinnie's words to express my amazement at how easy this was. Already Professor Tremont was talking about Kubanov. It was equally astounding that he was calling the Russian by his first name.

"He told me that you betrayed him, Doctor Lenard. That is why I agreed to work with him. He told me that you are an evil woman and I agreed with him. You took my reputation, my strength away from me and you took his friends away from him. Oh, don't look so shocked. He told me everything. How you had set him up to look like a criminal mastermind. How could you? He does so much good for his people. Not like you. No. You work with criminals and murderers. He showed me the photos of you and your friends. Such low class people you keep company with. Thieves and killers. You are evil!"

He was panting as if he had been exercising. It took some control to not react to what he had just said. This was another suspicion confirmed. It sounded as if Kubanov had indeed had me followed. Stalked might be a more appropriate word.

"Still saying nothing, huh? Well, I suppose Sharon fucking Stone wouldn't want to admit not doing her research. If you had properly looked into Tomasz, you would have seen how many people he had helped. He is one of the few people who really understand my pain, my grieving. He has been such a great support. That is why I didn't mind doing most of the practical organisation. He even helped me choose Luc. You've found Luc, haven't you? He's such a lost kid. I saw that the first day he came into my lecture, and again when he dropped out so soon after. I had to agree with Tomasz when he pointed out that Luc should get caught. That being in prison would save him from himself. You see how Tomasz has helped me when all you've done is destroy what I have been building?"

It wasn't hard for me to not speak up. Clearly Kubanov had used Professor Tremont's fractured emotional state to convince him that he was right to blame everyone else for life's unfairness.

"You can't even defend yourself, you witch. You are just like her. She also didn't defend herself. She never even took the time to answer my letters." His eyes lost their focus. He was retreating into memories. "She was never willing to accept responsibility for taking my Juliette away from me. It destroyed us. My wife was never the same, you know? Oh, what do you care? You only care about yourself and making sure everyone knows how clever you are."

"But you can't do anything to me, Claude." I put disdain in my tone. It wasn't easy. Observing this man's psychological deterioration was affecting me. "You are in police custody and I will walk out of here."

"Hah! That is what you think. I'm not done with you yet, you bitch. I don't care that I'm here. Everything is planned and in place. Nothing you can do will stop me now. Half of me died with Juliette. The other half when my wife died. I'm nothing any more. The only thing I have to live for now is to see you go down. You and that other witch."

I laughed dismissively. "How are you going to make me go down?"

"I will destroy you!" His face was red, veins standing out on his forehead and in his neck. I had successfully infuriated him. This was one deception I took no pride or satisfaction in. He leaned forward. "You will become a joke to the world. Oh, world-renowned Doctor Genevieve Lenard couldn't even stop a bomb. Not even when she knew about it long before the time. The world will know that you can also be weak and incompetent. I will destroy your reputation. I will destroy you all!"

He leaned across the table and continued shouting over and over that he was going to destroy me. We had lost him. He had gone into a place in his head where there was no peace. Despite our history and his wildly misguided plans, I knew it all came from a place of unbearable pain. I looked at Colin and shook my head. A second later the door opened and Daniel and the other two men stepped in.

I left the room with much more knowledge than I had before, but it weighed heavily on me. In the corridor I leaned against the wall, for once not concerned about hygiene. With only the greatest control was I able to not hug myself and fold double in emotional discomfort.

"Hey." Colin stepped into my personal space and rested his hands on my shoulders. "You did great in there. You know this. You also know that none of this is your fault."

Uncontrolled tears filled my eyes. "Rationally I know this. Why am I feeling so... so wretched?"

"It's called empathy, Jenny. Something he said must have resonated with you, made you understand his craziness."

I had never been accused of being empathetic. It was an aggravating misconception about people with autism. Just because I was non-neurotypical didn't mean I didn't feel. Didn't empathise. It would appear that Colin wasn't of the same opinion as the people of my childhood. They had called me cold, unfeeling.

It unnerved me that Colin understood me so well. That nobody ever understood me had become a cloak that I had worn almost all my life. Having that taken away from me was making me feel naked and vulnerable. It also made me feel light and connected. The cognitive dissonance Colin caused was not comfortable.

Often I considered people who needed reassurances weak. Why could they not use straightforward logic to reason themselves out of whatever self-doubt they were suffering from? I had to retract those beliefs. Colin's reassurances, him telling me things about myself I knew to be true, lifted the weight from my emotions.

"Hey." Colin squeezed my shoulders. "You are none of the things he accused you of and everything I believe in. You are kind, caring, loyal and want to help. Only sometimes you don't know how to communicate those things."

I awkwardly patted his hands on my shoulders. "Thank you. I needed to hear that."

"Doc!" Manny stormed out of the observation room towards us. "You were brilliant. I think you have to—"

"Manny, please don't finish that sentence. I don't ever want to do this again."

His face softened. "That bad, huh? I saw that the guy totally lost it."

"What's going to happen to him now?" I asked.

Manny considered his answer. "I'll put in a request that he be transferred to an institution where he will receive the help he needs."

"Thank you." I swallowed hard at the emotions strangling me.

"Doc, he was out of reality long before you wrote your article or spoke to him here. You have to remember that the info you got us might be very helpful. You just need to interpret it now."

I laughed weakly. "I need to sleep for at least four hours before I work on that. I need to create some emotional distance first. And I really need to rest."

Manny looked at Colin. "Take her home and make sure she rests. And for the love of God, play some Mozart for her. I'll get the guys here to start working on whatever they can."

We left with minimal goodbyes. The drive home was done in blissful silence. Colin had removed his hipster hoodie. I could see his profile in the soft lights of the streetlamps.

"I was wrong," I said into the silence. "About so many things."

"Which things, Jenny?"

"There are a lot of good people, caring people in this world."

"That is true." He didn't push for more.

"My experiences taught me that people don't even try to understand other people. It is so much easier for everyone to make fun of that which they don't understand. Mock it or declare it evil. It's been a human reaction to anything atypical since the beginning."

"And you believed this?"

"Believe. I still believe this." I looked out of the side window at the street flashing by. "But it doesn't apply to everyone."

"No?"

"It doesn't apply to Phillip, to Manny, to Vinnie, to Francine or to you." I started counting off my fingers. "Phillip has known me for six years and not once belittled me for being non-neurotypical. He was the first person to treat me like a normal human being. He gave me a job, an opportunity to be completely independent. He gave me a life. Then the rest of you entered my life. Manny is gruff, but his gestures proves that he cares about me. Francine wants to be my friend and Vinnie is a brother I never had."

"And me?"

"You understand me." I grew quiet for a long while. When I spoke my voice was raw with emotion. "It scares me."

We had reached our apartment building and Colin parked the car in the street. He turned to me. "I know it scares you, Jenny. A lot of this scares me too."

"What? Working with Manny or understanding me?"

He laughed. "I think working with Manny scares me more. Understanding you? It's not that hard. You're not that difficult."

Never in my life would I have thought to hear someone say those words. Not about me. And not when my entire life had been a fight to understand others and make myself accessible at least to some degree. Accessible enough to be part of society, even if only the fringes.

My thoughts were rudely interrupted by the buzzing of my smartphone.

I took the phone from its pocket in my handbag and swiped the screen. "Oh God. I have another package."

Chapter TWENTY-FOUR

"Vinnie is already on his way there, so you can stop arguing now, Jenny." Colin was speaking softer and slower. He was getting angry.

"We could've gone. It's a quick drive there and we are in the car."

"Still." He shook his head. "I'm getting out and going up. Coming?"

We had been arguing for the last ten minutes about collecting the package from the mailing service. In that time I had thought Colin was being rude by playing with his phone. Little did I know he was texting Vinnie about the package. I got out of the SUV and followed Colin into the building.

"I hate it when you disregard my opinions and make decisions without me."

We got in the elevator and Colin turned to me. "I apologise. But you know why I do this, right?"

We reached my floor and Colin gestured for me to leave the elevator ahead of him. A gentleman. He had keys ready and started unlocking the door to my apartment. I walked past him when he opened the door wide. "I know you do this to protect me."

"You don't have to sound so disgusted by that," he laughed.

Completely out of character, I threw my handbag on the dining room table. I walked to the kitchen to start the coffee machine. As soon as the coffee started filling the cup, I went back to the dining room table to carefully hang my handbag on the back of its usual chair. I smiled at the feeling of rightness and returned to the kitchen for the coffee. There was not going to be any sleeping tonight.

Colin disappeared to his room for a few minutes. By the time he came out, I was sitting in front of my computers with two cups of coffee. He joined me.

"I know you mean well," I said without looking away from the laptop monitor. When he didn't respond, I looked up. He was smiling.

"You're not alone anymore, Jenny. You don't have to carry your whole life all on your own. There are people who will help you."

"You mean overbearing men who just want to protect me?" There was no anger in my tone. Just a bit of sadness. "What if I get used to it and you disappear again?"

He flinched. "That was a mistake. Going to Russia and not telling you when we came back. It was all a mistake. I, we, are here to stay."

The rational part of me was fighting the illogical desperation to believe that. I looked back at the computer monitor. Work was safer. Made more sense.

"What are you looking at?" Colin asked.

"The thefts. I've been wondering why the thieves were told to steal those specific works of art. Maybe someone realised this and didn't say, but how did Kubanov know to get Jonas to tell Luc which specific works to look for in the security companies' systems?"

"Good question." Colin leaned back in his chair and sipped his coffee. "I would dare say that Kubanov already had Jonas hack those systems to have a look-see."

"That is such a silly phrase. You look at a system. Not look-see. It's redundant. Silly." I tilted my head. "Francine thought the same. I don't like that you're speculating like that, but it is a viable explanation."

"Hah. We'll make a gut-following guesser out of you yet."

I looked at him in horror. "Never."

"I promise to keep on trying, Jenny." He smiled and straightened. "Okay, let's see what these thieves stole."

We went through the police files of the five thefts, including the young thief's interrupted theft and Francine's great-uncle. It gave us seven works of art.

"What do an Alberto Giacometti bronze sculpture, a rare American coin, a Jackson Pollock painting, a Pablo Picasso painting, a Damien Hirst sculpture, a Francis Bacon triptych and an Amedeo Modigliani sculpture have in common?" I asked. Since Colin was an infamous art thief, I considered him the authority on this subject.

"Nothing. Not all seven of them. They are vastly different in era and medium, not even the artists have anything in common. Five of the artists originated from different countries. Nope, there is nothing that ties them."

I leaned my head back, closed my eyes and mentally started writing Mozart's Violin Sonata No. 21 in E minor. There was such complex logic in Mozart's compositions. It soothed over my frayed nerves and tiredness and brought clarity. My eyes flew open and I looked at the clock on my laptop. Two hours had passed.

Movement drew my attention to the reading area. Colin was pacing, his body screaming distress. He was speaking on his smartphone. The surge of adrenaline from my mental discovery turned into a heaviness in my stomach that made me feel slightly nauseous.

"You do everything they say, Vin. Don't fuck around with this. Don't be a hero." Colin's voice was tight, his grip on the smartphone even tighter. "Okay, I'll tell her. We'll see you soon."

He ended the call and turned to me. I knew my eyes were wide, my face an expression of worry. "What happened?"

"Vinnie is okay." He walked to the table and sat down facing me. "The same as the last time, he took all his toys to check out your package. One of his toys is a handheld biosensor."

I had never heard of or seen a biosensor, but the implications were clear. My heart rate increased and my breathing became shallow. "No. Please don't tell me this. No."

Colin took my hands in his. "Vinnie is fine. That is why I started this conversation with that sentence, so you don't have to worry. He's being decontaminated by the Hazmat team, but they're sure he's fine. I got him to agree to go to Paul to double-check in any case. Wait, I just have to phone Paul quickly."

While Colin arranged with Paul to make sure that Vinnie was one hundred percent free of any disease, I took the time to calm my breathing. Colin ended his call with a smile.

"Paul says that we're going to make him rich with all our visits this week."

My mind had never even covered those grounds. "Exactly who is paying for all these illegal treatments?"

"As long as no major surgery is involved, Paul appreciates my art greatly."

"You paint forgeries for him?"

"Yes, and he knows they're forgeries, so everything is above board. Okay, maybe not everything." He narrowed his eyes. "Calmer?"

"Yes. Tell me what happened with Vinnie."

"It was a large envelope in your mailbox. He scanned for all kinds of things with his not-even-on-the-market gadgets. The first thing he did was check for explosives or a bomb. There were also no electronics. Then he brought out this nifty biosensor that some nanotechnology firm is testing for release early next year. This thing lit up like a Christmas tree."

I smiled. That was a fun and apt analogy. "What was it?"

"Anthrax."

"Oh, no. Did Vinnie inhale this? Are you sure he's okay?"

"Vinnie only handled the envelope, he didn't open it. His exposure to it was minimal." His smile was wide and genuine. "Sometimes Francine's paranoia really pays off. She had indoctrinated him so much in the last few days with all her wild theories that he not only wore his usual gloves, but also a specialised mask when he checked your mail. The Hazmat guys thought he was a genius for doing that. He, on the other hand, is pissed off because he'll have to listen to Francine say 'Told you so' for the next few years."

"It's rather disconcerting how often she is right."

"True. Anyway, when Vinnie's biosensor went off, he phoned Manny and soon the Hazmat team was there. Their equipment is better than the handheld gadget, so they were able to determine that the amount of anthrax Vinnie was exposed to was minimal. Together with the gloves and mask, there is almost no threat."

"But he's going to Paul?" I no longer cared that there was any kind of illegality involved.

"He promised me, yes. So, the Hazmat team opened the envelope in those containment thingies or something. I didn't get all of that. The important part is that there was a lot of anthrax, but it was put in between the pages of a magazine."

I couldn't swallow. My throat was dry. "The academic journal my article was published in?"

"That specific issue, yes. Most of the anthrax spores were on the pages of your article."

I rested my crossed forearms on the table and dropped my head in the protective frame of my arms. It was surreal to think that someone wanted to kill me. In such an extreme manner, no less.

The sounds of my front door being unlocked made me lift my head. It was Francine. She was balancing her open laptop on her arm while closing the door. The excessive energy in her walk and the brightness of her eyes indicated good news.

"Was I right or was I right?" she asked.

"Your question doesn't make sense," I said. "It doesn't offer options."

"I was right. Vinnie was wrong. He's so going to eat crow. He is okay because I was right. It is a beautiful moment." She smiled and fell into a chair across from us. "You're going to love me."

"We already love you, honey," Colin said.

"You're going to love me more. Genevieve is going to love me. She's going to say she loves me. The two of us are going to have us a little moment. She's going to buy a constellation and name it after me." She closed her eyes and breathed deeply. When she opened her eyes, she looked marginally calmer.

And slightly embarrassed. "My mouth runs away with me sometimes when I had a super-cool breakthrough."

"Only gullible people buy stars within certain constellations, Francine. You can't own a star. I would never buy you a constellation. I would rather buy you another computer." The more I spoke, the more I realised that yet again I had most likely misunderstood. I was fully prepared to be smiled at, teased or humoured. I did not expect to see tears in Francine's eyes.

"You're the best friend anyone could ask for, Genevieve." She sniffed inelegantly and looked at her computer. "I know everything about Kubanov's baby brother, Pavel."

Her statement grabbed my attention. "Yes?"

"Well, he's dead. He died fifteen years ago."

"That's the same time his mother, their mother, died," Colin said.

"Fifteen years? Hmm. That's how many red daffodils Kubanov sent me." I nodded. "Yes, that would be the symbolism he wanted to connect to the flowers."

"How messed up can one individual be?" Francine pulled her laptop closer. "But there is more to the brother's story. Much more. When he was sixteen, he came to France on a holiday visa. He was here to work on a farm during the summer holidays. He might have inherited his father's abusive nature or his brother's sicko character, but he got into a heated argument with the farmer. The next day the farmer and his wife were found brutally murdered in their home. Naturally, Pavel was taken into custody as a suspect."

"Oh dear God." My hand covered my mouth and I stared at Francine.

"Yup, you got it, girl. At that time Kubanov was in the military, working his way up the ranks. He had enough pull and money to hire really good legal representation for his baby brother. He hired the law firm Raymond Godard was working for. The police had slipped up with some evidence and legal procedures. Godard could easily have had that case dismissed, but he never addressed the mishandling of evidence. Pavel was going to be tried as an adult and was sent to jail awaiting trial. There he was killed by inmates with some connection to Russia. Rumour had it that it was revenge on Kubanov. I think that Kubanov blames himself for the death of his brother."

"And the death of his mother," Colin said. "She must have committed suicide around the time that Pavel died."

"No, he doesn't blame himself." So much about Kubanov now made sense to me. "He would blame everyone, anyone, but would never accept such responsibility. Typical of a psychopath, he is narcissistic and a megalomaniac. He has delusional beliefs of greatness, of power, of importance. He also is pathologically egocentric. There is no real capacity in a man like him for attachment.

"His anger, bitterness and grudge would come from the blot that was left on his image because of the role he had played in the death of his brother. His image of greatness and power is something that he would protect at all costs. Kubanov would find someone to aim all the blame at and make that person his target. President Godard being the main perpetrator. I'm just a bonus."

"Holy hell, Doc." Manny stood in the front door and looked at me in horror. "Now it's the president as well?"

He looked haggard. I didn't know if I looked any better. It had been a tough night. Manny locked the door and joined us at the table. He lowered himself slowly in the chair.

"How's Vinnie?" I asked.

"The arsehole is fine. If I heard you correctly a second ago, we don't need to worry about him right now. We need to worry about the president. Speak to me."

I told him everything we had discovered and pieced together.

"Oh yes," I said. "I also found a connection between the thefts and President Godard. We know that Jonas aka DeathRabbit867 had ordered Luc Alain to search the security companies for specific works of art. Francine and Colin posited that Kubanov had already had Jonas search for it."

"Then why would he get Luc to search for it again?" Manny asked.

"To use Genevieve's fancy word, I posit that Jonas went in and out undetected," Francine said. "He knew how amateurish Luc is and knew that he would leave some sort of trace that would lead us to him."

"The scapegoat," Manny said. "Okay, so how did you connect the artworks to the president?"

"The artworks have nothing in common," I said. "Each originated from a specific country. If we look at this according to the chronology of the thefts, it gives us Switzerland, the United States of America, Spain, Britain, Ireland and Italy. Those were the countries in exact order that President Godard visited in his first three months as president."

"You're sure about this?" Manny asked and then he sighed. "I don't know why I even ask. Of course you're sure. But I need confirmation. Francine, can you check the president's itinerary for the first three months?"

"Here," Francine said after a few moments. She turned her laptop so that Manny could see.

Manny lowered his head and stared at her. "That was mighty fast, little girl. You have the president's itinerary at your fingertips?"

"Knowledge is power, handsome." She smiled at his irritation and pointed at the monitor. "Look. It's exactly like Genevieve said."

He look at the laptop, loathing around his mouth and eyes. With a heavy sigh he took his smartphone from the inside pocket of his coat.

"See his nice gloves?" Francine asked, pulling my attention to Manny's hands. He was wearing form-fitting black gloves with a silicone grip pattern on the palms and a light grey material on the tips of his index fingers. "I got him those. They're touchscreen gloves. Now he doesn't have to feel so helpless anymore."

Manny glared at her and turned his torso away from her while making his call. "Daniel, this is turning into a combined threat. Kubanov has a hard-on for the president. Where are they? Hmm-mm? Yes? And you are sure that everything has been checked?"

He finished the call and sank deeper into the chair. We waited, but he didn't speak.

"So?" Colin asked.

"They're still at home. It is after all half past five in the morning, a time when normal people are still sleeping and early birds start waking up. The president is already up, his wife and son usually get up an hour after him. Or that's what Daniel just told me. I don't really care. I'm tired."

It was the first time since I had met Manny that he had admitted being tired. It came as no shock since he had been the victim of a bomb blast less than seventy-two hours ago.

"Maybe we should all sleep for a few hours." Manny stood up. "I think I'm getting too old for this."

"Aw, handsome." Francine closed her laptop and also got up. "You're just a bit banged up. A little beauty sleep and one of Vinnie's breakfasts and you'll be as good as new."

Manny snorted. He looked at me. "I'm going to get some shut-eye. I think you should also hit the sack for an hour or so. Let's pick this up again in two hours. Frey, you can translate all this to her."

Francine winked at me and followed Manny out.

"I don't need a translation," I said. "It's crude English, but clear enough. What I do need is to know is whether this is it."

"What do you mean?" Colin narrowed his eyes. "What more can there be? We know that Professor Tremont wants revenge on you and the first wife, and that Kubanov wants revenge on you and the president."

"We also know that it will be a grand finale." I stared at the wall across from me. "It doesn't feel complete. I feel like I'm missing something."

"We've been at this since yesterday morning. Don't you want to sleep for an hour?"

"It wouldn't help me." I would never be able to fall asleep with the niggling feeling of an impending connection. There was only one way to find this elusive clue. "You go sleep for an hour. I need to work this out."

Colin sighed, long and heavy. "In that case, I'm going to take a shower, make coffee and let you Mozart your way through this."

"I told you not to use Mozart as a verb. It annoys me." I stood up stiffly. I had been in this chair for some time. "A shower actually sounds like an excellent idea."

Twenty minutes later, I walked out of my bedroom, refreshed after a scorching hot shower and dressed in clean clothes. Apart from the realisation that I was starving, I had had no epiphanies in the shower. I waited patiently in the kitchen for my coffee machine to spit out a strong Brazilian blend coffee. The aroma alone was enough to energise me. I grabbed a few of Vinnie's oatmeal cookies, picked up my mug and went to the dining room table.

Colin came in, his hair still wet from the shower. He had shaved and was wearing dark gray pants and an expensive-looking black sweater. He also looked refreshed.

"Silence or Mozart?" he asked, walking to the sound system.

"Put on Mozart's Symphony No. 26 in E-flat major, please." I took a large bite from one of the cookies. The opening sounds of the first movement filled the room and almost simultaneously I felt a shift in my mind. It was as if everything inside me aligned the moment I heard Mozart. I sipped my coffee and ate another cookie. This was not working fast enough. I put the mug on the coaster next to my notepad and closed my eyes.

It was the argument between Vinnie and Francine that made me open my eyes. They were in the kitchen, Vinnie cooking breakfast and Francine criticising his method of flipping pancakes.

I smiled. Then I frowned. An hour in my head and all I could do was confirm everything we had already discovered. Some of which had been mere hypotheses, but now I knew where to get the concrete evidence.

This was worrying. An urgency I did not often experience discomforted me. It was as if I needed something else to reach that hidden revelation in my brain. Whether it was more data, more Mozart or more sleep I did not know. What I was well aware of was the utmost importance of this revelation, this connection. Not even the mouth-watering smell of Vinnie's cooking could calm the tension gathering inside me.

My smartphone buzzed, making me jump.

"Hey, take it easy." Colin was sitting next to me, solving a Sudoku puzzle in a daily newspaper. "It's just your phone."

I reached for my handbag. "Well, lately when my phone beeps, it's some horrid email for a package or… God, this is from Professor Tremont."

"Impossible," Vinnie said. He was standing next to me with the pan in one hand and spatula in the other. "He's in jail."

I inspected Vinnie from head to toe. He looked his usual intimidating self. "Are you well?"

He smiled at me and leaned a bit forward. "As right as rain, Jen-girl. Even Paul says that there is nothing to worry about, so you can stop looking at me like that."

"Are you sure?"

"That you should stop looking at me like that? Yes." He smiled at my frown. "Yes, I'm sure I'm fine. Tell us about the email."

I first did another inspection of Vinnie's nonverbal cues. He wasn't lying. He was genuinely okay. I pulled my laptop closer and opened my inbox. "At the police station, Professor Tremont said that he had finished setting everything up. He must have scheduled this email to be sent at a specific time."

"What does it say?" Francine asked.

I stared at the screen, the *corrugator procerus* muscles pulling my brow into an even tighter frown. I lifted both shoulders. "'Bon Appétit'."

"Breakfast's not ready yet, Jen-girl."

"No, the email says 'Bon Appétit' and only that." I shook my head. "This doesn't make sense. If he had scheduled the email to be sent at this time, then it is obviously around breakfast time. But why would he wish us a pleasant meal if our eating has nothing to do with his great plan? Well, his and Kubanov's great plan."

"What's going on here?" Manny asked, walking towards us. I checked behind him and relaxed when I saw that he had locked the door. He still looked exhausted, but had also taken a shower and changed clothes. He was wearing a shirt that was so neatly ironed that I wondered if Vinnie had been doing laundry for Manny. For some reason that thought greatly amused me, and I smiled.

"What are you smiling at, Doc?"

"My own thoughts." Taking into consideration the tentative tolerance between these men, I did not think it wise to share those thoughts. I looked at my laptop monitor and my smile disappeared. "I got another email."

Manny walked faster and sat down across from me. Sombre. "What does it say?"

"'Bon Appétit'."

"What the fuck does that mean?"

"We were talking about it when you came in," I said. "There is no context and it doesn't make any sense."

"Hmm." Manny thought about it for some time before he looked at Vinnie. "Pancakes for breakfast?"

Vinnie looked into the pan he still wielded in front of him like a weapon. "I thought we all needed some unhealthy levels of sugar and calories to fuel us for the day."

"Are the president and his family still safe?" Francine asked as Vinnie walked back to the kitchen, mumbling about ridiculous suspicions.

"Yes. Daniel phoned to say that they have added to the

security detail. This morning the president will attend a function with his wife and son." He held up one gloved hand. "Before you get all upset, the severely neurotic presidential security detail have checked everything and double-checked it."

I was not convinced. The niggling just beneath my consciousness became stronger. "Where is this?"

"At their son's school. Since there are a lot of VIP children in the school, security is always pretty tight. The president was asked to not attend the breakfast concert this morning, but he refused. It's an annual breakfast the school hosts for all the kids and their parents. They get to enjoy a meal together while some of the kids play some instrument or something. Since there was no proof that he was being targeted at this event, he didn't want to take this very important milestone away from his son. Apparently the little guy had been practicing his Chopin non-stop for the last three weeks." Manny's mouth quivered. "Daniel said the bodyguards were convinced their ears were bleeding from hearing the same pieces over and over."

It was smooth. The transition from disjointed pieces of information into an all-inclusive, multi-faceted cognisance of everything that had taken place in the last week. I felt at peace with this new understanding as everything quietly fitted together providing me with the full picture.

"It's not the president or his wife who is the target," I said in a whisper. "It's their son."

My apartment was quiet. Nobody talked or asked questions. They just stared at me. Vinnie rushed back to the table, this time sans pan. I had their full attention.

"Think of the Bible verse on the post-it note. Exodus 20 verse 5, stating that the iniquity of the fathers will be visited upon the children. You thought it could have been me. Add to that this morning's email wishing me 'Bon Appétit'?" I looked at Manny. "There is a biological bomb at the school. Kubanov will be there to set it off, just like he was there when I stepped on the bomb and he was there to detonate the bomb that injured you."

"Whoa, Doc. You're going too fast here." Manny was pale. "What the bleeding hell are you talking about?"

I slowed down my thinking process and considered my words. Explaining myself was more complicated than I enjoyed. Every time. "The impostor on the videos was Kubanov. We've established that. He likes to show off and to be there for the action. Yes?"

Manny nodded.

"That combined with his past behaviours tells me that he will be wherever this grand finale he planned is to take place. I believe that is at the school. All the clues point to that. I can explain it to you in fine detail, but we'll be wasting time. You should be phoning Daniel right now to start looking for a bomb or some other delivery system that will spread a pathogen into the air at this event at the school. I think that it will be anthrax, but this is more speculative than anything else. Phone Daniel now." My last sentence came out as a somewhat loud order. One to which Manny responded immediately.

He pulled his smartphone out of his pants pocket and dialled. "Daniel, it's the son. It's the president's son."

Chapter TWENTY-FIVE

"Would you put a sock in it?" Colin snapped at Manny as we screeched around another corner.

"Then stop driving like the poet Sydney Goddphin and drive like a thief in a getaway car." Manny pushed himself deeper into the passenger seat and braced his feet against the foot panel. With his hands still bandaged and most likely sensitive, he was not holding onto anything.

I, on the other hand, was sitting in the backseat of Colin's SUV, the safety belt tight across my chest. My one hand was clutching the door handle, the other pressed flat on the seat next to me for balance. I didn't know why Manny was complaining about Colin's driving. He was speeding dangerously through the streets of Strasbourg. We had left the city centre's congested streets and were heading for the leafy suburbs where the school was located.

"Step on it, Frey. I want to be there five minutes ago."

"We'll be there in three. Stop your incessant nagging. You're worse than Vinnie when…" Colin stopped talking in order to concentrate on overtaking three vehicles, jumping the curb and bouncing back onto the road. "… he wants something."

"You compare me to that gorilla?" Manny sucked in air when Colin nearly collided with an oncoming car while overtaking again. He swerved in time and for a few metres drove on the shoulder of the wrong side of the road before slowing down and turning into a side street.

"You're okay there, Doc?" Manny didn't take his eyes off the road to look at me.

"I'm okay." I wondered if it was a lie. That would greatly depend on each person's individual definition of the word 'okay'. This unproductive reasoning in my mind kept me from panicking. I had never been in a car that was driven at such speed. The part of my brain that objectively observed things told me that Colin was an exceptional driver. Somehow that knowledge did not relax my tense muscles or stop me from biting down hard on my jaw.

The streets we were racing through now were lined with leafless trees. The current temperatures held the heaps of shovelled snow frozen. The sun that had greeted us when we left my apartment had now disappeared behind cold clouds. I wished for summer. And to end this perilous journey. We raced into a long driveway that led to impressive brick buildings spread over a sprawling property.

I was looking at my past. These were the schools my parents had tried to send me to. All prestigious academic institutions had the same look. The look that communicated money, success and intellectuality. To me it communicated pretentiousness, unhealthy ambition and a lack of love.

"Okay, cowboy, slow down. We don't want to make a scene here." Manny sat up. "They're expecting us at the gate."

We were stopped briefly by a police officer who pointed Colin to a place behind the main building. We passed many expensive cars in the parking area, some with drivers waiting inside heated vehicles. At the back of the main building were fewer cars. A bus was parked next to the doors leading into the building.

"Stop next to the bus." Manny fumbled with the seatbelt release button while Colin parked, facing the nose of the bus.

He glanced at Manny and smiled. "Need some help there, Millard?"

"Fuck you, Frey." Manny lifted his hand and waited for Colin to release the seatbelt. He mumbled his thanks and jumped out of the car.

Getting out of the SUV was not that easy for me. My hands were shaking as I opened the door and my legs did not feel as steady as usual. The adrenaline surge was affecting my mobility.

I took a deep breath and straightened my spine. A concert hall full of children and parents were in need of our combined skills. My dislike for this environment and the after-effects of Colin's driving had no bearing here.

I turned to the bus. It had only one door, which I found odd and interesting. The door opened and Daniel appeared at the top of the two lowered steps. There was no welcoming smile. "Come in, guys."

Daniel disappeared into the bus again. I followed Manny up the steps with Colin right behind me. I stepped into the bus that looked large from the outside and stopped. Colin bumped into me and looked over my shoulder.

"Um, Jenny, are you going to be okay with this?" he asked softly next to my ear, his British accent in place.

The bus had been outfitted with so much equipment that the pride I fostered for my viewing room diminished. At the back was a small conference table and chairs. Along one side of the bus were three computer stations, each with a keyboard and three monitors angled in a semi-circle. The opposite wall was covered in charts, touchscreen whiteboards and electronic equipment that I did not recognise.

Counting myself, there were currently eight people in the bus and it felt cramped. Claustrophobia tightened my throat. I could see that this bus was created to host up to a dozen people comfortably, but for me this was unimaginable. For extra strength I took five seconds to imagine Mozart's Piano Concerto No. 27 playing softly in the background. My breathing slowed and deepened.

"Please come in," Daniel said from the conference table. "We've been waiting for you. Let me introduce everyone so we can get to work."

I chose the least populated area of the bus, the computer area, to stand. I leaned lightly against a city map pinned to the wall. Colin was next to me, so close that we were touching shoulder to hip. I didn't mind. It anchored me.

Daniel started pointing at the men in the bus. "Next to me is Monsieur Aumont, the director of the school and board member. Next to him is Ian, the head of GSPR, the president's security detail. Ian's people are already in the ball room and around the school. We'll make use of that."

I studied the two men and came to immediate conclusions. The head of GSPR was a man formed by his service to the country. I doubted he experienced, or allowed himself to experience, soft emotions. His life was about being alert, protecting and leading. Monsieur Aumont was the exact opposite, possibly with the exception of leading. Even his features were similar to the people from my parents' social circles. High forehead, narrow nose, straight posture and arrogance in every muscle movement. I didn't like him.

Daniel introduced his other two team members in the bus. Pink was a name completely unsuited to the muscular man working between two computer stations. He was an expert in everything connected to information technology and electronics. He nodded at us without taking his eyes from the monitors, his fingers flying over the keyboard. His team mate, Charles, was the tactical leader of the team and stood close to the door, his arms crossed over his chest.

I glanced at the closed door behind Charles and flinched. Colin touched my lower back and brought my attention back to Daniel's introductions.

"Doctor Lenard is an expert in nonverbal communication."

"How is that supposed to prevent some imbecile from bombing my school?" Monsieur Aumont asked. Even his speech pattern was typical of this subculture. His question was asked with a cultured accent, in an apparent respectful tone, but his body language gave away his condescension. To him we were all inferior.

Daniel ignored Monsieur Aumont and finished introducing Manny and Colin. Both snickered when Colin was referred to as my assistant. I didn't bother to point out the mistake or try to understand Manny and Colin's amusement. I tried to focus on the situation and not the space that felt as if it was slowly constricting even more.

"Except for Monsieur Aumont, everyone here is fully briefed on the events of the last few days and how this led up to our presence at the school," Daniel said. "Monsieur Aumont understands that not all information can be disclosed to persons without needed clearance."

I had no idea what information Monsieur Aumont had been given and feared that I might disclose things better not publicly known. With a shudder, I acknowledged to myself that I currently found myself in a situation beyond my skill-set. I looked at Colin and he shook his head slightly. Since I had no context from which to interpret his communication, I turned back to what Daniel was saying.

"A quick rundown on what we have at the school. At present there are nine hundred and seventy-three people in this building. To our benefit, everyone is contained mostly in the ballroom and kitchen. Like I said, Ian's people inspected the premises thoroughly two days ago and again yesterday, ensuring the president's safety for this morning's event. Since the alert went out yesterday, they've upped the detail. There are presently eighteen of his people spread all over the school, in the ballroom, kitchens, everywhere. They are busy moving people out of the other areas, making sure that we only have the ballroom and kitchen populated. We were discussing sending some of our men in there."

"I don't think that's a good idea." All eyes turned to me and I regretted verbalising my thoughts.

"Why not, Doctor Lenard?" Ian asked.

"I believe that Kubanov is inside the building. The moment you send a team in there or start sending people out, he might release whatever pathogen he has."

Daniel nodded. "We came to the same conclusion, so we're keeping the status quo as it is. We have the Hazmat teams on standby outside of a safe perimeter. The last thing we want to do is trigger this man into acting rashly. So far we've been able to keep things going as is. Sending our guys in with biosensors will create a stir and most likely panic which is something we want to avoid at all cost."

"What do you recommend we do, Doctor Lenard?" Ian asked.

I was surrounded by alpha males, with the exception of Monsieur Aumont. What made this group of men exceptional in my eyes was their openness to cooperate. There were no territorial fights, no posturing, just a common goal and the need to find the quickest, cleanest solution to this situation.

"Sorry for stating the obvious, but we need to determine where the pathogen is and how Kubanov plans to deliver it."

The tactical leader Charles shifted from one foot to the other, restless to act. "This shindig is only for another hour and a half. We don't have time to figure this out."

Monsieur Aumont sighed loudly. He pointed with his sharp chin to some glossy pamphlets lying on the conference table. "These are the programmes for this morning's breakfast concert. It's all there. Even photos. As you'll see everything is planned to the minute."

Colin moved to the table and took two pamphlets. He handed me one. I glanced at it without completely registering what I saw.

"This event was planned under great secrecy," Monsieur Aumont continued. "No one outside of this school knew about this. An hour before the event started we alerted a selected few journalists. This is good PR for the school and for everyone involved. No one else knew about it until an hour before it started."

I cleared my throat. "These are teenagers with access to the internet, they have smartphones, use multiple forms of social media. Jonas, the expert hacker, would've picked up any communication about this if he had searched for this."

"I'm well aware of that," the director said. "The children in this school come from well-to-do families, families with political enemies, families that have entire security teams appointed to them. A lot of these kids have bodyguards. They understand the importance of keeping things under their hats."

We stared at him. I bit down on my lips to not say anything about his naivety.

"We're wasting time." Daniel looked at Colin. "Mister Goddphin, if you were going to set off a bio-weapon, how would you go about it?"

Colin stiffened. I knew that Manny had not told Daniel anything about Colin's background, yet the leader of the GIPN team had just proven his skill at reading people.

"Firstly, I would never do anything remotely like this." Colin leaned closer against me. "But I can imagine that Kubanov would have had this all set up months ago. If his motivation is to get to the president's son, he would have been here for some time looking for opportunities to exact his revenge in the most satisfying way."

"I agree," I said. "I believe that he's had someone here for a few months even to keep an eye on the president's son. He would not have wasted his time or energy with that. But today he would want to be here, to watch his handiwork."

Colin nodded. "Yup. He has someone at the school working for him and he got in as one of the temporary staff. Maybe the catering company, cleaning crew or even as one of the security guards."

"Impossible." The director lifted his nose to look down at Colin even though he was sitting and Colin standing. "All our staff, permanent and temporary, are vetted. Because we have diplomats' children here and other VIP children, a person entering these premises for anything other than a prearranged meeting has to be approved by the local police."

This man's arrogance pulled me back into my past. These people were never at fault, never open to learn and most definitely not open to change. I looked at Daniel. "He's not helpful. My professional opinion is that he will argue every decision you make and might even go as far as interfering. I suggest removing him from our discussion and keeping him contained."

My suggestion solicited many different responses. The director turned red in his face and spluttered. Charles and Colin chuckled. Pink stopped working on the computers for the first time since I entered the bus. He turned to look at me with surprise and respect on his face. Only Ian and Daniel maintained neutral expressions, but I had seen the micro-expression around Daniel's eyes. He had been surprised and amused.

"In this regard, I agree with Doctor Lenard." Daniel looked at Charles. "Please escort Monsieur Aumont out."

The director complained loudly and then resorted to threats. He had no qualms using his position and connections as leverage. I could see the fear beneath it all, but I knew it was not concern for the people in the school's ball room. It was fear for himself and his reputation. Charles took him by the elbow and pushed him out of the door. I was relieved. Now I could speak without the overwhelming concern that I might be disclosing national secrets.

"You are a goddess."

I blinked at Pink. He had completely swivelled his chair to look at me. I didn't know how to react at this exaggerated praise. He smiled at me and turned back to his computers.

"He's being looked after," Charles said as he stepped back into the converted bus. I closed my eyes briefly when he shut the door behind him.

"Doc, are you okay?" Manny moved to get up, but stopped when I lifted my hand still holding the programme and pointed it at him as if it were a stop sign.

"I'm fine. It's just cramped in here."

"Okay, boys and goddess." Pink turned and winked at me. "I have the school's security cameras on the monitors here."

"Well done, Pink." Daniel got up from the conference table and pushed past me. I sucked in my breath when his protective jacket touched me. He stopped behind Pink to look at the monitors.

"Pink?" I whispered to Colin to take my mind off the tight space.

"I'm a big fan of her music, Doc." Pink moved his head until he could see past Daniel to make eye contact with me.

"Oh." My smile was not genuine. I did not know what or who he was talking about and this sudden social acceptance was confusing. I reverted to work. "Pink, can you put the security footage on all the monitors here? That way we can all see it."

"Sure." Within seven seconds all the monitors in the bus flickered to life with black and white images of the school interior. I walked to the third computer station and stared at the three monitors.

"Is this a live feed?" I asked.

"Yes, it is."

"Hmm."

"What is it, Doc?" Manny asked.

I didn't answer him immediately, but continued watching the monitors. Each wide monitor was divided into six screens, showing different camera shots all over the school. I focussed on three. "This is not a live feed."

"Sorry to disagree with you, goddess, but it is."

"Look at cameras three, seven and ten," I said. Spending my days in a viewing room looking for the smallest clues had made me unusually detail-oriented. "The shadows—"

"Oh my God, you're right." Pink moved closer to the monitors. "The sun is no longer shining, yet here you can see it streaming through the windows. This must have been recorded earlier and put on a loop."

"We don't have eyes inside," Daniel said. "Except for Ian's guys, we are blind."

"Doc, you need to do something." Manny got up and moved to us. I retreated, but he followed to look me in the eye. "Do some of your Mozart voodoo and tell us where Kubanov is and where he stashed that bomb."

"I can only tell you where Kubanov is if I see him. Whether he wears a disguise or not, I'm sure that I'll recognise him."

"Our priority is finding out if there is a bomb, where it is and what it is," Daniel said. "And we need to do it soon. I don't want anyone inside that ballroom to even suspect that something is amiss."

"My guys are busy covertly looking at the ventilation system, the food and as much else as they can," Ian said. "The problem we face is time and subtlety. In order to not spook this Kubanov, we can't storm around. That means that we could really do with some ideas, Doctor Lenard. These guys tell me that this is not your first picnic with Kubanov. Maybe you can give us some insight into how he plans to deliver this."

Again everyone turned to me. I was not comfortable being the centre of attention. The pressure and the confusing, yet interesting word choices kept me from catching the message my subconscious was trying to deliver.

"I need to get out of here," I said as I walked to the door. "Space and time."

I didn't care if they agreed or not. If they wanted my help, they would have to accept my process.

I stepped into the overcast morning and pulled my scarf higher around my throat. I walked around the side of the building and stopped when I had a full view of the main entrance. It looked like most of these exclusive academic institutions. A sweeping rounded staircase led up to heavy wooden doors which were closed. The seven-story building had not been built in this or the last century. My knowledge of architecture was far too limited to guess its age and design.

I heard footsteps on the paving behind me. It wasn't the controlled footfalls of law enforcement men, but rather movement which would have been almost inaudible if other shoes had been worn. A thief's walk.

"I'm here," Colin said softly.

"I know." I didn't look at him when he stopped next to me. We stood in silence for a few minutes, my mind not reaching that elusive bit of information. I knew that the men in the bus were not idly waiting around for me. Most likely they were working all possible angles in desperate pursuit of ending this. They had the training and tactical knowledge how to handle situations like this. I was sure there were numerous operational manuals they had had to study on this subject. I had limited knowledge and no experience.

In all honesty I could not imagine the pressures of their lives. At this very moment I felt the oppressive weight of responsibility pushing down on me. These men were tasked every day with life-and-death decisions made under unimaginable stress and time constraints. I had been asked to help stop a potential bomb and was hard pushed to not succumb to the desire to return to my safe viewing room or home. Yet I would not. I knew in a small way I could help. If nothing else, I had to open my mind to that clue.

I inhaled the cold air and closed my eyes. Irrationally hoping that only a few moments of Mozart would give me answers, I gave myself over to the power of his Symphony No. 5, one of his childhood symphonies. It could not have been five minutes later when I opened my eyes wide and looked at Colin. I waved the crumpled pamphlet at him. "It's in here."

"What is?"

I stared blankly at him for a second, then ran to the bus. Soft footsteps followed me. The door to the bus opened before I reached it. Charles held the door and I rushed inside. On one of the monitors was the view from a security camera mounted on the bus' roof and aimed at the spot I had been standing. They had been watching me.

"Doc?" Manny's posture communicated readiness to act.

"Look at the breakfast programme." I unfolded the badly crumpled glossy paper. "They should be eating breakfast now. In half an hour there will be a speech by the president, followed by a final performance of all the children."

"Yes?" Daniel said, looking at the pamphlet.

"Look at the picture at the back. It must have been taken during their dress rehearsal. All the performances are by individual students. It is the final performance that includes everyone, like on this photo."

"Oh God, of course." Ian took two steps to the conference table and ordered two of his men to the stage.

"What is it, Doctor Lenard?" Charles was the only one who did not have a shocked or relieved expression on his face.

"Look at the smoke on stage. A smoke machine would be the perfect delivery method to get a pathogen out there. Not only would it be strongest around the president's son, but it would be all the children. Whichever adults are exposed to the spores would be an additional reward."

The next ten minutes were sensory overload for me. The interior of the bus vibrated with battle-ready alpha-male body language. All of them were barking orders into phones, two-way radios and microphones. Silence settled inside the bus, everyone waiting for feedback from the people they had been communicating with. Daniel was the first to receive news from his earpiece. His body stilled and then shuddered.

"Secured," he said to us. "They have the smoke machine."

Another few minutes of silent communications and Ian sank into the closest chair. "Son of a bitch, that was too close."

"Update?" Manny asked him.

"One of Daniel's guys got a biosensor from the Hazmat team and took it in. The smoke machine doesn't have any explosives in it, but the biosensor is reading a pathogen around the machine. They've secured the area and unplugged the machine. The Hazmat team is sending one of their guys in to secure the machine and take it in. After they tested the air backstage, one of my guys took the biosensor and discreetly tested the air inside the ballroom. So far we have an all-clear, but my guy is still moving around the ballroom. We're trying to attract as little attention as possible."

"Because we still have a Russian to catch," Pink said. "I can't get these cameras to work, boss. We don't have eyes inside."

"Well." Daniel drew out the word. People did that to give their brains time to come up with an answer or solution. "After the final performance we will make an announcement. We'll use the usual gas leak excuse, and say that it's not an emergency, only a security concern. That is why we could hold off a full evacuation, but we need them all to leave the building."

"What if Kubanov has a plan B?" Colin asked. Angry looks were aimed at him so fast, he lifted both hands. "Just asking. I might have had a back-up plan."

"What do you think, Doc?" Manny asked.

I shook my head and lifted both shoulders. "I don't know. He's arrogant enough to believe that only one plan was needed, that nothing or no one would foil his plan. But on this I refuse to speculate. Too many lives are involved."

The men discussed this for a few minutes. They were in full agreement.

"We need to get everyone out as soon as possible," Ian said. "We'll take the risk."

Charles unfolded his arms. "We'll secure all the exits, getting everyone to leave through the front doors. It might cause a bit of a bottle neck sending them out one by one, but that way we can control everyone leaving."

"We can station Doctor Lenard at the bottom of the stairs to check everyone coming out. Hopefully we'll flush out Kubanov." Daniel looked at me. "You sure you'll recognise him?"

"No. I can never guarantee a sure result of anything. It is simply impossible. I am, however, confident that I will be able to recognise his body type and involuntary nonverbal behaviour."

"That's good enough for me." Ian stood. "Let's move out."

"Doc, you're with me," Charles said and waited for me and Colin to follow him out of the bus. Pink was the only person to stay behind. Charles led us to the main entrance. "I'll set you up in the safest place you can imagine."

Chapter TWENTY-SIX

"This is not the safest place I could imagine." I stood stiffly at the bottom of the wide staircase. The wooden front doors looked even larger than they did from my earlier viewpoint.

"They've already won the argument, Jenny." Colin's voice had a smile in it. It annoyed me even more.

"I have three snipers aiming their rifles at me, Colin. How is that safe?" I turned to him, my lips tight and my eyes accusing. "Tell me."

"I'm only going to tell you the same as Manny and Charles told you." He stopped trying to hide his smile. "Those guys are looking out for you. They have the best vantage points. Two behind us and one in front? I'd say they have us covered."

"With weapons." I knew my words came out clipped and strong, but I had never liked weapons. After my first experience with Kubanov, I liked them even less.

"You remember the signal, Jenny?"

"Of course I do. I'm not dull." I turned from him in disgust. Charles had insisted I practice it seven times. How difficult was it to lift one's right fist into the air?

As much as I had wanted to, I didn't take offence. These men were more than the average police officer. Without anyone revealing my autistic tendencies, Daniel and Ian had noticed that I was non-neurotypical. They had not once treated me with less respect or courtesy, but had adjusted their approach to make it easier for me. My respect had been growing for them by the minute.

While Daniel and Ian's teams had been getting ready to herd all the children and their parents out of the front door, Charles had explained the strategy of the three snipers to me. Logically it had sounded good. It did not feel good.

Firstly, they were there to keep me safe. They also had direct communication with Ian and Daniel and would get the word to them the moment I recognised Kubanov. I wouldn't have to speak or interact or even point. I merely had to lift my fist.

They would immediately stop anyone else from exiting. Other officers posted on a perimeter around me would move in and apprehend whoever had exited before I lifted my fist. In theory it sounded like a simple and easily executable plan. Lifting my fist was an insult to my skill-set, but I had doubts.

My doubts became of lesser importance as the front doors opened and Manny came rushing down the stairs. He looked harassed. More than usual.

"Doc, we're running into some trouble inside."

"What kind of trouble?" My hands felt very cold as adrenaline forced blood away from non-essential body parts.

"There are too many exits. We don't have enough people to cover those, and help evacuating the people. Daniel's guys are covering the exits and Ian's people are stretched really thin."

"You can't possibly expect of me to help you with the people?" Had he lost all his ability to consider the implications of such a request?

"Not you." Manny sighed. I blinked a few times at the combination of desperation and disgust on his face. "I need Frey to help us contain these folks. Will you be okay out here?"

Colin moved to say something, but stopped when I looked at him with censure. "I have three men with sniper rifles supposedly protecting me. I dare say I'm safe out here."

"Thanks, Doc." Manny's *levator labii superioris* muscles curled his top lip. "Come on, Frey. Time to be your entitled, charming self."

Colin touched my arm. "Are you completely sure you will be okay?"

"Go, I'll be fine." I pulled my arm closer to my body.

"You'll remember the signal?" He nodded at my scowl. "Okay. You need anything, you shout for me, okay?"

"Go, Colin."

He and Manny ran up the stairs and disappeared into the building. Again I was staring at the closed doors with three high-powered killing instruments aimed at me. I shuddered.

Fortunately I didn't have any more time to think about that. One of the heavy wooden doors swung open and a GIPN team member stepped out. He tilted his head as he communicated into his headset. He straightened as the first person left the building.

One by one people came through the door. Men, women and children. The adults were all dressed befitting their stature. The children who were not in school uniform were in clothes that could have been costumes or trendy, youthful outfits. There appeared to be a system. First the woman would be sent out, followed by her child or children, the father being last to join them. Men and women dressed in black suits urged them to their cars. I had come to the conclusion that all the black-suited men and women were from Ian's team.

The majority of the adults leaving the building were exhibiting nonverbal cues of great agitation. They did not appreciate being in a position of lesser power, forced to follow orders. A few were exceptions and showed genuine cooperation and care within their family core. Not one of them was Kubanov.

One of Daniel's team members joined me. A brief sideways glance at his protective gear identified him as GIPN. There was no need for conversation and I returned to scanning each individual coming through the doors.

Recognition slammed into my consciousness with lightning speed.

There was no warning, no blackness threatening my peripheral view, no tightness in my chest. This was completely different than usual. I was fully cognisant of my environment, of every new person leaving the building, but my body was frozen. Books and the internet taught lay people only two responses to danger. Fight or flight. Very few ever mentioned the freeze response. This particular reaction in the face of danger happened more often than anyone acknowledged, but it was the first time it happened to me.

My muscles were completely unresponsive to my brain's desperate orders to obey. Practicing seven times was not going to help me now to lift my fist. Not even with Kubanov standing right next to me.

"You know it's me standing here, don't you, Genevieve?"

I hated feeling so powerless. I hated that I couldn't speak. I hated above all that he pronounced my name in the French way.

"I suppose this drama playing out in front of us now is for my benefit. How sweet. Everybody looking for me with such vigour."

I couldn't even move my head to look at him. It left me at an even greater disadvantage. I couldn't read his nonverbal cues. I couldn't tell if he was being playful in a sick psychopath manner or whether he was leading up to action. Did he have another bomb in the building that he planned to detonate with me watching here? I wanted to scream, but most I managed was an increased blinking rate.

"You have proven yourself to be much more than simply a worthy adversary, Genevieve." The genuine respect I heard in his voice grated my every value and belief. I did not want the respect and admiration of a man like Kubanov. "I underestimated you. But here's the thing. I don't often repeat little mistakes like this. You have revealed so much about yourself in the last week, Genevieve. I feel like I truly know you now."

The coward in me wished for an episode. Unaware of my surroundings, I would not have had to listen to his threat issued so conversationally. I was terrified to think of the ways that Kubanov now thought he knew me. Was this knowledge of me going to put those around me in danger? I knew Manny, Colin, Vinnie and Francine had skills and contacts to protect themselves. But what about Phillip? The man I had come to view as a mentor in all thing social?

"Don't worry." Kubanov sounded genuinely consoling. "Your cleverness today has completely foiled my plans. All these good people are safe from me. For today. Since those irritating Men in Black wannabes unplugged the fog machine, there is no other threat." He laughed softly. "Well, except maybe for the ladies running too fast in their high heels. Those things can be deadly."

Only part of my brain was now listening to him. He boasted about how he had planned this for months. How easy it had been to get Professor Tremont's cooperation. There was malicious pleasure in his voice when he told me how he had enjoyed the shock on Manny's face when he had detonated that bomb. He didn't tell me anything I didn't already know or suspect, so I gave his bragging less attention. I poured most of my energy into the other part of my brain sending messages to my muscles. There was a complete communication breakdown. I couldn't even feel the cold in my hands I knew for certain was there. None of my muscles reacted.

"Are you having one of your famed episodes, Genevieve? Do you even know that I'm here? It's a pity, really. I wanted to ask you if you liked the Beata Beatrix that I had especially painted for you. Personally, I thought it was a masterpiece. And the flowers. Did you like them? Oh well, I'm having a wonderful chat with you, so I suppose it doesn't really matter if you can hear me or not."

Another two families left the building as we stood in companionable silence. Not only was I fully aware of Kubanov next to me, I also imagined feeling the crosshairs of the three sniper rifles on my chest and back. Again I begged my right hand to form a fist and lift. Nothing happened.

"Actually, I hope that you can hear me. I want you to know that you might have won this time, but the next time you won't be this lucky. I'm a little strange like this, you know, Genevieve. Once I set a goal, nothing can deter me from achieving it.

"In your case, it would be to eliminate a target. You think you are so smart, but you lack a few things, Genevieve. Like ruthlessness and especially the ability to kill without remorse. Yes, you are not strong like that." He snorted. "Well, looking at you now, you are quite the weak little human, aren't you? Standing here all blacked out and useless to everyone. See that beautiful girl running to her mom? Yeah, I could kill her right now and you wouldn't be able to do anything."

Tears of frustration formed in my eyes and I blinked them away. If I could not get my body to respond, I would use my brain. And my brain was telling me that it was a wise strategy to let Kubanov think that I was not aware of his presence at all. Tears running down my face would take away the security he felt in taunting me.

"No, I'm not going to kill anyone today. Pity though. It would have been a stupendously remarkable day for me. Right now there are simply too many cops around. And of course the three snipers watching us right now. They are not even half as smart as you, Genevieve. You would have figured out by now that I was not a real cop. They're just too easy to outwit."

His voice lost its easy friendliness. "This is not over, Genevieve. You destroyed my reputation by taking away my forgeries. Today you have taken away my revenge on the man who killed my brother. A plan that has taken me almost a year to form to perfection. When you entered my life six months ago, I generously decided to include you into this plan. I was going to let you live through the embarrassment of having your reputation blown to bits. Pardon the pun. But I have changed my mind. I have something much stronger in mind for you now. Believe me when I say that you will suffer for this. I will get you, my dear Genevieve. Not today, not tomorrow, but soon."

I heard him walk away. The inability to do something, anything was possibly one of the worst experiences I had ever had. Another three families exited the building one by one before I could feel my fingers move. I inhaled deeply, closed my eyes and tried to lift my right fist. My fingers barely curled into a fist and my hand was shaking with the effort. With the same suddenness I had frozen, my muscles responded to my brain's messages. My fist shot up in the air.

I was gulping in air, my fist still raised. Uniformed and black-suited men and women rushed around me towards the door to intercept the man who had just stepped outside. Other members of Ian and Daniel's teams were halting the two families who had not yet reached their cars. Manny and Colin was running to me at the same time as two uniformed men.

"Don't approach her!" Colin shouted as he picked up speed. His British accent was gone. "Don't touch her!"

The two uniformed men slowed down and stopped a few metres from me, staring at me curiously. Colin reached me a few seconds before Manny. He covered my icy fist with his warm hand and tried to lower my fist.

"Jenny? Hey, I'm here. Let go, love." He pulled harder on my fist until my arm went stiffly down. He didn't let go of my hand, slowly opening my fingers one by one. He held my hand between both his, rubbing heat into it.

"What happened, Doc? Where is he?" Manny glanced at me, but quickly returned to scanning the grounds. "Where did you see him?"

"He was here." It sounded like I had been running, not them. I was winded. "He was standing right next to me."

"What the hell?" Manny turned his full attention on me. "Where is he now?"

"I don't know. He's gone."

Manny's lips tightened. He inhaled to speak and I knew it was going to be sarcasm.

"Millard, wait." Colin took my other hand, put both between his hands and continued rubbing them. He lowered his head a bit to be closer to my height. "Jenny, what happened?"

Angry tears filled my eyes. "I froze, Colin. I could hear everything he said, but I couldn't even move my head. He taunted me and spoke for such a long time. Then he walked away. I don't know where he went. All I know is that I heard him walk towards the parking area. He was wearing a GIPN uniform, so he could be anywhere."

"I'll get Pink to check the cameras," Daniel said. I hadn't

heard or seen him join us. He calmly spoke into his headset. Unlike me he had full control over his behaviour and reactions under this pressure. He finished his orders to lock down the perimeter and do a thorough search for Kubanov, and looked at me. "Tell us exactly what happened. As much as you feel comfortable with."

Colin moved to my side, standing close enough that I could feel his body heat. I wanted to lean even closer. I cleared my throat, shook my head a bit and pulled my shoulders back. I was stronger than this. Stronger than a conscious blackout. I aimed for calm control and told them in a voice as steady as I could manage what had taken place. I also included my initial analysis of the situation. Later I would like to watch any available footage for further analysis.

"There is nothing more I can tell you." I looked at Manny, Ian and Daniel and sighed. "I'm genuinely contrite that I failed you this badly. We could have had Kubanov."

"Doc, you didn't fail us." Manny lifted his hand to touch me and dropped it again. "We failed you. I should never have left you alone here."

The other two agreed heartily and tried in numerous sentences to make me feel better. They didn't. All it did was highlight how perceptive and sensitive these men were. And how much I had failed them. When Daniel emphatically stated again how much I had helped them, I turned to Colin. I knew my eyes were wide with the panic I felt building inside of me.

"Okay, let's get you out of here," he said and put his arm around my shoulders. Manny scowled at Colin as he pulled me tighter under his arm.

"You can't leave," Daniel said. "I'm really sorry. We've locked down the grounds and a five-kilometre-wide perimeter. The families have been given permission to return to their cars, but have been asked to wait for further instructions. The Hazmat team is checking the main building for any signs of airborne pathogens. You'll have to stay on the grounds."

"Inside or outside?" Colin asked me.

"Inside. There are too many people outside." Team members who were watching me. Who I had failed.

"The bus is empty right now," Daniel said. "Pink is in the school's security control room. Since it is in another building, he's there checking the computers to see if it's been hacked."

I wanted to say that I believed one hundred percent that those computers had been hacked, but Colin was already leading me towards the side of the building. He lifted his free hand and showed Manny his middle finger when the latter shouted that he'd be checking in on us soon and that Colin shouldn't get any ideas about escaping.

We reached the bus and Colin all but pushed me in and closed the door behind us. I walked to the back of the bus and stopped at the conference table, my back towards the door, towards Colin. Right now I didn't want to face anyone, least of all myself. One of my failings had always been judging myself too harshly. As I stood here, I didn't know if my self-judgement was too harsh or not enough. I had allowed an international crime lord to escape.

"Jenny, this isn't your fault." Colin was standing close behind me. He touched my shoulder and I shook my head.

"It is my fault, Colin." I turned around, tears in my eyes. "He was standing right next to me. Three snipers had their weapons trained on me. How is this not my fault?"

He rubbed my arms as if I was cold. "This was never supposed to be your responsibility. Daniel, Manny and Ian are trained to do this kind of thing. To put themselves in the line of fire. You were trained to observe people from a distance. Not to engage. You can't beat yourself up because your brain didn't allow you to deal with a situation you never even should have been in. There is no way you could have been prepared for that."

"Logically I know this, it's just…" My voice was thick with unshed tears. I could no longer speak past the tightness in my throat.

Colin tilted his head, his expression one of care and affection. It was the very last thing I needed right now. Cold logic and reasoning would have empowered me to regain control over my emotions. Colin's understanding and kindness brought more tears to my eyes.

"Oh, Jenny." He blanched. If I weren't so overwhelmed with these emotions I could have smiled at his micro-expression of male panic at the sight of female tears. That micro-expression gave way for sympathy and he opened his arms. He made it my choice whether I wanted physical nearness and comfort. For that I was more grateful than he would ever know. I chose the comfort.

As his arms folded around me and pulled me in even closer against his chest, I waited for the disquiet, the panic to set in. It didn't. Instead I felt safe and it was my undoing. An unstoppable sob escaped and I pushed my face deeper into his coat. For the long time it took me to quietly weep, he held me. With each tear, the frustration I had felt next to Kubanov left me as did the powerlessness and the anger that had followed.

How long I cried on his coat I did not know, but there was a large wet patch on his designer outerwear. I felt both exhausted and exhilarated when my tears eventually dried up. He continued to hold me. It was comfortable leaning against his solid body. Comfortable, safe and warm. I sighed and reached for a tissue in my pocket.

"You know these were purely tears of frustration, right?" I asked into his chest, blotting tears. "An expression of my outrage that Kubanov had escaped."

Colin's soft laugh rumbled in his chest. "You sure it doesn't have anything to do with you hating the loss of control?"

"That too," I whispered, hoping he wouldn't hear. He leaned slightly back and looked down at me until I looked up. The sharp forward tilt of his head gave him a double chin. I smiled.

"Feel better?"

I nodded. I knew I had to be looking fairly unattractive with the evidence of prolonged crying, yet I felt no embarrassment when Colin looked at me. That fact combined with the respect, the equality on many levels and ultimately the trust I had in him was exactly what I saw reflected on his face. All of the shelved observations I had made about my behaviour towards Colin came together to form a conclusion. Something I was too scared to name.

"You know, right?" he asked softly.

I nodded again. There was no point in pretending that I didn't understand what he was referring to. We had had an unstable start to our relationship, but even six months ago there had been a connection superseding simple friendship. The last few days had solidified a unique bond, something I never thought I would have. Something that I was completely unprepared for.

Colin didn't give me any more time to think and analyse. He lowered his head until our lips were a hairbreadth away. There was a moment's hesitation to give me a chance to move away. I didn't move and I felt the relieved exhalation of his breath softly against my face. His lips touched mine and it felt right.

The chaste kiss was not enough for me. I reached up with one hand, pulled his head closer and opened for a more intimate kiss. A shudder went through him as his arms tightened around me and he deepened the kiss. With my other hand I clung onto his coat, never wanting to let go. How was it that his closeness and the uncontrolled passion of this kiss made me feel so safe?

There was no panic, no desire to move away. Physical sensations overwhelmed me. The intimacy of our tongues duelling, exploring. His left hand lowering, curling around my butt and pulling me into him. I had never experience lovemaking so intense that I wasn't able to analyse every moment of it. And this was only a kiss. I had no awareness of my surroundings, my past or any thoughts of the future. It was like losing myself in my work. Nothing could distract me. Only Colin and this kiss existed.

"What the fucking, bleeding, holy hell is going on here?" Manny bellowed a few feet away from us.

Colin's body stiffened for a moment and then I felt him smile against my lips. He gave me one last kiss before straightening. I put my hand on his chest and shook my head. I didn't want this to turn into an ugly argument. This day had been difficult enough for me.

"Come on, it will be fun," he whispered. I emphatically shook my head and tried to pull out of his arms. He wouldn't let me go, but turned slightly so we both had a side view of the front of the bus. He looked at Manny. "Millard."

Manny ignored him and moved closer to inspect me. "Did he take advantage of you while you were vulnerable? Tell me and by God, I will arrest his thieving, criminal arse."

"Manny," I said reprovingly. "You can't arrest Colin for kissing me."

"Watch me." He gave Colin a quick glare before narrowing his eyes on me again. "You wanted this?"

I didn't answer him, but gave him a facial expression that I knew communicated that it wasn't his business and that yes, I did want this.

Manny stepped back, his mouth pulled in a sneer. "I should've seen this coming. Why didn't I see this coming?"

"You called him my boyfriend," I pointed out.

"I was sarcastic," he enunciated as if each word was a lone sentence. He threw his hands in the air and walked away. Staying true to his typical agitated behaviour, he quickly turned around and walked back to us, pointing a finger at Colin. "If you ever, ever hurt her, I will arrest your sorry arse and you will never see daylight again. Clear?"

Colin's lips tightened with suppressed laughter. He glanced at me and sobered slightly at my expression. He cleared his throat. "As crystal."

"Hmph." Manny rubbed his hands over his face. Twice. "Well, if you're done with your snogging, the president wants to meet with you."

Chapter **TWENTY-SEVEN**

"Vinnie," I looked at the empty plate in front of me and the empty dishes on the table, "this was spectacular. Thank you."

"Yes, Vin. You really outdid yourself this time." Colin leaned back in his chair with a satisfied sigh. We had come home late afternoon to be greeted by an array of different mouth-watering aromas. And to witness another argument between Vinnie and Francine. They were still glaring at each other.

Once Manny had led us out of the bus, things had happened very fast. Colin had refused to leave my side which had resulted in a nose-to-nose standoff between him and Manny. Ian had intervened and within two minutes the three of us had been whisked away in a presidential security vehicle to meet with the president and his wife. It had been an enlightening and interesting two-hour meeting.

"I still maintain that was the worst idea ever." Francine folded her arms.

"Francine!" Phillip, Manny and Vinnie spoke at the same time. Vinnie even shook a knife at her. He had insisted that we eat first before we had any discussion about what had happened earlier. I had thought it was a good idea. It had felt like days since I had eaten and this meal had bettered anything Vinnie had cooked before. Talking about me letting Kubanov escape would have destroyed my appetite.

Francine had been distraught to hear that we had met with the president and had not stopped with her paranoid ramblings about complete loss of privacy. She was convinced that we were all now owned. Like property. Phillip's presence had been both a pleasant surprise and a comfort. Assessing his nonverbal cues, he was highly entertained by Francine's paranoia.

"Just think about it like this," Colin said to Francine. "For any further research into a conspiracy concerning the government, you now have direct access to the source."

"Oh dear God help us all." Phillip shook his head.

"I'm making coffee." Vinnie stood up and looked between the table and the sitting area. "Here or there?"

"Let's take it in the sitting area," Colin said. He also got up and together with Francine helped Vinnie clear the table. I wanted to help, but there were too many people to bump into. My apartment was spacious, but I was not used to having five extra people in my space. It made the open areas feel cramped. Seven times already I had wished it had been summer so I could have opened the balcony doors for some illusion of extra space. And for fresh air.

Phillip and I walked to the sitting area and settled in the sofa facing the balcony. It was my favourite place. Manny joined us and fell into the other sofa. In the kitchen Francine was still making her case against the president having any knowledge of us whatsoever. She hated the idea that the president would know what she looked like, where I lived and a long list of other things she had been naming any opportunity she got.

"Why isn't anyone telling Francine that she wasn't the one who visited the president?" I asked Phillip. "She wasn't even mentioned at our meeting."

Phillip rested his one ankle on his other knee and dusted invisible fluff off his designer suit's pant-leg. "It's the principle with her. She is a well-educated woman with class and clothes to rival any of the rich people at the school you were at today. Outwardly, she would fit into any exclusive club. Yet she is more anti-establishment than I can honestly bear. She's a study in contradictions and I think she works hard to maintain that image."

Phillip's observation was exactly what I had thought about Francine. She had proven to be not only all that, but also strong, resourceful and determined to stop Kubanov despite all her misgivings about conspiracies and the like.

The others joined us, Vinnie carrying a tray with coffee and Colin a tray with an assortment of cakes. Vinnie placed his tray on the coffee table and went to the reading area to bring a wingback chair for himself. Francine sat next to Manny and Colin settled on the armrest next to me.

"How will we be insured against being arrested?" Francine was clearly not finished with this topic. "You know that I don't always colour inside the lines. How could you have met with those people?"

"Those people asked for our help, little girl." Manny shifted slightly away from her. "Helping the president find Kubanov and bringing him to justice is not agreeing to any of the nonsense you've been spouting. Being asked by the leader of a country to be part of a small investigative unit is a huge honour. You should be honoured and not turn your nose up at it."

Manny was not yet sarcastic and his body language also did not express anger. He was only mildly annoyed by Francine's incessant arguments. I understood where she was coming from. I also knew enough to not completely dismiss her paranoid theories. But this instance I believed she was sorely mistaken. She had not seen the president's body language when he had spoken to us.

"He was sincere both in his requests and his promise of secrecy," I said.

"Okay, wait." Vinnie sat up and frowned. "I've heard so many bits and pieces about this meeting that you guys had that I don't know what's what. Jen-girl, your version will be the most accurate, so tell us exactly what was decided."

"Nothing was decided," I said. "President Godard gave us the evening to think about his proposal and discuss it. The offer was simple. The president asked us, all of us in this room, to be part of a team to find Kubanov and make sure that he faces justice."

"What kind of justice?" Vinnie asked. Small muscle contractions under his eyes shocked me.

"The kind that includes courts and prison time, criminal." Manny glared at Vinnie. He must have also seen the murderous intent.

"What happened to that bastard? Do you know?" Vinnie asked in a challenge.

"A young police officer let Kubanov leave the perimeter line minutes before Daniel locked down the area. He had no reason to suspect that Kubanov was not who he pretended to be. By now he could be anywhere. And that is why we should be doing everything we can to find him and stop him."

"Just the few of us? No sweat." Francine was sarcastic. I recognised it from her curled lip and her hand waving around to include everyone.

I shook my head, still in slight disbelief at the strange turn my life had taken. "We were promised full access to any resources we need. That would include people and anything else. Ian and Daniel will continue to be our contacts in their respective fields. We'll be working as we did in the last week, from my apartment and office if Phillip agrees. All we have to do is dedicate ourselves to finding Kubanov. Then we can all return to our normal lives."

"And do you believe that?" Francine asked with wide eyes and a slightly open mouth.

"Of course not," I said with disgust. "I was quoting the president there. My life will never be normal again. Not with all of you in it."

The change in the body language around me clued me in that I had said something inappropriate. The laughter that followed meant it had amused them.

"I'm sorry. I didn't mean to imply that you are not welcome in my life."

Phillip turned on the sofa until he was facing me straight on. "Genevieve, I need you to listen very carefully to me. Don't apologise to us for being you. Your honesty is something unique. It is pure without any subtext. I think you brand of honesty is something that we all need in our lives. We are all here because of you, because of what you do and who you are."

"I agree," Manny said. He put his coffee mug down. "What Doc also didn't tell you is how she was congratulated on stopping a potential disaster and was given the president's wife's personal phone number."

I waved their compliments away. "This is not about me. It is about us. I could never have achieved any of this without you."

"Maybe, but the president's wife didn't ask me to become involved in one of her charities," Manny said.

"What's that about?" Phillip asked.

"Nothing important." I didn't want to be talking about this. "She asked me to attend charity functions with her. She supports a few charities that educate and help non-neurotypical people and their families."

"That's fantastic," Francine said. Gone were the conspiracy theories and paranoia. "Did you say yes?"

"I told her I would think about it. But that is not important now. We need to decide whether we are going to accept the president's proposal."

"Will they know where we live?" Francine asked, immediately shaking her head. "Scratch that. I'll make sure that our information doesn't get anywhere near the interwebs. Our data will never be found by anyone. I'll make Rousseau & Rousseau's system even more secure than it is already."

I knew Francine had the capability to do this. Even though I didn't feel the need for total obscurity, her paranoia was affecting me and made me grateful for any precaution she planned to take.

"What about Jonas?" Colin asked Francine. "Have you found him?"

"Of course I did. No one gets to hide from me. The little bastard was in Paris. Paris! I got Daniel on it and he got his people on it." A satisfied smile lifted her lips. "The Paris police are particularly paranoid about cyber-terrorists. He's not going to be writing any kind of code soon."

"Care to tell me how you got Daniel's number?" Manny asked. There was a warning in his voice.

Francine lifted her chin. "I told you I don't always colour inside the lines."

"What about the young thief you caught red-handed and Luc Alain?" I asked Manny.

"The detectives have kept their word and are helping the young thief out. He'll have to pay for his crime, but it won't take him away from school or caring for his grandmother. As for Luc Alain? He realised that this is no joke and that he's going to a real prison. He's currently trying his best to cut all kinds of deals, but it won't help him. He's going to serve out his sentence in jail."

While enjoying Vinnie's cakes we talked a bit more about the president's proposal. Francine was making strong arguments against being the government's little minions. Her body language consistently contrasted her words. Everyone had their opinions about working in such a team to ensure the capture of Kubanov.

I had no concerns about working with these people currently crowding my apartment. They had proven to not only be my peers on many levels, but also to be my friends. My main concern was to rectify a situation created by my lapse in control over my reaction to stressful situations. Indeed I was concerned about Kubanov's threats against my life, but it was the threat he was to everyone else that had me tempted to forego desperately needed sleep and start working on it tonight.

"I'm knackered." Manny pushed himself slowly out of the sofa. "You kids have a good night. I'm off to a shower and then to bed."

"Want me to come and wash your back?" Francine gave Manny a sultry look and burst out laughing. "You don't have to look so happy about it."

I had not seen happiness in Manny's micro-expressions. There had been shock and consideration, but not happiness. I was going to have to speak to Francine about that, to correct her. But it could wait for another day. The weight of the day's events combined with a filling meal was pushing me past my physical limits. I was too exhausted to care about words and phrases I didn't understand. By the minute other concerns lessened until my mind could solely focus on getting some much-needed sleep. It appeared that I was not the only one feeling thus.

Unlike our last case, I had no feeling of conclusion. We might have stopped Professor Tremont acting out psychotic fantasies of revenge, yet the satisfaction I derived from that was diminished by Kubanov's disappearance. Not even stopping the burglaries, catching the young thief, Luc and recovering most of the stolen goods comforted me.

"Stop micro-analysing everything, Jenny. Let's go to bed."

My eyes flew open. Colin was standing in front of me with his hand extended. We were alone.

"I am not having sex with you." My words reflected my outrage at his audacity. I became even more agitated when he pulled his hand back, laughing.

"It was not what I suggested at all." He chuckled again and sat down next to me. "You were falling asleep sitting here, so everyone left."

"I wasn't sleeping." It was the only response that didn't embarrass me any further. "I was thinking about what to do next."

"Yeah, I thought so." Colin smiled. "You were pretty lost in your thoughts, so the guys said their goodbyes and left. Phillip said he'll wait for your call tomorrow to tell him what you decided. He supports any decision you make. Vinnie will be in for breakfast tomorrow morning. Manny will be here early to talk about this whole president offer thing."

"What do you think about it?"

He sprawled on the sofa, rested his head against the back and stared straight ahead. "I think that there are some changes that all of us are going to make. My unmentioned career will need some adjustments."

We sat quietly next to each other for some time.

"Where were you born?" I asked.

Without lifting his head, he turned to look at me. He looked at me for almost a minute before he smiled. "Long Island, New York."

"Oh. Okay." I knew it was per capita income one of the richest areas in New York. Interesting. Again we settled in a comfortable silence, staring at the balcony and the darkness beyond.

"I don't like change," I said after some time.

"Sometimes change is good."

"It's always good. It forces us to develop, to grow. The growth and development I like. The change? Not at all."

"At least some things stay the same." He turned his head again to look at me. "I'm still here. Vinnie, Francine and Millard next door. Vinnie will cook and bicker with Francine and Millard will be his annoying self. The same as always."

I knew this wasn't true. Too much had changed between all of us in the last week.

~ ~ ~ ~ ~

Be first to find out when Genevieve's next adventure will be published. Sign up for the newsletter at
http://estelleryan.com/contact.html

~ ~ ~ ~ ~

Listen to the Mozart pieces, look at the paintings from this book and read more about the two Dantes:
http://estelleryan.com/the-dante-connection.html

~ ~ ~ ~ ~

The Braque Connection
Third in the Genevieve Lenard series

Forged masterpieces. Hidden messages. A desperate swan song.

World-renowned nonverbal communication expert Doctor Genevieve Lenard wakes up drugged in an unknown location after being kidnapped. As someone with high-functioning autism, this pushes the limits of her coping skills.

For the last year, Russian philanthropist and psychopath Tomasz Kubanov has been studying Genevieve just as she and her team have been studying him. Now forged paintings and mysterious murders are surfacing around her team, with evidence pointing to one of them as the killer.

Genevieve knows Kubanov is behind these senseless acts of violence. What she doesn't understand are the inconsistencies between his actions and the cryptic messages he sends. Something has triggered his unpredictable behaviour, something that might result in many more deaths, including those she cares for. Because this time, Kubanov has nothing to lose.

The Braque Connection is available as paperback and ebook

The Braque Connection
Third in the Genevieve Lenard series

Excerpt

Chapter ONE

"Jenny, wake up." A warm hand was rubbing my shoulder a bit too vigorously. "Wake up, honey-buns."

I bristled at the term of endearment. I had heard it used recently and it had offended me deeply. I considered such saccharine terms disparaging, something I couldn't associate with the voice calling me. I tried to open my eyes, but my eyelids would not respond to the message sent by my neurotransmitters. My cognitive function appeared to be impaired. Not even a frown formed on my brow as I attempted to ascertain where I was. It was disconcerting that I couldn't place the voice calling me, even though it sounded familiar.

A slow panic started to creep through me. Why could I not move? Why could I not remember things? I swallowed and tried to call up Mozart's Piano Concerto No. 27 in B flat Major. Mentally writing any of Mozart's compositions always calmed me. For the first time in my life, I couldn't recall one single concerto, étude, sonata or opera. Dread settled heavily on my mind. Forcing my thoughts away from not being able to move or remember, I focussed on what I could feel.

Pain. Intense, overwhelming pain. My head felt like it was twice its size and filled with wet wool. Had I been imbibing? I had not been drunk before, thus my knowledge was purely academic. What I was experiencing would seem to fit the symptoms of veisalgia, or in layman's terms, a hangover.

I continued my self-examination, ignoring the incessant voice calling me. Had my muscles not been so unresponsive, I would have been much more tense as my situation revealed itself in disturbing fragments. I was naked. Naked, on a bed and curled up against another naked body. My heart rate increased exponentially with this awareness. I had no recollection of how I had come to be here. My head was on a man's shoulder, my right hand resting trustingly over his heart. He was lying on his back, his right arm holding me against him, still rubbing my shoulder. I was on my side with my one leg thrown over his. I was cuddling. I never cuddled.

"Jenny, please wake up." Concern strained the familiar male voice.

I groaned. The deep voice vibrating against my ear increased the pain throbbing against my cranium.

"Honey-buns, wake up."

"Don't call me that." Forcing all my annoyance into my vocal cords resulted merely in a hoarse whisper. The chest under my head heaved with a deep breath.

"Oh, thank God." His chest shuddered. "How're you feeling?"

Darkness pulled at me and in my weakness I surrendered to its lure. The insistent shoulder-rubbing and irritating voice dragged me back to painful, paralysed consciousness. After a few seconds I realised I was keening. I swallowed the next monotone sound, but couldn't stop the groan. My head was pounding.

"Who are you?" I asked.

He drew in a sharp breath and slowly released it. "I'm your sugar-bunny."

Without the headache and worrying weakness in my limbs, I might have punched the chest I was resting on. As it was, it took immense effort to merely open my eyes. Pain that I had only read about stabbed at my eyes. I breathed through the nausea and looked beyond the naked chest under my hand.

We were in a bedroom, the bed comfortable yet firm under me. I was facing a wall, mostly taken up by a large window with the curtains drawn open. In front of the windows were two wingback chairs separated by an antique-looking coffee table. Elegant. The glass panes behind the leather chairs did not quite reach the floor or ceiling, but were large enough to afford me a full view of our surroundings. The pastoral landscape outside in the waning light of day was in sharp contrast to the turmoil in my mind. And it did not look familiar. In fact, it didn't look like anything I had seen in France. Where were we? Who was I with?

"Honey-buns, you need to get up."

I gritted my teeth and pushed myself up on shaking arms. I only managed a few inches, hoping it was enough to find out who was insulting me with such endearments. My eyes travelled from my hand to the muscular chest, neck and higher. Above the strong jaw with a few days' worth of stubble was a familiar mouth with uncommon depressed angles. I studied the *depressor anguli oris* muscles by his mouth for a few moments to determine whether the corners of his mouth were downturned in pain or distress. It was distress.

"Jenny?"

I raised my eyes and recognition slammed into my throbbing brain. I was naked in bed with Colin, the thief and art forger everyone called my boyfriend. His slow blinking and the elevation of his medial eyebrows evidenced deep concern.

"I am not your honey-buns." With great strain I moved my fingers, managing only a light pinch to his pectoral muscle. "And you are not my sugar-bunny."

His expression relaxed slightly. "We are naked in a strange place and that is what you want to argue about?"

"Colin." I collapsed back onto his chest when he smiled his relief at hearing his name in my still-hoarse voice. "Where are we?"

"Um, England?"

"Why are you questioning your own answer?" I wished I had the strength to look at his face. My expertise was in nonverbal communication, a skill I had learned out of necessity. Reading and interpreting body language did not come naturally to me. I relied heavily on my training to understand people's communication beyond their words. Being as weak as I was now, I only had Colin's words. "Why do you think we are in

England?"

He sighed. "We're in my cottage in England."

I had not expected that answer. There were a few important questions I knew I had to ask, but couldn't reach them in my mind. My neocortex seemed capable of only the simplest of reasoning. "Why did you bring me here?"

"Can you sit up?" He shifted under me. "We need to move. It might help."

I lifted my hand. Ten centimetres above Colin's chest, it fell back. I had limited control over my muscles. Dark fear entered my peripheral vision.

"Jenny, you have to try and stay with me." He turned, and I rolled away from him onto my back. My breathing was erratic, my heart racing. Colin leaned over me. "Come on, Jenny. Stay with me. We have to get you moving. Maybe it will get this crap out of your system. We have to be ready to go. I don't know what kind of danger we are in."

The moment I heard the word 'danger', the darkness swallowed me.

The Braque Connection *is available as paperback and ebook.*

Other books in the Genevieve Lenard Series:

Book 1: The Gauguin Connection

Book 2: The Dante Connection

Book 3: The Braque Connection

Book 4: The Flinck Connection

Book 5: The Courbet Connection

Book 6: The Pucelle Connection

Book 7: The Léger Connection

~ ~ ~ ~

Find out more about Estelle at
www.estelleryan.com
Or visit her facebook page to chat with her:
www.facebook.com/EstelleRyanAuthor

47201414R00216

Made in the USA
Lexington, KY
30 November 2015